Head Over Feels

Cover Photographer: Sydnee Rayl Photography

Cover Models: Kylie and Alex Katich

Cover Designer: RBA Designs

Adriana Locke, Content Editor

Marion Archer, Making Manuscripts

Jenny Sims, Editing4Indies

Proofreading: Kristen Johnson

Beta Reading: Andrea Johnston

Hard to Resist Series (Stand-Alones)

The Resistance

The Reckoning

The Redemption

The Revolution

The Rebellion

The Crow Brothers (Stand-Alones)

Spark

Tulsa

Rivers

Ridge

The Crow Brothers Box Set

DARE - A Rock Star Hero (Stand-Alone)

The Everest Brothers (Stand-Alones)

Everest - Ethan Everest

Bad Reputation - Hutton Everest

Force of Nature - Bennett Everest

The Everest Brothers Box Set

The Kingwood Series

SAVAGE

SAVIOR

SACRED

FINDING SOLACE - Stand-Alone

The Kingwood Series Box Set

Playboy in Paradise Series

Falling for the Playboy

Redeeming the Playboy

Loving the Playboy

Playboy in Paradise Box Set

Talk to Me Duet (Stand-Alones)

Sweet Talk

Dirty Talk

Stand-Alone Books

We Were Once

Missing Grace

Finding Solace

Until I Met You

Drunk on Love

Naturally, Charlie

A Prior Engagement

Lost in Translation

Sleeping with Mr. Sexy

Morning Glory

HEAD OVER FEELS

S.L. SCOTT

1

Radcliffe "Rad" Wellington

"Such an odd achievement for a guy who breaks up marriages." Tealey holds the crystal award in her hands. *My* award. One of the three *Big Apple's Most Eligible Bachelor* honors I've received. I keep the others at home because I don't want to boast too much.

"I don't break up marriages." I temper my defensiveness, noticing she couldn't care less about the Klein & Sable award right next to it. I'm pretty proud of winning my law firm's top honor this last year.

Trying to act casual by leaning back in my leather chair, I kick my feet up on my desk, and say, "They're already broken when a client walks through that door."

Relationships are complicated. I've traveled that road before—three times total. They lasted anywhere from two weeks to two months max. The frivolous notion of love never factored into those relationships, so no hearts were broken. *Particularly not mine.*

For me, dating is about companionship, something I

rarely crave. And since sex satisfies my physical needs, it's easy to separate the two. I have a contacts list in my phone that goes for miles, and the one thing they don't need is dinner and small talk. Their needs, just like mine, are met in the bedroom. No intimacy required. No dates scheduled. No food is involved unless they're into that kind of thing. *winks*

No hassles.

No strings.

No heartache.

Yet the golden-haired beauty in front of me, the only person I'd consider changing my current dating lifestyle for, can only—*will only*—ever remain my friend.

I may have been an innocent bystander when Tealey Bell ran right into me, but I don't believe in accidents. We may not be meant to be, but we were meant to meet. Her cheeks flamed as red as the strawberries that were squashed between us. She said something about being sorry while I momentarily got lost in her blue eyes. That is, until her gaze lowered to the mess on my shirt, and she said, "Bam, and here we are."

Bam is an understatement.

Tealey holds the trophy in the air. "It's heavy, like it holds the weight of bachelorhood inside." Her laughter is light, almost as if for herself.

I anchor my feet back on the floor. "I don't know about the weight of bachelorhood, but it definitely holds my reputation."

"Serial dater?" She lifts a brow. "Commitment-phobe?"

I could be offended, but she's right on the money. "That's fair."

She smiles, her eyes darting from the award and then back to me. "What do they base this on?" she asks. "Really."

"I don't know. Reputation probably plays a part. Financials. Looks, maybe?"

She'd make the worst attorney in the world. She's unable to hide her emotions since she wears her heart on her sleeve. Her displeasure causes her to purse her lips and narrow her eyes as if the award in her hands personally offended her. "You're more than connections and financials, Rad."

I quirk a smile. "Didn't know you cared, Bell."

She rolls her eyes but quirks a smile as she sets the award back on the shelf. It's slightly askew, similar to how she leaves me feeling. "Of course, I do. We're friends."

I sit back and take her in. She's as beautiful as she was the day she fell on top of me seven years ago. Her sweetheart face is a bit fuller, her hair a little lighter. It's long again after cutting it to make our friend Cammie feel better about a bad haircut.

But that's Tealey—the woman who came back into my life five days after our fateful encounter when my friend Cade started dating her friend Cammie, and our two groups merged into one.

Any hopes of dating Tealey Bell were squashed back then, just like those strawberries between us.

"I still don't get why that stuff is important."

"It's not. The title is utter nonsense, but the perks are nice," I say, trying not to let myself focus too much on her.

Our eyes stay locked for a few seconds before she averts hers again. "By perks, I assume that means having your choice of date every night of the week?"

This time, I sigh, tilt back in my chair, and fold my arms behind my head. "I wouldn't say *every* night, but it's good to have options."

"Options. *Okay ...*"

"It's for charity, so how can I say no?"

"No," she replies dryly but then grins. "Just like that. It's easy. Anyway, there are other ways to give back to your community than to . . ." Her brows pinch together. "What did you have to do to win this?"

"Have sex with prominent donors."

"What?" Her eyes dart to mine, the soft blues brighter in the afternoon sunlight flooding my office. "Please tell me you're kidding."

"That I need to tell you says everything."

Amusement dances in her smile. Returning to the award, she runs a finger down the side of it. "The phrase *most eligible* downplays the fact that you're not looking to become ineligible." Her brow furrows, displeased. "It's like false advertising to the women who think they can snag you."

"What exactly does snagging entail?" I'm an attorney, not a detective, so I have no idea where she's leading this conversation. I'm enjoying our chat but also wading through until she opens up about the real reason she's here. I know for a fact that Tealey didn't drop by to talk about my accolades, and she didn't just happen to be in the neighborhood, considering how far apart our neighborhoods are.

"Weren't you the one who said you prefer the wrong woman, so you have a built-in excuse not to call her the day after your tawdry affair?"

She's good with the details. Maybe she wouldn't make such a bad attorney after all.

"That was years ago, and tawdry is not a word synonymous with me. I'm top-notch and more than generous if you know what I mean."

I expect a laugh or knowing grin at the very least, but she silently crosses the room to look out the window instead. Her gaze lengthens into the distance of the Manhattan skyline. It's unlike her not to volley when I give her the perfect setup.

When the silence extends, I notice the change in her demeanor—all lightness being held hostage by the thoughts that appear to consume her. I sit forward again and pick up a pen. "It's quite a trek from Brooklyn for a one-hour lunch break. Anything specific bring you by?"

Hesitant, she exhales slowly. "Yes."

Her apprehension concerns me. She's not usually one to hide her feelings. "What's going on, Tealey?"

"Rad?" With her Bahama blue eyes set on mine, she drags her teeth over her lip. "I need . . . I need you."

The pen snaps, causing us both to look down at the ink on my hands. "Shit."

She rushes to grab a tissue from the box on the shelf and then to me. "What happened?" Taking my hand in hers, she starts rubbing my palm to no great avail.

Stopping her by stilling her hand, I ask, "You need me?"

"Yes, I need someone I can trust," she replies, returning to the distraction of my hands. Peeking at me from under long lashes, she adds, "A lawyer, and you're a lawyer."

Was it foolish to even consider the idea of her meaning anything more than needing my legal skills? Probably. Yet, because of the fool I am, I stupidly believed this was some long-overdue opportunity to . . . *to what exactly? Clenching my jaw, I run through what the hell I thought this could be—a hookup, a precursor to a date?* The whole situation with Tealey is impossible.

Fucking fool.

I switch gears, burying my personal feelings. "Why do you need an attorney?"

Losing hope for cleaning my hands, she looks around

the office as if her nerves have taken over. "Anything you can offer, advice or otherwise, I'll take."

"I'll help if I can. What's your concern?"

Whispering, she adds, "Preferably free." Embarrassment taints her cheeks as she drags her eyes away from mine. "I can't offer much in return—"

"Hey?" When she looks my way, somberness washes over her usually happy expression. "What's going on, Tealey?"

"I need a divorce."

As if the needing *me* didn't shock me enough, my jaw slacks as I realize I was wrong. She'd absolutely kick my ass in court by the way she throws tidbits out like bombs. I'm so confused by this curveball that I stumble through my next words. "I didn't know, know you were married."

"I'm not." *Thank fuck.* Her hand rests against her chest, and she adds, "It's not for me. It's for someone I'm working with."

"A case?"

Her eyes lower, dragging the corners of her lips down with them. "Yes, a woman I'm working with at the social services office. She has two kids. I found a place for them to stay for a short time, a safe place, but we're trying to help her move to Philadelphia, where her mother lives. Her mother can give her the help she needs with the kids while she works and then after school." Her expression is as soft as her tone. "She needs a divorce and permission to take the kids out of state."

I'm not generally an overly emotional guy. Many years of training myself to bury those reactions in court have served me well. But every now and then, my chest tightens, like it is now. She's so damn kindhearted. "You've never come to me before—"

"Misty Connor, that's her name. She's gotten terrible advice. One attorney told her to stay in the marriage and work it out for the kids." Leaning forward, she flattens her palms on the desk as if she has no other choice. "He's . . . awful, Rad. I can't go into the details, but she needs this divorce. She needs to be free from him. These kids need a stable home, and she and her mother can provide that for them."

Tealey's heart of gold shines through her plea. And I want to help her. I'd do anything to help Tealey, but it's not as simple as she thinks. "I hear what you're saying, but it's—"

"*I need you, Rad.* She needs you, and I need to do whatever I can to help her. I know this is a big ask. And . . ." Giving her time, she swallows, and then adds, "Her kids deserve a chance at a better life."

Shifting in my chair, I study the frown shaping her lips in a way they should never be and the sadness darkening her irises. Blowing out a breath, I look away and run my hand through my hair when my chest tightens. I remind myself to maintain a neutral expression and remain professional. "I hear what you're saying, but it's complicated to force a divorce on someone who doesn't want it. It can be a lengthy and emotionally drawn-out process. I'm assuming he won't sign anything if she gave it to him, correct?"

"She spent the night in the hospital when she once mentioned it."

Rage strikes like lightning. "Fuck."

"I know." She sighs through the defeat coating her tone.

Stay professional. Shuffling papers around on my desk, I distract myself from looking at her. I won't be able to handle the tears wavering on the edge of her lids if they fall. Seeing a woman cry is my weakness. *My mom . . .* I remember her tears too well. Tealey crying? No. I can't have that either. "Is there a restraining order in place?"

"She filed, but it was denied."

I should really have Ashley in here taking notes, but this is personal, so I pull a legal pad from my drawer and jot a few things down. "It shouldn't have been denied if there's a paper trail documenting the abuse." I look back up. "He's—"

"He's awful, Rad."

With our eyes locked on each other, I sense the words—fear, danger, and concern—she harbors inside but won't say. "I'll help her." I nod before setting the pen down before me and twisting it between my fingertips. "I take a handful of pro bono cases a year when I can. It's all I have time for lately. I'll take this one but on one condition."

"Anything."

"Get rid of her current legal aid. Whoever was assigned to her case is doing a shit job. I'm not interested in schooling someone on how to win a case. I'm interested in helping your client."

Tealey's shoulders ease as a small smile appears. "Thank you."

"I haven't done anything yet."

"You've done more than you realize. You've given me hope." She moves to her bag, pulls out a file, and sets it on the desk. "I brought this with me. I can get an e-copy for you if you prefer."

"I hate sounding like, well, an attorney since we're friends, but I have to keep things legal. I'll send over a contract. She'll need to sign it to retain me."

Worry creases the corners of her eyes. "Free of charge, right?"

"Yes."

Relief colors her expression with bright eyes, and a hint

of that pink in her cheeks kisses her skin. *Why does she have to be so fucking beautiful?* "Thank you, Rad. What can I do for you in return?"

"Nothing. It's fine," I reply, glancing down. "Really, it's no big deal." I'd never require a favor in return, especially not from her, but my mind goes to the gutter because yeah . . . *I'm an asshole.* A few good deeds can't change that fact.

She adjusts the strap of her bag over her head and settles it on her hip. "You're busy, and I've already taken up too much of your time. I need to get back to work before I'm late, and let's face it, I've already made this awkward by asking for a favor I can't return. I'm going to take the win and get out of your hair."

Our eyes connect one last time before she opens the door. Barely filling half the doorway, she says, "It was . . ."

I nod. "It was."

Smiles are exchanged before she turns and runs right into a Pepto-pink suit. "Marlow? Hey? Hi."

Just what I didn't need today. A groan rumbles through me.

"*Helllooo.*" The most boisterous and vain of our group, Marlow Marché arrives like she's late for a red-carpet event. She may annoy me sometimes, but there's also something strangely charming and captivating about her that draws people in. I just wish she wasn't making a show of things in my office. Marlow asks, "What are you doing here, Tealey?"

"I stopped by to visit Rad."

Marlow laughs, the sound echoing around the office. "Are you two having a party without me?" She nudges Tealey with an elbow and another giggle. "Meeting in the middle of the day is how rumors get started."

"No need for gossip," Tealey responds and then shrugs.

"I just needed to talk to Rad." Glancing at me, she smiles softly. "Thanks again. Call me later, Marlow."

"I will," Marlow says, nipping our friend's heel with the door as she exits. "Bye, Teals." As soon as the door is closed, Marlow leans against the back of it, her eyes piercing me from across the room. "When did the two of you get so chummy?" she asks, an insinuation embedded in the question.

I'd like to ask her why she's here, but I already know. A visit from Marlow only means one thing: she wants something. "We're friends," I reply casually. *Why do I feel like we were doing something wrong?*

"Yeah, but not usually outside of Jackson, Cammie, Cade, and me."

"It's no big deal. She just wanted to talk about some stuff."

She sags in relief and then pushes off the door. "Phew, I'm so glad she told you. That secret was killing me."

Even though I've known her as long as Tealey, I've never understood how those two became best friends with their night and day personalities. She struts toward me like she's walking a Paris runway, and I watch the whirlwind of a woman as her emotions twist around her, ready to usurp me into her drama, and I brace myself. "Told me what?"

"That she needs help."

It's not like Tealey to share individual cases with the group. Today with me makes sense since she needed help, but I'm surprised she'd tell the others. "Yes, we discussed the situation."

Marlow perches on the chair across from me. "Good. I was afraid I would have to get involved, and I just don't have time. I have appointments at the art gallery today."

"You don't have time to help a friend?" Taking the file

Tealey left with me, I open it. "Your best friend, I might add."

"How could I possibly help? Have her sleep on the couch for months on end? I offered her money, but you know Tealey. She has a saint's heart."

Why would Tealey be sleeping on her couch? "Wait, what?"

She looks at me like I'm dense. "Tealey's moving to Texas," she says as if I have comprehension problems. *Maybe I do.*

Tealey.

Texas?

What the hell is she talking about?

Rad

"What do you mean? *Tealey is moving to Texas?*"

"She was, but you stepped in to help her. Thank God. I don't know how I'd survive this city without her."

The sound of the pounding in my chest reaches my ears. "Slow down, back up, and say that again."

"I. Don't. Know. How. I'd. Survive—"

"Not that part," I snap, my irritation getting the better of me. "Before that."

"Tealey moving to Texas?"

I nod. "What do you mean she's moving?"

"What do you mean what do I mean?" She swirls her hand in the air like we're playing a game of charades. "It's when you load a car or truck full of your belongings—"

"Not funny."

I shake my head in disbelief that Tealey would move away and not tell me. *She was just here.* Why wouldn't she say something?

"Are you okay, Rad?"

"Yeah. Just confused. She was just here and didn't say—"

"I wasn't supposed to either, but since she told you, it's fair game to discuss." She pauses and blinks. "Wait, she didn't say what?"

The pit of my stomach grows heavier, and I swallow. "She didn't tell me she was moving."

Jolting her neck back, she shakes her head. "What do *you* mean?"

"It's when you don't reveal—"

"*Ha-ha.*"

I shift, the chair squeaking in protest. Why does it sting that she didn't tell me—especially when she had the opportunity? My mind races. Does she need help, or is something else going on? Is she moving for work? *Is this move set in stone? Is that why she wanted to make sure Misty's case was being handled by someone she trusts? Because she won't be here to see it through?*

"I wasn't supposed to say anything, but since you know . . ." Marlow flops into the chair, concern etched on her face. Despite Marlow's dramatics, she's caring at her core. She says, "You need to convince her to stay." *No shit.*

"How?"

"I can't share too much—" She sits forward. "Talk to her one-on-one and see what you can get out of her. I don't know why she's keeping it a secret from everyone. She didn't even tell Cammie. She can't leave us. Is there even an *us* without her?"

All valid points. "Why would she tell me the reason she's leaving if she won't tell you?"

"Oh, she told me." She flips her hair behind her shoulder. "I just wasn't really listening. I mean, how was I supposed to when the perfect pale-pink Birkin crossed in front of my eyes while we were at the bistro on 5th?"

Frustration creeps up my spine. "You weren't listening? Your best friend was telling you—forget it." Why am I not surprised that Marlow wasn't listening when her friend was talking? I know. We all know. Unless it's about Marlow, she's oblivious.

"She said something about a week."

"So talk to her again and get the details this time."

"Then she'll know I wasn't listening, and as you know, I've been accused of being a bad listener before. Not by her because she's too nice to say that, but by others."

Fucking hell. I take a deep breath to try to keep my cool. Me coming at Marlow in anger won't fix the situation or cure her narcissism. "This is ridiculous. You know that, right?"

"Ridiculous is losing my best friend when we have a chance to stop that from happening. Will you talk to her? Yes or no?"

Of course, I'd be happy to . . . if I thought she wanted my help. But instead of asking for it, she asked me to help someone else. *But that was typical of Tealey.*

Clenching my jaw, I tick through her visit. I was listening, offered to help her case, and participated in the conversation, which is more than she can say for Marlow. *Yet she told her.*

Still, despite my frustration, no way can I watch her move across the damn country. No. *Fuck that.* "You know I will."

"Great! I think the sooner, the better."

"She'll be home tonight?"

"Yes. Cammie and I were supposed to go over and help her pack, but it sounds like she has it handled."

"All right. I'll stop by and check on her." I glance at the file. "I need to drop something by her place anyway."

"Good. Now let's talk about me because I need to get going."

Clicking on my schedule, I double-check the appointment time for my next client, hoping to avoid her drama. "What is it? I'm swamped today."

Her hand lands on my file, her manicured nails tapping the papers. "I need a favor. An itsy, teeny, tiny favor."

"No."

She pouts. "I haven't even asked yet. You're in such a mood today."

"I'm in a mood every day, so if you'll excuse me." Despite her tailored pink suit, she relaxes in the chair like the indulged daddy's girl she is, apparently making herself at home.

"I thought you had to get going?" Marlow doesn't take hints very well, but let's pray she does today.

I need time to debrief the last few minutes before I walk into my next meeting. Usually, my post-Tealey ritual is to commit everything about her to memory.

Her pink-colored lips. An insight gleaned from our conversation. *But today?* Today, I'll be trying to make sense of this moving mess.

"Radcliffe?" Marlow snaps her fingers, pulling me back to reality

"What?"

She sweeps her long hair off to one shoulder and then leans in. "I need a favor."

Rolling my hand in the air, I encourage her to get to the point. "What is it?"

As if I have nothing better to do this afternoon, she opens a compact and eyes her brows, taking her time. Annoyance flickers in her eyes as she smooths a finger over it. "There."

"I have a meeting with a client soon, *sooo . . .*"

A smile rolls into place. "My dad is in town, and he wants us to join him for dinner tomorrow night."

"What's the catch?"

My desk phone rings. "Yes, Ashleigh?"

"Your next appointment is here," my assistant says.

"I'll be right there." I hang up and stand, reaching for my jacket hooked on the wall. I mentally calculate how long this meeting will run and how soon I can get to Tealey's for answers. "I need to go."

Marlow takes her bag and slips it to the crook of her elbow as she walks toward the door. "So that's a yes?"

"Sure. Fine." *Just fucking go.*

"Thank you, Rad. I can always count on you." She taps her Rolex before opening the door. "I have to run. My personal shopper is waiting. I'm already fifteen minutes late, so I'll text you the details. Ciao, darling."

Like a hurricane, she whips in here, destroys any plans I might have had, and races back out. I should protest, rushing to firmer ground to stand on, but she's gone, leaving me just enough time to check my schedule. As if I didn't have enough Marchés for the day . . . *Speak of the devil.*

I walk out, and Ashleigh flanks my side, handing me a file. She gives me the rundown at the pace of our fast walk. "Robert Marché. Movie producer with credits for three of the biggest films in the past five years. Net worth $350 million. Homes in Sun Valley, Los Angeles, Cabo San Lucas. A condo in Miami, and apartments in Manhattan and Paris. One daughter. Grown. Twen—"

"Twenty-eight," I fill in, "Robert Marché is Marlow's father."

With wide eyes, she asks, "Marlow, who just left Marlow?"

"The very one."

"Oh. *Wow*. Does she know he's getting a divorce?"

"After the conversation we just had, I'm thinking she doesn't."

Gripping a small laptop to her chest, she takes a deep breath just as we round the corner. "This should be interesting."

Maybe that's why he invited all of us to dinner tomorrow. He's going to tell her but wants her surrounded by her friends for support. That makes sense. And more so, maybe being surrounded by friends will remind Tealey this is where she belongs. We're basically a dysfunctional family, but we're family. "My thoughts exactly." I stop abruptly and lower my voice. "She can't find out from us. If she comes by for any reason, make sure we keep this under wraps."

"Yes, sir."

I've told her a million times, but I tell her again, "It makes me feel like my dad when you call me sir."

Ashleigh laughs but quickly quietens as a few eyes rise above the edges of the cubicles. "Unless the senior partners are around. It's just a hard habit to break. Anyway, I'm hoping you'll take me with you to the top when you make partner, and that means calling you sir, *sir*."

"You're my secret weapon. I'm not going anywhere without you." I push through the conference room door. "Mr. Marché, it's been too long."

Bob is a big man. From his shoulders to his hands, he loves to intimidate others with his large build. "Rad, you're always welcome to get some sunshine in California." Patting my arm, he almost knocks me to the side with his hearty hits, but I stand my ground because he's never intimidated me. "Palm trees. Beautiful women. Blue skies and the ocean. You need to come out for a visit."

"I do. But you're here now. Marlow mentioned you were visiting, but I assumed for pleasure." He's gone completely gray since I last saw him with white taking over the hair around his ears. Too tan to be a New Yorker, he fits right in with the Hollywood elite.

I refer to my right-hand woman. "This is Ashleigh Walters, my assistant."

"Hello," he says, a smile tugging at the corners of his mouth. Glancing at me, he lifts a brow. "I was hoping to speak to you alone."

Ashleigh doesn't need to be asked to leave but waits for me to confirm before exiting. I nod. "It's fine."

"I'll be at my desk if you need anything."

"Thank you." When the door closes, and we sit, I look across the table at him. "It's always good to see you, but I'll admit this comes as a surprise. Usually, when someone sits across from me during business hours on a Tuesday, it's to discuss divorce proceedings."

"Yes," he replies, his chunky fingers drumming the glass-top table. "I want to part ways with my current wife." *Of course you fucking do.*

"I'm sorry to hear that."

"We both know it's coming and long overdue." With a clip to his tone, he picks the lint off his sweater.

"So, you're here for legal advisement?"

"I want you as my lawyer."

"You have a team of attorneys for every aspect of your life." His last divorce attorney is probably still on retainer. "Do you mind if I ask why you want to work with me?"

"I like you. Marlow likes you. I've heard good things about your career, and I think this divorce is going to be a battle." Lowering his voice, he adds, "I want to keep things in the family." He clicks his tongue and winks.

I've known the man for years, but only through his occasional visits to his daughter. I'm thinking family is a bit of a stretch. "As much as I'm flattered, I think it would be wise to have an attorney in Los Angeles handle the case. California law is different—"

"Nothing you can't handle."

"I'm not licensed in California, but I can give you a referral—"

"No need." His hand goes flat on the surface with the same impatience Marlow displays. "I've made up my mind. You'll be representing me, Wellington. I'm filing in the state of New York. I think it will be cleaner here than in California. The Manhattan apartment has been considered my main residence for the past year."

Ah. The plot thickens. "In preparation for filing."

"California sees the divorce more equitably than New York."

"True. It's an equitable division state."

"But that doesn't mean half right out of the gate. Fair is not always equal."

He's done his homework. "Are you residing in the city?"

"I'm flying back and forth. I'm backing a new show on Broadway. It opens next month. For the filing, you can list the Park Avenue address."

"And I assume you had a prenup?"

"Yes, but I got lazy. I should have filed six months ago."

"Because?"

A scowl filters across his face. "The payout increases every six months. We didn't discuss this, but I have a golf buddy who got his prenup voided. What's the likelihood of getting that done for me?"

I do not—correct that—*should not* take this case. Red flags are already going up. Bob's latest divorce will be a high-profile case and splashed on every magazine in the country.

I've worked tirelessly for three years to prove myself, sacrificing most of my personal life to show how dedicated I am. Cade and Jackson have given me shit for missing baseball games, parties, and canceling dates with certain European flight attendants who were in the city for only one night. If I take this case and it goes sideways—*if I fail*—all my hard work would be wasted.

But if it goes right . . . I'll make partner by next year. It's an ambitious plan, but I'm willing to take the chance. *With caution.*

"The travel expenses back and forth to California will be costly," I say.

"I want the best, and my princess always talks about you being the best. This is your time to shine, kid." *Kid . . . time to shine . . .* I try not to roll my eyes. Since the comments are meant as compliments, I don't hold them against him. "I won't take no, Rad. Draft the paperwork."

Without an out coming to mind, I spy Mrs. Klein, a senior partner, eyeing me from outside her office. When her tap her temple, I know the signal. Bob Marché isn't just a big name in Hollywood. I need to take advantage of this opportunity that just landed in my lap. *It's expected.*

He holds his hand out. "Do we have a deal?"

I reach over and take it. "Let's get started."

Why do I feel as though I just sold my soul to the devil to make partner?

And yet, not thirty minutes ago, I felt as though I could make a genuine difference for the better in someone's life? *For Tealey.*

Fuck if my life didn't just get a lot more complicated.

3

Tealey Bell

The straps of my canvas tote dig into my shoulder as I feel around on the inside to find my keys. "See you tomorrow," I call behind me. I'm usually the one working late, but I need to get home to pack.

When I still can't find my keys, I kneel on the sidewalk and spread the handles wide to peer inside. "Ah." I snatch them out and resettle the bag on my shoulder.

"Bell?"

I look ahead to find the familiar voice but shake it when I don't see him.

"Bell?"

Over my shoulder, I spot the slate-gray car I was introduced to not even a month earlier. Nothing about Rad Wellington being in my borough or outside my office makes sense. "You lost, Welly?"

"Nope."

Smirking, I tilt my head to the side, still standing too far away to have a real conversation. I maneuver around two women in a hurry and lean down to see Rad in his full glory—his short brown hair mussed as though he's been tugging on it all day or just got lucky. *My stomach twists.*

I'm about to rest my hands on the open windowsill but stop myself, not daring to leave a fingerprint on this beautiful paint job. "What brings you to Brooklyn?"

"Want to go for a ride?" A rogue grin spreads across his face befitting the car—sleek and, dare I say, sexy.

"Where to?"

"My place." I raise my brows. It's not that I haven't been invited before, but it's never been just me—alone. I've only been there with the group. Rad and I are friends, of course. I even might have wanted to kiss him a time or ten over the years—how could I not? I'm a human, after all, and Rad is, well, Rad. He doesn't look at me as more than a friend. And that's probably for the best.

He's just always been Manhattan elite while I'm more grounded in Brooklyn.

"A bit forward, don't ya think, Mr. Wellington?"

"You asked." He smirks, staring through the windshield. His fingers tighten around the steering wheel. I'm not sure, but I think I catch the smallest of grimaces before he looks at me out of the corner of his eye. He leans over and pops the door open. "Hop in."

I look down the street toward my apartment. It's five blocks, an easy walk, but skipping another night of packing sounds tempting. I know better, though. It wouldn't be responsible to leave it until the last minute. "I really should go home."

"Come on. I'll treat you to tacos and margaritas."

He makes it so hard to say no when I really should go home and pack. "You sure know how to tempt a girl."

He gives me a sideways glance and chuckles. "So you say quite often lately."

"I've been too hard on you. I'm sorry. It's all in fun."

"I know, Tealey. Don't worry about it."

I open the door wider and slip onto the buttery leather passenger seat. After buckling in, I lean back, angling his way. "I'm starting to think the life of one of your 'perks' might not be so bad."

With our eyes fixed on each other, his smile falters. "Promise me you'll never settle for being a perk when you can be someone else's everything."

My heart starts throbbing, and my breath stills in my throat. He doesn't move except two blinks while waiting for me to answer a question he didn't ask. "All right."

He nods, appearing satisfied, and pulls into the flow of traffic. "Tacos?"

"Tacos." Running the tips of my fingers across the leather coating the dash, I say, "I think this is the most expensive car I've ever ridden in."

"I've been in pricier, but this car is my favorite," he replies with such confidence, though not a hint of arrogance is detected. "There's an envelope in the back. It's the retaining contract. No fees as promised."

I look behind his seat to see the envelope and take it, tucking it inside my tote. "Thank you. I know I said it before, but I really do appreciate you helping her and me."

"I want to help."

Though traffic slows, the city begins to tower as we cross the bridge. "Is the contract why you came to see me?"

"Actually, I wanted to spend some time with you. We don't get many opportunities." He glances at me. "Just the two of us."

Being under the steel and concrete bridge with the sun

blocked from most angles, I'm reminded how much I hate bridges. I grip the side of the seat with one hand and the belt across my body with the other. "On purpose."

"You don't spend time with me on purpose?"

I gulp down the fear threatening to creep up my throat and try to hold my tone steady. "No, I thought that's how you wanted it."

His eyes volley between the road and me, a little line digging deeper between his eyes. "Why do you think that?"

Shrugging, I shake my head. "I don't know. I guess because you never asked."

"Touché," he replies as confusion cinches his brows even closer.

Somehow, I find comfort in staring at him versus the brown cage surrounding the vehicle. "Actually, I asked once." I hate the shame mincing my words. "Junior year. I asked you to take me to a dance."

He's quiet for a moment, his attention on the bumper-to-bumper cars ahead, and then he says, "I don't remember that."

"Doesn't matter."

"Sure, it does. Hey. Are you okay?"

"Fine." I try to shake off the sinking feeling. "I don't like bridges. I don't even know why. Must be a fear from a past life or something. Who knows?" I roll my eyes because I sound ridiculous.

Reaching over, he covers my hand gripping the seat with his. The warmth brings peace to my racing heart as I keep my eyes trained on the veins of his hand. He asks, "What dance was it?"

I drag my gaze to his. "It was a last-minute ask, and you were busy."

He's steady in his voice and strength with his hand

gently wrapped around mine to keep it from shaking. "I'm sorry."

"It's fine. Really. I didn't even remember until just now. It was just a sock hop to raise money for a local shelter. A dance-all-night kind of thing. The social work department hosts one every year. I went to others."

"I should have gone with you, though."

"You made a donation, and that was the goal anyway—to raise money."

"It was 50s themed?"

"Yes." I smile at the memory. "That year, I had this great skirt—big and poofy with a poodle on the front and a matching sweater. It was the prettiest shade of blue."

"Like your eyes—" His hand leaves mine to return to the steering wheel before I even process what he said.

"Like my eyes?" My lids flutter without permission. *God, that's humiliating.* I don't think I've ever fluttered my lashes before, and now, I've gone and done it to one of my friends.

Then, as if he's entering evidence into a case in court, he states, "You have pretty eyes." *Direct. Professional. Affirmative.* A pregnant pause leads to him reaching for a button on the steering wheel. "Music?"

As a classical song hits fever pitch, like my face, he scrambles to turn it down. "Sorry," he yells before he can lower the volume. Hopefully, that was distracting enough for him not to notice me pressing my hands to my cheeks to lower the temperature of my embarrassment. *He noticed my eyes?* I get compliments, but not usually from Rad. Come to think of it, Rad doesn't say much of anything to me. Of course, that could be attributed to Marlow usually owning the conversations and Cammie discussing wedding details when we all get together.

An awkwardness permeates the air just as we enter

Manhattan, reminding me of the topic I've been avoiding. It may not change my fate, but I'd like his perspective. I ask, "Have you ever thought of leaving New York City?"

"No, never."

"Wow, that was fast. Never?"

His smile returns, but it's tight at the corners, guarded. "Correction. The easy answer is I have, but I wouldn't want to at this point in my career."

"The hard answer?"

"I used to think about leaving after college, but . . ." He pauses, seeming to debate with himself, which is something I've never seen Rad do. He's always sure of himself. Not in a bad way . . . and sometimes in a bad way. He's intelligent and confident. I guess he has a right to be arrogant occasionally.

"But what?"

The tension starts to ease as does his grip on the steering wheel. "You've always been honest with me, so I will be with you. When Cade and Cammie got together, and Jackson and I met you and Marlow . . . I don't know. It felt right. It made me want to stay. I mean, what would I do without Jackson texting me about food or Marlow wondering if I've seen the society page?" Chuckling through the sarcasm, he adds, "They're family."

I grin, but it's half-hearted as my gaze falls to the floorboard and my confession rolls off the tip of my tongue, "I stayed for the same reasons, but is it enough when the rest of your world is falling apart?"

The light turns green, but Rad stops to look my way. "What's going on, Tealey?"

I suck in a breath, my heart thumping, and try to steady myself. Admitting it out loud to my friends—to Rad—makes it more real. I'm leaving. *Them. My life. This city.*

I'm not ready, but with only a few days left until I need to be out of my apartment, I'd need a miracle to keep me here.

"If we're telling truths, I should have told you and the others already." I close my eyes briefly. "My apartment building sold. The new owners are demolishing it and replacing it with ten stories of modern condos. It's already been approved by the city."

"You're moving." His tone is somber without an ounce of surprise. "How soon?"

"By the end of the week."

I hadn't noticed his watch until a fluorescent sign gleamed off the large face. The man's all money. Always has been, but not in the flashy kind of way . . . other than that watch. Oh, and this car. His office and awards. And we can't forget his donations. "Doesn't sound legal. Owners must give proper notice. Less than two weeks is unreasonable, especially in New York. I'd like to look over your rental agreement."

I stare at the red light ahead as the car comes to a stop. "I was given two months' notice. I've been looking for a new place, but I can't afford anything in this market. The prices have gone up so much that even a studio in the cruddiest neighborhood isn't affordable on my salary."

"You can't leave."

"I also can't afford to live here, so I'm doing what I have to. That means leaving."

He grips the steering wheel tighter, and his jaw ticks. Finally, he looks at me out of the corner of his eye. "You've kind of become a habit."

"Yeah, a regular fixture like a lamp."

He whips his head my way. "What? No. Not like a lamp. Not like that at all." My face flushes when he looks away again. "Why didn't you say anything?"

I shrug. "I don't know. Everyone has so much going on in their lives. Cammie and Cade are planning their wedding. Jackson got a promotion. Marlow . . . well, Marlow is Marlow. And you're always so busy. I didn't want to burden you guys with my problems."

"You're the least burdensome person I know. You can always talk to me." He looks at me, and we exchange a grin.

"Trust me, it wasn't my first choice, but I don't have any other options, Rad. It's move back to Austin or sleep in a box outside the bakery. And while I have an unhealthy addiction to chocolate croissants, I think I'd prefer a bed and roof."

A storm creeps over his features as he pilots us in and out of a line of traffic.

"I'll miss you guys," I say. "I'll miss teasing you about your awards, our weekly dinners with the gang, and the seasons actually changing, unlike in Texas." Fidgeting with the strap of my bag, I continue, "Cammie's wedding drama and Marlow's *life* drama." I laugh, hoping it blocks the lump settling in my throat. "But we'll figure it out. Right?"

He doesn't say anything and just concentrates on the road.

Anxiety begins to bubble in my stomach as the realization that this is one of the last times I'll see Rad and one of the last days of life as I know it. "I'll be fine," I say, trying to talk myself out of panicking. "I just worry about my clients. I hope someone takes their cases that loves them like I do and —Rad!"

I slam forward against my seat belt as the car stops on a dime.

Rad twists in his seat to face me. "Move in with me." The on-the-fly offer feels too spontaneous in the moment, but when he starts driving again, he leaves it out there to linger between us.

"What are you talking about, Rad?"

He doesn't pause to second-guess his decision. Instead, he says, "I have an extra room for when my mom comes into the city. She only stays overnight a few times a year."

My head spins as I try to absorb what he's saying.

Move in with him? *With Rad?*

There are so many things to say, to ask, to think about, but all I can focus on is logistics. "Where will she stay if I'm there?" I ask.

"She can sleep in my room, and I'll take the couch. It's not an issue. I work a lot of late nights—"

"Too many."

"You work a lot, sometimes on the weekend. We'd hardly see each other."

"Are you being for real right now? This isn't a joke, right?"

He chuckles. "It's not a joke. It's a real offer."

His sincerity is overwhelming. He means it.

I force a swallow.

"If you're being serious . . ." I swallow again. "If I did this, it would be temporary, obviously. I would look every day for something affordable and would move out as soon as I can."

"There would be no rush."

Not what I was expecting.

I look out the window. Could this work out? Could I live with Rad? The mere thought gives me chills . . . and hope. "It could be fun, right?" I ask, our eyes meeting when he stops at the corner of his street. That gleam that shone on his watch reaches his eyes even though no signs are reflected this time. Earnestness softens that pesky, *and sexy*, line between his brows.

The architecture changes in this part of the city, mingling old with new so seamlessly. Potted trees with fairy lights anchor the entrances to prewar buildings with doormen in uniforms under each awning ready to perform.

I can imagine what the rest of our friends will say when —*if*—Rad tells them he offered to let me stay with him. They'd go berserk if I turn him down and throw out a million reasons for why this is a perfect solution. They'll beg me to stay. Especially Marlow.

We probably won't see each other much with his schedule and social calendar and my late nights and emergency weekend appointments.

It could work.

Maybe.

I'm suddenly realizing that I don't want to be responsible for breaking up the group. Those five people have my back. It's only a temporary solution, but one that keeps me near these people I care about so much.

I study him, searching his eyes for a truth he can't hide. To my relief, I can't find a lie. "Are you sure?"

He nods before easing off the brake. "Positive." He taps the steering wheel momentarily. "You still have your job, right?"

"Yes. I considered transferring."

"Then stay. With me."

Though I'm not sure this is the right thing to do, I take a deep breath and take the chance. "Then it's a yes from me, but I promise not to overstay my welcome. This will give me more time to find a new place to live instead of moving back in with my family."

A smile splits his cheeks. "I can't believe you considered moving back to Texas. You know we'd help you however we could."

"I know," I reply with a heavy sigh. "It's just . . . I'm the one who helps others in need. I don't want to put my problems on you guys."

"You'd rather leave us?"

"No. I'd rather stay. Texas was a last resort." I smile and look out the window. "I can't imagine leaving the city. It's become a part of my identity." Touching his arm, I add, "I want you to know that I'll pay you rent."

"We can worry about the details later."

Maybe he can worry about the details another time, but my money is accounted for down to the penny. Spying his modern and incredible building ahead, I know it's a conversation we need to have sooner than later. I'm thinking half the rent of his apartment is going to mean selling some things and dipping into my savings. "Or tonight."

"After dinner?" he asks, quirking an eyebrow, the corner of his mouth rising with it.

"Deal."

"Just one question."

"Okay." I grin, and say, "Shoot."

He slows the car on approach to the luxury residence. "When do you need to move in?"

"Friday. Is that too soon?"

Smirking, he shifts gears. "Perfect timing."

4

Rad

"You must love living here," Tealey says.

Pulling into the underground garage of the stream-lined, modern structure reminds me of how far it had come. It was formerly a dilapidated, bordering on condemned, four-story building that housed a tailor on the top floor, a pillow manufacturer on the third, a law firm on the second, and a deli on the first, dating back to 1921.

The bricks were crumbling around it and stood out like an eyesore on the prestigious block. The owner refused to sell it to anyone because of their visions of tearing it down and building an "ugly," as he called it, rectangle.

There's no changing the shape, but I presented him with an innovative design, and he sold it to me under the condition that I would live there for three years before selling. I bought the building as an investment, but I had no problem sticking to the agreement. I love this place. Although I dipped into one of my trust funds, I scored a deal and kept the elements that could be saved intact during the renovation.

"It's a nice place to come home to," I say, parking the car. "I guess you'll get to experience that too."

She looks at me and grins. I'll never get tired of seeing her like this.

We take the elevator, which opens into the apartment. She's been here many times over the years and even knows the code to get in the building, so when I hang my keys on a hook and toss my jacket on the back of the couch as I pass, why does it feel different with her following me this time?

Why do *I* feel different?

This is nothing more than a friend helping a friend. *That's all.*

I'm starting to wonder how many times I'm going to have to say that before I believe it.

Tealey leans against the bar and watches me as I roll up my shirtsleeves and then activate the lights on the same keypad. The lighting in the corners goes from dim to brighter, setting an ambiance usually reserved for the end of a rough day.

I enter the kitchen as she pushes off and walks the length of the windows from one end of the room to the other. "You're spoiled with the views you have at the office and your apartment. Does it ever get old?"

"No." I chuckle, checking my liquor cabinet. "I'm out of tequila, but I can order some."

"It's okay. No need. What do you have?"

"Water, wine, whiskey, whatever you want, you get?" Pulling my phone from my pocket, I set it on the counter.

"White wine."

"Sauvignon blanc from New Zealand, if I remember correctly."

"You do."

I pull a bottle from the wine fridge.

"What kind of tacos? I can order an assortment."

She smiles. "Sounds great."

I place an order and then pour her a glass of wine and a bourbon neat for myself. I take my time, giving me a few seconds to drink her in—the delicate curve where her neck meets her shoulder, the graceful way she stands with her arms clasped over each other, and the messy hair. I can't say I haven't thought about kissing her neck in the past or telling her that my crush has existed as long as I've known her. It would be a mistake, though, so I keep this silly crush to myself and hand her the glass.

"Here you go. The taco delivery is going to take a while. They just got hit with some large orders. Want to go to the rooftop while we wait?"

She pops to her feet. "Thought you'd never ask."

We're granted a cool evening with clear skies at the tail end of sunset. After not five minutes up there, though, the food arrives, sending me down to the street level to get it. I try to cool off before pushing onto the deck again. "Food is served."

Not an hour after sunset, Tealey's had her fill of tacos and is wrapped in a blanket on a lounge chair with her third glass of wine. She's been staring at the stars since we came up here. And I've been staring at her from the other side of the firepit. I can, for once, without getting caught because the rest of our friends aren't here.

"I've always loved it up here," she says, looking at me. "Comfort found in the middle of chaos. The peace reminds me of your mom's house in the Hamptons. Her property might be my favorite place in the world. Your mom is amazing as well."

"She happens to adore you, too." Kicking my feet out, I tilt back, searching for the stars among the skyscrapers. "She begs me to visit all the time." I spy her grinning out of the corners of my eyes.

"I can't even wrap my head around your life. It's so big. Does that make sense?" I understand the disbelief. My life was privileged, to say the least. *Still is.* Her eyes remain on mine, that comfort she spoke of reaching me. "You never talk about the divorce, only that it led you to become a lawyer."

"The divorce cost me everything—my mom's peace of mind and my trust in humanity. I set out to defend the innocent and ended up helping the highest bidder. No good deed goes unpunished."

"What happened?"

I take a deep breath. "The outcome of my mom's life, and mine by default, was decided by a judge who knew nothing about my family except for our finances and what gossip columnists shared. You ready for this?"

I don't expect her to answer, but she nods anyway. After taking a long pull of the amber liquid, I say, "When the judge awarded the properties to my mom, mainly due to my dad's philandering, he blamed me, and I overheard my father tell his lawyers that he'd be a lot richer if he'd worn a condom."

Sitting up, she covers her heart as if the ache is too much to bear. "That's terrible. I'm sorry."

"I'll say one thing about who I choose to defend. They aren't victims, but they share in their marital crimes and marriage misdemeanors like their spouses. There are no innocents when millions are on the line."

"I'm not judging you, Rad. You're a brilliant man who found a path that utilizes your cleverness. My skills don't pay well, but I feel my job utilizes my abilities. We're on a journey doing what we were drawn to do. With that said, everyone seems to be caught up in their own lives lately. I've been feeling somewhat disconnected." The gentle breeze can't whisk away the sadness hanging on her face even though I wish it could.

"Are you—?"

"I shouldn't have any more," she adds, waggling her empty glass. She leans her head against the pillow and directs her gaze back to the stars. "You know what Steve said when we broke up a few months ago?"

I know what I said—halle-fucking-lujah—though only to myself. Sitting forward, I rest my forearms on my legs and keep that to myself. No one in our group particularly liked Steve. He just never meshed with any of us, so there's no lost love between him and us and vice versa. But it was still a blow to her that she weathered alone. "What?"

"He told me I was boring and had big thighs."

What. The. Fuck?

Her tone didn't deviate, but that had to sting, especially since it's not true. My jaw clenches. I hope she can't see my reaction. I'm usually better at controlling it.

"I never liked that fucker," I say.

A burst of laughter fills the air, causing me to join her. "I know. That's why I didn't tell you guys."

"Why'd you keep that to yourself?" I'm shot a look that tells me she knows Jackson, Cade, and I would have paid him a visit. "Okay, then why didn't you tell Marlow?"

"She has a lot on her plate right now dealing with an upcoming gallery show." *Yeah, and meetings with her personal shopper.* "I didn't want to make a big deal out of it. I hate when people pity me."

How could she think we'd feel that way about her? "We

wouldn't pity you, Tealey. We'd probably treat you to a congratulatory dinner, though. He was such a punk."

"You're the worst," she says, but her laughter tapers off.

Leaning back again, I swirl the remaining liquid around the edges of the glass.

"I should have told you. You're just always so busy that I hate to be a—"

"I'm never too busy for you. I mean that." I catch her eyes on me before her gaze slips to the night sky again. "And for the record, just in case me calling him a fucker wasn't clear, I'm glad you're not with Steve."

"I love you for saying that." The warmth heard in her words fills my chest. This girl has always taken up a lot of space in my heart. Doesn't matter that she adds, "So much for letting the cat out of the bag." I'm not sure if she means her breakup with Steve or loving me, but I'll go with the latter.

She sits up, hugging a pillow to her chest. "He never liked you. That should have been a sign for me to dump him the first night he met you guys. God, how he ranted about Rad Wellington. I never really understood why he felt competitive with you. He's not even an attorney. He's an engineer for a pipe company."

I leave her to find her own answers to that question, though it doesn't surprise me to hear about his insecurities. Steve once cornered me to ask if I had a thing for Tealey. I'd made a joke, and she laughed. Everyone did, except him. I suppose my silence as I walked away didn't offer any comfort. Good. *Fuck him.*

Rolling her head to the side, she smiles as she stuffs the pillow behind her back. "I'll pay better attention with the next guy."

"There doesn't have to be another guy . . ." *What the hell am I saying?* I grab my glass and finish the remains. Distract. Distract. Distract. "The moon is huge tonight."

She looks up, but her knotted brows top a curious look that she aims back at me. Swinging her feet back to the deck, she leans forward, the fire flickering between us. "What do you mean there doesn't have to be another?"

I stand, gathering the glasses and the lighter. "Nothing other than you don't need to jump into another relationship." Glancing at her, I add, "See how things go on your own for a while." This time, the grin is subtle, but the round apples of her cheeks redden.

"You're right. I know you are." She sighs. "I don't even remember how Steve and I started our relationship. We went on a date, and the rest fell in line for a time."

"That's not love. That's a habit. Some habits are great, and some—"

"And some are like lamps." Standing, she grabs the blanket and stuffs it in the trunk. "Ready to show me the bedroom?" *Would I ever.* "I'd like to get a lay of the land." *Ah.*

"Sure."

I lead her back downstairs and drop the glasses off in the kitchen before making our way to the extra bedroom. Flicking on the light, I then step aside. "You can decorate it however you'd like. I'm sure it will be an upgrade to how bland it is now."

When she enters the room, the effects of alcohol have rested in her features. Quite a contrast to her gripping the seat under the Brooklyn Bridge. "It's bigger than I expected." Her fingers graze my arm as the tips slide down to the top of my hand before she's out of reach. "If I sold my furniture, I could probably fit my boxes in here instead of renting a storage unit. But I can't afford to buy new stuff. I need to save as much as I can for the security deposit and moving expenses."

"I can cover it if you'd like—the moving costs. Save your money for a few new pieces. Do you still have that futon from college?"

She starts laughing. "It's not so bad."

"Start with replacing that piece of junk."

With a little laugh, she pushes the curtains aside and looks out the window. "I might get rid of it. I should. It's so uncomfortable." Turning back, she adds, "But I'm not taking your money, Rad, not borrowing or accepting a loan. I could have followed in my parents' footsteps and become a physical therapist. They make a good living, but that wasn't my goal. Unfortunately, my chosen career doesn't pay much, but it's my dream. It pays enough to get by. I just . . ." I lean against the doorframe and watch as she explores the room. Her eyes find the window, and she pauses. "I'm not sure my job is the dream I imagined in my head."

It's interesting how I've known her for so many years, but tonight, I'm seeing more of who she is on the inside. The dynamics of six can overshadow the individual. She's more than the pretty face, the girl with a great smile and charitable soul. She's more than the few parts I've seen. I've wasted so much time keeping her at a distance that I've missed being a part of the story. *She's ethereal. And I want more of her.*

She sits on the bed and then lies back with her arms spread and her eyes closed. "This bed is what heaven must feel like."

"My mom likes it too." At that, she smiles softly. "If you could do anything, what would it be?"

. . .

SHE TAKES a deep breath and then exhales slowly. Turning her head toward me, she props herself up on her elbow. Excitement flickers in her eyes, a wild confession that has me fixed on her every word. "I would start a program to help kids in need. I'd raise money to help them however I could from getting them off the streets to getting them nutritious meals to after-school programs and tech training."

Impressive. And so Tealey. "Do you want to continue working on the front line, or would you ever want to be behind the scenes?"

"Depends on where I'd be most effective."

"Why did I not know this? Do the others?"

Shaking her head, she says, "No one ever asked."

So humble. "You have a big heart, Tealey."

"And a small bank account. I should have asked you way before falling in love with this bed, but how much is half the rent?"

I give her a look. "You aren't paying me anything. Save your money for the new place."

Bolting upright, she's apparently gotten a second wind. "No way. I insist."

I suspect her current rent would be about a quarter of what one of my tenants would pay. But I'm not going to throw that in her face.

"My studio in Brooklyn is sixteen hundred a month, so I can pay you the same while I'm here."

Almost two thousand a month for the dump where she lives? That building should have been condemned thirty years ago.

"You'll need money for the new place, so why don't we cut a deal and say two fifty? You're only getting a room. That way, you can save and get ahead."

Her eyes stay locked on mine as if she'll find another answer. "Really? You'd be okay with that?"

"I'd be fine with you staying for free. The room doesn't go away when you're not here, so I'm used to covering my expenses."

Standing, she comes to me as if we're those kinds of friends, the kind that touch and hug and—*oh fuck*. Maybe we are those types of friends. "You're an amazing man, Rad." She pats me on the chest. "You know that?"

"I'll take amazing." I angle toward the door to lead her out but stop. "By the way, I'm glad you dumped that fucker." That elicits a chuckle from her.

Her smile slides away as she looks up at me. She sighs. "I wish I could find a guy like you. You're too good to me."

"A guy like me?" Tealey wants a *guy like me*?

"You drive me around in your fancy car, and you feed me, give me shelter . . ." Her hand flattens on my chest, just over my heart. I cover it with mine, trying hard not to have her hear my nerves through a hard swallow. The light from the living room shines in her eyes, and another smile appears. "Thank you for everything you're doing, but also for sharing your story about the divorce with me."

Fuck it. I swallow the lump in my throat down, not even apologizing for how loud it is. "I'm glad I did as well."

I don't think she realizes that she's patting to the beat of my heart. "Being here already feels like home, but speaking of, I should go."

"I'll call a car to take you home."

"Thanks." She's gone from the room too fast for my liking, leaving me alone. "Fuck me," I mutter under my breath. The woman has me spinning like my liquor.

I catch her picking up her bag. "You've made my week,

Rad. Hell, my month. Thank you for letting me move in."
She comes closer and nudges me with her elbow. "Roomie."

"Roomie . . ." I'm not sure this is how I imagined our
relationship going. Utterly confused now, I scratch the top of
my head. What the actual fuck am I doing? The woman who
I've pined over for more than seven years, and that I'll deny
if put on the stand, is going to be sharing the same roof as
me—breakfast, dinner, late nights.

I'm so fucked.

5

Rad

"I'm walking in now."

"Walking in where?" Jackson asks on the other end of the call.

"To the restaurant."

The phone goes silent, long enough for me to make sure I haven't lost the connection. When I put it to my ear again, he asks, "Are we talking in code because I'm confused?"

I swing the door open and step inside. "Dinner. Tonight. Marlow. Her dad. Your sorry ass. Ring a bell?"

"I don't know what you're talking about, Rad. You're having dinner with Bob? I didn't know he was in town."

"What do you mean? We're supposed to be here, pretty much now."

After giving the midtown steakhouse a quick scan, I approach the host. Wearing a white shirt and a skinny black tie, the host asks, "Do you have a reservation?"

Holding the phone against my chest, I reply, "Marché."

"Ah, yes. Your party is already seated. Follow me." He turns swiftly and guides me through the restaurant.

Holding the phone to my ear, I whisper, "You're already here. You're such an asshole."

"Wish I knew what the fuck you were talking about. I'm sitting in my apartment. Just turned on the game. I take it you're not coming over?"

The host stops at a booth in the corner where Marlow and her father are engaged in a lively conversation. I pause, wondering where everyone else is, before turning around and heading back out before the Marchés have time to notice me. "Are you serious?" I whisper through gritted teeth. "You're not at this dinner."

"I don't have a clue about that dinner."

I push the door and step out onto the sidewalk, starting to sweat under my suit. I tug at the collar, and gripe, "Why aren't you here?"

He starts crunching on what I can assume are Cheetos. The man eats them like he holds stock in the company. "Guess I wasn't invited."

Motherfuck. I pace the sidewalk with the phone glued to my ear. "How can I get out of it?"

"Doesn't sound like you can, man."

"I should be able to on principle alone. She told me he wanted to have dinner. I assumed it was with everyone, not just with me and her and Bob."

"Sounds cozy." He chuckles. "But if she didn't tell you, and then you assumed, I think that means it's on you. Anyway, bright side—you get a free dinner. Her dad loves to splash the cash around."

I'm sure, but I'd rather not be here at all. "Yeah, okay." I roll my eyes.

"Cade is on his way to my place, so it's safe to say he

didn't know about the dinner either. Just go in, have a good meal, and come over later."

I sigh. The high I was riding all day after spending last night with Tealey has faded. Rubbing my forehead, I pinch my eyes closed. "Yeah, you're right."

"Rad?" Marlow calls from behind me. "We already have a table in the back."

Glancing back over my shoulder, I give her a nod and then point at my phone. "I'll be right there." She disappears back inside. I grip the back of my neck and then tell Jackson, "Don't drink all the beer. I'm heading over afterward."

Determined to make the most of this dinner, I hang up and re-enter the restaurant, passing the host. "I see them." I'm hoping this isn't about his divorce, but a dinner among friends. I remain hopeful as I cut through the bustling restaurant.

Checking my watch, I say, "Right on time," when I arrive tableside. "How are we?"

Bob is dressed casually in a short-sleeved button-up, repping California to a T, and Marlow is in designer from head to toe, per usual. She has great style, albeit eccentric some days. She smiles. "Fantastic. You?"

"Peachy. No one else is joining us, or everyone's running late?"

She pats the booth beside her. "Dad thought it would be fun for the three of us to catch up." Red flags fly up as my gaze darts between them. Not only is there no backup for me in managing Marlow if this goes off the rails, but she'll flip if she finds out I met with her dad just yesterday. *Thanks, Bob.*

This should be fun . . .

Reaching forward, Bob and I shake hands. "Good to see you again, Mr. Marché." I slide into the booth.

"Bob works." His gruff voice is loud enough to draw the attention of the surrounding tables. "Marlow and I were just discussing cryptocurrency. I'm dabbling. Got any good tips for me?"

"Just dabbling myself. It's like the Wild West. You never know if you'll strike gold or lose it all."

Marlow sits in the middle of us with a big grin, playing innocent. She knew it would only be us when she invited me. It would have been nice to be in on the plan, especially since he's now my client. The omission means it was on purpose and leaves me in a vulnerable position. Do I treat him like a client or her dad? I've known him for years, and we've always been friendly and gotten along, but things have changed in the past thirty-six hours. And more than just professionally. I shoot Marlow a glare. I may not know why she only invited me, but everything she does has a reason behind it.

When she whispers, "Don't hate me," my face must say everything I haven't. Moving on like everything is A-OK, she says, "We ordered drinks while we were waiting. Whiskey neat, right?"

"That works." Make it a double if he tells Marlow I'm representing him before the first course.

"So, here we are . . ."

She's quick to add, "Let's order. I'm starving."

The drinks are delivered, and I immediately take my glass and tip it back, my manners flying out the window. A buzz in my pocket has me slipping my phone from it and peeking down at it. Jackson: *Damn, dude. Five minutes in and Miami is up by two. That wager you let ride is gonna be mine.*

It's tempting to shit-talk back, but again, I'm riding the professional line here.

"Everything okay?" Marlow asks, leaning over with the menu in hand.

"It's Jackson. He's watching the game."

"Football?"

"Basketball."

"Ah." Returning her attention to the menu, she taps it. "I'm thinking about the halibut."

I decide on the steak and set the menu back on the table. Glancing up, I ask Bob, "How's your stay in New York?"

"Lots of meetings. There always are when money is involved." Setting his napkin on the table, he slides out of the booth. "Will you excuse me? There's a producer at the bar who I've been trying to connect with while here."

"Sure," Marlow says, but as soon as he leaves, she looks at me. "I'm so sorry, Rad. I hate putting you in this position, but I was nervous about this dinner, and I knew you would back me up when the shit hit the fan."

"Why are you nervous, and what shit are we talking about?"

We both glance toward the bar just as Bob reaches it. When we turn back, she grabs a frantic hold of my wrist. "I think he's going to cut me off, and then what will I do? I'll be homeless and will have to sell my belongings to Sotheby's to auction off to the highest bidder or, worse, the only bidder."

"Slow down, Marlow. Maybe he just wants to have dinner with you."

"It's bad news. I can feel it. Something is off." Tapping a nail to the wood table, she says, "He's been here for weeks but just told me the other day. He's been busy in endless meetings, and his current wife isn't here. It's fishy if you ask me."

"Or he's been busy working," I say. I'm not proud of myself for lying, but again, this is where we are.

"You're probably right. I'm glad you're here anyway. I knew you could temper the situation no matter how it plays out." Rolling her eyes, she laughs. "He loves you."

I catch sight of Bob returning and whisper, "I'll run interference if you need it, but I want you to remember that anything he says, you can handle."

She nods and looks up. "How'd that go, Daddy?"

Bob arrives with the server, and says, "Better than expected. We set up a meeting for Friday."

After we place our order, Bob angles toward Marlow. As much as I don't want the fact that I already know about the divorce coming out, that beats her being financially cut off. "Marlow, sweetie, I've been meaning to talk to you, and Rad being here seems like a fitting opportunity." Here it comes . . .

Her eyes widen as her breath catches in her chest. "What is it?"

"I know you'll be disappointed, but I'm getting a divorce."

I cringe, knowing what comes next.

She blinks in disbelief. "You've been married for less than two years." *Not what I expected.*

"It was a whirlwind. We met at Cannes. The food. The awards. The parties." Bob reminisces as if it's a bygone era. "As you know, we were married before we returned to LA. Not my best decision."

Marlow drops her head in her hands. "Not even two years." Popping up, she asks, "Does the press know? TMZ? Page Six?"

"No. Only my attorney, and now you."

She gasps. "Does Lorie know?"

"Yes. She found out when I caught her fucking the chef

for crafts services on her latest film. She's agreeing to keep this as hush-hush as possible."

"For a fee, I'm sure."

"Of course. You know how these things go in Hollywood."

"I do. Too well because of you. This is humiliating. They'll stalk you and Lorie, and then they'll come after me." She tosses her napkin on the table with anger. "Why can't you date like a normal person? You don't have to marry every woman you meet."

I have her back, but this is not something I can fix for them. Feeling like an intruder to their conversation, I sit back as far as I can within the confines of the red leather booth.

The space allows me to remember how beautiful Tealey looked covered in a blanket on the lounge chair, stars shining down, and the sound of traffic becoming the city's soundtrack.

I've not lived with a woman before, so I'm not sure what to expect. When I lived with Jackson and Cade back in college, that was a mess. Hence, why I now live alone.

Wonder what it will be like to wake up with Tealey there, to have her as the last person I see at night? Will I see her, or is she right that we'll hardly see each other?

Given I haven't heard anything from any of the guys, I'm guessing Tealey hasn't told them she's moving in with me. Is it something I should do, or is this a secret? I can't imagine why we'd hide it. We're all friends. I'm just one helping another . . . another that I'm not sure that I've been great at hiding the torch I've carried.

Torch might be taking it too far.

Lantern?

Flashlight works, I lie to myself.

Who am I kidding?

I thought I'd see Tealey at this *group dinner* tonight, which made it worth it to miss a game when I have a large bet on the line. *I wonder how long's a reasonable time to stay here?*

When Marlow downs her wine like a shot, I do what any good friend would do. I hold my finger in the air when a server passes by and point at the empty glasses. Judging by his hustle to the bar, I'm thinking he can read my desperation.

Marlow says, "I'm tired of your bad decisions wreaking havoc on my life. Why can't I have normal parents?"

I might have called her spoiled any other time, all in good fun, because she relishes the role, but this time feels different. She's upset.

I reach over and awkwardly nudge her in the arm. "I think—"

"Because your mother ran off with an Italian race car driver, that's why." Bob's smarting words cause Marlow to flinch from the impact. "That's when our lives were so-called 'normal' and look how that turned out. So calm down, Marlow." *Yikes.* Rookie mistake. Telling any woman to calm down explains his divorces. "You didn't even like Lorie."

A red wave crawls from the base of Marlow's neck, spreading to her jaw and settling in her face. She tightens her mouth, and says, "Don't tell me to calm down."

"Listen—"

"No, you listen. I didn't dislike Lorie. I just don't bother to get to know them anymore. What's the point, Daddy, when you're going to turn around and divorce them so quickly?"

"The point is, I'm a sucker for a beautiful—"

"Too-young-for-you models, actresses," she says, ticking off her fingers. "Flight attendants, my friends—"

"I married Deandra, so I think that makes her more my friend than yours."

"Oh, trust me, Daddy. She's not my friend anymore, but she was in high school and one of the few people I thought I could trust. Why do you think I left California?"

That's a lot to unpack, and I'm thinking that won't happen tonight.

The drinks arrive, allowing each of them to catch their breath. Marlow crosses her arms and looks across the sea of people while Bob looks at me. *Shit.*

Covering her hand, Bob returns his attention to his daughter. "I've hurt you and caused you pain. I'm sorry, sweetie. That was never my intention. I'm not always the best with this kind of stuff, so I'm glad you have Rad to rely on."

Marlow's scowl softens. "I don't want to fight with you. I'll weather the paparazzi storm like I always do."

"That's my girl." Bob grins like he's saving the day he just shit on. "I have a surprise for you if you're up for it?"

He knows the way to Marlow's heart. Her eyes brighten along with her disposition. "What is it?"

"I've been so proud of how you've pursued your passion and landed a job at the gallery. You've really pulled your life together." Signaling toward me, he continues, "Rad's in your life, and well, I know living in the city is expensive, so I thought I could help you two lovebirds with a little nest egg."

Wait, what? Lovebirds? Nest egg?

"Lovebirds?" Marlow asks, sounding just as confused as I am.

He pulls his napkin back onto his lap with a grin. "Yeah,

I know you two like to keep things under wraps, as we say in the industry, but I want to buy your apartment. Then you won't have to carry that burden." Eyeing me, he adds, "Fewer hours at work means more time to play at home. Right, Rad?"

"Um . . ." I'm thinking now is not a good time—*personally or professionally*—to disclose that Tealey's moving in with me. "Right, sir," I answer begrudgingly, feeling caught between my job and my life.

Although Marlow's not hurting for money, her dad's offer is chum in the water. Not sure how she's planning to break it to him that we're not together, but by her wide smile, she's already fallen hook, line, and sinker into this plan.

Since I'm one-half of the future owner of this purchased apartment, I'm thinking now would be a good time to speak up. "Although we appreciate the offer—"

"Thank you, Daddy." Marlow throws her arms around him. "We'll take it."

"Uh."

She turns to me. "Don't worry. It will all work out how it's supposed to."

Between gritted teeth, I say, "It's too generous."

Shrugging, she laughs. "He wants to."

"I want to. I like to keep things in the family. That's why I asked you to represent me. You can run interference with the press. You can't break client privilege, and since you're dating Marlow, they won't drag her into the media this time. It's a brilliant plan."

And here I thought Marlow was the mastermind behind tonight's dinner. I think she did as well, but Bob's outplayed us both. It actually is a brilliant plan. I don't know whether to be impressed or worried.

He takes a long pull of his scotch, and then adds, "My baby girl snagging a prestigious East Coast bachelor, a Wellington, at that, will bring plenty of good PR. And you won my daughter's heart, so everyone wins."

Everyone does not win, namely me.

Two things:

Firstly—Why the fuck would he assume Marlow and I are dating?

Secondly—Tealey will be pleased to know that I figured out what snagging entails.

I start, "I didn't snag—"

Her index finger swings in her father's direction. "Back up. You *retained* Rad because you thought we were together?"

"Yes, and because he's good at what he does."

Shooting me a hard glare, she says, "I wasn't told."

"I—"

"Shh!" Holding her finger straight up, she stares at me, and then she bites her lip, her expression morphing from anger to . . . *oh shit*. As the puzzle pieces fall into place, I realize she's already two steps ahead. "Weren't you trying to make partner?"

Am I about to be blackmailed into marrying Marlow?

What the fuck?

My swallow is as deep as the Grand Canyon. "I am."

"So, winning a high-profile client's case would help you achieve that?"

"There's no guarantee."

"You're under oath. Is that a yes or no?"

"I'm not under oath, but yes, it would help."

A smile that could win the title of Miss America settles across her face. "I'd call that a triple win then."

My phone buzzes on the seat beside me. When I glance

down, Jackson's sent the latest score. Not only have I lost all logic when it comes to this asinine idea but I'm also about to lose one thousand dollars.

At this point, I'm certain my eyebrows have become one with my hairline. There aren't enough hours tonight to wade through this absurd scheme, but no way am I just agreeing to please them.

They have some solid points, but I need to get out from under this Marché madness, find fresh air, and clear my head.

There must be a solution that serves us better than lying to the world and each other to get what we each want.

And I'd really like to know why Bob Marché thinks I'm dating his daughter. Because that is utterly crazy.

Kill me now.

6

Rad

"No." I storm down the sidewalk in front of the steakhouse, pacing as my mind tries to process this mess. The clicking of Marlow's heels has haunted me on each pass, except this one. I stop and turn back. Crossing my arms over my chest, I take a stance. "Absolutely not. This is bordering on unethical."

"It's not unethical, Rad." She smiles, tilting her head. "It's a favor for a friend, at best."

"At worst, it's fucking with my job." Her dad left already, leaving us standing here to sort this disaster out. Pointing toward the restaurant, I add, "Your dad admitted he only hired me because he thought we were together. Why would he think that?"

"I don't know." Crossing her arms, she matches my stance, facing me head-on. Marlow's never been the damsel in distress. "I'm telling you the truth. I've never said or insinuated anything was going on between us. I really don't know why he'd assume that."

"Me being the one sitting by your side at dinner doesn't help quell any assumptions."

Marlow cringes. "I understand why you're mad. Mad Rad." Her slip of a smile eases the edges of irritation. "Look, we can both benefit from this plan. If we just pretend for him, for just a little while, I get an apartment—an investment in New York real estate, which is priceless. And you look good to your bosses, getting you one step closer to that partnership."

"Bob gets the cover of attorney-client privilege by working with me, and you're protected from the paparazzi until the case is settled. And then what?"

"And then some celebrity will screw up and grab the headlines back."

Somehow, this farce started to make sense while we ate our three-course meal. But now, back in reality, not so much. So why am I considering going along with it? She assumes it will all go as planned, but it has the potential to go bad.

What if the gang finds out? What do we say? Maybe we should tell them and be up front. Once we start this, how do we end it? And more importantly, how will this affect my new situation with Tealey?

I roll my neck to the side and then the other to release the tightness of my muscles.

"Please, Rad. This only works if you're on board. I won't blame you if you're not. It's nuts, for sure. But it will mean everything to me if you do this one little thing for me." She uncrosses her arms and then says, "No kissing involved because ew."

"Thanks for the unsolicited ego check," I deadpan. Although she is right.

"You're like a brother, so definitely no kissing or

anything weirdly romantic." She pats me on the shoulder as if I have cooties to prove the point.

Cocking an eyebrow, I say, "We agree on that."

Hope flashes through her eyes. "No romance. No flowers or dates or anything even remotely relationship-y." She shivers. "Even thinking about that grosses me out. No offense."

"None taken."

She sighs. "Look, I can see you don't love this. I don't either. But think of it this way—my dad uses people to get what he wants all the time. Hence, the fifth marriage you're about to dissolve. So, let's use this to our advantage."

She must sense my frustration waning because she goes in for the kill.

"We can use this to set ourselves up for the future," she says. "Purchasing my apartment is nothing to my father, but it would be everything to me. It would . . . it would allow me a breather and allow me to catch up on some other expenses. I make decent money at the gallery, but you know how high the cost of living in this city can be."

She has a point. *Several.*

"And you, Rad Wellington, were born to be partner. You're living the bachelor life to its fullest, but maybe one day you'll want a wife and kid. It could happen," she says, biting her lip. "Maybe. Anyway, what position do you want to be in when that day comes, if that day comes? Working eighty hours a week for base pay or working forty and making a cut of the profits? You'll have more time to pursue your other interests and more income to do it. It's a chance that some never get. And honestly, it hurts no one. It's only a little show for my dad. He'll be back in LA before you know it, and then I can tell him we broke up. This is ours for the taking."

I tilt my head back and look at the sky. *She's right.* I hate it that she is.

If I do this and it works—I'll definitely make partner. I'll have another successful case under my belt and making partner before I hit thirty would allow me to relax a little and have a life again. More time to watch games with the guys, visit my mom more often in the Hamptons. It would set me up for life and would be the cherry on top of a dream I've had since I was seven years old.

Images of spending time with Tealey on the weekends crowd my other thoughts. My head snaps back to Marlow as I shake those thoughts out of my brain.

I need another drink. I can't get ahead of myself.

"So, what do you think, Rad?" What do I think?

I think this is nuts.

I take a deep breath. "If this charade is only for your father and not the whole damn world, I'll agree."

Raising her hands in surrender, she replies, "That's all. I swear."

No matter how many times I try to riddle through this mess, I know there's no figuring out something that will never make sense. I give up and finally relent for a friend. "Fine."

"We agree not to tell my dad until that deed is in hand and you're the star of the firm."

"I'm already a star."

"Come on, Rad. Promise me."

"Okay. I promise." We shake on it.

"Tealey always said if there's one person we can always count on, it's you." *She does?* Why do I like that she thinks so highly of me? Marlow adds, "She's right. I knew I could count on you."

She's trotting toward a cab at the curb, so I'm not left

with enough time to change my mind on this scheme. "Hey, where are you going?"

"I have a date."

I check the time, and it's just gone nine. I give her respect for double stacking her night. She handled her business, and now she's off to have fun. I should follow her lead.

Swinging the back door open, she waves. "You're the best, Rad."

I tuck my hands in my pockets and smirk. "So I'm told."

Laughing, she adds, "Don't wait up for me." She's grinning when she ducks into the back of the taxi.

While Marlow's off to see some guy she's *actually* dating, I'm standing on the street corner like an idiot. That's my cue to leave, and hopefully, I can catch the end of the game with the guys.

I don't get four blocks when Jackson texts me the final score and types: *Thanks for the payday, sucker.*

Sighing, I text: *Remind me to never let it ride.*

Jackson: *Why would I do that when I just won from your poor judgment?*

I chuckle. Me: *Cade still there?*

Jackson: *He just left.*

Me: *I was heading over there, but I think I'll head home instead.*

Jackson: *Early morning for me, so I wouldn't be good company for long anyway.* There's a game on Thursday.

Between my caseload, Tealey moving in, and now this Marlow madness, I reply: *A lot going on this week. I'll check my schedule.*

Jackson: *All good. Have a good one.*

Me: *You too.*

Although I'm heading in the same direction as my apartment, I'm not ready to go home. I lean forward and tell the driver, "Change of plans. Brooklyn."

Cars honking. The city lit up at night. People crowding the sidewalks. It doesn't matter if it's a Tuesday or Saturday night, the city is always awake and thriving. The thrum of New York beats inside me, and I sit back and let it fight against the adrenaline coursing through me. That's something I usually reserve for court but going against the Marchés is similar. The only difference is I think I just lost my case.

Tealey asking if I'd ever considered leaving has me looking at the city again. I've become so used to the hustle of the streets that it had become a blur in my mind, a place I was sleepwalking through to get to my job or go home with not much life between.

If someone were to ask her, she'd detail out some exciting life that she imagines I lead. It's interesting enough to pass time, but is it fulfilling in the ways humans desire?

I think it used to be.

Now, I'm not so sure.

As we cross the bridge, a new rush runs up my spine. I shouldn't be fixated on Tealey like I've been since we're just friends, but I'm starting to believe that she might put some excitement back in my life.

Friend.

Roommate.

Whatever we are, I'm liking this energy she's injected.

Deep in the borough away from the bridge, the cab turns down a street and then cuts across another. I recognize the block, though I don't think I've ever been here at night. Come to think of it, I'm not sure I've been in Tealey's apartment at all.

I pay the driver and get out. Looking down the street in

one direction and then the other, it's distinctively quieter on her block than the parts of Manhattan we drove through to get here.

After verifying the address once more, I walk to the door. I'm about to knock, but some guy on the first floor smoking a cigarette asks, "You don't live here. Who are you here to see?"

"Tealey Bell in 3B."

The lines in his brow are smooth, and his expression lifts. "Why are you here to see her?"

"We're friends. *Good friends*." Since that doesn't seem to satisfy the old guy, I add, "She's moving in with me this weekend."

"Chad Mellington, or something like that."

"Close enough." *That Tealey's talked about me has to be a good sign.*

He stamps the cigarette on the brick windowsill and says, "I'll buzz you in."

I wait only a few seconds before I hear the buzz and the lock release. I pull the door open and enter the building, only to be greeted by the same guy. "She tells me you have a nice place."

"I do. It's not too far from Central Park."

Rubbing his fingers together, he oohs. "Money. She deserves better than this dump." He pats the wall. "Well, what are you waiting for? Go on up."

I go but stop on the bottom step and turn back. "What's your name?"

"Meisler. Joey Meisler."

"Nice to meet you, Mr. Meisler."

Nothing impresses this guy. Without another word, he eyes me up and down and then returns to his apartment.

Dilapidated is an understatement. The handrail

wobbles, and the stairs sound like they're about to break under my feet. There's a distinct smell of old cigarettes and chemical cleaner in the air. On the second floor, the sound of a gameshow blares through the thin and dusty walls as I climb higher. When I reach Tealey's floor, I glance down the hall to see the apartment number—3B.

There's no sneaking with floors this creaky, but it's noticeably cleaner, and the bad odors don't linger up there. I knock on her door and then shove my hands in my pockets to wait.

The door swings open, and there she is—hair twisted in pink rollers and a T-shirt that hangs to her knees, fuzzy pink slippers, and what appears to be a face mask. Without looking up, she says, "What'd you forget—*Oh!*"

I smirk.

Her fingers rip the white sheet from her face, and she starts scrubbing her fingers across her skin. "What are you doing here?"

"I was nowhere near your neighborhood, so I thought I'd stop by."

Her shoulders ease as she laughs. "Well then, since you're here, come on in."

7

Tealey

"Did I interrupt?" Rad asks, his voice as smooth as jazz, as is his smile that leaves me weak in the knees. It's probably just the glass of wine I had earlier.

"No. No. Not at all." *What's a little lie?* I wasn't prepared for Rad Wellington to be standing outside my door, much less showing up out of nowhere on a random Tuesday night. I can't say I'm bothered by his presence, but a little notice would have been nice.

I take a deep breath and steady myself when he steps inside.

"So, yeah, this is my apartment." I rush to toss the mask in the garbage. Bending down, I use the side of the toaster to check my appearance. *Oh crap!* I wipe the food from my face, but when it doesn't disappear, I lean in for a closer look, only to discover it's a crumb stuck to the toaster.

I shake my head and quickly swipe over my face again, rub in the serum, and then start plucking the rollers out of my hair. Of all the times I decide to use my spa supplies before the move, naturally, it had to be the night he stops by.

Not that this will do much to make me feel better about how I look right now, but I still try. I toss the rollers in a basket beside the bed and then sit down at the end, trying to act like I'm not freaking out inside. "What brings you by?"

He's sporting a charcoal-gray suit and white shirt, and his tie hangs loosely around his neck. His dark hair is disheveled, and there's a distinctive dusting of scruff covering his jaw from a long day's work. As if he couldn't get more handsome, he proves me wrong. "I always considered you more of a Monica," he replies, his gaze skimming over me.

I shift awkwardly, resting one fuzzy house shoe–covered foot on top of the other. "It's a sleep shirt. Wait, really?"

"Really is it a sleep shirt?"

"No. You think I'm more of a Monica than a Phoebe?"

"Sure," he replies casually.

Glancing down at the shirt, I'm reminded of when we found these from a street vendor in Times Square. I love my I'm-a-Phoebe *Friends* shirt despite its thin fabric and thread-bare hem . . . I just don't love that I chose to wear it tonight. It's not my fault, really, considering Cammie was wearing something equally comfortable. How was I supposed to know Mr. Eligible Bachelor of the Year, or whatever that award is, would show up on my doorstep. "Marlow bought these for us."

"Let me guess. She got Rachel, Cammie got Monica, and you were left with Phoebe?"

"You're very good, Counselor."

"Thanks. It's really just that Marlow is predictable."

I've always considered that part of her charm. She's . . . reliable that way, which allows me to manage my reactions to some of her outlandish ideas. Like the time she talked us into pretending we worked for the hotel where Chris Hemsworth was staying so we could try to meet him. If our street clothes didn't give us away, the lack of key cards and ability to explain what we were doing to the manager did.

When Chris saw us being berated by the manager, he came over and said we were with him. We scored a meeting, a photo, and he had his driver take us back to our dorm. "I'd say she's predictably unpredictable."

Narrowing his eyes above a slight grin, he asks, "Marlow or Phoebe?"

"You're probably right on both." I hold up a finger. "Also, I like Phoebe. She's great—funny and artistic. I'm okay with being a Phoebe in my trio. But whatever." I wave away the nonsense filling my brain.

As if he's afraid to take another step, he remains standing near the door.

"The futon is covered, but you can sit here?" I pop up and offer him the end of the bed. "Or I have a chair over there if you'd like?"

"I'm good." After he takes in my tiny apartment, his brown eyes land back on mine.

I don't make apologies for what I can't afford, but a tinge of embarrassment winds its way through my veins. He lives in the lap of luxury, and here I am, not even making ends meet in my one-room apartment. I shift under his curious gaze and look down.

"What brings you by?"

Bending, he catches my eyes. "You okay, Bell?"

There's been no judgment on his behalf. There never has been, so I'm not sure why I would feel even a hint of shame. I raise my chin and nod. "I'm fine."

"I wanted to see how the packing was going." He can

easily see over my head to scope out the place because he's tall like that.

Tall and dark.

Handsome.

Intelligent.

I digress . . . "I'm almost done." I move to the kitchenette to busy myself. "Make yourself at home. It's a mess in here, so you're welcome to sit wherever you find space."

"Don't worry about me," he says as he walks toward the window. Moving the curtain to the side with his fingers, he spreads the blinds and looks down the street.

Rad Wellington is too big for this space. He's meant for wide-open lofts, penthouses, and rooftop terraces. It's utterly fascinating to see him in my apartment. The entire place could fit in his spare room. Makes me wonder how it will feel to be living in his space—airy and spacious or like I'm staying in an Airbnb, where it gives the façade of feeling at home. "It's been a while since you've been here, huh?"

Glancing back, he says, "I don't know that I've ever been here." He moves around a stack of boxes and finds the end of the futon in front of him.

I get two bottles of beer from the fridge, and when I turn back, I catch him searching the apartment. I'm assuming over the lack of space a man his size requires. "It's a . . . cozy place." He's polite enough to call it cozy versus tiny. "Why haven't I been here before?"

Shrugging, I set the bottles on the counter and dig through a drawer for the bottle opener. "I don't know. Maybe because it's completely out of your way?" A draft breeze runs across my bum, and I lower my arms, realizing I've been flashing him my ass. I duck behind a smaller stack of boxes and tug at the hem of my shirt. With my shorts being closer to him than me, I'm stuck.

His eyes narrow as he runs his fingers through his hair. "What are you doing?"

My spine stiffens. "Just standing here?"

Touching his chest, he angles his head. "Are you asking me?"

"The English language deems that it was indeed a question, but I didn't mean to pose one."

Scratching the bridge of his nose, he furrows his brow. "Why are you hiding behind those boxes?"

"I'm uh . . ." Sighing, I ask, "Do you mind closing your eyes for one minute. I need to grab a pair of shorts, and unfortunately, those shorts are closer to you."

He looks to his side and reaches down to a pile of clothes I'd dumped on the futon earlier. The lace of a hot pink thong wraps around his finger, and he stills. I stop breathing altogether, frozen to the spot—horrified, mortified, and every other *fied*—that he's seeing my underwear for the first time.

Sure, I wear comfy clothes on the daily, but I like to keep things spicy underneath. Sue me . . . *oh wait, he's a lawyer and could.*

When the slyest of smirks plays along his lips, my heart thunders in my chest until he sets it to the side to take hold of a turquoise pair of running shorts and asks, "These?"

I press my hand to my forehead and gasp for air. "Those work." He tosses them to me and then turns just before I reach for them. After slipping them on, I step out of hiding. "All good."

His hands are in his pockets, and he's looking as dapper as ever. "Are you going to give me a tour?"

"Sure." I laugh, moving next to the bed. "Look left, now right. That's the kitchen. Behind me is the bedroom. Behind you is the living room. That concludes our tour for today.

Don't forget to tip your guide." I give him a wink and click my tongue.

There's a sweetness to his smile that's not often seen. Although I do remember seeing it last night when we were on the roof deck. It looks nice on him.

He chuckles. "Tipping the tour guide. You might be more Phoebe than I realized."

"Probably. *Oh!* I have beer . Would you like one? I also have one or two pieces of pizza left from dinner if you're hungry. Cammie ordered an extra large."

"You don't have to go to any trouble."

"It's no trouble, Rad." I return to the drawer and start searching through the junk to find the bottle opener again.

He comes to stand beside me, his arm brushing against mine. He twists the metal top off one bottle and then the other. "They're twist off."

"Ah. Guess it's obvious I only keep beer in the fridge for company."

There's no great rush to leave. Standing next to each other, he glances over, giving me a charming boyish smile. It reminds me of when we were in college with no real responsibilities in life. Grades and part-time jobs. Afternoons spent studying in Central Park and lattes down in Washington Square. The six of us were inseparable.

Life loves throwing curveballs. All we can do is step up to the plate and swing. "Pizza?"

"No, I'm good," he says, now grinning to himself. He returns to the futon and pushes the clothes pile to the side before sitting down. "You like pizza, but it looks like you cook, too."

I settle on the bed, leaning against the headboard, but glance at the dishes in the sink. "Yeah, I'm broke, so I have to cook."

"You meet us out for meals."

I laugh lightly, and then say, "That's why I eat *in* the rest of the time." When he doesn't laugh, I bite my lip, feeling awkward. "I do enjoy cooking, though, so it works out."

"You can cook whenever you want when you move in." The way his head tilts down and his eyes study me, I'm curious what he's thinking. "I have a lot of top-of-the-line cookware that never gets any action."

"I can relate," I say under my breath.

"What?"

Ack! "Um, I can make use of those pots and pans. Cooking for two will be more fun than for one."

I stare at him while he takes a long pull from the bottle.

Oh.

My.

God.

Captivated by the way the light brings out the golden centers of his eyes, I stare at him. His magnetism has my tummy tightening. Those eyes, his broad shoulders, the tailored suit, sexy-messy hair, and darkening eyes as they devour me with a look—Good lord, this man is perfection.

Why have I never been so affected by how utterly gorgeous he is before?

I've always thought he was incredibly attractive, but we're friends. He's gone out of his way to make sure there was no opportunity for it to be anything else, and honestly, that's probably for the best.

So why am I suddenly wishing we could be more?

My insides tighten.

It's a futile thought. I know it.

We can't.

We shouldn't.

I shouldn't. I should leave the man alone. He clearly has

enough attention from the world and doesn't need me drooling all over him. Especially since he's being so kind and offering me a place to stay.

Be smart, Tealey. And then mop up the drool when he leaves.

I force myself to look away from him, then down two large gulps of beer, praying he won't second-guess his offer to me after my awkwardness. When I turn back—*Damn, why does he have to be so hot?*

He smirks and just about does me in, but then he licks his lips, and I find myself biting mine. He asks, "Should I open a window? You look a bit flush."

"I'm fine. So fine." I clamp my mouth shut, turning my gaze to the ceiling. *What am I doing?*

He says, "It will be fun to have a roommate."

"Roommate." Good reminder. *Great, in fact.*

Roommates.

Friends. *Only friends.*

But if we're only friends, why am I now staring at him like there's a possibility of more?

God, I'm in so much trouble.

8

Tealey

Rad always looks incredible in his tailored suits, but seeing him with his shirtsleeves rolled up, a large watch wrapped around his wrist, and a towel draped over his shoulder while washing dishes brings a whole new meaning to erotica. Watching a man doing chores is divine, but when they offer, even when they didn't dirty the dishes, it's swoonworthy.

As if reminiscing about how he renovated his building, images of sweaty and shirtless Rad racing back, he tries to do me in with domestic duties. I still don't know how in the hell I got distracted by other guys back in college when this Adonis was right there all along. I check to make sure the air-conditioning is working before I reach the brink of spontaneous combustion.

After he insisted that I pack as he washes the dishes, he dries them and sets them on the drying rack. Time has gone too fast, fun always making it fly. Not that packing is fun, but spending time with Rad has been tonight. "I rode in a cab, but I can take one or two boxes back with me if you like."

"Oh, uh . . ." I look around, thinking what would be easy to carry.

The veins in his forearms are mesmerizing as they work together while he tosses the dish towel behind him on the counter.

Fanning myself, I say, "I, um . . . clothes, maybe my dishes . . . hm." He's too distracting, so I cross the room, spying my treasured box of mugs I packed earlier. "I have this box I worry about moving. I'd hate for anything in it to get broken in a truck."

After drying his hands, he hangs the towel on the rack's hook. He turns to eye the box and then steadies his gaze on me. "I'll handle it with care."

Needing to cool down under the heat creeping up my neck, I tug the collar of my shirt away, but I'm quickly reminded that it's already hanging off my shoulder, so I play it off and tug on my earlobe instead. His eyes follow the motion, but then he clears his throat, checks his watch, and says, "I should probably get going."

"You don't have to leave if you don't want."

He pauses and then grins. "It's getting late."

I glance at the time on the microwave, and my disappointment is hard to hide behind my weak smile. "I didn't realize the hour. I have to be at work early tomorrow."

Rad comes closer, and though his hand lifts, he's quick to lower it back to his side. "Can I help in any way?"

Shrugging, I reply, "It's just packing. Nothing I can't handle."

"I wasn't talking about the packing. You have a lot of big changes happening, life coming at you fast with the move . .

. and Steve." His voice quietens at the end as if he doesn't want to verbalize the name.

"I'm fine with the breakup. It was going to eventually happen. Sooner is better than later." Not sure why I felt so comfortable talking about my ex with him tonight—as I've normally only shared with Cammie and Marlow about this sort of stuff—but it's been one of the many things we've talked about. It's been so nice, and I think spending the last few hours together has brought me comfort in our new, evolving relationship. "I didn't love him. Not in the forever kind of way."

"Is there a temporary way?" Empathy fills his strong features as the new crinkles beside his eyes soften.

Angling my head, I stare at the drying rack, fixating on the water dripping from the dishes. "I'm . . ." Crossing my arms, I peek over at Rad. "I don't know why I'm acting this way. I'm fine. I really have been. I don't even think about him, except—"

"Except when you do?"

"Just the mention of his name triggers something inside me," I grumble. "It's that the breakup wasn't enough for him. He had to implant an insecurity." Tossing my arms up, I let them fall to my sides. "Honestly, I was fine with my thighs. Am I perfect? No. But I don't need to be. I exercise and eat decently healthy. I try to stay in shape—"

"You don't have to justify anything to me, Tealey. I know my opinion doesn't matter regarding your body, but trust me, nothing's wrong with it."

My heart clenches, but I stop myself from audibly awing.

He finally sits on the bed, and it wasn't until then that I think he's been trying to avoid it.

"And from a guy's perspective, there's a lot right with it, like all of it is pretty great." As if cleaning the dishes wasn't enough, he decides to swoon me to death with his sweet-talking. "Come here."

I sit beside him, the sides of our legs pressed together as I tuck my hands between my thighs and look into his eyes.

"It's easy for me to tell you that he's not in your league, but I'm not sure you'll believe me." Rubbing the back of his neck, he clears his throat. "When I said he was a fucker, I meant it, though." The left side of his mouth lifts as he stares at me out of the corners of his eyes.

"You can tell me that anytime." I grin. "He hurt my heart. He didn't break it. But his words still sting."

His arm wraps around my shoulders, and he whispers, "You're the best thing he ever had, and he lost you. Don't look back, Tealey. He doesn't deserve a second of your thoughts."

I look down when my breathing picks up. Though my nightshirt blocks his hand from touching my skin, the heat is felt between us.

His hand slides from my arm and returns to his lap. I hear him swallow in the silence of the room, and then he says, "If he'd asked you to marry him, I wouldn't have let you walk down that aisle." Caught off guard, I look into his earnest eyes. His words are just as gentle as his gaze, albeit direct. "None of us would have let you."

I toe the box near my feet, unsure how to feel about his admission. Betrayed? Mad? *Lucky?* Yes, lucky. Lucky to have friends who care so much that they'll risk offending me in the short term to protect me in the long run. I know where their hearts lie, and it's not the same place Steve's did, which is why we broke up.

His eyes remain on me unapologetically, like his confession. "I didn't mean to put you on the spot. I just thought you should know that we always have your back." The heaviness that crept into the apartment begins to splinter, and he adds, "I just wanted to check on you because even though it's been a while, it's still not easy when a relationship ends."

"You take dating in such stride. I wish I was more like you."

His expression hardens. It's just a moment, but enough to catch the change in his disposition. "I'm glad you're not. You're not cynical. It's one of my favorite things about you. Your heart is wide open. Never change, Tealey Bell."

My smile grows ridiculously, I'm sure, across my face. "You have favorite things about me?"

He shakes his head and reaches to rub the back of his neck again but stops and stands instead. "That list is too long for tonight, and I should get going." He rolls his sleeves back down and puts his suit jacket back on before reaching down to take the box. A slight clang of the mugs bumping together rings, and he says, "I'll be careful."

Despite wanting to, I shouldn't keep him any longer or delve into that favorites list he apparently has of me. We've been friends for so long, but no matter how close we are, or weren't, some things between us have been held back on both sides.

I'm glad we're remedying the situation.

"Thank you." I push off the bed and go to the door. I stop and look at him once more. "I'm glad we're friends and . . . and that we have this chance to get to know each other better." I should feel awkward, the two of us standing here alone for what feels like the first time, but I don't, though. Nothing but hope rises inside me and brings a smile to my face right now.

"It will be good, a long time coming and nice to have your company."

I could overanalyze that he said *my* company versus a

general anyone's company, but instead, I take it for what he means and look forward to watching our friendship grow. "Yeah, it will be a nice change for me too." Opening the door, I let him go first and follow him down the hall. "And I promise to stay out of your hair, so you can carry on with life as usual."

He stops one flight down, and a crinkle of his brow is smoothed just as quickly as it appears. "It's funny because you being in my hair is one of the things I'm most looking forward to." His laugh is so genuine—deep and soothing—a blanket that warms me in the hollows of the building. "You can start staying there tomorrow if you'd like."

"I might take you up on that. I'm almost packed, and it makes it kind of chaotic to be around."

We continue down the stairs, and I push open the door. When he comes out, he sets the box down gently and pulls his phone out. I briefly catch a rideshare app on his phone before he pockets it again and retrieves the box. "I've been meaning to ask when you want to tell the others?"

"Oh, uh, it's not a secret, so anytime. I did tell Cammie tonight. I didn't know you wanted to wait."

"No, I don't. I also didn't know. It's not a big deal. Anyway," he says, walking to the curb, "if Cammie knows, Cade knows, and you know it will travel down that gossip vine from there."

A blue sedan pulls to the curb and rolls down the window. A guy leans over the console, eyeing us, and then calls, "Rad?"

"That's me." Turning back to me, Rad says, "I'll have a key sent to your office tomorrow. Use it when you're ready." He pauses, briefly glancing at the driver. "I'll be home late tomorrow."

"I'm not your mom—"

"Most definitely not." *A wry grin spreads across his lips.*

My curiosity gets the best of me, though. "Got a hot date?" I try to sound casual but fail miserably. To distract him from my ridiculousness, I rock forward and poke his stomach . . . *Whoa.* Hard as a rock.

"I'd rather be there to help you settle in, but . . ." Him having a date or even a girlfriend shouldn't disappoint me . . . *still*. I hate this feeling, the drop of jealousy that poisons a good time. "I have to work late. I've added a new case to my load, and well, I shouldn't have taken it on, but I needed to."

"You sound like me."

The driver lays on his horn. This time, I'm the one looking away when I hear the rattle of an old window open. Mr. Meisler dips his head out the window. "Knock it off. My wife's trying to sleep." He spies us but remains expressionless as he lights up a cigarette. "Nice night."

Rad says, "Don't hesitate to call or text me if you need anything, anything at all." I don't know when the inches between us disappeared, but the tips of our shoes touch as he stares into my eyes in an unfamiliar way. "I should go."

"Yes, me too."

"If I don't see you at your place tomorrow night, I'll see you Friday."

"See you when I see you."

I start the short walk back, each step away from him a little heavier.

"Hey, Bell?"

When I look back, he says, "He's a fool for letting you go."

Melting might be more Marlow's speed, dramatic, but he sure has a way to make a girl feel special. "You're not so bad yourself, Welly."

He grins, big like I do, and then gets in the car with my

precious cargo. I type in the code to open the door, but before I go in, I watch the car drive away.

"He's a good kid, like you, Tealey."

"Thanks, Mr. Meisler." I swing the heavy metal door open and ask, "So your son is taking you and the Mrs. in?"

"Yep. They have a pool and a float with my name on it. I'll be living the high life out in Jersey."

I laugh. "You're making me jealous."

"Nah," he says, waving me off. "Sounds like you'll be living the good life in Manhattan."

"It's not too shabby."

Rubbing his fingers together, he adds, "He's all money. I could smell that expensive cologne from here, and phew, *that suit*—class all the way."

"He's nice, too."

"That's good. Real good."

"Good night, Mr. Meisler."

"Night, Tealey."

I take the steps by two but grab my cramping side when I reach my floor and huff all the way to my door. Inside my apartment, I lean against the back of the door and close my eyes, releasing a breath that's felt held since Rad showed up on my doorstep. My body sags under the release, and I can't help but noting that it's the best release I've had in a while.

Desperate times . . .

Why did I think moving in with him was a good idea? How am I going to face Rad day in and day out? When his soulful eyes are on me, it feels as if he can see right through me. As if he can see the feelings blooming inside and the thoughts that want to be verbalized.

After all these years, I have questions about what this is with him, questions that can't be asked because what if . . . what if he answered them?

Surely, it will get easier to be around him once I move in. It has to be, but what if laughter and good times bond in ways that blur the line of our friendship? And why is my heart racing like the first time we met?

Pulling my head from the clouds and my heart from floating away, I sink into reality. I remind myself that I must pack before I'm too sleepy to finish.

Rad said I can stay there tomorrow, and although it's sad to leave this place behind, I'm looking forward to a new adventure.

I take a box with only a few things in it from the corner and try to keep my mind on the task at hand instead of what tomorrow brings. But a smile crosses my face when Mr. Meisler's words cross my mind. "Sounds like you'll be living the good life in Manhattan."

I will be, and he's right about Rad as well. He may be an eligible bachelor, a catch, and all class to most, but tonight, he showed me another side to the man behind the awards. He showed me his heart.

When he says he would have stopped me from marrying Steve, I believe him. It wasn't his words that convinced me, but the look in his eyes. It was the same look he gave me when he said Steve was a fool.

With sweet words like that being shared, I'm even more excited to see how our relationship grows from here. I'm not foolish enough to think it could be anything more than friends, but I'm happy to finally build on what we've always had.

Looking around the room, I sigh. "It's going to be a late night."

Less Rad. More packing.

Tealey

Beginnings—of a relationship, adventures, and new opportunities—are always exciting.

A siren in the distance wakes me just prior to my alarm going off on my phone. Though still drowsy, I let my mind drift to Rad and wonder if such things are heard where he lives.

Remembering him stopping by last night just to check on me has me grinning by the time I open my eyes. I stretch my arms over my head, catching the first signs of light daring to slip in through the blinds. Normally, I'd groan and pull a pillow over my head, but this morning, I sit up, feeling buzzed for the day even before I've had coffee to do the trick.

I pop up and plant my feet on the ground. There's just enough room to stand in the sea of boxes on the floor. Even though Rad invited me to move in early, I was too tired, and my mind was stuck on other things, namely him, to finish.

There's not much but enough to keep me busy for a few hours.

Something about seeing all these boxes, my life and belongings, hidden in brown cardboard brings a wave of sadness. This is it. My last day.

I won't hear Mr. Meisler yelling, "Shuddup," or smell Mrs. Russo's secret red sauce simmering when it wafts from the second floor. No more sirens in the night or sanitation guys yelling in the early morning hours. Okay, I won't miss the last two, but the first two for sure.

The housewarming present from Cammie, a coffee pot, no longer sits on the counter. My surprise birthday present from Marlow, a rosebud vase I fell in love with two years ago when we were shopping at the flea market, was wrapped in paper and packed away. The guys gave me a framed photo of all six of us on the beach in the Hamptons two summers ago as a gift for Christmas. Its spot on the windowsill now sits empty.

Memories of the experiences that have shaped who I am usually fill this apartment but are gone and hidden today. I wrap my arms around myself, my throat thick when I swallow. My mom would tell me to keep moving forward and not to wallow.

She's my best cure for the blues, and I know she's always up early, so I make the call. She answers on the first ring. "Good morning."

"Good morning," I reply, rummaging around to make sure I didn't forget anything. I don't know what I'm looking for, but I feel lost without my usual morning routine. I'm not even close to being ready to go to Rad's tonight. I stop and sigh, the weight of worry pressing down on me. "I'm scared, Mom."

"Don't be, darling. You'll land right where you're meant to be."

"Is that here or back in Texas? Should I have come home?"

"I'd love to have you here, but I have a feeling you're more suited for the Big Apple these days."

I'm already smiling, my chest feeling lighter. "Change is good," I say, hoping I'll believe it. I don't. Not quite yet.

"Change is good. Look how well you've been since the breakup with Steve."

Logically, I know I'm better off, but should it have been so easy to part ways? I've been more hurt by his parting commentary than the absence of him.

Ugh. Like Rad said, he doesn't deserve another second of my time or any emotion of mine. "Yeah. Just moved right on." *He sure did.* "What are you doing this morning?"

"Having a cup of coffee on the back porch and listening to the birds starting the day with a song."

"By looking at the time, you better get a move on this morning."

"Is that a moving pun, Mom?"

"No," she says with a laugh I miss so much. "It's don't get fired advice."

I pull the string of the blinds and let the sunshine in. "It's good advice."

"Remember, Tealey, home is where the heart is. You're always welcome to return, but something tells me your life is there. So put on your strongest armor and face this new challenge head-on."

That seems to be all I need to find the strength to charge forth. "Thank you, Mom."

"You're welcome. Remember what I've always told you. A new chapter starts with a fresh page."

"It's time to live a new story."

I DUMP my bag on my desk before making a beeline for the break room in desperate need of coffee. Last night, I accidentally packed some of my morning routine items, so it took me longer than expected to get ready, and I had no time to stop for coffee.

As soon as I have a hot cup in hand, I return and straighten my cubicle in preparation for the day, and then send Rad a quick text: *I can't make it tonight. Still too much to do.*

Three dots wave across the screen and then disappear.

Wave, and then gone again. Then a message populates: *Anything I can help with?*

Me: *No. Just need more time.*

Rad: *Good luck.*

Me: *Thanks. I need it.*

I set my phone down and take another sip of coffee.

My co-worker Peggy wishes me a good morning on the way to her desk. "Misty's in the waiting area."

"She is?" I stand and tilt to see down the aisle. "I have news for her." After kicking my bottom drawer closed, I head to the waiting area and signal for her to come back. "I have good news." I return to my chair and direct her to one of the two others that fit in the cramped space. She pushes her long brown hair from her shoulder and lets her shoulders sag. Concealer can't hide the dark circles under her eyes, and the faintest of smiles appear to be a chore.

"I could use some, but I don't have much time. I can't be late to work again."

I open the file. "This is an agreement to work with one of

the best divorce attorneys in New York. He's taking your case pro bono, so you won't have to pay him."

She studies the papers as she twists the straps of her purse in her lap. Looking at me, she asks, "He's really going to help my kids and me? There's no catch?"

"He is. He was moved by your story." Resting my hand on my chest, I say, "I know him personally. He'll do everything he can to help you." I pull a pen from a mug I keep on my desk and set it on top of the papers. "I read through them. It is a legal document, but there's nothing to be concerned about. It's giving him the right to represent you with your permission. If you agree, you sign here, and then I'll contact your current legal aid to inform him of our plans to work with Mr. Wellington."

"I trust you, Tealey." She picks up the pen and signs. When she sets it back on the desk, she stands, gripping her bag to her body. "Deacon is allowing me to visit my mom this weekend with the kids." Her voice is so soft that I stand and lean in closer to hear. "It will give us a few days to plan."

"That's good. All the pieces need to be in place. Mr. Wellington will make this divorce happen on your behalf. I just know it." She looks relieved.

"Thank you for everything. I'm just so grateful."

We wrap our arms around each other, and before she leaves, she says, "I don't know what I'd do without you."

"I'm here when you need me."

She nods before lowering her head and quietly leaving the center. I flop into my chair and drop my head into my hands. She's one of so many, and the realization that I can't help everyone in need overwhelms me some days.

I'm more tired than usual today from the late night, but my heart still hurts. Taking a deep breath and exhaling slowly, I regain my composure, take a sip of coffee, and then return to the front to assist the next person.

It's a steady stream of clients all morning. By lunch, I'm operating on coffee and a countdown to the end of the day. I'm about to sneak eat a package of crackers I store in my desk when I hear Peggy's voice from the other side of the cubicle. "How's the sexy roommate?"

I'm laughing too hard to reply to Peggy right away. It's not the first time I've heard someone call Rad sexy. It happens practically every time we're at restaurants or in bars, the beach, and at parties. Okay, it pretty much happens anywhere that man goes. But the roommate part is what sends me into a teenage fit of giggles because yeah, that incredible man is my soon-to-be roomie.

"Wait, how do you know?"

She says, "A certain smooth-talker called to tell you the key is being made and will be delivered later. Since you were busy, I took it upon myself to satisfy my curiosity."

I'd roll my eyes, but she cracks me up too much to be annoyed, so I find myself smiling instead. "Ah, I see." I lean against the feeble cubicle wall and peek over. "I assume the door is locked?"

"Yes."

"Well then, officially," I say to Peggy, "I move in on Saturday."

"And unofficially?"

"Tonight." I giggle again, my grip tightening on the top rail of the barrier. Peggy's not only a great resource for me but she has also become a friend.

She rocks back in her chair, smiling up at me. "I read all about him in that Manhattan Movers and Shakers column last weekend online. Full-spread article with photos. *What a hunk.* I know you're friends, but I didn't realize how good of friends you were to be shacking up together. Tell me some-thing, Tealey. How are you going to sleep, knowing that man is just mere feet from your bed?"

"Like a baby," I say, pretending to doze off. But my lids open, and I lean down so no one else can hear me except her. "I've tested the bed. It's luxurious."

"Tested, huh?" She's all ears, interest piqued. She turned sixty when we celebrated that time, but I have a hunch she's been the same age for at least five or more years now. She always says she wished she'd settled down and had a family, but her life was too big back then. She modeled in Europe, worked at the Macy's downtown, and then turned to social work. Now she says she lives vicariously through me. She's incredible, and selfishly sad for me, she's retiring this year.

Resting her chin in her hands, she's eager for more details.

Bursting out laughing, I roll my eyes. "I've laid on the bed. *By myself.*" I throw my arms up. "Just to get a feel for it."

"Was he with you when you got a *feel for it*?"

"You're so naughty, Peggy," I say, still laughing. "And we're not shacking up together. We're sharing a very large apartment. We could pass each other in the night and not notice. That's how big it is."

"Since you brought up how big it is . . . you're stronger than me, sweetheart. There's no way I could live with him." Grabbing a stack of papers, she taps them on her desktop and then lowers her voice. "It's been too long since my vagi-na's seen the light of day."

"I can't speak to you, but if it makes you feel better, I'm in the same boat."

"All I can say is buy extra batteries then. You're going to need them."

With a goofy grin, I push off the small wall as images of

Rad talking to Peggy swirl in my head. I wish I could have heard that play out. As soon as I sit down, she looks over.

Scanning our surroundings to make sure the coast is clear, she then turns back to me. "Rumor has it we're over budget. There might be cuts." My stomach drops.

"What rumor?"

This time, she rolls her eyes. "Lowell blabbing on speak-erphone to a friend the other day."

Job cuts? Have I assumed too much? Do I have job secu-rity, or should I consider putting a backup plan in place?

She stands with the papers tucked to her chest. "Don't worry. We run out of money every year, so I'm not worried. Not yet."

"Because you're retiring."

She perks up. "Jersey Shore, here I come."

Mr. Meisler was right—sounds like Jersey is the retire-ment hotspot.

"I need to talk to Lowell," I say, "so maybe I'll ask him directly."

Peggy laughs. "You do that. You do that, honey, and report back to me."

I laugh nervously. "I don't think I have the guts."

"Well, neither do I. I guess we wait and see what happens."

When she goes to the back room, I'm left with my own thoughts. Lowell is full of a lot of stuff, but insider informa-tion is usually not one of them. I bet he was just talking nonsense.

Hopefully.

But if he's not, the thought of locking myself into a new lease with no guarantee of a job adds a new concern to the mounting pile.

I walk down the hall and knock lightly on my boss's

door. Lowell's kicked back with his feet on the desk, and his personal phone is pushed to his ear like he's some high-powered attorney with an incredible view of the Manhattan skyline, *basically Rad*, instead of working in a government-funded office in a section of Brooklyn that doesn't get the hype like the DUMBO area near the bridge.

Annoyance crinkles the right side of his face. "What is it?"

"As you know, I have to be out of my apartment—"

"I know this." He rolls his hand in front of him. "Everyone knows. Get on with it."

I recoil. His rudeness and impatience smack of Steve, and my insides brace. "I still have some packing to do."

"Hold on."

I wait, but then he drops his face to the linoleum and shakes his head. "Not you. You need time off? You can use your lunch at the end of the day. If you need more than that, fill out the time-off request form, and I'll consider it."

I'm feeling stuck. My stomach already rumbles from the thought of not eating until tonight. I can't afford time off, though. I need the money. "Can I sacrifice two lunches instead of time off?"

"Yeah, whatever." He spins away from me in the chair, and says, "Where were we . . .? Ah, yes, so you were wearing the pink number—"

How does someone so careless and heartless end up working in a social services office? It can't be for the money, so I'm always puzzled why Lowell is here. And since he's my boss as well, I had another reason to move away.

I shake off his bad vibes and focus on the fact that I will be at Rad's tonight, and technically, it's mine now as well. At least in the short term. I'll never be able to afford something that nice, so I'm going to savor every minute in that beautiful place.

I might even relish in Rad as well.

Who am I kidding?

I already do.

10

Tealey

My smile is instant, my heart beating faster to meet the joy I feel seeing my two best friends waiting for me. My pace picks up as I hurry toward my building. "What are you guys doing here?"

Cammie, dressed in yoga pants and a sweatshirt, waves. "We thought you could use reinforcements."

Marlow stands in sleek white pants and a fitted black silk top, not looking like she's here to pack. She's holding a tray of drinks, though, so I won't complain. "And I brought coffee."

I readjust my bag on my shoulder and hug them. "Thanks for being here."

The three of us have been best friends since we were assigned to the same tour group on the first day of freshman orientation at New York University. Although we couldn't be more different, we clicked, and as the saying goes, the rest is history.

Cammie grabs the handle of the door. "When you texted

that you'll miss a few lunches to finish," she says, punching in the code, "we figured we could knock it out quicker together."

"There's not a lot left to pack, but I appreciate you being here."

Marlow wraps her arm around me. "We're always here for you."

Although I know she won't pack much, her being here, with coffee I might add, makes the chore not so bad. "Mocha latte?"

"You know it."

We file up the stairs, and after I change clothes, I come out of the bathroom and say, "I'm moving in with Rad," more for Marlow since Cammie already knows.

Marlow's eyes widen, and then she smiles. "You are?"

"I am. He offered, and I accepted. We're a match made in roommate heaven." I fold the flaps of a box down while Cammie drags tape along the seam. Realizing how that might be taken the wrong way, I add, "As friends, of course. Friendly roommates. That's all. Nothing to see or discuss. We probably won't even see each other much. Just two friends—"

"We get it." She winks at Marlow. "It's platonic." Double wink. My mouth drops open as she grins and adds, "No one thinks otherwise, Teals."

Marlow relaxes on the couch, shoes on the floor, her legs tucked under her, and her shoulders shaking with laughter. "I'm happy that worked out. I told him the other day to help me convince you to stay. I guess he worked his magic." She smiles mischievously and then clicks her tongue and winks.

"Okay. Okay. Enough. He's not working any magic on me," I snap. "It's only temporary, and he has a spare room, so—"

Cammie laughs. "I think you're handling it great. Keep calm and carry on and all that." She points the tape dispenser at me. "I mean, why would you feel otherwise? Just because you're moving in with the one guy you've crushed on forever . . . What could go wrong?" She stands, looking at me expectantly with the tape dispenser, ready to battle the next box.

Marlow adds, "When so much could go right." Remembering how he said my body has so much right with it has my cheeks heating. I play it off as frustration.

"There is not going to be any wrong or right with Rad. We're friends. You guys know this better than anyone." I busy myself with the box flaps to avoid their stares and the questions I spy populating in their eyes.

"I've been thinking about this," Cammie starts, worrying her lip. "Are you sure moving in with him is a wise idea? This will either bring you closer or destroy a good friendship. It could ruin . . ." She catches herself before she says the words.

I say them instead. "The group dynamic. I worry about that, too, but I can't live on your couch." Trying to lighten the mood, I add, "Cade made it more than clear that you two have christened that thing fifty times over. Anyway, you guys need your couple time, *alone*." Reaching across the box, I squeeze her hand. "So it wasn't even an option to ask."

Marlow pushes off the futon and holds the flaps in place. "I want to help."

"Then help," Cammie snaps, causing Marlow to recoil. "Grab another box and get to it." The screeching of the tape breaks the standoff of silence that follows.

Reaching down, she lifts a box to the top of the stack and says, "Cade's right. The stress is getting to you."

After Cammie zips the tape over the top, she sets the

tape down and hugs Marlow. "I'm sorry. I'm the worst."

"You're not the worst. You're awesome. You just have a lot going on. We'll get through it, and so will you, and then you'll live happily ever after."

When they both finish hugging, and the tension evaporates, I move a box to a stack by the door.

She peeks inside a box on the bed and says, "I would have offered my couch, but it's really not made for sleeping."

Cammie and I exchange a knowing look, and then she laughs. "It's not even made for sitting. It's for looks, Marlow, and the most impractical sofa ever." The red velvet couch is so overstuffed, it's stiff, hard like a rock. Sleeping on it would be impossible.

"I like what I like." Marlow shrugs. "And I'm rarely home to ruin it." Swift to change the topic of conversation, she asks, "How's the wedding planning?"

Cammie bends to tape down the edges of an extra-full box. "Good. I think. I don't know. I promised myself I wouldn't worry about it tonight, and Cade told me to take the week off from it. Everything that needs to be done is done, so he's right. I should." She laughs to herself, but anxiety weaves through the sound. "I just worry everything's going to fall apart. He's been a good sport, though, and is just worried about me."

"I think Cade's right. Nothing will happen this week to ruin your whole wedding. If something comes up, we have months to get it fixed. Just let us know, and we'll help."

"Thanks. I'm going to try to focus back on life this week, give myself time to decompress." Since all the boxes are taped up, Cammie moves into the kitchen and opens a cabinet. "We're on for Saturday too. You secured the storage unit?" She gasps.

Her gasp causes both me and Marlow to startle. With my

hand over my thumping heart, I ask, "What?"

"Where are your mugs?"

"Oh, good lord, Cammie. You scared me." I start to giggle. "I sent them with Rad last night."

"*Whaaaaaat*?" she says, smiling like she knows a secret. It's not a secret that he was here, hence why I said it like it was no big deal.

It's no big deal . . . *or is it?* They are a part of my heart. *Oh God*, did I send a piece of my heart home with Rad last night? My subconscious is a devious bitch.

"He came by to check on the packing and said I could start staying there tonight." I do a quick sidestep I learned in tap class when I was five and add jazz hands, cracking myself up. "Don't make a big deal out of this."

Leaning against the counter, she holds her hand out, ready to tick her fingers. Oh great. I roll my eyes, bracing myself, which is something usually reserved for Marlow. Speaking of . . . she joins in the fun and stands next to her. Two against one. *Even better. . .*

I cross my arms defensively over my chest. "Bring on the mockery. Let's do this and get it over with."

Cammie touches her index finger. "I want someone to love me like I love coffee."

I restrain my grin even though that mug is one of my favorites. "It's a classic." That barely earns me a smile.

Marlow asks, "And that ugly, brown 'Happy Birthday, Gerald' mug?"

"That awesome flea market find is already at Rad's."

"I'm surprised your mug collection left the premises. I would have thought you'd be personally escorting them to the city."

"I love mugs, but I felt they were safe with him."

Marlow laughs as she returns to the futon. "I can't wait

for Rad's reaction when he sees them." Touching her chest, she adds, "We've been good friends keeping your addiction under wraps."

"You submitted my story to *Hoarders* to be featured in an episode."

"Although true, does one need that many mugs?"

"No," I reply, holding my chin up as I defend my mug-loving ways and sit on the bed. "But I think the real question is do I love them? Yes. *I do*. Do they make me smile? *Absolutely*. Quippy mugs are sort of my thing. It's a collection. I have one to fit every mood." I point at a lone box by the door. "For the record, though, I did set a few aside in the donation box."

Cammie pads across the room and looks down. "Three? You have like two hundred. As Marlow said, I think you are past love at this point and well into obsession. Did the 'Happy Accidents' mug make it?"

"Bob Ross is an American treasure. Of course, his mug made the cut. Anywho, what kind of collector would I be if I broke up the band, Yoko?"

Her hands plant on her hips, and although Cammie tries for serious, she can't contain her grin. "Yoko did not break up The Beatles. They were already splintering."

"Whatever you have to tell yourself to sleep at night."

Giggling, she flops down on the bed next to me and lies back. "You're ridiculous, Teals."

Marlow smirks to herself. "I think it's great that you took them to Rad's. He needs a little chaos in his life."

Knowing she's not intentionally insulting me, I ham it up. "Are you calling me chaos? I thought I was fun. Phoebe fun."

"You are fun with a side of chaos," she replies, "fun chaos."

My brow furrows. "Fun chaos?" I shake my head. "Fine, I'll be the fun chaos." Packing takes precedence again, so I drag myself to my nightstand and start tossing stuff into my suitcase. "I found out that our budget's run out at work."

Marlow crooks her head. "Quarterly or yearly?"

"I didn't get the details."

"It's only May."

The vibe in the room changes. I know they're looking at me, probably worrying about both my passion and my paycheck. I agree, so I don't look at them. I don't even know why I brought it up. It probably won't even happen anyway. I do feel better getting it off my chest, even if I now have two sets of wary eyes directed at me. Cammie asks, "What does that mean?"

"Cutbacks. We run out of money every year, though, so I'm not worried."

"We know," Marlow says, "And then every year, you accumulate weeks on the clock and don't get paid. You can't keep doing that." Ideally, no, I wouldn't, but I'm left with no choice.

"Would you suggest I let people suffer?"

"I'm not trying to be heartless. I'm worried about *you*. You deserve to be paid for your efforts and the hours worked."

"And to have a life outside of work, especially if they aren't paying you," Cammie adds."

"I agree, but what am I supposed to do?"

Sighing, Marlow huffs, sending her bangs flying up from her forehead. "I don't know. I just worry about you."

"I'll be fine."

Cammie sits up, resting her weight on her hands behind her. "What if they shut down the office?"

A deep-seated fear bubbles to the surface. It's one I've

tried not to think about without knowing any specifics. But it's always there in the back of my mind.

What if I lose my job?

What if I sign a new lease and then lose my job?

How long can I stay at Rad's? Those details haven't been worked out. I know that I refuse to be a burden to him or cramp his lifestyle.

What if I end up back in Texas after all? I'd have to get new certifications, and would I return to my parents' house? Tail tucked between my legs . . . Off the top of my head, I reply, "There are other centers I can transfer to."

She nods, and when I glance at Marlow, she's staring at her lap. This topic is a real downer. My stomach interjects its own opinion with a growl.

Marlow sits up abruptly. "Hey, how about we go out for dinner? My treat."

I suggest, "There's a new Thai restaurant one subway station away. I've been wanting to try it."

"Thai sounds great," Marlow starts while slipping her heels back on, "but Louboutins do not belong on the subway."

Cammie pops up. "No worries. I'll order a car."

As I slip on my sneakers, I listen to them chatting about everything and nothing. It's good to be surrounded by the sound of friends and them showing up without me even asking—I'm a lucky girl.

I just hope that it carries me through this stint at Rad's and that moving in with him will only bring us closer and not the alternative. Although it feels a lot like everything's on the line, I suck down my worries and grab my purse.

Marlow opens the door. "You ready?"

For dinner or Rad? Either way, I say, "As ready as I'll ever be."

11

Rad

"Hey, you," Tealey says, smiling like I just brought the sunshine with me. "You're full of surprises lately."

When she greets me in the lobby of her workplace, her light hair is in its usual state of catastrophe on top of her head, and honestly, I find it so incredibly sexy, but the temptation to pull the pencils holding it together is strong. Flushed cheeks match her lips, all under sky-blue eyes hidden behind glasses I didn't know she wore.

The past few days have felt longer than usual, and now I understand it's because I haven't seen her.

"Yeah, it's called fucking off." *Why am I sweating?* You'd think I wasn't a seasoned attorney used to intense situations. *Is this intense?* It shouldn't be. I tug at my shirt to allow air under my collar.

Her laughter fills my ear. "I have my share of struggling-to-concentrate days. More lately. What's going on?"

I dig in my pocket and hold the metal tight in my hand. When I open my palm, the only excuse I could come up with to see her today lies in it. "I had a key made for you. Wasn't sure if you want to move over tonight."

My other hand tightens around the brown paper bag, crinkling in the quiet of the office. We both glance down, but I use the time to look her over. The tail of her white shirt hangs loose in the back over a baggy gray skirt, leaving no figure to be found. I already miss her sexy little body I was eyeing the other night when she was revealing her shoulder and those great legs. And I haven't been able to get her ass off my mind all day. Hence, the special delivery, which now feels like an utterly ridiculous idea as I stand in front of her.

When her glasses slip down her nose, she's quick to adjust them with her index finger. Turning shyly to the side, she takes them off and tucks them in her pocket. With her other hand, she takes the key, the tips of her nails scraping gently across my skin. "You didn't have to bring it all the way to Brooklyn."

"No trouble."

"Thanks," she says. "The girls helped me finish packing last night. It's only a day early, but I'm looking forward to sleeping in your bed." Embarrassment flashes through her eyes. "My bed. The spare bed."

Chuckling, I hold up the bag to help her out. "I also brought you lunch."

She blinks twice as her brows rise in surprise. "That's so sweet, but you didn't have to do that."

"I heard you were working through lunch."

"Just making up the hours I needed to leave early this week. How'd you hear?"

"Jackson ran into Marlow last night."

"Ah." Tugging at her skirt, she seems to give up on the ill-fitting garment and reaches for the bag. "What did you bring me, Rad?"

I'm about to respond, but she closes her eyes and takes a deep inhale, exhaling with a moan that has my body unable to decipher between her craving the food or having her in my bed. Dirty thoughts I shouldn't be having rush my veins.

I'm surely going to hell.

She's way too nice to get mixed up with the Bachelor of the Year three years running. I can't even act right when I'm near her anymore. I went from zero to sixty for her, and she's looking at me like I'm a dead end.

"Hope you like hot and sour soup." I already know she loves that soup because she always orders it when we eat at an Asian restaurant. I've also eaten enough meals with her to know the two foods she hates—mushrooms and anchovies. Every week when the group meets, she chats with the server about what to try that doesn't include those two ingredients. "I told them to hold the mushrooms."

She shivers while scrunching her nose, being utterly adorable. "I hate those little fungi." Taking the bag from me, she says, "How'd you know?"

"I don't like them either," I lie. *I love mushrooms.*

"Do you have time to come back? I can show you my fancy cubicle." She waggles her hips.

"Absolutely."

We only travel about ten feet before I'm in a cubicle not much bigger than my desk. Two chairs are squeezed into the space, so I angle to sit.

Perking up, she asks, "You got the contract yesterday, right?"

"I did. Thanks for sending the retainer. I have my assistant gathering records so we can start laying the groundwork for the divorce."

"Thank you."

"You don't have to thank me every time."

"I'm just grateful."

"I'm glad you came to me."

When a door grates against its hinges, she stands up and looks around, then sits back down. "If my boss stops by, pretend we're working together," she whispers. "There aren't many people I dislike, but Lowell is at the top of the list. The city placed him here two years ago because they want a business degree judging how we operate. We have a very tight budget. I get that, but sometimes someone needs more than food assistance and a pat on the back." She leans forward in her chair, sliding across the cracked plastic mat.

My idea of what she did for a living felt distant from my life, never touching my shores, but seeing her office and hearing her stories puts it in perspective.

She's even more amazing than I knew, and I already thought highly of her.

She continues, "Our job can entail taking five extra minutes with someone to help prepare them for a job interview or find other financial resources. Lending a nonjudgmental ear can change a person's life. He doesn't get that. He only understands dollars and cents." Waving to clear the air, she takes a deep breath and raises her chin. "And he refuses to pay for some of my extra hours. If anyone can relate to long and demanding days, though, it's you."

"I hate it sometimes, but it comes with the territory. I'm also compensated for the work. You're not."

"No one goes into social work to get rich." I receive a pointed look, but then her expression eases. "I wanted to help people. I'm helping people . . . ten hours a day. I hate complaining. Sorry for the rant."

"Rant away. You're too damn good-hearted, you know that?"

The compliment leaves her grinning, too. "Someone's

got to counteract the cynicism in the world." She winks at me.

"Touché. The world needs more Bells and fewer Wellingtons."

Pulling the container from the bag, she laughs. "Lies. Your mom is very charitable."

"Ha! She's not even a Wellington anymore, but I'm not sure she ever felt one with the name anyway."

I'm caught in a laugh when our gazes connect. Through shared smiles, our laughter fades, but our eyes stay fixed on each other. It's quick, but in that one look, something more than our sense of humor tied us together.

She says, "It's not only your mom who's wonderful. You give people hope, a chance to make a new life."

"I've never heard a divorce lawyer made out to sound like a saint."

"It's all about perspective."

"Well, from my perspective, you're the saint who's *actually* giving people hope and a new start in life."

She smiles again but doesn't look at me as she pulls off the lid of the container. As if she doesn't want to discuss herself, she sighs. "Hot and sour is just what I needed today."

"Comfort food."

When she finds the spoon, she offers it to me. "Do you want to share?"

I hold my hand up. "No, you go ahead. I ate earlier."

Tealey starts eating as I look around at her personal belongings. It's cute like her with the knickknacks. There are only a few, but enough to show her personality. Picking her coffee mug up, I read, "There. They're. Their? . . . *Ohhh*." I chuckle.

"Grammar jokes. Lame to most, but funny to me." She

pulls open a drawer. "I have snacks if you want a candy bar or gum."

Various packages of gum slide around, but the Mars bars and Milky Ways are stacked in a clear bin. A clipped bag of chips and a few pieces of root beer candy are shoved in a white bin along with pencils, Sharpies, and what looks to be feminine products. "What else do you have in that drawer?"

"Survival tools. Coffee. Candy. Spoons. Mugs. Tampons. Baby food." She shuffles stuff around. "And a knife."

"What kind of knife?" Tealey wielding a knife was not something I had on my bingo card. *Impressive.*

"A switchblade. I was thrown against the wall once when I denied benefits to someone. I felt horrible about it and gave him twenty dollars. Guess it wasn't enough." Anger burns in my veins, and I clench my fists. He physically attacked her. Twenty bucks wasn't what he was after. It's bullshit she was put in that position.

"What the hell, Tealey? I never heard about that."

"I think you were in Aspen at the time." She starts eating again, leaving me stunned. What the hell? I was skiing when I should have been here for her. No one could have predicted the attack, but I had a right to know and make my own decision on how to react. "Why didn't anyone tell me?"

"We didn't want to put a damper on your trip," she says as if the attack was nothing. "And now we have a security system."

I never thought about her job being dangerous. Glancing over my shoulder, I stare at the front entrance. Anyone could walk in off the street, and her cubicle is the second closest to the door. "That's good, but how will another attack be prevented?"

"Sometimes people do desperate things. That's the

only time I've ever been threatened. Every other time I had met with him, he was fine, even optimistic about the future."

I'm not going to harp on this to her, feeding a fear that I'm sure she's tried to bury. But I'm glad she's letting me in, sharing parts of herself that I never knew about before. Sharing her life with me—the good and bad parts. We all have them in varying degrees. I just hope her life isn't on the line because of her chosen career.

Pushing aside my feelings on the matter, I turn back to her. I shift on the chair that was never meant to be comfortable and redirect. "You ready for the move?"

"Ready to get it over with. Cammie has a clipboard and printouts. I suspect it will move fast if she has her way. If Cade has his, he and Jackson will be drinking beer and taking their time."

I chuckle. "That's for sure."

"Not sure if Marlow will be there. She said she will, but . . ." She looks around conspiratorially. "Cammie and I have our suspicions that she's secretly dating someone."

She brings a spoonful of soup to her lips and grins before shoving it in her mouth. There's something in her eyes—an amusement—and I want to ask her about it, but I don't.

"This soup is so good," she says, the words punctuated with more gusto than I've ever heard over a liquid.

I might have ulterior motives—to see her, feed her, make her smile. It worked, and I give myself a mental pat on the back. *I did good.*

"She's single," I say. "She doesn't have to sneak around."

She's quick to shrug, and then using her spoon to talk, she says, "That's my point. Why is she sneaking around when she doesn't have to?"

I think I got lost somewhere in this conversation when I got distracted by Tealey's smile.

She says, "Marlow loves to talk about her dates; the good, the bad, and the ridiculous. She loves to share the details, and we love to hear them. That's like our group M.O. when it comes to dating. No detail is off-limits. But she hasn't said a peep in a week or so."

"Maybe she hasn't gone on a date worth talking about this week."

She plants her elbows on the desk, resting her chin in her hands. "You're close with her." *Not that close.* "Do you know anything?"

Only that she roped me into some scheme to get an apartment out of the deal . . . A hookup possibly the other night, but nothing out of the ordinary. "No."

"Bummer. I was hoping for insight." Though she starts eating again, her gaze keeps flicking to me. She then takes hold of her water bottle, twisting the cap on and off, seeming to contemplate.

"Something on your mind, Bell?"

As if the acknowledgment comes out of left field, she pulls her attention back to me. "I'm told I ask too many questions." She sighs softly. "Hazard of the job."

"Are you wanting to ask me a question?"

"I don't mean to pry."

"You can ask me anything. That's what roommates do. We pry into each other's lives."

Under rolling laughter, she asks, "Is that what they do? Pry into each other's lives?"

"I don't know." I laugh. "It's been a long time since I've had one. But I imagine getting to know the person you live with isn't an intrusion. It's a part of building a friendship. Right?"

She thinks about it. "The other night was nice." She looks down, shaking her head. "Not that we'll be spending much time together after I move in. You have a life. Your work. I know you're super busy. I just meant—"

"I know what you mean, and I'm looking forward to spending more time with you as well."

I watch her smile bloom. "Thanks."

That smile is one of the reasons I came here, but now I'm starting to think I'm driving this friendship off the rails entirely. Nothing good could come from us hooking up, yet I've put myself in a position as though it could.

What am I doing?

The last thing I want to do is hurt Tealey, and that's what will happen if we date. Romantic relationships aren't my thing. They require more time than I have to give. The sound of a bell that needs tuning buzzes, and I stand abruptly. "I should get back to work and let you do the same."

Disappointment contorts her expression. "So soon?" Then she checks the clock on her desk. "I guess you do."

Ducking out from the cubicle, I take a few steps, needing the space between us to allow more rational thoughts. She stands, resting her hip against the side of the short, upholstered wall, and a smile anchors the stars in her eyes. "Whoever said divorce lawyers can't be noble is just plain wrong."

"Do people say that?"

"Rumor on the street." She rocks back on her heels, giggling softly, and tucks her hands into her pockets.

"I guess if they thought otherwise, I'd be out of business."

Her laughter feels better than anytime I won an award. She says, "Your reputation is safe and will remain intact. I promise. I'm like Gringotts vault."

Confusion wrinkles my brow. "I don't know what you're talking about."

"Gringotts." Her eyes go wide. "From *Harry Potter*."

I tighten my lips and shake my head. "Never read the books."

A gasp echoes around us before her hand covers her mouth. She comes closer and plucks lint from my lapel. Her eyes remain focused on my chest when she whispers, "There's an indescribable feeling of magic, like anything is possible. Have you ever felt that?"

"I have." With you. *What am I saying?*

Her gaze slides up to mine, her chest noticeably rising and falling as her hand flattens against my jacket. "You have?"

What am I doing?

Stars still shine in her eyes as if I'm one of the good guys.

A heaviness starts pressing on my chest as silence overcomes the fun, and the hour demands my attention. I do the impossible and take a step back, away from her, and clear my throat. "Sure. I saw the movies."

"Oh," she replies, her hand falling to her side. "Thanks for the soup."

"No problem."

"And for delivering the key."

"My pleasure." Rubbing the back of my neck, I keep my eyes on her and say four words that feel more like a beginning than a goodbye, "I'll see you tonight?"

Leaning against the wall again, she crosses her arms over her chest and smiles. "See you tonight."

12

Rad

Clearheaded.

Reasonable.

Straightforward.

I sigh as I think back to the old me—the old me that I'm starting to miss. This dazed and confused version of Rad Wellington that comes out every time I see Tealey is starting to bother me. Why? Mostly because it's silly. There's nothing between us. We're the same *friends* that we were last week.

So what if she's moving in? It's temporary.

When did temporary turn into opportunity? Fuck, drop it.

Needing my ego kicked in the ass, I text the man for the job.

I drive deeper into Brooklyn to a neighborhood that hasn't been reinvented with prices to match the rest of the borough—a hidden gem. The homes have been here for generations and still have chipped paint, rusty awnings, and people parked on their porches who wave at strangers.

Jackson, Cade, and I would make the long run from my building, *literally run*, and stop here to recover before heading back to the city. I should start running that route again. With the spring breeze blowing in through the open window, it feels good out here, like my lungs are free to breathe.

I park where the street dead-ends and the East River is the only thing separating me from Manhattan, then get out and wait. Cade parks next to me and gets out. Tugging at his belt, he looks around. "We haven't been here in a few years. Good to see some things never change." When he shakes my hand, he asks, "What gets you out of the city, Wellington?"

The question feels loaded, although I know it's not. While I'm sure he's curious about my last-minute text to meet by the water, there's no way he knows what's on my mind—that she's on my mind, and I'm worried about that.

"I checked in on Tealey. I needed to get her a key and wanted to see how she's doing," I say as naturally as I can.

"Cammie told me Tealey's staying with you until she finds a new place. Could take a while in this market."

"I don't mind."

He picks up a stone and fiddles with it. "Didn't know you had it in you."

Staring at the water and ignoring the smirk on Cade's face, I ask, "Helping a friend out? Thanks . . . You guys really think I'm an asshole, don't you?"

I glance over at him.

He tosses the stone into the dirt and kneels to pick a weed. His brown is pulled together as if he's actually having to consider my question. "No, not an asshole," he says finally. "You've isolated yourself in a lot of ways since graduation."

This is news to me. "We watch games together all the time."

He shrugs. "I wouldn't say all the time. Sometimes."

"Sounds like you miss me." I pop his arm with my elbow.

"I wouldn't go that far." Laughter bellows from him as he discards the weed. "I've been buried at work and spend most nights planning this wedding. I'd marry Cammie today at the courthouse if she'd let me. But a big wedding makes her happy, and her being happy makes me happy." He looks down and kicks the curb. "What I'm saying is I know busy. I get that you're busy and want to make partner to break some record at the firm, but are you happy?"

Am I happy? Is he wanting to talk about real feelings? I'm surprised by the changing tide of his mood. I might have contacted him to help me see things clearer, but instead, the water feels muddier than before, causing my chest to tighten. "I wasn't expecting a therapy session, Cade."

"Sometimes we get what we need, not what we want."

I could apply that to many aspects of my life, but the words hit home more today.

Stepping over the curb, I get closer to the water's edge. "Why didn't I know Tealey and Steve broke up until this week?"

"Refer to my previous statement."

Fuck.

He adds, "And I can't say I lost sleep over their breakup. Cammie was thrilled when she heard, but don't tell Tealey." He studies me. "If it makes you feel better, I hear everything from Cammie."

I cross my arms over my chest, watching the water lap at the shore. We don't need to fill every minute that passes between us, but so much seems to have changed overnight.

Work is a nightmare, and now I have Marlow and Bob throwing a wrench in things.

Why does the best opportunity I have come with strings that dangle into my personal life? And it's not like my personal life isn't complicated enough. I now have these foreign feelings starting to become more familiar with each passing day for Tealey, who has always only ever been out of reach moving in with me. There's the logistics of that life change, too.

I wish I could sort all that out myself. I should be able to. I'm Rad Wellington—I sort other people's shit for a living. So why can't I make sense of all this?

Here goes nothing . . ."I've had some things on my mind and wanted to get your opinion."

"I'm here. Might as well make the most of it."

I take a deep breath and then confess on the exhalation, "I need answers, a solution to a problem I can't seem to riddle myself out of."

Something in my tone must strike a chord because he says, "You know I'll help if I can. What's going on?"

Confusion on his face greets mine. Rubbing my chest, I say, "Emotional crap I can't seem to shake."

To himself, he mutters. "Emotional crap?" Then he squints his eyes at me, reading me like a wide-open book. "Feelings?"

Bingo. Feelings for Beginners—the CliffsNotes version. That's what I need. A crash course in why the fuck I'm suddenly turning soft. I'm not even thirty, dammit.

I shove my hands in my pockets. *Why is this so fucking embarrassing to talk about?* "There's a lot of shit going on, and most of it I can't talk about."

"Stuff at work?"

Nodding, I briefly glance over at him. "Cases I'm working on."

"Trouble with women?" *Stuck in an agreement with Marlow wasn't on the agenda, but it's something I have to contend with.* "In business?"

"You could say that."

"Are you going to make me work for every last tidbit?"

"You're doing a good job so far," I reply sarcastically.

He volleys right back. "Thanks, Dad." Pacing, he adds, "Trouble with women in your personal life?"

I blow out a breath.

I wouldn't say that I'm having a problem *with* Tealey exactly. But maybe that *is* the problem. It's so easy to be with her—a newfound fact since I've stopped my self-imposed ban on being alone with her. *For this very reason.*

It's not really my fault. Who wouldn't want to spend time with her? She makes me laugh, smile, and forget about the pressures of work. I'm funny around her, more intelligent, more interesting. She makes me feel that way, at least.

Around Tealey Bell, I'm not just a high-profile divorce attorney. And, for some reason, I like that.

"So, women in your personal life too?" Cade asks again.

"Probably." Because I'm going to be in a whole lot of trouble if I keep letting my time with Tealey veer off sideways into areas we shouldn't travel.

A hot pink lace thong comes to mind, and I can't say any of my thoughts on those have been platonic.

Cade would kick my ass if he found out. Tealey's like a little sister to him and Cammie. She spends the most time with them, eating dinner over there at least once a week.

Not sure if he's joking since his expression turns serious when he crosses his arms over his chest. "When did this start? Are there any other symptoms?"

"Clammy hands. I've got 'em." I hold up my hands and then press two fingers to my wrist, fighting a smile "Racing pulse. And sometimes," I say, restraining a chuckle. "I even hear birds singing, but when I look around, there are none." Cade's eyes grow wide as he pretends to be concerned. "What's wrong with me? Give it to me straight, doc."

He moves in front of me, his large frame blocking the view. "Hate to tell you this, but you're either about to have a heart attack or . . ."

"Or?" He sounds so serious, keeping me on pins and needles.

"You might be in love."

I think my performance was too convincing, maybe even Oscar-worthy. "I think I'll get a second opinion." I burst out laughing.

In love?

Me? That's a stretch.

Who would I possibly be in love wi—*Shit.*

Blond hair. Bright blue eyes . . . Nah. Not possible. I even cringe at the term crush. Infatuation probably works better. It was a short-lived infatuation back in college.

Nothing more.

Never has been.

Holding his hands up in surrender, Cade says, "I'm just a Sunday afternoon armchair sports enthusiast. I can write you a prescription to watch a day of sports to get your balls back, but that's the best I can do." I receive another well-meaning pat on the shoulder. He finally breaks into a grin, a shit-eating one at that. "But here's the good news. Although I know it's scary for you to develop feelings for the first time, worse things could happen, Rad."

I let my posture sag, you know, to add dramatic effect

from learning that I might have caught a case of "feelings" for the first time. "Like what?"

Stepping back a few feet, he laughs. "Like having an *actual* heart attack."

"Don't put that into the universe."

"Eh, you've never been superstitious," he says, kicking a rock into the grass.

"There's a first time for everything."

He punches me in the arm, and teases, "Like joining the love club."

"I'm not in love, Cade." Even though we're joking around, I don't know why his words hit close to home. My neck is itchy under the collar, so I pull at it. *Ah, fuck it.* I tug my tie loose and undo my top button. "And I'm definitely not in the club."

"It's good in the club. The club serves tacos every Tuesday. Do you get tacos every Tuesday?"

"I don't want tacos every Tuesday. I had them on Monday, and I'm pretty fucking sure they taste the same."

"Sex whenever you want it."

I cock an eyebrow for two reasons. *One*—I don't want to hear about him getting sex. It's just a reminder of how long it's been for me. Not long for some, but for me, too long. *Two* —I know for a fact he doesn't get it whenever he wants it. Cammie is in control of that relationship hands down. "You're reaching."

"Very funny," he replies humorlessly.

Shrugging with a smirk, I say, "I have my moments." Moving around the car, I lean against it. "As entertaining as this has been, I need to get back. I have work to do before tonight."

"What's tonight?"

"A guy who gets tacos every Tuesday and copious

amounts of sex shouldn't be interested in my boring life as a bachelor."

Cade pulls a face, rolling his eyes. "C'mon, Rad. If you're not fessing up about who you love, tell me you're finally calling that fitness model back. Just one more night living the life—"

"Vicariously?"

"Nah. You just seem like you need to get laid."

He's probably right. My dick is messing with my head. I'm about to get in the car, but add, "And stop saying I'm in love. It could ruin my reputation."

"And make people think you have a heart? Don't worry, you picked the right profession to throw 'em off the scent."

"Look who the funny guy is now."

"Back to the fitness model. Angela?" I nod, letting him have his fun. "She's no Cammie, but damn, dude, she's worth a callback. If you're not calling her tonight, who are you calling, or should I say falling for?" I should have known I'd get interrogated. Even a hint of blood in the water summons the sharks.

"I'm not going out, calling, or falling, asshole. I want to help Tealey settle in. It's her first night at the apartment."

"Way to let a guy down. I thought I was going to get some juicy details." He opens the door to the car. "Not that Tealey's disappointing, but you know what I mean. She's . . . just Tealey."

"Yeah. Just Tealey." My throat thickens, the words leaving a bad taste in my mouth.

Getting in his car, he starts it and rolls down the windows. "When you're ready for your second session, give me a text."

"Yeah. Yeah." I open the car door. "Any words of wisdom before I go?"

"You're asking a guy who's getting married soon. I'm smack dab in the middle of mixed-up emotions and taco Tuesdays." I imagine that wasn't the dream he had growing up.

"So no second thoughts?"

Cade shakes his head, his hands gripping the wheel. "Nope. I have it good, and I know it. I'm not going to lose it."

"Cammie's a catch."

"She is." Leaning over the console, he eyes me through the passenger side of his vehicle. "If you're not going to tell me who the unlucky lady is, then the next time you need advice—"

"I'll go to Jackson."

Shooting me the bird, he laughs. "Probably best."

Chuckling, I say, "The city beckons."

"Thanks for slumming it. Good luck, brother."

"Thanks." *I'm going to need it.*

Rocks crunch under the weight of his tires when he pulls away. I stay a minute longer, taking in the view and sitting with my thoughts. I'm not in love with Tealey.

It's just a heavy dose of attraction.

And complicated, like we've been since the moment we met. The risk outweighs everything. I'm not willing to lose what we have—and what we're currently building—by fucking her and expecting it to be the same as it is now. That's what will happen if we cross that line. I'd only hurt her and disappoint her. I don't do relationships, and she doesn't seem to go without very long.

No way. I'm not a relationship guy.

The screen in my car comes to life with a text from Tealey: *I can't believe you've never read Harry Potter.*

I start laughing and record a text to send: *He played Quid-*

ditch, and I played squash. We had nothing in common to inspire me to spend that much time with him.

Tealey: *I'm impressed by the Potter reference. Thank you for lunch. The soup was good. The company, even better.*

Me: *You're welcome, but the pleasure was mine.*

Tealey: **rolling eyes emoji* Save the charm for your ladies.*

Me: *I don't have ladies, but I do know this great woman who can be quite charming herself.*

Tealey: *You're making me jealous *winky emoji**

Me: *Spoiler alert: it's you. *winky emoji**

Tealey: *See? Charming.*

Me: *I'll take charming for $200.*

Tealey: *Who is Rad Wellington?*

Love is definitely ruled out. Love can't be this much fun. I deal with the aftermath of experiencing it every day.

Tealey: *This has been fun, but sadly, I need to run. Thanks again for lunch. It was a great surprise to see you. Maybe I'll see you tonight if you don't have to work too late.*

Me: *We'll see how things go. Make yourself at home.*

I drive away, letting her texts mix with Cade's wisdom. That's probably not a wise idea, but it's all I've got, and he just might be right.

Despite the years of friendship, Tealey's and my relationship feels different, like riding a roller coaster that sends you soaring and your stomach dropping.

Whatever this is, she has me seeing things, and by things, *I'm referring to us*, in a whole new light.

13

Tealey

Moving sucks.

Unless it's to one of the most beautiful residential streets in Manhattan.

The driver helped me unload the five boxes I managed to cram in the car with me, and I scooted each one inside the door to the building. Though the lobby is small, it's airy, and it almost gives it an atrium feel instead of a place to enter or check your mail. Light floods through the black-framed floor-to-ceiling windows, and the shadows from the surrounding buildings crawl across the walls. The plants are a welcoming touch.

I get the boxes in the elevator, and when the door opens to his apartment, I turn off the alarm system. Using one foot as a doorstop, I shuffle the boxes into the apartment.

The elevator buzzing subsides, replaced by the sound of the door closing behind me. And then silence.

Staring down the short hall into the space, I smile,

feeling like I've finally made it in this city. It's a delusion I'm perfectly content existing inside of while living here.

I kick off my sneakers and then sashay into the living room like I'm the queen of the castle and go straight for the windows. The sun is hidden behind the tops of the buildings, but there's enough light to see ten blocks down the avenue in one direction and probably more in the other.

I spin in the expansive space, something I couldn't do back at mine without stubbing a toe on the bed or futon. I feel so comfortable here that I wonder if I can ever go back to a shabby studio without remembering that time I stayed in this apartment. Anything I can afford will pale in comparison.

So I might as well make the most of it. Taking my time, I run my fingers along the windowsill and over the console under the TV.

The marble in the kitchen has charcoal-gray veining, reminding me of Rad's suits and how incredible he looks in them. It's cool to the touch and tempting to press my heated cheeks against.

I bend down and open the wine fridge. Taking full advantage of making myself at home, I pull out the bottle he opened for me the other night. I search two cabinets before finding the one with shelves of different styles of glasses, one for anything you can imagine, from whiskey to champagne. Then I pour myself a drink.

Sipping my wine, I explore the rest of the apartment, except Rad's room. He left the door open, but I don't dare walk in. That would be a complete invasion of privacy. He'll never know that I peeked, though.

I move into my new room to plan. There seems to be plenty of room in the closet, and I feel spoiled for having my own bathroom. Setting my wineglass on the dresser, I return to the hall and drag each box back to the room, taking the time to unpack each one. Other than the rest of my clothes, I'm officially moved in.

Not ready to settle in for the night, I top off my glass and curl up on the couch. Night falls, and though there's cloud coverage, I love the feel of the darkness consuming the large space.

I grab a book from my room and flip it back to where I left off...

"I don't even know your name, so more than a drink might be a bit presumptuous."

He sticks his hand out. "Jack Dalton. I was named after my dad's favorite writer, and there are rumors," he says, lowering his voice and looking around before his eyes land back on mine, "that we're distantly related to the Dalton Gang. It's nice to meet you."

"Jack Dalton." A warmth covers my cheeks and down over my chest when our hands touch. It's ridiculous that I still blush at my age, but I do, and I might be falling for his overly confident act, something I would never do back in LA. "So you're an outlaw, huh?"

Dropping the smile, he looks away briefly as if checking the surroundings for eavesdroppers. His expression lightens when he turns back. "I guess you could say that, but I prefer Jack."

"Jack. I like Jack, but I think I'll call you Dalton. Seems more fitting."

Chuckling, he says, "I can handle that." He takes a sip of his drink, then looks me over. "Holliday is a beautiful name."

My heart starts to race from his sweet words and the sincerity in his eyes. "My mom was a little quirky. I think she heard it on a soap opera once or a Christmas special. My friends call me Holli. It's more normal."

"Normal sounds boring, and nothing about you is boring."

"WHAT ARE YOU READING?"

The book flies from my hands and slides across the wood floor. "Rad!"

"Hi, Tealey."

"Good Lord, don't sneak up on people like that." His tie is hanging undone along with the top two buttons of his shirt. The smile on his lips makes me think he caught me doing something naughty. Not naughty, but definitely heated.

"I actually didn't sneak. I walked right in and said hello."

My heart is still racing when I realize where it landed . . . at the toe of his right wingtip shoe. His shoes are so shiny that the book reflects against the leather. I gulp, slowly getting up as if he's easily spooked. "Sorry I didn't hear you," I say, trying to sound less weird about being caught just before I was hoping to read a sexy scene. "I got lost in the story."

"Must be a good book."

"It is. Really swoony."

When his eyes flash to the paperback at his feet, I scramble to mine, slipping in my socks on the slick floor. I lunge for it, but he picks it up and turns it over in his hands to read the back cover copy. "*The Resistance*? What's it about?"

I don't know why my face feels hot. It's a romance. The world needs more love in it. "It's, um . . . there's this self-made heroine."

"You've got my attention."

"She meets a famous rock star, but she doesn't know he's famous." Refusing to look him in the eyes to save me the embarrassment, I stare at his hand as he flips through the book.

"It's a romance novel?"

"Yes."

There's not a judgmental bone in his body or his expression right now. His interest might even be piqued by how he's studying the pages.

I try to swipe it from his hands, but he turns and holds it in the air. Looking up, he reads, "'You don't choose when. You don't choose where. And you don't get to choose who you fall in love with.' *Huh*." Tapping the book, he's still looking at the cover when he hands it back to me. "What's this guy's name?"

Rubbing my foot along my bunched-up socked ankle of the other, I take the book and hold it to my chest. "Jack Dalton. His rock star persona is Johnny Outlaw."

"The man knows what he's talking about." He tugs his tie off as he heads for his bedroom.

"Yeah, he's good with his tongue." I clamp my hand over my mouth. "Words! He's great with words," I add, hoping he didn't catch what I said. I'm quick to deliver the book to my nightstand and return, attempting nonchalance when he walks out.

The tie is gone, and his sleeves are rolled up, revealing his sexy forearms. "My mom loves romances—books, movies, songs. She was always reading before she went to bed. She'd tell me that after a long day, a book was the perfect escape from real life."

"She's right."

In the kitchen, he leans on the island with his palms to the marble, and says, "But can the average man live up to the expectations set by a fictional hero?"

I enter the kitchen and stand on the other side of the

island from him. "You have nothing to worry about. There's nothing average about you." I drop down to get the bottle, thinking I'll just polish off the rest of the wine tonight.

When I pop back up, he's staring at me. I ask, "What?"

A smile etches its way onto his face, and then he shakes his head. "Nothing." As soon as I open my mouth, he's already moved on—physically and literally. The bottle of bourbon is pulled from the cabinet before he grabs a lowball glass from the other. Dropping a large custom ice ball from the freezer into the crystal, he's already pouring.

It's fascinating to watch him wind down. I've just performed the same routine to burn off the edges of the day, to dull them. It's not a habit, but I'll take it tonight.

He takes the first sip, savoring it with an extended blink of his eyes. When he reopens them to find me staring, he looks at the glass shyly, and that great smile of his grows.

"What are you thinking about?" Maybe I'm wrong for asking what seems like a standard line for a guy, but the innocence of his reaction has me so curious.

"You. *And me*. Us." It wasn't embarrassment I saw, but thoughts of us that had him smiling like that?

Now I'm grinning. "Care to share?" I ask, returning to the couch with the bottle. The remaining wine only fills a quarter of the glass, but that's all I need.

"It's nothing."

"Two nothings now." I laugh. "Whatever you're thinking about must be really good." I drink my wine and slide my legs under me as I angle to face him.

His eyes search the ceiling as though he'll find the answers up there. "Do you need help unpacking?"

"I'm good. I only brought a few boxes and have already unpacked them."

Checking his watch, he looks up with a mischievous

glint in his eyes. "Want to do something fun?"

I glance at the clock in the kitchen. "It's late. After ten."

"And we're up anyway."

"It's a Thursday?"

"We used to party until dawn back in college on Thursday nights. Anyway," he says, waggling his eyebrows, "no one will be the wiser. Except us."

"Are you wanting to go to a bar?"

"I haven't eaten since lunch. I found a stale protein bar in the break room around six, but it was as hard as a rock and had expired two years ago." Rubbing his stomach, he says, "I'm starving."

"We should go eat. I only had a package of peanut butter crackers back at my apartment." Excitement zips through me, and I stand. "Just give me a minute to change. I'm a mess."

"Don't change a thing. You always look great."

Looking down at my blue yoga pants and baggy NYU sweatshirt, I reason that I've looked worse.

As if he senses the debate in my head, he says, "I know this little hole-in-the-wall place. Good food. Dim lights. Great company."

I grin, heading to the bedroom to retrieve my purse. "You had me at dim lights."

When I snatch my bag from the dresser, I catch a quick glimpse of myself in the mirror that hangs above it. Little makeup survived the day, but for some reason, I've never felt more beautiful.

When I walk back out, he already has the elevator waiting. Stepping inside, I lean against the back railing. "You coming, Welly?"

Biting his lip, he releases it, allowing a grin to spread. "Right there with you, Bell."

14

Tealey

"No one expects hot dogs. You know, like the Spanish Inquisition? Monty Python?" My shoulders drop when my joke doesn't land, and I shake it off. "Never mind." I take a big bite and then wipe the bun crumbs from the corner of my mouth. "Guess you weren't a fan."

"I didn't watch a lot of TV growing up. I played the hell out of *Grand Theft Auto,* though. My mom would have killed me if she'd known."

"Never played. More of a reader, in general, myself. Basically, a total nerd."

"I doubt that. And even if you were, there's nothing wrong with being studious."

Mustard splats his shirt. "Fuck," Rad grumbles when an air bubble loosens from the pump. "There goes this shirt." He doesn't let it deter him, and he covers his dog with precision.

"Good gracious, Rad. Save some mustard for the other customers."

"What can I say?" He shrugs, dipping his tongue out to lick a splat on the back of his hand. "I like mustard."

"Understatement of the year. Do you like hot dogs because I'm not sure you have enough for that much condiment usage?"

"Hey. Hey," he says, nudging me lightly. "I didn't judge your lack of condiments." He feigns offense behind a teasing grin and cold shoulder, hiding his hot dog from me. "Leave my mustard alone, Bell."

Laughing, I grab my root beer and head for a table by a window. When he sits down, I say, "Fine. Since you bought dinner, I'll honor your drowning-in-condiments-hot dog-loving-ways by making this an official hot dog judge-free zone." I take another bite of my condiment-free-best-way-to-eat-a-hot dog late-night dinner and moan in pleasure.

His lips twist as he uses his dog to point at mine. "Not judging, but why do you eat your dog plain?"

"Condiments have a time and place—"

"Seems like a hot dog would be the right place to pack on some mustard or ketchup. Relish. Onions. Get crazy with the sauerkraut. Look around. It's the right time to live on the edge and smother that meat."

Bursting out laughing, I cover my mouth, but it's too late. All manners are gone as I lean back, holding my stomach. "Oh my God." I choke down what I'm chewing and then start coughing. Shoving a napkin over my mouth, I'm still in hysterics, trying to catch my breath. "There will be no," I try to speak, waving my finger, "meat smothering tonight."

"Oh fuck," he mutters, dropping his head in shame. A chuckle shakes his shoulders, and then he starts laughing too. "This never leaves the two of us."

"No way. The girls will get a kick out of it."

Scrubbing his hand over his face, he peeks over it at me. "Kill me now then. If they know, Jackson and Cade know."

Unguarded and a bit bashful, I'm seeing a new side of Rad, one that's more carefree and closer to how he was in college. The last of the giggles peter out, and I take a sip of my soda. Still hunched over with my elbows on the table, I rest my chin in my hand, unable to stop smiling. "This is fun."

"Yeah, I'm glad we came out, even if I did have to endure your mocking."

"Nothing you can't handle, Counselor." Looking around the low-key restaurant, I sit up. "I didn't take you for the hot dog–shop type, so I have a feeling living together might be eye-opening."

"I'm full of surprises."

"I haven't lived with anyone since Cammie before she and Cade moved in together. If living with you means late-night hot dog runs, I'm all in." I couldn't wipe the smile from my face even if I tried. It feels good to laugh again, to forget about the usual daily stresses, and to be starting down a new path.

Holding his cup, he taps it to mine on the table. "Here's to new traditions." We both sip, his already gone, the ice screeching in protest. When I take a bite, Rad inhales his hot dog in three bites. *Such a guy.* "This eases the pain of working late."

The early spring night is cool enough to keep warm in my sweatshirt, but I still shiver, not from the weather but from an excitement that wriggles up my spine. "I feel rebellious being out this late. I'm usually curled up in bed reading or asleep with the TV on by this hour."

With Steve, I would have been listening to a lecture

about how irresponsible I was being on a work night. I don't miss those lectures about everything. I don't miss *him*.

We may not be on a date, but sitting here with Rad has been the highlight of my week. I think I judged him all wrong. He's still dressed for work sans jacket and tie, but he fits in with the casual vibe of the restaurant as though he belongs. I say, "I always thought you were more uptight."

Amusement widens his eyes. "Most people do."

"I've seen you relaxed at the beach, and we've been to hundreds of parties together over the years. You're one of my friends, someone who easily makes my top six."

He chuckles. "I've earned that sixth spot."

Reaching over, I cover his wrist with my hand. "I'm only teasing."

"It's probably true, though, and that's okay, Tealey. I'm willing to work my way to the top." There is nothing innocent or bashful about that smirk. I'm dead. Gone to heaven . . . or maybe this is hell. Considering one of my "friends," my sixth closest to be exact, just told me he's working his way to the top of my list and then killed me dead with a smile that could land me in his bed . . . Yeah, Rad Wellington knows exactly what he's doing using that loaded weapon on unsuspecting victims like myself.

"I, uh, um, oh my . . ." He leaves me stumbling over basic English, so I use a napkin to wipe the drool from my chin and then shove the hot dog in my mouth because nothing I say right now will make any sense anyway.

"Since we're on the subject of friends, I've been thinking about the unique opportunity we've been given."

I take a quick sip of soda. "Oh, yeah?"

"To strengthen our relationship. Not that it's weak or anything, but—"

"It's okay. I know what you meant. What's the opportunity?"

"We have a chance to really get to know each other. We're both single and work way too much. The little free time we have will probably be when we see each other at home."

"I'm following." As I finish my hot dog, I think about all the ways this opportunity could go, filling in blanks that aren't even on the table. Pulling my head out of the gutter, I say, "We could spend some of that time together."

"Take tonight. There's no pressure or dress code. No expectation or—"

"Demands. We get to be ourselves."

He nods, looking at me like he believes in me. It's been a long time since I've seen someone look at me like that and even longer since someone felt that way. *Other than my mom, of course.* "That's just what I was thinking. You're easy—"

"Slow your roll with that rumor, Counselor."

Chuckling, he says, "Easy to be with."

I laugh, the corners of my mouth lifting as I tilt my chin down. "Not much better."

Rubbing the bridge of his nose, he says, "I'm blowing it."

"No, you're not." I reach over and take his hand. The heat between us causes me to note our connection before I set it on the table. "You're doing just fine." The thumping in my chest is loud enough for the entire city to hear as I try to swallow the nerves that have crept in.

When I look at him, he seems to be having the same struggle. His soulful brown eyes lift to meet mine, and then his hand reaches over. Taking my hand in his, he says, "This is the start of . . ." He gulps. "Of a great friendship." Snapping his cup up, he stands. "More soda?"

Shaking my head, I'm left bewildered by what just

happened. The sentiment is still spinning in my head and chest. Was he suggesting more than friendship there? That's impossible. This is Rad I'm talking about. Mr. I don't do relationships. *No,* I'm reading the situation all wrong, interjecting a fantasy of mine where it doesn't belong.

Rad Wellington is off-limits—if not for our friendship, then because of our living arrangement. With so much going on in my life—from my living situation to my job and relying on his offer to stay with him—I can't screw this up by confusing his kindness for flirting.

Scooping up the trash, he tosses it in the bin, and then says, "Guess we should—"

"Yep." I stand, and we walk toward the exit. "Call it a night."

"I was going to say have a nightcap, but you're probably right since we both work tomorrow."

He holds the door open for me. Mentally kicking myself for the wrong assumption, I don't stop or look back because then I'll look and sound desperate, making it awkward. "Probably for the best," I say, though I don't believe a word of it.

The conversation on the way back is kept in safer territory, like the weather and the neighborhood.

I find myself walking a little slower when I step off the elevator into the apartment, not ready for the night to end. It's late. We work. I know all the reasons it makes sense to go to bed, including how much longer it will take me to get to work tomorrow, but that doesn't loosen the knot in my stomach.

I'm being silly. It's midnight. *Go to bed, Tealey.* Stopping at the edge of the living room, he looks back at me. Thumbing over my shoulder, I say, "Guess I'm heading to bed."

Rocking back, he nods. "I'm going to work for a bit. Let me know if you need anything."

"I will."

Like a dead man's walk, I move into the bedroom and close the door, leaning against the back of it. Closing my eyes, I try to tame the thoughts running rampant through my mind. Everything from what it will be like to see him first thing in the morning to throwing him on the couch right now crosses my brain.

Even with those thoughts competing with my rational side, I still have no regrets about moving in with him. Things will calm. Although we've known each other forever, this is new to us. Things will settle as we get used to being around each other.

A rap on the door has me jumping halfway across the room. Straightening my hair before I remember it's in a knot on top of my head, I call, "Yes?" and swing open the door.

Rad's holding a mug; *One of my mugs, to be specific.* "Do you know where this came from?" He walks away and stands where the kitchen meets the hall. When I follow him, he shifts to the side to reveal the open cabinet in the kitchen full of my other mugs. "Or those?"

"I . . ." *Is he mad? Curious if the mug fairy visited while we were away? Or fine?* His temperament is too even to read into. "I do know where those came from." I reply, whispering, "They're mine."

Twisting the mug in his hand, he furrows his brow. "Kiss my . . ."

"Ass. Kiss my ass. Get it?" I point at the donkey on the mug.

"I get it." *Nothing.* I don't even receive a sly grin like he usually gives to lowbrow humor. Glancing at me, he asks, "But why do you have it?" No cute smile or chuckle follows.

That mug is one of my favorites, too. I sigh, feeling like I might be in trouble. Did I make myself *too* at home *too soon*? I simply claimed an empty cabinet. And since I had him carry my preciouses over here and told him to handle them with care, I thought he understood the gravity of my love for mugs. *I assumed wrong.* "Sometimes, I let my cups speak for me. Speaking of squash—"

"We weren't speaking of squash."

Snapping my fingers, I say, "Keep up, Welly. I'm continuing our conversation. *Quidditch.* Squash. Remember the text?"

I can see when the memory returns by the small smile I receive. "Right." He sets the mug back in the cabinet and peruses the selection before glancing at me. "Squash."

"Huh?"

"You said, speaking of squash. The floor is yours."

I hop onto the counter, and ask, "What do you get when you drop a pumpkin?"

I'm finally rewarded when he can't hide his smile. "Squash."

"I've riddled it around my head for days, trying to come up with something about squash."

Giving in to the grin, he chuckles. "You did gourd. Bah dun dun."

Rad rubs the back of his neck, a tic of his, while looking back at the cabinet. "Back to the mugs . . ."

"Cammie didn't think you'd mind since you only had four mugs in that large, lonely cabinet, but if you don't like them—"

"You can leave them. I don't mind. I just wasn't expecting to find them . . . *or so many.*"

My pride shines as I admire the colorful cups. "It's quite the collection, a thing of beauty."

"It sure is." His voice is quiet, so I look at him. He looks away, grabbing a bottle of water on his way out of the kitchen. "Well, good night," he says, walking into his room. The door closes behind him, leaving me in the kitchen alone.

"Well, alrighty then. Good night to you too." I close the cabinet, unsure how to feel about that interaction.

I return to my room and shut the door quietly, forcing my thoughts to focus on getting ready for bed instead of what just happened with Rad. As soon as I crawl under the covers and turn out the light, I hear soft footsteps on the other side of the room approaching the door.

But then I hear them distancing into silence again.

My curiosity is getting the better of me and tempting me to open the door and ask if he needs me. But I shouldn't. He would have knocked. So there is absolutely no reason to walk back out there. *None whatsoever.*

Not even to check to make sure everything's okay. We're fine. It just got a little awkward at the end. The man has a million things on his mind, and I know for a fact that I'm not one of them.

Maybe not for a fact. But I have my suspicions.

15

Rad

This is the biggest mistake I've made in years.

Why'd I ask her to move in with me? *Why the fuck did I choose to torture myself like this?*

Friends? With Tealey? I scoff. *Yeah, not possible.*

I could barely sleep a wink knowing Tealey was only down the hall from me. I could sense her in the apartment . . . so could my dick. I haven't had to take a cold shower over a woman in a long time, until now.

Even pumping iron at three o'clock in the morning didn't work out my frustrations. I added a five-mile run to help burn off the adrenaline. My mind finally cleared in the quiet early morning hours. I took another shower, hot this time, to lull my mind and muscles into getting some sleep.

Using the light of the early morning, I meander into the kitchen after little sleep. I start the coffee machine, so it begins heating the water, and then go to my cabinet for a mug. Opening it up, I grin. With the new distractions in my apartment, I'd forgotten about the mug collection.

The ass mug seems to fit my behavior best regarding how I ended our night, so I grab that one and set it on the coffee stand. When it's filled, I take the steaming cup with me and sit on the ledge of one of the windows.

Even at this hour, the city is dotted with lights, and when I crack a window to get fresh air, I hear a melody that only someone who loves Manhattan would love—the honk of horns, the sound of laughter escaping an open window nearby, and the vibrant hum of the streets coming to life.

The wood floor creaks, and I look over my shoulder to see Tealey, dressed in pajamas covered in images of cats, tiptoeing out of her room. She's quirky, much more than I ever thought before. I smile from the sight of her, though, and from her choice of sleepwear. "You live here," I say. "You don't have to sneak around."

Her spine stiffens, and her shoulders shake with laughter when she finds me in the darkness. Holding up a glass, she says, "I needed water."

"Help yourself."

She moves into the kitchen and starts filling her glass. "Can't sleep?"

"Not well," I reply.

"Me either." Crossing the room, she sits down on the sill facing me, her eyes dipping down over my body. I didn't think to put a shirt on, not used to having company. I guess I'm lucky I pulled on a pair of sweatpants.

She leans against the brick column dividing the windows and gazes through the glass. Sticking her hand near the opening, she rolls her gaze back to me. "Spring is my favorite. When the bitter cold of winter is behind us, but the heat of summer has not yet set in."

Her bare knee is bumped against the thick cotton of my pants, and despite learning to share a space with someone again, I can't stop thinking about how much I like having a connection with her—the laughs, smiles, and little touches we've shared.

Jesus Christ, Wellington.

It's been all of ten hours since she moved in. Get your head straight. Make small talk, for fuck's sake. "I tried to be quiet."

"You didn't wake me." Closing her eyes, she inhales. "That coffee smells so good." I like seeing her at this time of day. There's no tension in her shoulders, and her eyes are wide, taking in the world. It's as if her body knows it can wake up with the day.

She straightens and starts padding across the floor. "I think I need a cup."

I stand with my back to her and look out the window. If I don't, I'll stare at her in ways that I worked out in the middle of the night . . . or so I thought. I have no perspective at this hour.

"Nice ass," she says.

I whip back, thinking I heard wrong. "My ass?"

There's not much light still, but enough to see her cover her stomach as silent laughter takes hold of her. "Oh my God, Rad." Bursting out in laughter, she continues, "I meant the mug, but said—" She grips onto the edge of the counter as if she needs the support, bending over in a fit of giggles. "I did say . . . *I said ass*. I said it and yep . . ."

Laughing, I glance at the mug, forgetting I'd chosen this one. But hearing her and seeing her on the verge of tears causes me to laugh, too.

With her body still shaking in laughter, she plants a hand on her face and runs it into her hair. "I'm delirious."

"I think you're quite entertaining at any hour, but this

might be my favorite." A few more chuckles run through me before fading.

"Yeah, I definitely shouldn't be allowed to people before coffee." She opens the cabinet and stands staring at the mugs with a big smile on her face. I'm still stuck on the fact that she just told me I have a nice ass. The longer she stares into that cabinet, the more I start to believe that my ass might be too much of a distraction for her. Let the woman have her coffee without fucking with her.

Or shift and let her enjoy it.

I face the windows, sipping my coffee, and when she opens the fridge, I watch her in the reflection. She pulls out the creamer but still doesn't pick a mug. I'm sure the chaos of the cabinet stumps her as it did me. Mugs aren't something I want to think about before having my first cup. *Or ever.* I don't tell her that, but I appreciate the uncomplications of a simple white coffee cup.

The cabinet closes, and she says, "I might try to rest for another hour."

Although she's not asking me, I turn back and nod. "Searching for the perfect mug to use can be exhausting."

She returns the creamer to the fridge. "That's funny, Welly, or it's early."

"Guess we'll never know." Smirking, I shrug.

"I'll give you the benefit of the doubt." She gives me a wink, and then wordlessly, she slips back down the hall and closes her door.

Turning back to the outside, I look up, scanning the sky for stars to enjoy the last moments before dawn breaks.

Tealey Bell is distracting in ways that don't truly bother me. I just can't seem to figure out why. Cade's diagnosis comes to mind, but that was us messing around.

Love is the furthest thing on my mind and love with

Tealey . . . "Don't be ridiculous, Wellington." I run my hand through my hair, refusing to let that idea sink in. My personal life is sidelined for my career. I have no time to indulge in attraction when I have a full load of cases. *Making partner.* That needs to be my sole focus.

At this rate, I should either try for more sleep or just go to work early. I choose the latter since I'm caffeinated. Since my body's already been scrubbed clean twice in the past four hours, I get dressed.

Before I leave, though, I wash up the mug, returning it to the cabinet, and then stand in the kitchen debating if I should leave a good-morning-I'm-off-to-work note or text for Tealey. We're roommates, not dating. So I'm out the door before Tealey leaves her room.

On the car ride to work, I let my regular driver deal with the traffic while I check emails to get a preview of the day ahead, starting with my schedule. I have court this morning and then meetings all afternoon. That means another late night of research to prepare for next week's court hearings. My work is literally never fucking done.

That didn't bother me at one time, but over the past couple of weeks, I've lost some of my enthusiasm for the job.

Cade wasn't wrong. I have missed a lot of my friends' lives simply because I have a job that requires an unreasonable number of hours. *And maybe because, for the first time, there's someone at home I'd rather see or enjoy a meal with instead of eating stale protein bars in the break room.*

RUNNING OFF ADRENALINE AND CAFFEINE, and after having two cases settle in my clients' favor, I sit with Ashleigh at a café down the street from the office. Though there's no time built into the day to take off, I needed a breather.

After sipping an espresso, she sets the cup down, the china clanking together. "Want to talk about it?"

My gaze flicks to her. "Talk about what?"

"What's on your mind? You've been staring at that intersection for five light changes like you're going to be tested on traffic patterns." She nods her head to the right. "You haven't even noticed that a cat is sitting in a stroller at the next table."

I glance at the stroller. Sure enough, there's a tabby contentedly sitting inside. Our eyes meet, and it meows. "Only in New York."

"Yep, only in New York." She turns her attention to her laptop and runs through a list of files that need to be verified before entering evidence, talking through each one with me. She's right. I've been staring off into space until she says, "Mr. Marché's initial offered wasn't accepted, as we expected. In addition to sparing their reputations, his soon-to-be ex-wife has sent a list of demands to keep the settlement locked."

"And?"

"I've sent you the list." She turns her monitor to face me.

I lean down and scan the list. "Some are reasonable." I glance at Ashleigh. "She wants to release a statement, but doesn't want to allow his side? We'll be pushing back on some. When am I scheduled to meet with Bob again?"

She types, and then replies, "Two weeks. I wouldn't normally suggest this, but Marlow has also requested a business lunch that day. Would you like me to make a reservation for the three of you? Two birds. One stone?"

"Confirm with Bob first, but I think it makes sense. If he's open to discussions in front of Marlow, make a reservation at Highland on 5th." There's no other reason to meet with Marlow. Our agreement has gone rather well so far. Without Bob, we've had no reason to put on a show.

She types, but then her fingers still. "You're working too much, Rad. I can tell you're burned out."

"You are, too."

"No, I leave well before you do. Sometimes, I actually leave on time. Other nights, you practically push me out the door. When you do, it gives me time with my boyfriend. We go out, to the movies, to a Broadway show, or stay in, but I have downtime. You left the office after ten and were back there before seven. That kind of schedule isn't sustainable." She looks at me thoughtfully. "I know you want to make partner, but does it have to come at the expense of every-thing else?"

I finish my espresso, keeping my eyes fixed on the plain white cup . . . plain, like my life. Thinking of the cabinet at home, what once represented me and my orderly life, now represents the color and humor Tealey's brought to it.

Ashleigh's not saying anything I don't already know. Reaching beyond the job description to voice her concerns, she has me seeing the situation in a new light. I shift in the chair, and say, "I want to make partner. It will come at the expense of my personal life. I'm willing to sacrifice that in the short term. But even if I chose not to, we need to reeval-uate our case load." I sit forward. "The last thing I want to do is burn you out in the process. I can't go it alone."

Her smile is tight, but she nods. "I'm here if you are."

The server sets the check on the table. She's quick to slot it in the credit card machine, and hand it back. We're left alone. When I sign the receipt, I set the pen down, and say, "Everything will work out just how it's supposed to."

She pulls her purse onto her shoulder, her smile still

barely deviating from a straight line. "I hope that one day you find a reason to leave work behind, to even skip out of work early, a reason to make you smile again, and most importantly, that you get everything you've ever wanted, and it brings you the happiness you deserve."

Her words hit me with a dose of reality, though I play it off by tucking the chair under the table. She sees through the façade I thought I was so masterful at projecting, but there's no judgment. Ashleigh knows I'm going to pursue my goals to the fullest, and I appreciate her support.

Greatness comes from personal sacrifice. My father lives by that motto, even today. He gave up my mom and two other wives. *He gave up me.* That's his legacy, though he'd claim otherwise.

He's alone now.

But is that what I want? Is that how I want to end up in life? Working hard only to have no one to share it with? *Fuck, am I having a quarter-life crisis?* No. This is my life. It's normal to be doing this, and often alone. *Isn't it?*

"You've isolated yourself in a lot of ways since graduation . . . I get that you're busy and want to make partner to break some record at the firm, but are you happy?" Cade's words ring in my ears.

Happiness will come later. Now . . . now is about winning cases and moving up the ladder.

Greatness comes from personal sacrifice. *Live with it, Wellington. This* is *your life.*

16

Rad

Is it wrong to wake up early in hopes of spending time with Tealey?

So much has spun on its head since Tealey moved in with me. When I get home, no matter the hour, she's waiting for me on the couch with popcorn or some other snack that hits the hunger spot so we can watch an episode of *Ted Lasso* together. She could binge through the first season, but I love that she waits each night to watch one episode with me.

We text each other throughout the day just to touch base. When I manage to get home before dinner and have time to give her a heads-up, she has ingredients spread across the island, and we cook together. From spaghetti Bolognese to her family's take on shepherd's pie, everything tastes better when we're doing it together. *The food is delicious as well.*

If we're too tired, we go out or order in. It's never a big affair. It's the two of us spending time together. Just how I like it. Beats how I used to work all hours or how I spent my free time preparing for the next day. I'm now driven to get as much done as possible at the office.

We still go to our weekly dinners or brunch with the others. I probably spend too much time hoping to catch her eye from across the table. When I do, she smiles and winks at me.

It doesn't matter that we're surrounded by others; she makes me feel like I'm the only one who matters. I've come to realize she's the best part of my day.

Opening the cabinet this fine Saturday morning, I grin like an idiot. Tealey Bell occupies more than my thoughts. She's managed to move into my place and claim space of her own. My life prior is now full of empty memories.

"Good morning."

"Fuck." I slam the cabinet door shut, startled. I take a breath, and say, "You shouldn't sneak up on people like that."

"I didn't sneak," she says, grinning. "I walked right in. No sneaking involved." Moving to the fridge, she laughs. "Guess we're even. What were you doing staring into the cabinet anyway? If the mugs bother you that much, I can pack them back up and keep them in my room." She turns her back as she reaches for the creamer—the creamer that also showed up with the mugs.

"No."

Straightening, she scrunches her nose. "All right. Settle down. I'll leave the mugs." It's incredible that she just got me to convince her to leave her cups. Then I spy the sly grin that creases her cheeks.

"Well played."

She shrugs. "What can I say?"

"Got Rhubarb?" I read the front of her T-shirt.

Glancing down, she runs her hand over her chest. My

jaw slacks. Oblivious, she says, "It's an underrated vegetable if you ask me."

I narrow my eyes in confusion. "Did I miss the rhubarb bashing?"

"No," she replies on an upbeat. "Just showing my support." Handing me a mug, she asks, "Coffee?"

Taking it, I spin it so I can read what she's given me. "Let's bone?"

Let's. Bone.

"Uh, mm, er . . ." I readjust, not even subtly, because damn, is Tealey flirting with me? "Um."

"It's funny," she says. "He's a skeleton."

"Yeah, I got it."

Touching my arm, she goes on about where she found this "gem" and how it cracks her up. But my mind has jumped at the opportunity that the mug provided and is in the process of undressing her. She looks from the cup to me and then gasps. "Oh, God. Let's bone. Did you think I was asking? *Oh, my God.* So embarrassing."

"No, it's okay. I know you were only joking. It's funny. Ha. Ha. Ha." Nothing sounds real about my nervous laughter.

She stops to stare at me, placing one of her hands on her hips. "I wasn't flirting. I know you're thinking I was, but trust me, Welly, I'm usually more clever than 'let's bone.' God, I hope so."

I'm pretty sure she doesn't have to use a line to get a guy to bed. "I didn't know women used lines?"

"I'm sure they use them on you all the time. What gets your attention?"

You. *Fuck, that was close.* I run my hand through my hair, glad I've retained some self-control. "I'd have to think about it, but my place or yours usually works."

Her mouth drops open. "For anyone?" Her arms flail.

"All they have to do is approach you and ask if you want to have sex, and it's an automatic yes from you?"

Detecting a note of disgust, I lean against the counter and cross my arms over my chest. "No," I reply flatly. "I don't have sex with everyone who asks, insinuates, or flat-out hits on me."

"Asking your place or mine is straight up hitting on you."

"Tealey, I hate this fucking term, but I'm not the *manwhore* you think I am. Fuck, I haven't had sex in a while."

"I hate that term, too. Doesn't make you a whore because you like sex whether you're a man or a woman." I can respect her principles, but she's traveling down the wrong path in this conversation. Then she asks, "How long has it been?"

"Okay, slow your roll. That's not what I was—"

"Last week? Last night? Last month?" A twinkle dances in her eyes. "Don't tell me. I'm better off not know—"

"More than a month ago."

"Oh," she says, her eyebrows raising. *Why'd I say anything?* I don't normally need approval regarding my sex life, but for some reason, I want hers. "I—it's been longer for me."

The two of us stand there with no embarrassment to hide, so we both nod and turn back to the task in front of us. She pours creamer into her coffee, and I'm quickly reminded of how she teased me about my love of mustard. I ask, "Do you even like coffee?"

"What do you mean? I love coffee." She takes a sip.

"You added a shooter to that cup of cream."

"What can I say? I also love creamer." After blowing on the top of the liquid, she takes several small sips with her eyes on me. She has a stubborn streak, and I guess creamer is the war she's choosing to challenge me on.

"How can it be hot with that much cold creamer in it?"

She spins and nudges her heel into my shin. "Stop teasing." *She's adorable.*

"But teasing you is so much fun." My phone buzzes, so I dig it out of my pocket. I have the move scheduled, and noticing the time, I say, "There's a chance we'll be late if we don't leave soon."

With coffee in hand, she says, "Hint taken. I'll finish getting ready."

I smile. "Meet you at the elevator in five."

She dances her way back to the bedroom like a ballerina, not spilling a drop of her drink. "I'll be quick."

Tealey Bell has a way of brightening any gray day. Still entertained by this morning's coffee talk, I return to wait by the elevator with a smile on my face and use the wait to scroll through emails on my phone to pass the time.

"I'm here. I'm here," she says, closing the bedroom door behind her. "You can stop tapping your foot now."

I didn't realize I was tapping my foot. Bad habit. My patience these days is razor-thin—not with her but with everything else.

Looking sprite and ready to take on the world, she asks, "Are you ready for the big move?"

"Are you, is the question. It's the last time you'll be there."

She looks toward the windows on the other side of the apartment. When she turns back to me, she says, "I have to be, don't I?"

"It's hard, I know. If you want to talk about it—"

"I'm fine," she replies, not sounding convincing. "Do you have a travel mug?"

"Yeah, let me get that."

I dip down in the kitchen and grab a double-walled lidded mug from a drawer. Handing it to her, I say, "I mean that, Tealey. I'm here for you."

She smiles. It's softer around the edges, but I'll take it. "I know. Thanks."

"Anytime."

Giving me a once-over, she says, "That's a nice shirt. You sure you want to wear white? The possibility of it getting dirty is fairly high, so if you're an odds man, you might want to change."

"An odds man?" I start laughing. "I think I'll take my chances."

"Don't say I didn't warn you . . ." *Sounds a lot like famous last words.*

17

Rad

"It's eight fucking thirty in the morning. Does everyone have to drive like bastards?" Horns are blaring, and I've been cut off twice. If I get so much as a scratch on my car, I'll lose my cool.

"How exactly do bastards drive?" Tealey grips the seat with fear.

"You're witnessing it." She briefly glances my way with pursed lips. "The other drivers, not me." With raised eyebrows, she sips from her travel mug, totally judging me. "Fine. I'm one of them."

"I know you're excited to move my stuff into storage today, but we're not in a hurry, Rad."

"Sarcasm noted, and traffic sucks," I complain, rolling my palms on the steering wheel. "Is everyone in this city heading to Brooklyn for the weekend?"

"You insisted on driving when we could have taken the subway."

I throw a look her way. "Yeah. *No.* Not my idea of a good time."

"There's a great farmers' market on Saturday mornings. Maybe people are in a hurry to get their fresh veggies."

"Like rhubarb." Hitting another red light, I look her way.

"They're great in pies," she replies offhandedly, turning her gaze out the side window.

In the quiet, I take the time to digest the underlying current running between us. This feels natural, almost to the point of normal, which is a quick turnabout to how we used to be in each other's company. I glance over at her, liking the way she looks in my car and enjoying having her in my life. "You're right."

"About the pies?"

I chuckle. "About racing to Brooklyn. It's not so bad driving a little slower."

Poking me in the arm, she says, "And the company's good."

I angle my head toward her, leaning a little closer. "And the company is *definitely* good."

When we arrive at Tealey's apartment, Jackson and Cade are loading the futon into the back of the truck. I park in a delivery zone. Tealey and I get out and walk closer.

"Nice of you to join us," Cade says, wiping the sweat from his brow.

"I'm sorry we're late," Tealey starts. "Rad insisted on driving."

"He never was one for the subway," Jackson adds, stepping onto the metal ramp and walking backward into the truck.

Apparently, I need to add my two cents into this conversation. "Why take the subway when I can have the love of my life drive me?"

"You let Tealey drive?" My jaw hangs open. *Wow.* I fire Cade a look of warning to tread lightly. I didn't expect to be put in the hot seat by my best friend.

"No, I drove—"

"Good morning." Cammie breaks the ice that had frozen me to the spot. My gaze darts to Tealey, who appears genuinely interested in my answer, then to Jackson, who's chuckling. Cammie asks, "What'd I miss?"

"Nothing," I reply curtly, stalking toward the truck to kick Cade's ass.

She claps her hands twice. "Then let's get it done, team. We have lots to do. Hop to it. Cade, I need you upstairs after you load the futon." Turning to Tealey, she adds, "I have a few questions about the boxes in the corner by the bed."

I dare to look Tealey's way again, unsure of what she thinks about Cade spouting shit into the universe like it's a fact. But her gaze is now trained on the building, and she replies, "On my way."

They head to the apartment, and I detour to the truck to walk off my aggravation. "You're an ass, Cade, you know that?"

"It was a joke," he replies, lifting one side of the futon. "She knows that. You know that. Hell, we all know that. No one thinks you and Tealey would ever hook up." He laughs. "The odds of that are the same as you letting her drive your car."

"I ..." *Wait. What?* They all know that Tealey and I would never hook up? Why would they think that? Why is it so outrageous to consider that she and I might be a match?

Something about that rubs me the wrong way and adds to my irritation.

"Guess I must be ignorant when it comes to my own fucking sex life," I tell Cade.

He quirks a brow. "I didn't say shit about your sex life. I assume you have that handled." He groans as he moves the end of the futon around to get a better grip. "I will say that after our little chat the other day and your admission about feelings . . ." He grins. "I'm wondering if you didn't trip into love. The question is with who?"

"Whom."

"Whatever," he replies, setting the futon down.

Jackson carries on by dragging the large piece of furniture to the back of the truck. I don't think he's heard a thing Cade and I were talking about, and I'd like to keep it that way. Lowering my voice, I give him my in-court glare, the one that levels my opponents into oblivion. It's my legal superpower. "I'm not interested in revisiting the conversation from the other day."

Jackson comes toward me and jumps off the truck. "What's wrong with you?"

"Nothing," I snap.

"Yet you're defensive about it." Jackson pats my shoulder when he passes in front of me. "That's called being grumpy. Come on, grumps. There's not much to move. I want to get it done in time to watch the game this afternoon."

We get to work, which gets me off the hook from more awkward, ill-timed conversations and happily distracts me from overthinking it.

After a few trips up and down the stairs, I wipe the beading sweat from my forehead when I walk into the studio apartment again. Cammie instructs me to carry the nightstand. When I pick it up, Tealey is entering the room. She wipes her own brow, then busies herself with a bag.

The piece of furniture is heavier than it looks. Are the drawers lined with stone? When I reach the second floor, my grip slips on one side, so I set the nightstand down to rearrange. I wrestle with it again until I get a hold of it and start forward, my view blocked while going down the stairs. "Am I the love of your life, Rad?"

"Shit." My grip slips, and the nightstand tilts forward. I grapple to hold it, but the drawer shoots like a rocket, crashing to the floor, and the contents fly everywhere.

Tealey gasps and drops to her knees, scrambling to grab stuff before I have time to set the nightstand down. When I do, I say, "I'm sorry. You startled me." And then drop to my knees to help.

"Don't look, Rad." Her voice pitches as she shoves whatever is buzzing behind her back. "Or listen. Close your ears!" she commands.

"I can help."

"No!" she shouts, panic filling her features, her hands shielding very little from what I can see on the floor. "Look away. Please."

I turn my back to her, but not before I catch sight of little foil wrappers. *Lots of them.* Buttons are clicked, the buzzing stops, and the sound of crinkling is heard as she gathers the packets that scrape against the floor.

Although I have no right to have any say in her life, I didn't need the in-my-face reminder of her . . . *I clear my throat* . . . activities with other men. Sure, she had . . . *has* every right to a sexual social life, but I prefer to block out that aspect and never think of her with another man again. "Don't worry—"

"Worried? Try mortified."

Though I probably shouldn't disobey her request, I do. Reaching down, I start picking up the packets that skid next to me, giving her credit where it's due to help temper her reddening cheeks. "You're being responsible." Tossing the packets in the drawer, I add, "And taking care of yourself."

The humor's lost on her, judging by how red her face is and her scowl. "We will never speak of this."

"It's perfectly fine."

A hand is clamped over my mouth. "Never, Rad!"

"Got it," I mumble from behind her fingers.

When she lowers her hand, I hear a heavy swallow before she sets her eyes on me again. "I was kidding with you when I asked if you loved me. I knew you were talking about your car."

I hand her the last packet, which she takes while squeezing her eyes. "Ugh. I'm never going to live this down, am I?" She tosses it into the drawer and then gets up, shoving the drawer back into the nightstand.

As if I've said something, I'm shot another look. But then she softens, and a smile leads to laughter. "Just to clear up any assumptions you might be having, Cammie gave me a box of one hundred condoms as a gift a few years ago."

Considering the number of condoms we just picked up, I can only assume she hasn't used many. And I'm not upset. I grin. "They expire, you know?"

She sighs. "It was supposed to be a gag gift. That's all. I actually forgot about them. I never use that drawer." She pauses, panic striking her eyes. "Almost never."

She clears her throat, flustered and searching for an out, but then lays into me again, "With all that I had going on at work, with the move, and searching for a new place, I forgot to clear out this drawer. Happy?"

"Um—" I'm not quite sure how to answer that. "I'm not sure my happi—"

"I didn't even think about it until I saw you carrying the nightstand." Why is she so upset? She's spinning over something she doesn't even need to worry about.

"You don't owe me an explanation, Tealey." I stand back

up with the nightstand wrapped in my arms. "I'm going to take this to the truck."

"Can we pretend this never happened?"

"Your secrets are safe with me."

"Which secrets?" She smirks.

"Right. That never happened." She gives me a little wink. I'm a bit slow this morning, but I finally caught on. "Also, never look in my nightstand." I give her a wink right back.

"Ooh, do tell. What do you keep in your nightstand, Welly?"

"Nothing that innocent eyes like yours should ever see." I start down the stairs again, chuckling.

"Gah, I'm so intrigued now. Why do you tease me so?" She trails me, giggling.

"Because it's fun."

"Yeah. Yeah." I don't have to turn back to know she rolled her eyes. And she won't see the big grin I'm wearing the rest of the way down the staircase. I can't even explain why I'm in such a good mood, other than she just makes me happy.

When I hand the nightstand to Cade, who's standing in the back of the truck, he says, "About time, man. At this rate, it's going to take all morning."

"There's not much left." He turns to pack the nightstand against the mattress. I rest against the bumper, and ask, "Did you guys know she has a mug collection?"

Jackson starts cackling. "Everyone knows that."

"I didn't."

Cade hops down, tapping my forehead as he passes. "Because you haven't been paying attention."

I swat him away. Although he might be right, I can't give him the satisfaction. As a matter of fact, when I give it some thought, I know he's right. When she's in a relationship, my attraction to her is dead on arrival with nowhere to go. It was easier to keep a wall, even a poorly built one, between us than seeing her with another guy.

Tealey Bell is off-limits because she has always been on my mind . . . *not because she is*. It's been a good tool to protect my thoughts from straying her way, though one I've failed miserably at lately.

All I can deduce is that is why my mind has been all over the place with her, why I suddenly feel the need to see her face, wonder what she's wearing, and figure out why she has so many damn coffee cups.

When she was dating someone else, it was easy to admire her but not pine when I'd see her at dinner with the group or joke across a table at brunch.

Pine?

No, that's not what I do.

I don't *pine*.

". . . shirt." I'm about to bat Cade away again but realize it's Tealey tapping me on the shoulder. "Your shirt," she says, rubbing my arm.

I glance between my sleeve and her eyes that are fixed on my bicep. With her teeth tugging on her bottom lip, I lose my train of thought. "Huh?"

She lowers her hand to my stomach. "And here. That's two spots." My body tenses under her touch, curious where she's heading next.

"Two spots?" I repeat like an idiot who's being rubbed by a beautiful woman . . . oh, right. I take her hand, stopping her because we're entering dangerous territory with my mind going dumb and my body reacting on its own.

She looks up, and I might be mistaken, but seeing a gleam in her eye, I'm wondering if she already knows. "You've got something black on your shirt. Looks like grease." She carries on, oblivious to how she has my entire being responding to her touch. Holding her hand up in front of her face, she analyzes her fingers before turning them toward me. "Yeah, definitely grease."

The connection felt when she ran her nails across my palm to take the key amplifies under the pressure of her touch today. We don't usually touch, but I'm wishing we did because every time we do, I feel it throughout my entire body. "Grease?" I ask.

She pokes the two spots again. "Don't worry. I might be able to bleach it."

Cammie calls her back to the entrance of the building, and she goes running. As much as I like having her hands on me, the view when she walks away is so damn good.

I catch Mr. Meisler watching me, and he waves me over. "Hey, how're you doing, kid?" he asks when I approach. He sips his coffee, eyeing me.

"Pretty good, sir. Yourself?"

"Not too bad."

With a cigarette tucked between his two fingers, he points at the truck. "I saw what was happening, and it seemed you were blowing it."

Glancing at the truck, I turn back, confused. "Blowing what?"

"Your chance with Tealey. She had her hands all over you, and you stood there like a doofus."

I shake my head, chuckling under my breath. "No, you've read the scene all wrong."

"Have I?" He takes a drag, then shakes his head as well. "I don't think so. What I saw with my own two eyes was a young woman looking for a reason to give you attention. And you blew it."

Tealey and Cammie walk to the truck, deep in conversation with their arms full of coat hangers. Tealey stops. "Hi, Mr. Meisler."

"How're ya doin', sweetheart?"

"Great." She walks out of earshot.

He says, "You get one shot, two if you're lucky. She got rid of the jerk. Step up to the plate and take a swing."

I don't even know why I'm entertaining this, but I cross my arms, feeling smug, and play along. "I'll hit a homer."

"And be her hometown hero. I'm telling you that little lady is giving you the same look Mrs. Meisler gave me when she was still Miss Garcia. I, as the kids say, put a ring on it. Forty-one years later, we're retiring to Jersey," he says as though he's won the lottery.

I look over my shoulder, and Tealey's tee lifts, exposing her waist and the top of her workout pants. I indulge, appreciating the way the fabric hugs her body.

It's been a few months since I've been with anyone. Schedule conflicts and late nights are putting a strain on my dating life. *Damn, she's sexy.* If I keep staring, I'll need another cold shower.

Am I developing feelings or just staying the course with an attraction?

Fuck these mixed-up emotions.

Tealey's hot. Simple as fucking that. It's out there. Now I can deal with it and move on. Feelings are complicated, but I can control attraction. I've seen the destruction of too many relationships that should have never started in the first place to fall into that trap. Hell, I make my living off it.

All I have to do is remind myself not to pursue Tealey Bell.

Easy.

Or is it?

Seeing all the boxes loaded and her apartment snug in

the back of the rental truck, it dawns on me. Tealey and I are more than just an attraction. I've had my feelings packed up like her apartment for so long that I denied owning them.

But now I realize these emotions won't stay boxed for long. Not when the mere sight of her has me running to catch up. "Ready?"

"As ready as I'll ever be."

She smiles and then rests her head on my shoulder. When I step up to the plate and wrap my arm around her waist to hold her closer, I know I'm screwed.

18

Tealey

If buying homewares with Rad is wrong, then I don't want to be right.

Leaning against the counter, I set my biscotti next to a whole slew of items the saleslady appears to have talked Rad into buying. The moment we walked into the store for me to check out their selection of mugs, she smelled a sucker.

Riffling through the items, I hold up a garlic press, and ask, "Do you need another one of these?"

He comes around a display table with a blue oven mitt on his hand and a matching apron hanging around his neck. "I already own one?"

"Yes." I move it to the side. "In the drawer behind the lemon squeezer."

"I have a lemon squeezer?"

Since he doesn't even know he has one, maybe he'll let me take it with me when I move. That is, if the realtor ever calls me back.

The crinkle of his brow is so cute. "You do." I've only lived with him a few weeks, but I've done a thorough investigation of his supplies and utensils.

He slides the squeezer across the counter next to the garlic press. "Guess I don't need two." Picking up my tin, he asks, "Biscotti, that's all?"

"Your kitchen is stocked, and I don't need to buy anything before I move." Plucking the mitt off his hand, I then reach up. "Duck." He dips his head, and I remove the apron. "You don't need these. That's just spending money to spend money."

"The marinara stained your shirt last week, so I was actually buying them for you." My heart gets stuck in my throat, making it hard to swallow. I look down at the set, somehow managing to swallow the sweetness down, and ask, "For me?"

Thumbing over his shoulder, he grins. "If you'd prefer another color . . ."

"No, it's perfect. Thank you." I hug them to my chest. "And you picked it, which makes it even better."

"The blue is pretty. It reminds me of your eyes."

"Miss?" Holding my tin, the saleslady smiles. "Sixteen dollars and twenty-seven cents."

But how am I supposed to function like Rad didn't just drop that compliment on me like it's nothing? To me, it's everything.

"Miss?" I look up when the older woman tugs my attention back to her again. "Would you like this gift wrapped?"

"Yes, thank you," I reply, taking a breath that feels needed at the moment and lift on my toes. I point at the bottom paper on the dowel. "Pink, please."

The more time Rad and I spend together, the more our comfort level grows. Less than a month ago, he felt like a stranger in many ways as he did a friend in others. Now, we're shopping together like a married couple.

Angling toward me, he leans against the counter. "Who are the biscotti for?"

"Your mom. I don't want to arrive empty-handed, and she loves coffee like I do. Voilà—biscotti."

"She's looking forward to seeing you." He turns to the saleslady, and says, "I'll add it to my total."

"You don't have to do that, Rad. She's hosting all of us for the weekend. I can buy her a gift."

"It's all good, Bell. No worries."

While he faces the counter, I lean against him, looking across a sea of pricey kitchen items. He pats my hip, and I pat his. Not only has our comfort level grown but also our friendship. I feel safe with Rad in unexpected ways, like now. We're a team and in this together, whatever this is. It's ours and ours alone.

I sort of love that we're living this secret life away from the others.

When the items are wrapped and tucked in the bag, I peek around him and get a glimpse of the total before his black card is charged. My eyes practically bug out of my head. He's spending hundreds on things he doesn't even know if he needs.

How can he spend all that money without so much as a second thought?

Taking the bag by the handles, he lowers it to his side as we walk toward the door.

Maybe it's the way his hand just barely braces to my back when he opens the door with the other, or how he makes me feel special every time he looks at me. But then I ask, "Why did you buy all that stuff?" He grins sheepishly.

"I've enjoyed cooking with you. Figured we could use a

few more gadgets to play with." I'm not sure I'm buying his response.

I think he just likes spending time with me. As if Rad couldn't get sweeter... *he does.*

If I'm being honest, he's dreamy, too.

The street is in the shade of the building as we walk to the restaurant for our weekly meetup with the gang. Rad glances at me. I say, "Thank you for buying the biscotti."

"My pleasure."

After thinking about how good it's been to build on our relationship, I didn't think *his pleasure* was going to be what stuck with me, but now I can't stop thinking about it and wondering how he likes to be pleased. *And who's pleasing him?*

Is he meeting someone during the day for a lunchtime rendezvous? Or sneaking out after I go to bed for a midnight quickie?

Most importantly, why do I care?

And do I have a right to care?

I look at his free hand hanging by his side through the corners of my eyes. The heat of his fingertips was still scorching through my satin shirt. *What is happening?* He barely touched me, but my skin is on fire, wanting to feel the burn one more time.

I think I need to check out a dating app and get myself back out there. Craving human touch, *his to be precise*, isn't appropriate. Rad's my friend, my roomie—

"It's just around the corner," he says.

"What is?"

He chuckles. "The restaurant. What did you think I was talking about?"

Rolling my hand next to my head, I reply, "Sorry. I have a lot on my mind."

"It's okay. Want to talk about it?"

"No. Definitely not." I hate that I snap, but what am I going to say? I'm thinking about you touching me in completely inappropriate and non-platonic ways? Yeah, I don't think that'd go over well.

"Okay. Noted." I stop walking. When he stops a few steps ahead of me and looks back, he asks, "What is it?"

"I don't want you to not ask me questions. I want you to ask, and I want to tell you, but sometimes. . ." I look at my shoes and fidget with the seams of my jeans.

"Sometimes what, Tealey? You can tell me anything."

Looking up, I sigh heavily. "I know you say that, and I know you mean it, but I don't know." I start walking to catch up. "I think I need to talk to Marlow."

"All right." He pops out his elbow. "Let's go, and you can talk to Marlow."

Why does he always have to be so understanding? If he'd pushed me a little more, I would have confessed everything. But now is clearly not the time, so I slip my arm around his and settle for the physical closeness instead.

"WE'RE ONLY MISSING Cammie and Cade," Jackson says, rubbing his stomach as he rests back in his chair.

Marlow tips her glass back and finishes the last few drops of wine. "I'm starting to think this is how it will be from now on."

Since it's something I've thought a lot about as well, I say, "I hope not."

Rad reaches for his glass. "Things are changing. We're changing. It's not a bad thing. It's life evolving."

With an exhaustive exhale, Marlow's patience has worn

thin. "Why does life always have to change? If it's not your father divorcing, it's Mother's botched fillers or praising an artist's work while stroking their ego when you hate the art they make. Or your friends getting married and losing them for the better part of a year while your other friends are too busy for you."

Rad, Jackson, and I stare at her. I think my personal problems need to be put on the back burner. Reaching over, I take her hand and hold it. "We'd never forget about you. I'm sorry if I've made you feel that way. There's been so much going on—"

"Tealey, I know. It's just been stressful, but I'll be fine. I always am."

Marlow's gaze lengthens to the front of the restaurant. When she looks at me, she smiles. "I'm lucky to have you guys in my life."

Jackson says, "We're the final four."

I say, "We'll always have each other." I find comfort in the exchange of knowing looks. Whatever happens, we will always be there for each other. The restaurant comes back to life around us, invading the moment bonding us together.

The back of my hand grazes the side of Rad's unwittingly, but I let my own desire to be touched again overwhelm my common senses and leave it just a beat or two longer. I can place the blame squarely on Rad's shoulders, his biceps, those sexy forearms, and strong hands. But he hasn't crossed any boundaries despite what my body would love to beg him to do.

He's made me believe that I don't need to settle for some guy who doesn't cherish me when I can have a man willing to do anything for me. Not saying that's Rad. Just saying that he's given me back my self-confidence.

Looking at my beautiful friend, I've learned that even

the strongest need reassurance. "I'm only a phone call away, Marlow."

She nods. "I'm just missing how it used to be."

It's probably the first time in adulthood that I'm looking forward to the future more than I enjoy living in the memories. I'm loving the new direction in my life. I take her hand and give it a squeeze since I can't share the same sentiment.

The night has written its last chapter, and we say our goodbyes. In the back of the taxi, the lights from outside flash across Rad's face in a myriad of colors when he rolls his head in my direction. "Did you have a good time?"

"I did. You?"

"Yes, but you were too far."

"Too far from what?"

"Me," he states.

My breath stops hard in my chest as his words send my thoughts spinning. What does he mean I'm too far? I try to riddle through any reasoning but still can't land on anything that makes sense, so I say, "I was next to you, not more than two feet."

Reaching over, he takes my hand and holds it on the seat between us. "Like I said, too far."

This is confusing, him holding my hand like he's my boyfriend while my pulse races us home. Pushing the boundaries of our friendship in a new direction? Or me reading too much into it?

Tired of fighting the pull I feel toward him, I squeeze Rad's hand, and whisper, "Too far." I scoot across the vinyl seat and lean my head on his shoulder. "This is better."

Moving our joined hands to his leg, he taps his lap twice, making me wonder if he's as nervous as I am. His skin is a bit rough, and his grasp firm. The heat between us is causing a chemical change in my body's makeup. That's all I can come up with to explain this deep-seated desire to kiss him.

But I don't.

I can't.

Not with Rad, though his words from dinner come back around. *"It's life evolving."*

By how close the two of us have become, we're evolving with it. Only one question remains. *Are we evolving as friends or into something more?*

19

Tealey

Rad has a morning routine, and apparently, a low-hanging towel wrapped precariously around his middle while getting coffee is a part of it.

I'm not complaining. But seeing the most eligible bachelor in Manhattan walking around shirtless and fresh from the shower is toying with my emotions . . . *and my libido.*

What the heck has gotten into me?

Rad . . . well, not into me specifically.

That towel is really the gift that keeps giving, at least Monday through Friday, and the best way to start a day. Me sipping my coffee, sitting on the windowsill. Him with that towel he catches when it begins to slip . . . unfortunately, he's good with his hands.

Wait, maybe that's not so unfortunate.

Clearly, I need a day off. Glad my Friday was approved and that Marlow, Jackson, Cammie, and Cade are busy doing their own thing in this SUV. This three-day weekend to the Hamptons couldn't have come soon enough. His mother and the others will surely help douse the fire burning inside me.

Although it would be easy to blame that charcoal-gray terry cloth that refuses to stay tucked at his hip for confusing the matter, and when I say matter, I mean awakening my sexual desires, it's not the only culprit.

I flat out blame Rad himself. Despite the pretty women I side-eye when Rad and I are out and about together, I have the privilege of drinking in his full devotion like a deserted woman in need of water. *Wait, that's not right.* A woman in the desert in need of a drink? A fish out of water?

Ugh! He muddles my thoughts.

Not to mention how he snuggled me into his side on the way home from dinner that night last week. What was with that? And then in the elevator to his apartment, nothing. What is a girl supposed to think? That it's just the way Rad shows his friendship?

Maybe, since those are the only times he's shown that kind of affection toward me. The pressure is mounting, and I haven't been brave enough to use my vibrator at the apartment in fear that he'll hear the buzzing again.

I should have taken advantage last night since he left to help his mom get the house ready for guests. Now it's too late.

Yet because of the damn towels and more than two hours stuck in a car traveling, I've spent most of today thinking about how hot he is. This is what he does to me. *Mounting pressure* . . . Muddled. I can't even think straight because of those damn towels, the deep V that I saw water droplets trailing down last Tuesday, and a minimum of six abs. There might be more. It would be rude to stare longer than I already had.

So there's only one thing I can do. I must now dedicate

my life to the pursuit of confirming just how many muscles he has on that washboard stomach of his.

Yes, now would be a good time to remember he's not mine—not to claim, not to flirt with, not to think about beyond our temporary arrangement.

I've seen at least fifteen apartments in the past three weeks, and any that Rad saw, he refused to even consider. So temporary is already longer than I expected. He's been a great sport about me staying and even told me not to rush into a rash decision.

I appreciate how he's looking out for me. He's been such a gentleman, and here, I've been acting like a dog in heat. *Not very nice of me.*

Yes, this weekend is needed. Hopefully, it will offer a nice distraction, taking my mind off everything it shouldn't be on, and I can relax.

As soon as the car pulls onto the driveway, I see Rad walking out of the house to greet us. Dammit. Why does he have to look like he just stepped out of *GQ*?

Every. Dang. Time.

His mom hurries from the house right behind him, waving from the porch. Amanda Allison is pure joy. When the car comes to a stop, Marlow swings open the passenger's door and groans, "Why do the Hamptons have to be so far from the city?" She's already stretching her arms in the air when my back-seat door opens.

Rad smiles at me, trying to kill me dead on this seat. "Hi," he says, offering me a hand. "It's a big drop."

Freaking gentleman.

"Hi." I slip my hand in his and hop out. He moves to the back, *too fast for my liking*, to start unloading. Stepping onto the lawn, I smile, closing my eyes, stealing only a second to take it all in. "Listen. Not a siren or horn to be heard."

Marlow laughs. "Those sirens lull me to sleep each night."

"You can hear them in your palace in the sky?"

Coming around to this side of the SUV, she taps my arm. "I bought a noise machine that plays the recorded version. Too much quiet leaves room for my mind to wander, and I don't want that interfering with my beauty sleep."

Cammie and Cade are already on the porch hugging Amanda, so I drag my large bag from the floorboard and hike it onto my shoulder. Before I have a chance to start walking, Rad's taking the handles from me. "Let me." I peek up to find the gold in his eyes brighter in the sunshine. "How was the ride?"

It takes me a second to get my bearings. "Noisy. Marlow snored with her headphones on. Jackson was watching a movie on his phone but forgot his earbuds. Cammie was dealing with the wedding planner. Cade tapped the steering wheel to a beat in his head for at least two hours."

Chuckling, he asks, "And what about you? What did you do to pass the time?"

"Daydreamed." The confession makes me giggle, and I'm grateful he can't read my thoughts . . . or know what I was daydreaming about.

"Must have been a good daydream."

I nod. "It most definitely was."

Marlow calls out, "Rad, do you mind taking my bags upstairs?" She goes inside the house without taking them with her, including the small Vuitton train case she was holding.

"I can help," I add.

"It's okay. You should go inside and join her. It was a long drive. By the time I get the luggage to the rooms, you'll probably be ready to freshen up."

"I don't mind."

He chuckles. "I insist. I missed my workout this morning anyway, and Jackson can help. Go on up and enjoy." He winks. Calling out to Jackson, he says, "St. James, get your ass over here and help me with the luggage."

"Thank you. I appreciate it."

Amanda comes down the steps with her arms open wide. "It's so good to see you again, Tealey."

Wrapping my arms around her, I say, "It's been too long." There's comfort in her arms and such kindness felt in the hug. She leans back and looks at me like a doting stage mom. "You're more beautiful every time I see you. How are you?"

We exchange smiles, and I notice a silver streak running through her hair that wasn't there the last time I saw her. It only adds to her sophistication. "I'm doing well. How are you?"

"Wonderful. I'm so glad everyone could come this week-end." She wraps her arm around my shoulders, and we walk toward the porch together. The gray shingle home with white trim and white columns leaves me in awe every time I see it. It doesn't matter that I've visited a handful of times over the years. This house is beautiful down to the smallest detail and so inviting.

"I am too. I needed a break from the city." Maybe from your son and those towels, but I think it's wise to keep that last part to myself. "I love coming here."

"The cottage needs life breathed into it and nothing like the young to fill it with excitement." She refers to her home as a cottage, but at six thousand square feet, I'm thinking the quaint term isn't quite fitting.

When we reach the porch, she turns back, and says,

"Good to see you, Jackson," making sure she's greeted every guest.

He waves. "You too, Ms. Allison."

"Amanda."

"Got it. Amanda."

She laughs, turning back to me. "He can be such an Eddie Haskell sometimes."

"Who?"

She waves her hand. "Never mind. Are you hungry? I set out snacks, and since it's reached cocktail hour, let's have a drink. I'd also love to hear more about your apartment search this weekend. Rad said you haven't found anything suitable yet."

That's interesting since I've found probably five options, but it was him who wasn't on board with them. I glance back over my shoulder, catching Rad's eyes on me as he drags the luggage across the lawn. He grins, and I return a smile.

"Absolutely."

As Rad's apartment is warm with original brown brick walls, black-framed windows, and darkish wood floors, Amanda's home is bright and airy with whites and soft colors. I can only dream of owning a home like this one day.

The house is bustling with laughter as champagne is being popped, and various conversations are overheard as we enter the great room. The gang has arrived and already made themselves at home.

The table for eight has been transformed into a buffet of snacks, and a full bar is set up at the far end. "You've gone to too much trouble, Amanda."

"No trouble. I love having all of you here." Patting my back, she says, "Go on in. I want to check on a few last-minute details."

"I'm starved," I say, joining Marlow at the buffet. We round the table filling our plates, and at the end, she offers me a glass of white wine, then she goes outside on the back deck to join the others.

My hand clashes with another just as I reach over for the last frosted sugar cookie. My eyes dart to the culprit. Those golden centers still shine without the sun when Rad sports a playful grin. "I don't think so, Welly." We're both quick to grab for the cookie, but I win and take a victory bite. "I'm sure the snickerdoodles are just as delicious."

He growls. "You're lucky you're cute, Bell." He snatches a snickerdoodle, tearing into it as he walks outside.

With my mouth too full to talk, I stare at the back of him.

Rad Wellington thinks I'm, *me—Tealey Bell*, is cute.

Feeling giddy inside, I go outside to join the others. I just wish I could stop staring at Rad like we suddenly have a secret.

"I'M THINKING alcohol and swimming in the ocean *at night* isn't our best idea."

Cammie tipsily skips across the lawn. "Probably not, but it sure is fun."

Jackson, Rad, and Cade are already at the beach because we're women who took 'too long to figure out which suit to wear,' as Jackson put it.

He's right. It's not like there's a beach full of single, hot guys waiting for us.

"What took you so long?" Rad calls to us.

I take that back.

Cammie runs and jumps into Cade's arms, sending him to his ass under fits of her giggles.

I tighten my sweater around me. The bonfire surrounded by red Adirondack chairs nestled in the sand is a welcoming sight to behold. Next to me, Marlow holds two bottles of champagne.

"I brought reinforcements," she says, her sleek black suit and sweeper sweater hanging open.

Jackson holds up two bottles of bourbon. "So did I."

"Great minds." She smiles at Jackson as she sits next to him.

After tossing another log on the fire, Rad finds me. His smile is set just like his gaze. "Where's your suit?"

"In Manhattan." I shrug. "I knew I forgot something."

Marlow pops the champagne. "I offered her one of mine, but she refused."

"There was no way in Hades I was going to wear that . . . *body floss*. Nope, no way. I didn't want to scare the sharks."

Rad furrows his brow, giving me a look like I'm crazy. Before I can read too much into it, Marlow shoves a red cup of champagne in my hand, and says, "Maybe you'll change your mind if we get you drunk, and you can show off that great body of yours."

"It will take more than a cup of champagne to get me naked."

"Shots?" Jackson asks, already filling a line of cups.

"I'm good," I reply, holding up my cup.

He hands Rad and Marlow a glass. "Here's to spending time with my best friends on a Friday night," Jackson says, holding his shot in the air. Liquid sloshes out the side. "Time with you is almost as good as a random swipe right."

"That's disgusting," Marlow says right before downing hers.

Settling into the chairs, we sit around the fire, Rad plopping down next to me. The heat of the flames licks the air as we revel in tales of the past. Drinks are poured. And refilled. And topped off again. Laughs are shared and, in the case of Rad and me, too many glances and brushes of our hands when we reach to warm them by the fire are exchanged to be written off as accidental.

Heat builds between us. I'm not sure if it's the alcohol that's making me think he's watching me with an intensity that's usually reserved for work, or if it's really happening.

Before I can make sense of it, Cade picks up a squealing Cammie and heads for the water.

Jackson pulls off his shirt and peers down at Marlow. "I'm going in. Wanna come?"

"God no," she replies, waving him away. "It's freezing."

"Then why'd you wear your suit?"

"Because I look damn good in it."

He laughs. "It will look better wet."

She cocks an eyebrow. "Whatever you're thinking, don't, Jackson." But she starts laughing, kicking up sand with her feet. "Stop looking at me like that."

"Like what?" He shrugs.

Pointing at his face, she says, "Like that."

"How about a five-second head start?"

"What? No." She glances at me. "Save me, Tealey."

"Don't look at me. This is between the two of you."

She pleads, "Rad?"

"Nope," he says, hands in surrender. "But if I were you, I'd start running."

"Damn you, Jackson!" Pushing out of the chair, she takes a sharp right and laughs as she starts running down the beach.

The night is quiet, disturbed only by the crackling of the fire and the laughter of our friends in the water. I tug my sweater around me and watch Rad pour another shot of bourbon. There's something written in his features that I can't quite name.

Damn champagne.

He sits back in his chair, sipping the amber liquid.

"Are you having fun?" I ask him.

"It's only slightly disappointing."

"Why is that?"

A slow, sinful smirk crosses his handsome face. "I was hoping to see you in that body floss."

I burst out laughing. "Yeah. Right."

"I was."

"You're so flirty." I laugh, but my cheeks heat anyway. "Must be the bourbon."

"Maybe it's the company." He nods toward the ocean. "We could freeze our asses off in the ocean."

The flames cast shadows over his face, making his jaw look more angled and his cheekbones higher. Even his lips look more kissable.

"We could go freeze, or you could keep me warm," I say before I realize that I'm even saying it.

Wasting no time, he moves his chair even closer to mine, and his arm comes around me as if he'd been waiting for the invitation. "You're flirting now. Must be the champagne."

"Probably."

We exchange a smile that simultaneously fills me with warmth and sends a shiver down my spine.

Rad trails his fingertip along the back of my neck, dragging it slowly down my shoulder. He watches me with a satisfied smile on his face.

"I really was hoping to see you in that swimsuit, Bells."

Emboldened by both the look in his eye and the alcohol, I smirk back at him. "And I was hoping to see you shirtless. Guess we both lose."

The fire crackles in front of us. It's as if it spurs Rad to life, and he leans forward. My breath hitches in my throat.

His lips part, but before he can say—or do—anything, Cammie runs from the water.

"I need a hot shower." She grabs a towel from a chair and keeps running to the house with Cade close behind her.

"Night," he says.

I look at Rad again, the moment we had now lost.

"I think I'll head back, too," I say, climbing to my feet and ignoring the way my stomach clenches. It demands a release to the tension we just built.

If only . . .

"I'll see you in the morning," I say, giving him the best smile I can manage under the circumstances and turn toward the house.

"Bells."

I pretend I don't hear him and keep walking.

I don't know what just almost happened between us, but I'm sure it's fueled by the alcohol.

Just keep walking.

I don't want to embarrass myself and lose both a place to live and my best friend all in one night.

20

Tealey

A gentle knock on the door has me sitting up in bed. "Yes?"

"You still up?" Rad whispers from the other side of the door.

Not sure what he's doing here, I push off the bed and answer it, leaning my cheek against the painted wood. "Hi."

He smiles. "Hi. The day got away from me before I could talk to you."

"About anything specifically?" My stomach flutters with the butterflies I brought in from the beach.

His gaze drops to our feet. Everything slows when his eyes meet mine again, and he says, "I've been thinking about you."

I lick my lips and swallow as my spine straightens, not wanting to be slouching during such a confession. Gripping the door, I ask, "You have?"

"I have, and I was thinking . . . *wondering* . . . Well, I haven't exactly used words to show you what I'm thinking. And I want to change that. I've held back in fear of you saying no. But I've been thinking about us and the possibility of more. More of us." He looks down briefly, and if I didn't know Rad as well as I do, I'd think he was nervous. But then he looks back up with no hesitation. "I want to know if you've been thinking about me . . . *about us* . . . like that as well?"

Do I confess my sin? Tell him how I've started to fantasize about him? What turns him on and hoping that damn towel would drop? And that with every touch, cuddle, and smile, I've felt more and more attracted to him?

Or do I shut this conversation down and bury my feelings in the sand tomorrow when I go to the beach?

His eyes search mine in earnest, so I say, "I . . ." I take a quick breath and exhale. "I have thought about you. A lot, in fact." I didn't know I could shock Rad, but I managed it.

"Really?"

I'll blame the alcohol tonight for my slippery tongue and deal with the repercussions in the morning. "Terribly naughty thoughts."

"Even better." He cups my face and kisses me.

His lips against mine.

Mine against his.

Rad is kissing me. His mouth is embracing mine, and I'm wasting time thinking about the fact that he's doing it instead of participating. Just when I lean in for more pressure, he pulls away too soon. "Did I screw up by telling you?"

"You didn't screw up." I tug him inside the bedroom, and this time, I kiss him. I just do it, moving on instinct, following my heart . . . *and my desire.*

21

Rad

For everything I've done right in the world, kissing Tealey Bell tops the list.

Soft lips mold to mine.

A hand that rubs gently over the roughness of my cheek.

The way her body lifts on her toes, increasing the pressure and deepening the kiss, makes me think she was telling the truth when she said she'd had thoughts about me.

She drops back down, our lips parting, and we look at each other. Neither of us rushes to apologize or call those kisses an accident. No. We both plead guilty to the offense of wanting it with each other.

Her chest rises and falls as she looks at me to say something or make the next move. I tilt my head, resting my forehead against hers as our jagged breathing evens.

Closing her eyes, she whispers, "No take backs."

I chuckle between us, angling back far enough to take her in. When her eyes open, I reply, "Never."

Her gaze shifts away, and I hate that anything but a smile resides on her face.

Don't read too much into it, Wellington. Keep perspective. It may not have been more than a kiss to her.

I cup her cheek and run my thumb over her soft skin. "What are you thinking?"

Her body language reveals her walls are down, a comfort even now that we've strayed outside the lines of our friendship. Taking my hand and holding it between hers, she keeps her eyes trained on the bond between us. "Have you thought about kissing me before, or is this the bourbon talking?" Glancing up briefly, she adds, "I've had a lot of wine, and I'm not sure how much you've drunk."

I weigh my options, knowing so much depends on how I answer. I could hide behind the alcohol, but I don't want to. Tilting her chin until I can see the blues of her pretty eyes again, I go with the truth. "I think about you all the time, Tealey."

"Why haven't you been on any dates lately?" she asks, gripping the front of my shirt.

"Lately?" I scratch the back of my neck. "Hm." *Why haven't I?* I could list so many things, like how she talks with her hands when she's excited to how I work through lunch so I can rush home to be with her before the golden hour disappears. That she uses my lemon squeezer and then asks me to use my strength to get the last drop from the fruit squeezed into her water. How she touched me after the move, and I can still feel the ghost of her fingers grazing across my skin. But what made me forget about being with anyone else was when I realized that Mr. Meisler was right.

Sometimes, I catch Tealey looking at me like I'm that sugar cookie she stole earlier, and she just wants to take a bite. *So fucking hot.*

Not to mention when the light hits her eyes and—call me a narcissist, but I like to think they sparkle just for me. And those lips, fuck, I've dreamed about kissing those pink lips. As a matter of fact, I want to kiss them again.

I shift again, hoping she can't see *or feel* what she does to me. Or maybe she needs to so she understands exactly why I'm not returning any of the texts or calls I'm receiving from other women.

Nothing like going with the truth . . . "You want to know why I haven't been on any dates lately?" She nods, her body still as I rest my hand over her heart. It's fast and steady, matching mine. "Because in so many ways, I'm already dating you. We've been pretending we're not, but I think you feel this connection as much as I do."

"Friends can spend time together and not be dating."

"That's not the case when it comes to you and me. Not anymore." *Fuck.* What the hell am I doing? Running my hand through my hair, the thought of ruining everything we've become has me on edge. "I didn't come to the Hamptons thinking this would happen or that I'd be telling you any of this."

She says, "But we're here and . . ." Reaching for my hand, she holds it between both of hers. "I've been happier spending time with you than I have been in years. I thought I was wrong for feeling this way, to think about kissing you and the possibility of what could happen after that, like I shouldn't be enjoying our time together so much. I already told myself I can blame the wine tomorrow. Tonight, though, I'm glad I can finally tell you how I'm feeling inside."

"How do you feel?"

"I feel if we kiss again, we might not be able to be *just* friends."

I look at her. Really look at this beautiful woman. Her hair lies in thin cables of soft waves against her small shoulders. Her lips are plush like the softest cotton and have a slight swell since they left mine. Even the thin sweater she's wearing can't hide the gentle slope of her breasts. But it's the way she looks at me, seeing me as the man I want to be, the one who could deserve someone like her, that gives me the most hope. "I don't think we've been *just friends* since the day we met, Tealey."

The revelation shimmers in her eyes as she pieces my confession together. "You haven't been dating because of me?"

"Pretty much," I say, keeping my voice low but my honesty loud and clear. "That was for me."

She reaches up, sliding her hands into my hair, and pulls me closer. "Kiss me again, Rad."

Our eyes close, and our lips come together. My worries are lost as our lips meet like this was their destiny. Maybe it's because this feels too good to be bad, but I deepen the kiss, and our tongues embrace.

My body feels like a live wire, every part of me alive and reactive. The tiniest moan escapes her, and I swallow the sound as her arms tighten around my neck, holding me even closer.

But we need to breathe, so our lips slowly part and our eyes open. I keep my forehead against hers and then whisper, "Wow," feeling every part of the word and left speechless to form sentences.

"Wow," she says with a sweet giggle as she pulls back enough to see my eyes. "What do you think?"

I can't play it cool. I grin like a kid locked in a candy shop. *Unsupervised.* Her nails scrape lightly along my scalp, and a smile slowly spreads across her mouth. "I think I'm going to need more."

"Kissing?"

"All of you." We fall back together on the bed and kiss until we're breathless again. We kiss until the innocence of mewls becomes moans of pleasure, and our bodies tangle together. We kiss because I never want to stop kissing this amazing woman.

I'm not sure of the time or how long we've locked lips, but she falls to the side of me, lying in the spray light from the lamp we never bothered to turn off.

I revel in this juxtaposition of the situation—the rush to do everything with her, *to her*, and the contentment of kissing her all night long. *Emotions. Feelings.* I admit to having them all, especially the hot and heavy ones I'm having right now.

I've let the cat out of the bag, and there's no turning back now.

I'm not just sexually turned on, but it's as if she's flipped a switch inside me. I'm seeing her in a whole new way, yet the same woman I've always known is right here next to me, looking at me like she sees me the same way.

Rolling closer, I kiss her head, wanting to memorize every detail of this moment, *of her*, of the way her lips take possession of mine and claim me as much as I want to claim hers.

So delectably enticing, I don't want this night to end. I press my hand to her cheek and run my thumb over her bottom lip. She looks wanton and wild, so incredibly sexy. *Is this really happening?*

But I catch a glimpse of my watch and know time is our enemy. "It's almost midnight . . ." I don't want to go, but I need her to want me to stay.

I slide my hand to the curve of her neck, feeling her racing pulse. She runs her fingers into my hair, and whispers, "Stay."

"We might get caught." *Why do I always have to be so fucking rational?*

"We can lock the door."

Works for me. I bounce out of bed, not needing to be told twice. Just as I touch the doorknob, it spins and opens. Sucking in a breath, I hold it, securing myself to the wall with my palms glued to the sheetrock and heels pressed to the baseboard. The door stops just before reaching the tips of my shoes.

Tealey flies up onto her knees. "Marlow? What are you doing here?"

"Saw your light still on and wanted to talk." She starts closing the door. "Is that okay?"

"Leave it open!" Tealey blurts and then cringes. "Sorry," she whispers, "but we can leave it open unless you think it would be better closed." She winces again, her gaze avoiding mine. Probably because she knows I'm silently shouting "what the fuck" in my head.

"Sure." Tealey gets off the bed and grabs Marlow's hand. "Let's look at my view first." She drags her to the window and opens the blinds.

Marlow says, "There's nothing to see but the driveway and cars."

I rush into the bathroom, leaving the door open just enough to have a crack to spy on them through. I should have escaped, but I'm not ready for my night with Tealey to end, so I'm willing to wait Marlow out.

"I know. That's my point," Tealey replies enthusiastically. "There are no trash bags piled at the curb or broken bottles smashed in the street. Look, there's no twenty-four-hour laundromat sign shining into my room or people lined up down the street to get into the after-hours club. There are only two cars and a front lawn."

Marlow turns to her. "How much did you have to drink tonight?"

"Not much."

Sitting on the bed, Marlow says, "My dad is getting a divorce. *Again*."

I'm surprised she hasn't told Tealey. And maybe I should feel bad for eavesdropping, but I'm stuck regardless.

Tealey says, "I'm sorry. I know you've struggled with his patterns for a long time."

"My whole life." She pulls a pillow to her chest, and I've never seen Marlow look more vulnerable than she is now. "I think he's the reason I have no desire to settle down. What's the point if we're just being set up for a messy divorce?"

"Not all marriages end in divorce, Marlow."

Yeah. That's my girl. Keeping the faith.

Wait a second. I stop myself from banging my head against the door. *Barely.* How can I support that side of the defense when my whole career is built on the opposite argument? More importantly, when did I become an optimist? All the kissing we did must have shorted my oxygen supply.

Tealey says, "My parents have been married for almost thirty years."

"They're the exception." Marlow sighs, lying down. "But I have a feeling that I'm going to follow in my parents' footsteps. "One day, my looks might fade, and then my husband will be looking for my replacement. I'm going to be old and alone—"

"When you love someone, you see their beauty is deeper than the surface. My mom always told me it's a blessing to age."

"Why?"

I lean back against the shower, listening. Tealey pauses, and then says, "Because then you have lived a long life and can appreciate the beauty of your journey." The silence stretches between them, and then Tealey sighs thoughtfully. When I peek out, she's lying next to Marlow, and they're both staring at the ceiling. "If someone falls in love with your soul, the outside doesn't matter so much, does it?"

I kneel, thinking this might be a while, and I'm not in such a hurry to leave anymore when I'm learning so much about Tealey.

Marlow says, "I don't know anymore."

"You're beautiful, Marlow, but you're more than your looks. You have this great way of convincing anybody to get what you want. Look at your gallery. You put it on the map by talking reclusive artists into showing their work. You have incredible style and fantastic taste in friends. If I do say so myself." I can just make out Tealey through the crack of the door. "But you're smart, so clever, and funny. And though you don't often show it, you have a big heart for those you care about. You're always there for me, and I can tell you anything."

"Tealey?" Marlow starts and then goes quiet. I hear a pillow being tossed to the floor, and she sits up. "I've been keeping a secret from you, and I feel awful about it. It's not even that big of a deal, so I don't know why I've been mum."

Tealey sits up, resting her hand on the bed. "What is it?" I hear the worry in her tone, and I can't help but feel somewhat sick to my stomach as well. What is she going to tell her? Now I feel bad for staying. *Should I cover my ears?* Thinking Marlow deserves the respect of privacy, I raise my hands.

"I'm dating Rad."

I freeze—my hands not having a chance to reach my ears.

What the fuck?

I get to my feet, ready to explain, but stop and still again when I see Tealey stand and cross her arms over her chest. *Shit. Shit. Shit.*

I absolutely hate the pain I can see in her eyes. *She believes Marlow.* Fuck. Glaring at Marlow, Tealey grits her teeth. "What do you mean you're dating Rad?"

22

Rad

"For my father," Marlow says, like everyone should know what the hell she's talking about.

Fucking hell.

I knew this arrangement would come back to bite me in the ass. I just thought it would be professionally. Meanwhile, Tealey appears rather calm after this bombshell was just dropped on her. Still, not moving a muscle, except her eyes, she shoots me a hard glare, and then she says, "Explain. In detail."

The woman's got the patience of an angel.

Marlow stands and starts pacing, making this worse by dragging this out. *Fucking tell her, Marlow!* She finally speaks. "I asked Rad to come with me to dinner with my dad."

Tealey's silence on the matter worries me. What is she thinking? *Are we done before we've begun?* Talk about having the worst timing. I want to be kissing her again, but instead, I'm tucked between a towel warmer and the shower, spying on her through a one-inch crack of the door with panic rising like bile as Marlow feeds her bits and pieces of the story.

Tell her it's a favor.

Tell her it's pretend.

Tell her we aren't really dating.

Tell her the truth, dammit!

If I had my way, I'd clear this up in two point four seconds. Not drag it out for dramatic effect like Marlow loves to do.

Tealey says, "You hate dinners with your dad, so I'm trying to understand how this is different? You had a date with Rad, or he was there for moral support?" *Thank God. This will finally be cleared up.*

"What's wrong with your chin, Teals? You're all red." I lean forward to see Marlow leaning close to Tealey.

"It's nothing." Tealey touches her chin, but then says, "I must be breaking out. Tell me about Rad." *Come on, Tealey. Don't doubt me. Please don't doubt us.*

"He was there for moral support." Phew! I sink back and take a deep breath. "My dad has always loved him, so I felt he could temper the fires between us."

"I'm missing something. Is there more to the story or was all that just for dramatic effect?"

Marlow sits back down on the bed next to her. "My dad adores him. Thinks of him like the son he wished he had instead of me."

"I'm sure that's not true. Your father dotes on you."

"Maybe." Sadness drips from her sigh. *Go on . . .* "He's really come around, but it's sort of, kind of come at a cost."

"Which is?"

"He told me he's getting his divorce but was thrilled to hear Rad and I were together."

"Why would he think you and Rad are dating?"

Thank you, Tealey.

"I don't know." Marlow shrugs. "He just did, and neither of us rushed to correct him."

"Rad didn't?"

"No."

"Why not?"

"Because Rad gets something from it. Why else? Guys never do anything unless there's something to gain."

No. No. No. I growl. *Don't do this, Marlow.* Don't plant those doubts about me.

Marlow laughs, but there's no humor in the sound. "If we play along, like the happy couple, we both gain something for it. Why else would he agree?"

"He agreed?" Tealey walks to the dresser. With her head dipped down, she rubs her brow. "Agreed to what?" She spins back and snaps, "Give me the short version, Marlow."

"Geez, you're so moody, Teals."

"It's late, and I'm tired, and a big part of this story is still missing. Are you dating, or was he there as moral support?"

"Moral support but for the sake of my dad, we're dating." *Thank. Fuck.* I didn't think she'd ever get to the truth. "For some reason, the man who can't seem to settle down wants me to. I don't know. It's probably to get me off his payroll."

"You work for your dad?"

"No, I just get an allowance. I was speaking metaphorically."

When Tealey starts pacing toward me, she squints to spot me in the dark. Not sure if she does, but I mouth, "I'm sorry." *Just in case.*

When Tealey whips back around, she says, "So this scheme you've thought up is about money?"

"It's about an apartment in Tribeca, actually, and I didn't

make this up. As I said, my dad assumed we were together and offered to buy my apartment as a gift, a nest egg, for us."

Rubbing her temple, Tealey stares at Marlow like she's grown a third eye. "This makes no sense." She releases a hard breath. "I think we should continue this discussion in the morning."

"Okay." Marlow stands and then throws her arms around Tealey. Tealey doesn't make a move. *Shit.* I have a feeling the option to kiss her all night might have just flown out the window.

Marlow takes a step back, and this time, she's the one staring at her friend. "Are we okay?"

Tealey gives her a nod. "Fine. I'm just tired."

"Okay." Marlow walks to the door and turns back. "You seem tired."

Another nod but no words are spoken, so Marlow keeps talking. "I thought you'd get a kick out of me and Rad dating. As if . . ."

"Yeah, completely unimaginable."

Marlow's head jerks back. "I wouldn't go that far. We have a lot in common."

Tealey crosses her arms over her chest, and I'm praying she doesn't take the bait. This will only end badly for all of us. She asks, "Like what?"

Marlow needs to read the room and her best friend's temperament. *Nothing good, Marlow. Walk out now*, I will with my mind.

Never willing to take anyone's advice, she replies, "We both come from money and well-known families. There are differences that only we understand."

"As opposed to the average suburban family, like mine?"

Oh, fuck. Do I let this go on?

"Well, yeah. Like—"

"I don't want to hear anymore tonight." Tealey holds her hands up in front of her, putting an end to this torture . . . *for both of us.* "I was tired before, but now I have a headache."

Is that for Marlow or me?

"Okay, well, good night, Teals."

"Night." The door is shut, but I don't see or hear any movement. When the lock catches, Tealey says, "You can come out now."

I'm careful, each step tentative as I walk into the bedroom. I'm not greeted with a smile, and there's no relief found in her expression. Her arms are crossed, and she asks, "You're dating Marlow?"

That I'm having to address this at all as if I've done something wrong, I reply, "I'm not dating Marlow. Not officially." I reach for her, but she takes a step back. "Not like how I want to date you."

Her eyes go wide, her head thrown back from a scoff. "Me? We're not even dating, and now you're telling me you're with her, but you want to be with me?"

Tangled webs are really not my thing. Ever.

Most of all, I don't want to lose Tealey because of this absurd charade.

"Will you listen to me with an open mind?"

"It will be a struggle, but I'll try."

She moves to sit at the head of the bed and crosses her legs. She appears calm, willing to hear me out. Calm is good. Listening is great.

Keeping my voice down, I say, "I went along with his assumption to ease tension between her and her dad. I guess he assumed we were together because none of you were there, like usual." I shrug. "It's weird that he'd think that because nothing was going on and still isn't." Distracted by those sexy lips of hers, my thoughts muddle.

"Rad?" *Two snaps.*

"Huh?"

"You were saying that nothing is going on and . . .?"

I rack my brain as to what we were talking about, and the words miraculously reappear. "I'm dating Marlow so she gets the apartment and I make partner at the firm."

"So you *are* dat—"

I hold my hand up this time. "I'm not really dating her. He thinks we're dating. Actually, he thinks we're getting married."

"What? You're engaged now?" She huffs and gets out of bed while shaking her head. "This is too much, Rad. I don't know what's going on here, but I think it's best if you leave. We can discuss this tomorrow."

I stay right where I am. "No, I want to talk about it now because you're making assumptions—"

"Me?" She points at herself in disbelief. "I'm only going off what the two of you have told me. Apparently, you're tangled up in some weird love affair in a scheme to make money and get property. Is that the gist of it?"

Stepping forward, I take hold of her hands. She reluctantly lets me. "Not at all. We agreed to pretend only in front of him through his divorce and him giving her the property deed." Holding her hands to my chest as if she'll slip away if I don't, I say, "You can think I'm a terrible person for making the best out of a bad situation, or trust that the thing with Marlow is nothing more than what we've said. I'm not interested in being with her. She's not interested in me."

"Rad . . ." Her eyes turn down, and her head follows.

"I'm right here, Tealey. Right here with you. You're all I want." She looks up, so I beg, "Please believe me." When I have her full attention, I kiss her cheek and whisper, "I've waited a lifetime to be with you."

Any anger that she was harboring in her eyes disappears. I don't get one of her beautiful smiles, but her fingers fold around my hand. "I really don't know what kind of deal you two have made, but the truth always comes out, so I'm going to give you the benefit of the doubt. Tomorrow, I want the full story with both of you sitting there. But tonight . . ."

"Anything, Tealey." I brush her hair behind her ear, still holding her hand to me.

"I just want it to go back to how it was before Marlow said anything." Taking her hand from mine, she then stretches her arms around me. "I can't say when I started having feelings for you, but I can't stop them either. All I can ask is that you please don't hurt me."

Engulfing her in my arms, I kiss the top of her head. "I won't."

She looks up, her chin on my chest. "I don't need a rushed response. I want you to think about it."

Sitting on the edge of the bed, I pull her closer until she's standing between my legs. "I don't need time to figure it out. I already know the answer. You're giving me a chance, and I won't blow it. I promise not to hurt you, Tealey."

A gentle smile finally slips into place, and she says, "After what just happened, is it wrong to want you to stay?"

"What does your heart tell you?"

Her smile blooms brighter. "To kiss you again. What do you think I should do?"

"I think you should listen to your heart." She leans in, and I cup her face. We come closer with only an inch or two between us, and I say, "I need you to make me a promise."

"Okay." Her breath is heavy, but her expression is light and playful, intrigued by the suggestion.

"If I stay, you're going to have to promise you won't ravage me."

Already laughing, she rolls her eyes as she pushes away. I catch her hand and pull her to my lap, wrapping my arms around her. She tilts her head as giggles escape her. "You're ridiculous, Welly. You know that?"

"I do know, but women find me irresistible. What about you?"

Rubbing the back of her hand along my cheek, she says, "Utterly irresistible." This time, she cups my face and kisses me. When we roll back on the bed with her on top of me, I know. I just know . . . *Tealey Bell is going to be the death of me.*

23

Rad

The problem with lies is they multiply.

Sneaking out of Tealey's room just as the sun begins to rise, I almost make it to my room before everyone wakes. *Almost . . .*

"What are you doing up so early?" I whip around like I'm a burglar busted. Cammie's eyes are still tired, but her smile–unsuspecting, *thank God*—is there.

"I, uh, wanted to watch the sunrise."

Looking down the hall through the window, she says, "It's just rising."

"Yeah, it was great . . ." I reach for the doorknob to my room. "I'm going back to bed. Seen one, you've seen them all. Good night . . . technically morning." I slip into the room and shut the door, ashamed of all the lies I'm caught up in. What am I doing?

I have this thing with Marlow hanging over my head that needs to play out. Also, I figured Tealey and I would be taking it slow until we figure out what we're doing. I know neither wants to alienate us if things don't work out. That means I need to find some time to talk to her privately today before we get carried away, which I'm finding is way too easy to do.

Until we can have that conversation, is it worth lying to everyone to be able to be with Tealey?

Hell-to-the-fucking-yeah.

Okay, Wellington. Settle the fuck down.

That feels like an entirely impossible task, considering I just spent hours kissing my dream girl until our lips went numb. Not really, but as soon as I had the chance to hold her in my arms, I took it. I don't think I've slept that well in years. The short number of hours don't matter. I found peace wrapped around her.

After climbing in bed, I toss and turn, the bed feeling colder without Tealey next to me. How can such a small thing take up so much room . . . in bed . . . *in me?*

It's just not the same without her, so I finally give up, get dressed for the day, and go downstairs. I see Cammie and Cade are on the back porch through the large windows framing the lawn and ocean in the distance. My mom is in the kitchen putting the finishing touches on platters of fruits and pastries. Glancing up, she smiles. It's the kind that makes me feel like a kid again—loved—and, although I proved her wrong many times, like I can do no wrong. "Good morning, son."

"Morning, Mom."

"How'd you sleep?"

Images of Tealey on top of me, her fingers running through my hair, and our bodies against each other come to mind. *Fuck. Don't get hard.* I could have come through my clothes, but we'd stop, she'd giggle, and then we'd kiss again, doing it all over again.

"Like a baby." Coming around the large island, I kiss her on the cheek. "You?"

"I love having you under my roof again. It gives me a sense of peace, knowing you're safe."

"I'm always safe even when I'm not here."

"You'll understand one day if you decide to settle down and have kids."

She's never pressured me to get married or give her grandkids, but she's not shy about her dreams of it happening one day.

"I need to accomplish a few things first."

That gets her attention. "First. I like that. Also, you don't need to accomplish more. You're very accomplished already. So, I have a feeling it's not a *need*. It's a *want*." She turns to me and holds a honey bun up to my mouth. "I want you to leave your troubles in the city and try to relax this weekend."

I bite the bun and nod. "Yes, ma'am."

When she starts carrying a platter to the table, I follow with the other and then seek out the caffeine I need. I pour a cup of coffee, missing the routine I've fallen into of choosing a punny mug to make Tealey smile each day. I didn't even realize we had a routine to miss until now when faced with a sea of white cups.

The mugs are funny, but it's the company I'm craving the most. Our mornings begin with a quick chat in the kitchen before work, and most nights, she falls asleep on the couch when it gets late. I don't wake her right away because I like the sound of her peaceful breaths at midnight.

I don't want to miss any of it, not even for a weekend. I glance at the stairs, hoping to catch a glimpse of her coming to fill the Grand Canyon–sized hole in my chest again.

When I don't see her, I walk to the buffet, wondering if eating enough honey buns will do the trick.

"Good morning, Amanda." From just hearing the sound of Tealey's voice, I'm smiling before I even look up. When I do, I'm not disappointed.

Wearing a yellow sundress hitting just above her knees, she walks across the marble floors in little white sneakers. Her hair is loose with soft waves streaming past her shoulders. Those beautiful blue eyes stare into mine, and if I'm not mistaken, her lips are swollen from our kissing. I try to act normal, but she makes it damn hard not to stare.

My mom says, "Good morning, Tealey. You look like sunshine today. Yellow is your color."

Mom's compliment deepens the pink in Tealey's cheeks, matching the shade of her lips.

"Good morning, Rad," Tealey says, tugging at a strap as if she's suddenly self-conscious. When she joins me at the buffet, she asks, "How'd you sleep?"

"Amazing." I lean down, resting my forearms on the counter next to where she's standing at the coffee pot. "How'd you sleep?"

"Like a baby."

"That's what Rad said," my mom says with a bowl of berries in her hands. "Glad you're enjoying the getaway." She holds her finger up. "Tealey, can you do me a favor and try to get Rad to forget about work and relax this weekend?"

Tealey smirks while I try to hide my amusement. "It would be my pleasure, Amanda."

That sly vixen. I whisper, "And mine."

"How about I take the berries out back and leave you two to chat?"

I turn back, worried I wasn't sneaky enough. "You don't have to leave, Mom."

"I was heading to the back porch anyway." The door closes behind her, and Tealey and I are alone.

She leans down, matching my position. I cock an eyebrow, and say, "I have an idea." With our fingers aligned on the cabinet, I move mine to press against hers. It's not enough because apparently, *now* when it comes to her, I want more. I lift my little finger and wrap it over hers.

Catching a smile on her face, she laughs. "What is your idea?"

"I know a way you can help me relax."

"Does it involve a bed, a locked door, and just the two of us?"

I lean a little closer, my eyes locked on her lips. "It does."

"That—"

"Why are we up so early on a Saturday?" Jackson bellows as he enters the great room. I pull my hand back to my side and stiffen upright.

While I move around the island, putting distance between Tealey and me, she replies, "Because a beautiful day beckoned us to enjoy it."

Jackson heads straight to the table. "I'm starved." He glances at us. "Have you guys eaten?"

"No," I reply. "Go ahead. Anyone up for a walk on the beach?"

"Me." I expected Tealey, but it's Cammie, coming in from outside, who takes me up on the offer. "I'd love to go. We never get to talk anymore."

It's not like I don't want to walk with Cammie. She's great, and I always enjoy spending time with her. I just thought this would go a different way. "It has been a while."

"All that champagne and . . ." Tealey eyes me. "Activity last night has me famished. I'm going to make a plate and join your mom on the deck."

Cammie grabs a pair of sunglasses from the counter, anchoring them on her head, and then looks at me. "Let's go."

When we start crossing the lawn, Cade cups his hand to the side of his mouth. "Just have her home by curfew, brother."

I shoot him the bird.

"Inappropriate, Radcliffe," my mom says just before we're out of range. I chuckle because sometimes it's fun to push her buttons.

Stopping to blow him a kiss, Cammie quick steps to catch up with me.

When we reach the beach, she leaves her shoes on the edge of the lawn before dipping her toes in the sand. I kick mine behind me, and ask, "How's life treating you?"

"Good. You?"

"Good." She's a good friend, but I'm not sure what I'm supposed to say, so I just start talking. "Actually, every time I open my mouth lately, I seem to get caught up in another person's plan."

Using her hand as a visor, she looks up at me. "You're spread too thin."

"It would help if I could get work under better control."

"I'm coming to realize I have no control. My whole life revolves around planning this wedding, so much so that I've forgotten how I filled my time before this took over. At this stage, I'll be lucky if Cade marries me. I've become a nightmare to live with."

"He loves you. Crazy in love with you. So I'm sure he doesn't mind. We should all be as lucky as him. He found his soul mate and his much better half."

We stop with the wind at our backs and our toes in the water. "Honestly, he's the better of the two of us. I can't wait to put this extravaganza behind us and just be married to him." She looks at me. "Tealey said you're not working late every night anymore."

"Some nights. Whatever I can get away with." I shove my hands in my pockets, unsure of what I want to share versus what I like keeping private for Tealey and me—like last night.

She starts walking again, so I do as well. Approaching a large pile of driftwood, we part and walk around it. Hidden from view of the house, she asks, "Can we talk about the secret you're hiding?"

My eyes shoot to her. "What secret?"

At the edge of the ocean, she pushes a log toward the water with her foot. "Tealey told me about you."

"She did? When?" Cammie nods. *Fuck.* "I assumed we weren't telling anyone this weekend." Scratching the back of my neck, I redirect my gaze to the horizon. "It just happened." When I look back at her, I ask, "We haven't even had time to discuss it."

This really surprises me. Cammie's one of her closest friends, so I understand her sharing secrets, but I'd think that Tealey would talk to me first. Still shocked, I start rambling, "It was one kiss, and then that led to another, and hours later—"

"Hours later?" She gasps, her eyes going wide. "You kissed Tealey?"

Locking my lips, I don't say another word because anything I say could be used to tease me relentlessly.

"You kissed Tealey for hours last night?" Cammie's mouth hangs open as she waits for me to answer.

Distract. Distract. Distract. Shit. I've already fucked this up. "What were you talking about?"

"Oh, no. Too late for that, Rad. The cat is so far out of the bag that it's down the street." Stepping up to me, she squints and points her finger at me. "You kissed Tealey. Tell me everything." Her tough-guy act cracks, and she giggles in delight. "*You kissed Tealey.*"

Tealey is going to kill me. "You can't tell anyone, Cam. Tealey and I agreed to keep everything on the down low until we figure things out."

"She must be freaking out."

"Why would she freak out?"

"What do you mean why would she freak out? She's crushed on you since the day you met. Strawberries. Hard as rock abs. Chocolate eyes."

"Chocolate eyes?" Stepping closer, I say, "Never mind. She's crushed on me since the day we met? She said that?"

"I've had to listen to that story so many times over the years." She can't contain her smile. Neither can I because Tealey Bell has been attracted to me as long as I've been attracted to her. This affection hasn't been one-sided. "I always knew you two were meant to be, but I didn't see it coming just yet."

"Neither did I . . . What do you mean by just yet?"

The water drifts over our feet, and though it's cold as ice this morning, we don't move. We just let our feet sink into the sand. Shaking her head at me, she laughs. "You were kissing for hours. Making out like teenagers last night. Apparently, I'm not the one who's gone crazy." She pokes me with her elbow. Tealey and Cam are a lot alike that way. "Making up for lost time much? Yeah."

Swirling her finger willy-nilly in the air, she adds, "You two are the crazy ones. Crazy for each other. I knew it!"

"You've gone mad with power, Cam. It was a tidbit in a deep well of information. It's not like we had sex." *She laughs.*

"You can downplay it all you want, but people who don't want to have sex don't kiss for hours." She grabs a stick and draws a big heart in the sand. "Sex is next, my friend, and I cannot wait." Looking back at me, she says, "That came out wrong. Rest assured, I have no intention of being there or wanting to see anything regarding you or her or you two together having sex." She laughs, carving *RW loves TB* in the center of the heart.

I should be willing a wave to wash the sand art away, but instead, I'm standing here like an idiot admiring it. Not because it's particularly clever, but the idea behind it speaks to something deep inside me.

Cam says, "You really like her." Not a question or a revelation. There's no giddy laugh or teasing tone. Her softer joy is still seen in her expression, genuine in her care. She wants the best for Tealey, but I also know she wants what's best for me as well.

"I do."

Coming over, she bumps me with her hip. "You're going to make me cry, Rad."

"Why?"

"Happiness. For you and her."

"I appreciate that, Cam." Looking back in the direction of the house, I'm reminded of everyone being there, people I'd normally not care about sharing things with. But I can't do that just yet when it's Tealey I'm seeing. Especially not with the Marlow situation still unsettled. "Do you mind keeping this between us? Just give me a little time, give *us* that time. Tealey seems happy, so I don't want it ruined before—"

"Before what?"

The question plagues me because I don't have an easy answer. "Before I fuck it up."

She throws the stick in the distance and nods. "Love is complicated, but don't doubt what you know is right."

"Love? That's a little heavy-handed, Cammie."

"I've waited more than seven years for this day. Don't ruin it for me."

Wry is an understatement when it comes to her grin. I ask, "Don't ruin it for you?" I roll my eyes. "You're not the only one who's waited years."

"I won't tell the others." She locks her lips with an imaginary key and then tosses it out to sea. "It will stay our secret."

"Thanks." Nodding down the beach, I ask, "Ready to head back?"

In a matter of weeks, I've become the master of deceit. I really need to turn things around. I need to talk to Tealey, and I need to talk to Marlow.

We pick up our shoes and cross the lawn. Cammie jogs onto the porch and plants her behind on Cade's lap. I'm not sure where Marlow and my mom has disappeared to, but Jackson scrolls on his phone, oblivious to our return.

Tealey looks more beautiful than I've ever seen her— windblown hair, a strap slipped over her shoulder, and a look in her eyes that tells me she feels as happy as I do inside. She smiles, resting her head back on the rocking chair. "Good walk?"

Cammie's phone rings. "Hello?" She plugs her ear and then stands. Pointing at the phone, she tells us, "Sorry. I need to take this. Wedding stuff." She walks down the steps into the lawn again with Cade by her side.

"It was," I say. "Insightful." It still surprises me that she told Cammie about last night. I chuckle, remembering how I tried to sneak out of Tealey's room this morning. I don't feel betrayed. Instead, there's a sense of certainty that she's given me. If she told Cammie, that means no regrets are haunting her. I feel the same. *No regrets.*

"Walks with Cammie always are." Tilting her head back, she closes her eyes and soaks up the sun. "She once told me that there's someone for everyone. It's only a matter of what you're willing to compromise."

"She thinks you should settle?"

She opens her eyes and smiles. "Compromise isn't settling. It's learning to live with the things you can and knowing what you can't."

Mugs with funny puns—*punny*—and sarcasm, some even tipping to the vulgar side, come to mind. And I don't know when it happened or why, but a cabinet full of mismatched mugs doesn't bother me anymore.

I find them quite endearing, like Tealey.

Does that make Cammie right about us? *"I always knew you two were meant to be."* Are we meant to be, or is that just wishful thinking on Cammie's part?

I like Tealey, but I still think we need to take one step at a time to allow us to sort through the details of our plans and how those plans might need to evolve.

Jackson sits forward. "I thought I'd get away without anyone noticing, but Nick's texting."

"Nick Christiansen, your brother-in-law?"

Holding the phone, he says, "We had an account go sideways a few months back. I got it back on track, but we're left making amends to the client."

"You don't control the stock market," I say.

"They sure think we do, though." He stands and goes inside. Just over Tealey's shoulder, I watch as he cuts across the great room and goes upstairs.

I shift my gaze back to the beauty in front of me. Taking her hand, I ask, "Is now a good time to talk?"

"I'm free. Where should we go?"

"Follow me." I get up and hold the door for her. I lead her up the stairs and to my room.

"This doesn't seem that private."

"It is." I lock the door behind her, but then I direct her to the door in the corner.

Her eyes volley between me and the door several times before she says, "You want me to go in there?"

I open the door for her since worry is pinching her brows together. But then her expression morphs. She dips inside with a huge smile on her face. "You have your own private media room?"

A black L-shaped couch anchors the space, a remote-controlled screen hangs from the ceiling, and a skylight with a light-blocking shade is large enough to spot constellations on a clear night. "Perks of being an only kid."

"It's amazing." She walks to the large couch and sits. "Close the door."

I light a candle in the corner before I lock out all the light streaming in from the bedroom.

Lying back on her elbows, Tealey kicks off her shoes and gets more comfortable horizontally. I don't think she realizes how much she affects me. I brought her up here in hopes of talking about last night, but seeing her lying there with her skirt bunched around her thighs and that distracting strap refusing to stay put, talking is the last thing I want to do with her. She pats the cushion and says, "Will you lie with me, Rad?"

I sit beside her and run my hand along her cheek. I follow the line of her cheekbone with kisses and then stop on her forehead, savoring that I get to do this. Her hands run up the backs of my arms and then higher, her grip tightening and pulling me closer.

She must know that I want her desperately. But it will be more than just sex for me. I look into her eyes, knowing she was always more than a crush. I've never shared this level of connection with anyone before. Leaning down, I kiss her once more before lying down beside her on the couch. "I plan to do more than lie."

With our bodies aligned, I'm gentle in touch, though I want to do so much more. I run my hand along the curve of her breast and dip into the valley of her waist. She wraps her arms around my neck and pulls me closer, kissing my face, and then whispering, "If you're worried, I'm not breakable."

The words have me pausing with my eyes closed and forehead tipped to hers. The gravity of what we're doing weighs down on my shoulders. Not because I don't want it—

because fuck, she's a goddess—but I don't want to fuck it up. Tealey's not just a hookup or a late-night date.

"No, but we don't have much time, and you deserve more than quick sex in a game room."

"I'm okay with it. Trust me, Rad. I want it." At least I know I'm not alone in my desire. She tilts her head, and her hair splays across the cushion—the light and dark in contrast.

Smiling, I kiss the tip of her nose. When her arms tighten around my neck, she kisses me again, and whispers, "Let's make the most of the time we have."

She's right.

I don't have time to make love to her like I want, but I won't miss the chance to make her mine.

24

Tealey

I broke my promise.

How could I not ravage him, though?

The man is undeniably sexy.

Dipping my fingertips under the band of Rad's shorts, I run them over the muscles of his lower back and then deeper, covering that sexy incline of his ass. Rad is the perfect male specimen. I've earned an advanced degree in his anatomy after so many mornings were spent studying him wearing those towels.

It's as if he knew I'd break, considering that was the promise laid on the table. *Bed, in our case.*

I love the way he feels lying on top of me, the slow grind that makes me want to combust, and the goose bumps he shatters across my skin with each kiss he places with care on my body.

But that's just it. I don't want him to place gentle kisses with care. My body is winning this battle over my head, and as I start to ravage him, I want to be ravaged right back.

Up two inches, Rad. Just do it. Touch me like I want you to. His hands have roamed from my hips to my ribs where he's tentatively holding me like I'll wriggle away. I won't. "Rad?"

"Hmm?" he hums with his lips pressed to my neck.

"You can touch me."

Popping his head up, he looks into my eyes. "I am touching you."

"Like *more* touching me."

His brows lower, and he asks, "More touching you?"

I want more. My body wants everything I'm one-hundred-percent sure he can give. I grab his hand and place it on my boob.

"We can start here."

"Ah." He starts to laugh, not even trying to hide his amusement. "And here I was, struggling to figure out my next move and how far you wanted this to go."

"Mystery solved. Now back to our previously scheduled program." I wrap my arms tighter around his neck, bringing him back to where he left off.

But he pops up again, his eyes set on mine with a spark of determination. "You know I want to touch you every-where, but I thought you'd want me taking time in the fore-play part of the program versus jumping to the post-game celebration."

"I like celebrations."

His lips part as if he's going to say something, but not one to miss a golden opportunity *(Thank God!)* he squeezes my breast while kissing my mouth. Our hips start a seduc-tive dance when a buzz amps up the interaction.

Panting, I grab his shirt wanting that vibration a little closer to my—"My phone," he says, ripping away the sensation.

"Huh?"

Rad readjusts himself . . . *oh, his phone.* "Fuck," he says, tossing it on the carpeted floor. "Sorry." Leaning back down, he starts kissing my chest while palming my boob. "Is this where we left off?"

I start laughing, running my nails over his scalp. "I thought you were introducing electronics into the mix."

His eyes find mine in the darkened room, his hair wild from my tugs. "You'd want that?" *He doesn't sound upset about the possibility.*

Sinking back on the cushion, I rest my arms behind my head. "I think we both know I'm not opposed to battery-operated options." His phone starts vibrating again, and we both look at the screen when it lights up. "Does Cammie normally call you?"

He glances at the phone and reaches for it. "No. Should I answer it?"

"Probably."

Rolling off, he lands with a thud in a push-up position and quickly answers, "Hello?" His eyes dart to me. "Yeah. I was showing her my . . ."

When he stalls, I whisper, "Movie collection."

"I was showing her my movie collection." He whacks his forehead and mouths, "What the fuck?"

Their conversation goes on for what feels like forever. I whisper, "Hang up." *What are they doing, swapping fishing stories?*

Finally, he says, "Okay." Rubbing his brow, he glances back at me. "I'll tell her. Mm-hmm. Yeah, okay. Bye."

Sitting up, I ask, "What's wrong?"

"I don't know. She's looking for you, though."

Worried about what's going on, I'm already reaching for my shoes. Not sure what has happened to upset Cammie, I quickly slip on my sneakers. Looking up at Rad, I say, "I'm sorry."

"Don't be." He tucks his phone in his pocket and smirks. "Sooooo?" He rocks back, still grinning.

"So?" I stand, quickly attempting to flatten the wrinkles out of my skirt and failing.

"You have a naughty side, Miss Bell."

Sliding the strap of my dress back onto my shoulder, I smirk as I walk past him and tap his chin. "If you only knew, Mr. Wellington." My eyes are still adjusted to the darkness behind me, so I squint in the bright light flooding in through the bedroom windows.

My hand is caught, and I turn back. Looking every bit of the fantasies I've had about him—hair a total sexy mess, lips plush and red from kissing, bedroom eyes that tempt me to stay—I suck in a staggered breath, wondering if I'll ever get used to the fact that I get to kiss Rad Wellington. *He never disappoints.*

He says, "I intend to find out."

I'm pulled into his arms once again and kissed like we might never have the chance again. Releasing me, he leaves me breathless. "And for the record, Miss Bell." He glances back, rubbing his thumb along his bottom lip. "Kissing you is even better than I thought it would be."

When he walks away, I melt into a puddle of swoons.

I bite my lip and watch as he slips into the hallway. I think I'm going to need a minute, so I catch my breath, holding my hand to my chest. My heartbeats demand every bit of my being until I steady myself, and my knees regain their strength. *That man* . . . He has me on the edge of combusting again, and this time, he only used his words.

Taking another deep breath, I then wobble to the door, thinking about how much my life has changed in such a short time. I could never have predicted that moving in with a friend could turn into one of the best decisions I've ever made.

I'm not sure when my life decided to flip on its axis, but I'm glad it did.

When I enter the great room, everyone is already there. "What's going on?" I ask. I didn't expect to make an entrance, so I move to the island, hoping to blend in. Marlow is rubbing Cammie's back when Cade says, "We just lost our wedding venue."

My mouth falls open, but before I can say anything, Cammie's crying and running into my arms. "The pipes," she says, sniffling into my hair. "Burst. Flooded the ballroom."

Holding her in my arms, I stroke her hair. "Oh, no. What are they going to do?"

She turns, throwing her arms up in the air. "There is no fixing it in time. The carpets are ruined, and the wood floors are bowed." When she faces me, she adds, "Tealey, it's a historical hotel. We searched for a year for that location."

I nod. I remember visiting at least fifty venues. She stepped into that ballroom, and that was that. I go to her again and hug her. "I'm so sorry."

"Months," she says. "They said it will take months to fix." Swiping tears with the back of her hand, she lowers her head. "It's ruined. My wedding is ruined just like the carpet. The wedding is a month away. Twenty-seven days to be precise."

She angles on my shoulder to face Cade. One look exchanged between them, and they know; they understand everything that's not being said. When she moves into his arms, he kisses the top of her head.

Marlow, who has remained silent, crosses the room and grabs a bottle of champagne. "Anybody need a drink?"

"I do," we all say at once.

Amanda is quick to her feet, pulling glasses from the shelves. As they start pouring drinks from champagne to wine and whiskey, I sit on the couch, leaning forward. Rad comes from the other side of the fireplace where he'd been standing and sits beside me. Resting back, he stretches his arm across the back of the couch behind me.

My stomach twists in concern as my thoughts race through options that can fix this for my friend to make her day as special as she deserves. But I keep coming up blank. I take a moment to fall back, seeking comfort in my proximity to Rad.

We can't touch the way I'd like, hold hands to silently show we care. A deep-seated bitterness stretches inside my chest that I know I can't share this news with Cammie because she's panicking and doesn't need me shifting any attention off her priorities. And I'm still confused about what to do with Marlow because I know she'll feel my relationship with Rad would affect the outcome of her arrangement with him. I still haven't gotten much in the form of details, but Rad's shown me that I'm important to him, and he's here how he can be.

I slide my gaze to his, and all I hoped for is felt inside me —safety and that calming comfort I needed. A wave of peace rolls through me, and I say, "I know this is stressful for you, Cammie. You've put so much into the planning and dreaming of the day, but remember, it's about the marriage, and I know Cade would marry you anywhere."

"We're going to end up in city hall in front of the justice of the peace."

Cade moves to sit on a barstool and brings Cammie to

stand between his legs. Wrapping his arms around her waist, he says, "But we'd be there together."

Marlow hands Cammie a glass of wine and Cade a lowball of whiskey. "Lots of famous people have gotten married in a city hall. Like Marilyn Monroe to Joe DiMaggio. Matt Damon and Keira Knightly. Not to each other, of course. Carrie Bradshaw and Big. Or was that at the library?" Rolling her eyes, Marlow laughs. "I don't know about that one, but getting married at city hall is so romantic and freeing. You show up and confess your love only for each other." She sighs sweetly.

She rarely shows it, but it's nice to see Marlow's soft side. *Is she actually a romantic at heart?*

"I can't look on the bright side right now." Tears free themselves from her lower lids, following in their predecessors' tracks. "Everything is falling apart."

My heart hurts for her. "I will help however you need, Cam. We can find an even better location. I promise you."

She looks up, her face already blotching. "I can't put more on your plate, Teals. You still need to find an apartment."

"It's ok—"

"There's no rush for Tealey to move," Rad says. "She can help you. We all can."

His mom finishes taking a drink and sets her glass on the counter. "I know it's not how you imagined your day to be, but you're always welcome to have the wedding here. I've hosted many events on the lawn. The weather will be beautiful next month." Holding her hands up, she smiles. "No pressure from me, but please know that I'm happy to host your big day if you want."

Cammie's stifled sniffle has Cade holding her again. Collecting herself, she walks into the kitchen. "Thank you.

That's so generous." Amanda and Cammie embrace. "We'll definitely consider it."

Marlow says, "Wherever it is, we promise to make it the most beautiful wedding ever." She hands me a glass of wine and Rad his usual bourbon.

When Marlow sits on the other side of Rad, Jackson shoots her a look from the other side of the coffee table. "The service around here is lacking."

She raises her chin into the air. "I'm not your server tonight."

"I'd leave a big . . .*tip,* sweetheart."

The glass stills in my hand, the edge pressed to my lips. *Uh-oh.*

Her gaze slices the air as she levels him with a look. She says, "If that's your version of flirting, Jackson St. James, then you have a lot to learn about women." They've always been hot and cold. This weekend, they're pure ice.

"Flirting?" He scoffs. "You wish." Knowing we all just witnessed him lose this round, he goes and grabs a beer from the fridge.

With that sideshow moving to the next town, I say, "I think we should take a breath and reconvene to discuss the options we come up with later. Does that sound like a plan?"

Marlow's already opening the back door. "I'm getting fresh air."

Amanda's right behind, tucking her hair behind her ears. "Fresh air is a great idea."

Cade angles to kiss Cammie's cheek. "Why don't we lie down and try to take a nap? Emotions are high, but once rested, we can come up with an even better plan."

She nods. Glancing at me, she says, "Thank you," before taking his hand and going upstairs.

Jackson is lost in his thoughts, the argument with

Marlow seeming to affect him. That's unusual. He's such a happy-go-lucky kind of guy, so I'm surprised he'd think twice about it. Taking another long pull from the bottle, he then lowers it and says, "I'm going to catch up on some work in my room."

"Okay, man," Rad says. When we're alone, he scoots a little closer. "Let's go for a ride. Just you and me." There's a renewed happiness reflected in his eyes. It's hard to look away from him when he exposes an emotion he usually hides.

"Where do we go?" *From here?*

His arm tightens around me. To everyone else, we only look like friends, but for us, it's a connection that's deeper than appearances. I cherish these small moments together that feel stolen from an ordinary day. "We can go into town to do some shopping."

"That sounds fun. I just need to get my purse from upstairs." We walk into the foyer, and I take a few steps. With my hand on the banister, I shift onto one foot, feeling a little nervous. "I want you to know I don't regret anything."

He smiles, and it's so genuine that my heart squeezes. "Me neither. No regrets whatsoever."

I smile and start running up the stairs.

"Hey, Bell?"

Just before I reach the landing, I turn back, already grinning. "Yeah?"

"You broke your promise and ravaged me."

Laughing, I say, "I think you set me up to fail."

"How so?"

"You know how irresistible you are, and you used it against me."

"What's the point in owning the tools if you don't use

them?" He starts chuckling, and says, "Can't blame me for using all my best assets." I smile coyly.

"Don't worry, Welly. I might have a few *assets* of my own. Don't say I didn't warn you."

His tongue slides across his lower lip as he takes me in from head to toe and back again. "I just bet you do."

"Revenge is going to be so sweet that I can already taste it." With a wink, I take the last step nice and slow, giving one of my best assets a little wiggle so he can see exactly what I have to offer.

"You're killing me, Bell."

"I haven't even gotten started."

25

Rad

I thought we'd at least reach the town of East Hampton.

I thought wrong.

In a restaurant parking lot five minutes from the shops, we're in the back seat of my mom's Mercedes SUV. It's not as roomy as I thought it would be back here. But Tealey and I are managing the best we can. I'll take cramped spaces with her than extra legroom without.

Maneuvering to the floorboard, I lean over her while she lies on the leather seat. I kiss each of her inner thighs, her moan music to my ears, encouraging me to do even more. That and her saying, "More, Rad."

She's lifting her ass off the seat, seeking her own pleasure. Her hands are frenzied through my hair when I duck out from under the dress to study her face. She has me hard, her arousal speaking straight to my groin, so I'm pressing against the edge of the seat to no avail.

"Move down, baby," escapes my lips with a rush of breath yanked from my chest. Keeping my eyes on her face,

I dip my hand under her dress and don't waste time dancing around where we both want me to be. She's too close not to take her to the edge.

One finger, then two. I swipe through the slickness and start fucking her, wishing it was my dick instead.

"I want you," she says, pushing the back of her head into the seat. With one hand, her nails scrape across my back, and her other twists the seat belt around it. "You feel so good."

She rocks against my hand, our bodies moving as much as they can in the confined space—hands and arms, legs, and heated breath. Everything becomes one as we both teeter toward the cliff.

Nails dig into my skin as I watch her start to fall apart under my ministrations. As she tugs my hair, I revel in her possessiveness, letting her take what she needs from me. When her mouth opens and her eyes roll back in her head, I continue to thrust my fingers while her body trembles around me. My name rolls from her tongue in a plea to fall with her.

I'm so hard, so ready to come, I'm not far behind.

Just as she finds peace in the aftermath, I don't hold back. She sinks against the seat, her body soft, as I build momentum. Grinding against her leg, I kiss her neck. I brace my hands to the side and keep seeking my own release. I might be raw when my orgasm hits, but it feels so fucking fantastic to come, the tension ripping through every part of me. "Tealey, fuck."

My upper body sinks into Tealey's arms, covering as much of her as I can. Doesn't matter that my legs are cramped to the side and twisted on the floorboard, I close my eyes and savor the feeling of what we just shared.

When her breathing shallows, I push up, balancing

vicariously above her. "Shit. Sorry." I move her hair back from her face. "Are you okay?"

"I'll survive," she says with a smile. "Anyway, I like to feel the weight of you on me. There's something so . . ." She looks away. "I don't know what I'm trying to say." A giggle escapes, and she kisses me as if that distraction technique will work.

I regain my strength and try my best to hold her by shifting underneath her. She molds herself to my body, the scent of the beach in her hair, and her breath warming my neck.

"I want to be with you, Tealey," I say, already knowing that I've never felt this connected to another woman before. It's as though, in such a short space of time, that she's become my best friend. The one I want to share all things with. Be home early for. Be up to have coffee with. *Want desperately in my every day . . . everything.*

I think I underestimated my crush. Kissing her temple, I close my eyes and pull myself back together.

She moves to rest her chin on my chest, and whispers, "We are together."

"More than now. I want to date you. Take you out or stay in. Whatever we decide to do, I want to do it with you."

I run my fingers through her hair, admiring not only the beauty before me but also the person she is on the inside. *Can I be the man she deserves?*

My forehead is kissed, and I close my eyes, savoring the feel of her lips. The feel of her nose rubbing against the side of mine has me opening my eyes. "I want that, too."

Guilt sinks in. "I wanted to romance you, give you flowers, *hell,* at the bare minimum, a bed." She grins.

"I don't need any of those. I just want you."

A bang on the glass has me jumping and gathering

Tealey in my arms. I turn over my shoulder to see a thick, gray mustache under dark eyes and bushy eyebrows. The window is fogged, but his words cut through the glass. "The restaurant is opening soon. You need to leave the premises."

Tealey scrambles off my lap. Hoping to get the security guard to move along, I say, "Thanks. Will do."

I can't reach my shoes, so I wait for Tealey to do what she needs to first. Pulling her skirt down, she asks, "Why did we think this was a good place to . . . Heavy pet?"

I start chuckling. "Heavy pet?"

"Make out? Get off? Whatever you want to call it."

Reaching over her, I pop the glove box but don't see any wipes. Checking the console, I find a Valentine's Day pack of tissues. Seems fitting and will have to do. We both do a quick cleanup. We're both fully dressed so it only takes a moment to collect ourselves and fix our appearance. I can't care that I'm a sticky mess, not when I'm a mess because of Tealey.

I steal a glance at her, my heart attaching in new ways— protective, selfish . . . A four-letter word that starts with L comes to mind.

Like.

I can handle that. She turns back and whacks me on the chest. "Get a move on before I die of embarrassment."

"No one is going to die. He's a security guard. He doesn't care what we're doing in here as long as we're done when his shift starts at five."

She pops the door and steps out. "Let's get a move on then."

"Someone's awfully demanding post-orgasm."

"Shh," she says with a finger pressed to her lips.

I chuckle and get out of the car, readjusting as I walk around the back of the vehicle. Glad I wore a loose shirt today to cover the . . . evidence. We close the front doors at the same time and steal a quick glance—me still laughing and her sitting with flaming red cheeks—before I start the car. Rubbing her leg, I lean over. "It's okay. No one will be the wiser. Now, give me a kiss, Bell."

"Look who the demanding one is now."

"Only when it comes to kissing you."

She leans over and gives me a kiss I'll never forget. "You, sir, are going to get more than a kiss the next time we're alone."

I definitely underestimated her assets. She's not afraid to use any tool in her arsenal.

I'm a lucky bastard.

I AM SO grateful Tealey forced me into a shop and, again, for the baggy shirt.

We were dodging questions like bullets as soon as we walked in the door. Holding up the bag was a great distraction. I tossed it to Jackson as Tealey and I ran upstairs under the guise of freshening up. If they only knew . . .

The water didn't even have time to heat because I took the fastest shower in history and jetted back downstairs.

Cammie found the chocolate.

Jackson had grabbed the graham crackers.

Already out the door, Cade was starting the firepit, which left Marlow holding the marshmallows. She asks, "Where's Tealey?"

"I don't know," I reply, hoping she can't tell that we were up to no good. She takes her glass, and says, "We need to talk about my dad's situation when we get back to Manhattan."

"Will do."

Marlow starts for the back deck when Tealey enters the great room. Marlow says, "There you are."

"I wanted to change clothes and get more comfortable," Tealey offers. Wearing sweatpants and a faded NYU sweatshirt, she pads into the kitchen in thick, bunched-up socks. The woman could wear anything and make it sexy.

I start checking emails when Tealey opens a bottle of water. Marlow says, "Heading out. Are you coming?" I glance up, but the question is directed to Tealey.

Tealey replies, "Be right out."

The house grows quiet as the crew moves the party outside. Buried in a page of unread emails, I catch the subject line: Update – Misty Connor. I click it first and read the email from Ashleigh.

"What's wrong?" Tealey rubs my shoulder, a look of concern worrying her eyes when she feels how tense I am.

"We finally heard back from the judge. He granted your client, Misty, a restraining order. I filed the paperwork before I left Manhattan."

She releases a deep breath, and her expression brightens. "That's great news. I'm surprised a judge was working on Saturday."

"It went through last night, but now it's in place."

"Does she know?"

"I had a call with her on my drive, explaining how it would work, and Ashleigh made sure she knew it was approved this morning when she received word."

"I really appreciate this, Rad." She smiles, leaning against me. "Can I reward you with a s'more?" She holds up a s'more. "It's all ready to heat over the pit."

"I have other ideas on how you can reward me, but if

those aren't on the table, I'll take the next best thing." I take her perfectly made treat and head out back.

Tealey starts laughing and is quick to follow.

Tonight after dinner is about the same as last night, except we stay around the firepit.

Cammie has made a concerted effort not to worry. Or maybe she just hides her stress well. The guys and I tossed a football around for a while after eating too much, but now we're enjoying the clear-sky night and the sound of the waves crashing onto the shore.

My mom's gone to bed, and the gang seems to be winding up.

Cammie pokes Cade over with her toe. "You guys were rambunctious tonight."

"Every night," Marlow adds.

Jackson sits on the arm of her chair and rubs her shoulders. "You love it, and you know it."

Marlow laughs. "You say that, but I really don't. I like my men like my wine—"

"Palatable?" he jokes. "Or rich?"

"Both." She grins unapologetically. "But I was going to say strong, bold, and with depth." Pushing him off her chair, she says, "Basically, the opposite of you, you big lug."

Though their fighting is entertaining, my mind is elsewhere. I still haven't had a chance to talk to her about our arrangement or ask Tealey how we want to handle ours. I'm hoping I can put at least one of these conversations to rest tonight.

We're among our friends, shooting the shit like we've done a thousand times before, yet it's Tealey I'm drawn to. Seeing her snuggled inside the sweatshirt that practically swallows her whole, I get it. Her lips part, and although I can't hear her, I reply, "Hi."

I keep my eyes on the beauty across from me who's leaning back in the chair, head tilted to the side with heavy eyelids. Conspiratorially, I nod toward the house. She grins, and I feel like I just won the jackpot. She stands. "I'm going to bed."

"I'm wiped," I say, faking a yawn and raising my arms for a good stretch. I call over my shoulder to the group, "Good night."

A chorus of, "Night," follows, but the rest is lost in the sound of the ocean. Just out of their sight, I tug her by the shirt, pulling her toward me. "Want me to keep you warm?"

"I want nothing more."

Holding out a hand, I show her what I brought with us. She laughs. "You brought graham crackers? Deviously delicious."

"What can I say? I'm still hungry."

Tealey takes the small package and kisses me quickly before dashing upstairs. I'm right behind her, and this time, I remember to lock the door.

The flirting ends, and the two of us stand there in the light of the small lamp she turned on. The crackers are on the nightstand, and she toes the carpet. "Alone again."

"Being alone with you is my favorite place to be." I cross to her and cup her face, kissing her until her hands grab my wrists. Slowly reopening my eyes, I then lean my head against hers. "I'm free to kiss you for as long as I like."

She kisses the underside of my jaw, "To explore, to date, to be whatever we want to be."

"Exactly." Her hands slide down my arms and then to my chest, lower until her hands reach under my shirt. I'm okay with this. I'm more than okay with all of this because it's with her. It's something I never thought would happen to me, but I'm starting to see a whole new opportunity. A relationship might actually work out how it's supposed to, even for a cynic like me.

I kiss her shoulder and then whisper, "Turn around."

She does a slow spin. I pull the sweatshirt over her head, and when she tugs her socks and pants off, I finally get a good look at her in a bra and pair of white cotton panties. *So fucking innocent.*

I don't have as much patience with my own clothes. I'm practically kicking them to the floor until I'm left standing in my boxer briefs.

Tealey's already climbing into bed when I join her. You'd think after years of keeping my distance that getting into bed with Tealey Bell would feel weird, but it doesn't. *It feels right.*

She feels right.

We lie there for a minute, and I assume she has a million things racing through her head like I do. Every thought I have is landing on one theme.

How do I make this last past the weekend?

26

Rad

"What if your opinion on my body did matter?" Her voice is only a whisper between us, but her nervousness is heard in the question.

I turn to the side to find Tealey already facing me. Her eyes search mine for answers to a question I don't understand. "What do you mean?" I ask.

"You once told me that your opinion doesn't matter regarding my body, but it does. It matters to me, and you said there's nothing wrong with it, but a lot right with it. Did you mean that?"

I caress her cheek. "I meant it." She smiles, scooting her body closer. I move in, closing any gaps between us. "I like you, Tealey."

"I like you, too, Rad."

I pause, debating how to approach the delicate subject. I'd rather think through this logistically, which is my forte. But now, I have feelings involved that subtract some of my rationale from the equation, so I decide straightforward is best. "I'm not sure where you stand, but I want to be with you and *only you*."

She grins. "I'm not standing. I'm lying right here with you. This is the only place I want to be. Where does that leave us beyond this bedroom door?"

"Our friends might understand—"

"Or they might not." She looks down, doodling circle eights on my chest. "I don't want to take away from Cammie and Cade's wedding either, but this announcement would do the trick."

Wrapping my arms around her, I pull her entirely, *and selfishly*, against me. "I agree. It's great timing for us but might be bad timing for the overall situation. What do you suggest we do?"

"Is there anything we can do other than keep us a secret?"

"For right now?" I kiss the top of her head, hating that life is leaving us no choice. Because this woman deserves to be hugged and kissed whenever she wants it. Not only behind closed doors. "I don't think we have any options."

She kisses my chest. "Only for now." I nod. She whispers, "As soon as the wedding's over—"

"The minute it's over."

I can feel her cheeks rise against my skin. Kissing her once more, I add, "But for tonight—"

"We should probably slow things down again." Not the answer I wanted to hear. Tilting her head back, she smiles. "I heard that huff. I said slow, not end, Welly." When she wiggles her brow, it's game on.

"Did you just waggle your eyebrows at me?"

"I did. What are you going to do about it?"

I slip my hand under the covers and slide up the top of her thigh.

Her mouth opens.

I pull the covers down and run my tongue over the top of her breast the bra left exposed.

Her tongue runs over the corner of her mouth before the softest of mewls is released. My cock reacts by hardening.

Disappearing under the covers altogether, I anchor myself by holding her hips with my hands and then kiss beneath a little pink bow on the top of her panties. I lift the covers to watch her.

She bites her lip.

I hook my fingers around the edges of the cotton and begin to leisurely pull them down until she bends her knees and lifts so I can remove them altogether. I stop, though.

Enough light penetrates the blanket for me to see the beauty of her body. A curve from her waist to her hips leads my eyes to where it meets her thighs. Her perfect legs. I start there, wedging my shoulder under the right thigh while kissing the inside of the other. I can't resist going deeper with her, tasting her, feeling her heat on my tongue.

"Rad?" she asks on the end of a pant.

"Yeah?" I run the end of my nose along the side of her thigh.

Breathless, she says, "Being with you like this . . . it's still new."

I pause, wanting to reassure her and rid her tone of any insecurity. I lift the covers until our eyes meet. I can imagine my eyes reflect the same desire I find inside hers, but I want to take away any doubts she may have. "As fast or slow as you want to go. You're in control."

I love the sweet smile and nod she gives me. *How did I deserve such trust?* I already know this is not where and when we'll have sex for the first time. It won't just be the freedom to be together. It will also be about the freedom to express ourselves. I want to hear her yell my fucking name at the peak of her orgasm.

After that, I'm going to take my time and have her do it all over again. I want to experience her and listen to every noise she makes. I want her to feel free to moan and cry out and scream as I bring her to orgasm. *Something I've fantasized about for so long.*

I will my erection to go down, but nothing works. Her scent surrounds me, enticing me, so I push my hips against the mattress, trying to find some sort of relief. The more I hear and feel her losing control, the more the discomfort in my boxers grows.

No way am I putting my needs before hers, though. I started this, and I intend to enjoy every inch of this sublime body of hers. I start making love to her pussy with my mouth.

Touching.

Kissing.

The sheets are fisted around me, her hips bucking against my mouth until I hold her still again. This time, I fuck her with my tongue until my hair is pulled as she releases under a barrage of heavy breaths mixed with my name being whispered.

Licking.

Sucking.

Writhing beneath me.

Her body shivers with a giggle as she comes back down from the heavens. I climb up next to her and fall on my back. She lies there with her features at peace, her eyes closed for only a minute or so before turning to me. "You were right."

"About?" I grin in response, though I have no idea what she's about to say.

"You're very good when you're bad."

"I'm not usually one for *I told you so*." I move her hair behind her shoulder just to see her graceful neck. It's the spot where her neck meets her shoulder that draws me to kiss her right there again. "Why do you taste so sweet?"

Her chest vibrates with laughter. "It's the s'mores." Maneuvering on top of me, she bends down until we're nose to nose. Her little body rocking on my middle has me gripping her hips and holding her down harder. A rumbling growl builds strength inside. "You feel so good, you naughty girl."

"Guess what?"

"What?"

Escaping my grasp, she slips under the blanket. "Want to see how bad I can be?"

Yes. *Fucking yes!*

I WANT to have sex with Tealey.

I'd sacrifice the chance at partner, give up my apartment building, and sell my soul to the devil to taste a piece of heaven. The samples are good, but I need more. I *want* more with her. *I want her.*

I haven't had sex for . . . well, a long damn time. I should be climbing the walls. I should be a grouchy ass who's best avoided. But I'm the opposite.

Doesn't mean I won't race home to get this woman alone. I'll be breaking the speed limits if it gets me there five minutes sooner.

I wave one last time to Mom before rounding the bend and leaving the others driving home in the SUV in my dust. Reaching over, I walk two fingers down Tealey's thigh. She hasn't made access easy by wearing jeans, but I think I'm up for the challenge. "What kind of underwear are you wearing?"

She laughs, her head pushing back on the seat rest. "Wouldn't you like to know?"

"Yes, I would." I smirk and then chuckle. "That's why I'm asking."

"None," she replies, her eyes trained out the windshield.

I start braking, and her hands fly forward to brace herself against the dashboard. "Rad, what are you doing?"

"You can't tell me you're not wearing anything under those jeans and expect me to focus on the road."

"If you focus on the road, though, you'll get to see under these jeans sooner."

"I know a restaurant parking lot nearby. *Hint, hint.*"

A smile is quick to appear. "Too much security patrolling the property." She has a point. "I have an idea."

"Where?"

"Your apartment in Manhattan," she deadpans and sits back again.

A honk causes me to look in the mirror. Tealey turns to look out the back just as Cade speeds past us in the SUV, flipping us off. Sending me a look, she asks, "Are you going to let them beat us home?"

Home.

I can't lie. I love hearing her call my place home.

"No fucking way."

The last we saw of the crew was outside Medford when we all decided to grab snacks and get gas from a convenience store.

I tried not to worry about the Oreo cookie crumbs falling on Tealey's lap and didn't say a word when popcorn kernels fell onto the floorboard of my baby. Not a peep from me was heard when she dropped a jelly bean down the side of the seat, but I might have been squeezing the steering wheel.

If I weren't still fixated on the fact that she says she's not wearing any underwear, the rest of our trip might have gone a different way.

But as soon as that elevator opens into the apartment, I sag in relief. "It's great to be home."

27

Tealey

"Too tired?" I ask, smoothing a section of Rad's hair to the side that's hanging over his forehead. He looks at me, and the devilish smile on his face makes it hard to breathe.

"Depends why you're asking." He takes hold of my waist and moves in, dipping his head to my shoulder and placing little kisses there. *I'm thinking we're on the same page.*

We haven't made it five feet into the apartment, but I couldn't stop the anticipation building on the drive back of us finally being alone and free to do whatever we please. Now, I'm so turned on my body feels like a live wire.

Rolling my head to the side, I give him more access to my neck. He pushes my hair aside and leaves lingering kisses on my skin. "Is this better?" His breath gives me goose bumps.

The ember inside me has been lit, and the burn of desire for this man is insatiable. We've been adding kindling to this fire for days, and now it's beginning to consume me. Taking his hands, I start leading him to my bedroom. "I'm not going for better. I want spectacular. Are you up for the challenge, Welly?"

"I never shy away from a challenge." Scooping me into his arms, he carries me the rest of the way.

"I was hoping you'd say that."

I get comfortable on top of the mattress as Rad settles between my legs. It's not the first time we've done this. We've become experts in the art of making out, but this time, it feels like the love we're making is reaching deeper than the physical part of our bodies connecting.

We're alone.

Endless hours alone with him is what I've wanted since our first kiss. Now that I have it and his complete attention, this feels like a step we can walk back from. Seeing him go into it wholeheartedly has me leaving my nerves behind and enjoying it. "Take off your shirt," I say a little too eagerly.

"So demanding, Miss Bell."

He still gets up and undresses completely, which I appreciate. Why drag out what we both want anyway?

With my hands behind my head, I watch unabashedly. Maybe I should feel some shame, but I've never seen or been with a man so sculpted as he is. He's a work of art, and I gratuitously take him in from head to toe and every delicious inch between. He works too hard on that body not to appreciate the effort he puts in. It would be rude of me not to.

That roguish smile.

The dip of his head as his eyes remain on me.

Those abs. *THOSE ABS.* I want to shout about them from the rooftops. I want to thank every crunch that made them possible.

While I'm busy fanning myself, he asks, "You look like you're enjoying this."

"I am. Very much," I purr, letting my inner thoughts speak for me. Pinching my fingers, I kiss the tips. "Compliments to the chef."

Chuckling, he slides his hands up the sides of my hips, pops the snap of my jeans, and works the zipper down. "Your turn."

I bite my bottom lip and lift, letting him strip my legs bare. "You weren't lying," he says. I look down and am quickly reminded. I could let my insecurities take hold of me and ruin the moment, but this feels too good, too right, to get caught up in that mess tonight.

"Why would I?" I ask the sexiest man alive, currently pinning me to the mattress just from the look of lust blazing in his eyes.

Lifting my leg over his shoulder, he kisses the inside of my knee and then down my thigh. "God, I love you."

We both freeze, but I know what he meant. "Never heard a thing."

Carrying on like that three-word phrase didn't come from his mouth, he presses his hands to my belly and slides under my shirt. When his lips reach the curve of my hips, he squeezes my breasts.

Hot breath covers my core, and my back arches in response. I'm already so turned on that I'm willing to skip the foreplay to get to the main event. I start by pulling Rad higher. "Come here."

His elbows anchor him to the bed on either side of my head, and he runs his finger along my lower lip. *Slow. Savoring. Seductive.* He kisses me, and whispers, "Not until you come, beautiful."

Beautiful. My heart dances in his words.

If I weren't already lying down, I'd thud right to the ground. He moves back down, his lips covering me. Kissing my mouth is romantic, but kissing my body exactly where I want him draws a moan from deep within myself.

The magic of his tongue, the way he holds me as though I might slip away, has me on the verge of falling. "Oh God, Rad."

The pressure picks up, and he sucks harder, dives deeper, his fingers teasing the spot that will send me into pure bliss. My mind floats with the stars as my body tremors through the release.

Sinking into the mattress, I didn't realize I was fisting his hair until I stretch my fingers. "I'm sorry."

"Don't be." When he crawls up my body, I feel his erection hard against my thigh. Our kisses become hurried despite the sense of peace I feel inside. He kisses my neck, and I kiss his.

Licking his Adam's apple is a glorious thing. Each weighted gulp is a reflection of how I make him feel. I love it. "I want you, Rad."

"Thank fuck because I want to be inside you so badly." The hunger in his voice and the growl rooted in his words make me squirm even more. But then he pushes up. "Fuck. I'll be back."

"What?" I lift to my elbows. "Why?"

He's harder to read under the scrutiny of his own frustration. "I didn't come prepared."

"You haven't come at all. Not yet," I say, winking.

Kissing me quick, he says, "Punny girl," and then gets up.

"Just in case you've forgotten, I do happen to have a stash of condoms."

"A large stash, from what I remember." His snark has

reached his grin before he leaves the room. As if he wasn't already sexy, that smirk causes me to rub my thighs together like a dang cricket, wanting him down there again. "Did you bring them with you?"

"I might have one or two, or ninety exactly in the box over there."

I can practically see the calculations spinning in his head. The answer isn't hard to figure out, but the images populating are probably stumbling blocks. To lighten the mood again, I say, "Sadly, one was lost in the move."

"It's probably still on the stairs. Should we go check?" When he chuckles, it makes me happy that we can laugh about it now.

Digging through the box, he widens his eyes. "Damn, woman. What am I going to do with you?" Holding up a handful of condoms, he says, "I can't say I'm too upset over the fact that you have so many left."

"Got big plans there, Welly?"

Tossing them on the mattress, he says, "I sure do," and then dives back on the bed. "Because once we make love, gorgeous, I'm going to take you again, and probably again after that."

"Where are you takin' me?"

"Straight to heaven, baby."

I burst out laughing. "Wowsa. That was a doozy of a line. I wasn't prepared. But the way you're throwing around that sweet phrase *making love* has me thinking you might be the one going to heaven."

Tugging my top off, he says, "You won't be needing this."

"In heaven?"

He clicks his tongue and winks, and then runs a finger down my chest between my breasts. "You're too goddamn beautiful. You know that, Bell?"

"No, keep telling me," I say, lifting to plant a kiss on his head.

His eyes dart to mine, and he stares in all seriousness. "You're so beautiful that it was hard to look at you over the past whatever number of years and realize that I'd never have the privilege of telling you how I feel."

My heart thumps against his hand that flattened to my chest, my secret of how he makes me feel felt between us. I caress his cheek and give a gentle smile. "You say the most romantic things. If you're not careful, I might believe them."

He smiles and kisses me on the lips. "I hope you do one day."

Wrapping my arms around his neck, I hold him close. "Don't go falling in love, Counselor. It never ends well, remember?"

"I'm sorry I ever gave you that impression."

"What impression is that?"

"That true love doesn't exist."

Still embracing as much as I can in my arms, I whisper, "It does?"

He lowers his gaze and kisses my chest again. I'm not sure if he's avoiding the question or distracted by other things, namely me naked underneath him. So, I say, "It's okay. We'll just file that under other things we'll never mention again."

"For now, it's probably best, Miss Bell."

I'm not going to spend time overanalyzing what just went wrong when I'm not willing to take that step and say those words either. Instead, a craving I have for him has become an ache in my core.

"As you please, Mr. Wellington."

The cockiest smirk of all time lands on his face. Leaning down, he kisses the top mounds of my breasts, leaving me squirming and panting for more. "The death of me," he mutters under his breath just before he begins sheathing himself.

"Don't tease," I say, watching him. Purposely teasing him, I run the tips of my fingers down my neck and over one breast, then the other.

"There won't be any more teasing. I plan to follow through when I make love to you." He positions his body over mine, and I can't resist feeling his solid muscles. I wrap my arms around his neck and pull him down to me, kissing him hard with intention one last time before we cross that final line.

Make love, where my heart, body, and soul are invested in him. This is something I want to share with Rad.

With a slight shift in our bodies, he pushes in. My eyes close, and my head dips back, my back arching and my breath shortening as we become one. The stretch and burn that I've come to know with him flicker to life inside as the heat we create has me shedding the sheet from our bodies. I move against him, wanting more—harder, faster—and more of him. *All of him.*

There's pleasure found in the scrape of his five o'clock shadow against my chin. I've come to yearn for the rawness I feel after kissing him, the burn a reminder of how hot his mouth is against mine. God, this man doesn't just do things to me. He does everything to me—makes my heart beat heavy in my chest, causes goose bumps to cover my skin, and has me believing that we're more than friends with benefits, trusting his words and the way he makes me feel inside and out.

Beautiful.

Respected.

Sexy.

His body takes mine as I take his, meeting him thrust for thrust, pulse for racing pulse, trading my harsh breathing for his, and begging for more. He chants, "I've wanted you for so long . . . so long, baby." Baby falls from his lips in lust, from a deep desire he can't control, just between us. Even though he says he's wanted me since we met, it still feels surreal to be with him now.

"Rad . . ." His name is my mantra that plays on repeat.

"God, you feel so good."

It's too much—his deep voice, the rhythm we find pushing us to our limits, toward that cliff, the feel of him everywhere—in, out, and all around me, taking me body and soul. Kissing my neck, he dips his hand to rub just the right place above our connection. "So good."

Our bodies are still bonded when his eyes lock on mine, his biceps carved of stone when he rises above me, my own personal Michelangelo staring back at me. A growl vibrates through him, spurring him to pump harder.

He kisses my cheek and works his way to my ear, whispering, "I won't . . ." His brows pinch when the words appear too heavy a burden to share.

As I run my nails along his jawline, my own feelings bloom inside. I ask, "You won't what, Rad?"

On the tip of a breath, he replies, "I won't ever hurt you."

I lift and kiss where my fingers were. "I know."

We lose ourselves in each other with kisses and thrusts, moans, and names uttered as prayers.

Begging for this to last forever, I'm conflicted as I race toward the finish, feeling too good to take things slow. I watch his stomach muscles tense and flex, his biceps working to pump and push, hold and move, a dance between what he wants and his body's desire. Incredible is not fitting for this man.

The coil tightens my core, and I take a breath to release the pressure, but there's no holding back any longer. We fall together this time, lost in our passion and the sound of love being made until my heart escapes my soul, choosing to embed it into his chest instead. "Oh, my God. Yes. Rad." I squeeze my eyes closed as my body awakens.

"I need you, baby," he groans as if the words themselves pain him in his pleasure. He follows me, drifting into the sweet abyss. Then his body collapses on top of me, his weight locked in my embrace.

He was right. *Pure heaven.*

He rolls to the side and tries to catch his breath. I'm not sure how long we lie there before our heartbeats regulate. I look over at him. "I didn't think it could be like that."

"You asked for spectacular," he says, his breath grazing across my skin.

"You delivered." I reach over and run my fingers through his hair. "It was spectacular."

I smile and then kiss his head and his temple, rubbing his back until he catches his breath. "You're pretty spectacular yourself."

Night arrived before we had a chance to say goodbye to the day. Finding my hand between us, he brings it to his lips and looks my way. With only the light from the living room slipping in through the door, it would be so easy to fall asleep in his arms. And I almost do until I hear him say, "You're spectacular."

If there's one thing I've always loved about Rad, it's his motto of not saying anything for the sake of appeasement. I know they're not just words to him.

They're his truth, which becomes mine because when I'm with him, I feel spectacular. He has given me that power.

Sliding onto my side, I drape my leg over his and rest my head on his chest.

His heart is beating fast and strong, and I begin to fall— floating in this bliss, finding sleep, and into love.

28

Rad

I had sex with Tealey Bell.

Made love.

Did the deed.

Hit a home run.

Whatever I want to call it, it happened, and I haven't stopped grinning since. Except when we slept, though I'm pretty sure I smiled all night since my cheeks hurt when I woke up.

"You must have been having sweet dreams last night," she says, her eyes still trained on the paperback resting on her lap.

"Why do you say that?" I ask, not because I don't know the answer already but because I want her to know.

I lower the newspaper and look at the beauty on the other end of the couch. We woke up early since we went to bed around nine after wearing each other out. The sun hasn't even come up, but I'm already wishing it was a weekend so we could spend all day like this.

She looks right at home here, and that brings me more pleasure than it probably should, considering she'll be living in her own space again one day.

My grin is gone.

Long brown lashes tap above her eyes when she looks up at me, free of makeup but more stunning than ever. I give in and start smiling because whether I get her for a month or a year, I'll take her and appreciate the time instead of wasting it.

She says, "Because you grinned all night like you just scored your favorite candy."

"I did."

There it is—the sweet blush that covers her cheeks, eyes that can't hide how a simple compliment makes her feel, and the twitch of her lips as she tries to hide that pretty smile. She can't. Just like I can't.

"I don't know anyone who still reads a newspaper. You know they have the news on your phone, TV, and pretty much everywhere you can get Wi-Fi these days."

I chuckle. "I like holding something in my hands. I stare at a screen most of the day and then again most nights. It's nice to take a break and read the old-fashioned way." Leaning forward, I tap the top of her book. "What about you? There are e-books and audiobooks, but you're always reading paperbacks."

"I guess, like you, I like the feel of it in my hands, and I bought this book used to give it another life." She holds it to her nose. "I love the smell of the paper, the dust from the old shelves, and the life this book has lived before it became a part of mine." She rests her head sideways on the back cushion, and her smile is so right. Wriggling her feet over to me, she tucks them under my legs. "Can you play hooky today?"

"There's nothing I'd rather do than spend the day with you." The newspaper crinkles in protest when I lean over to kiss her. She meets me halfway, and our lips press together. "But I have court this afternoon."

Flopping back to opposite sides of the couch, she says, "I'd take this morning."

"Is that something you can do?"

"I have so much stockpiled time off and nothing scheduled that someone else can't handle."

"Then, why'd you have to use your lunch hour for the move?"

"They only count full days and I didn't want to use a day when I only need an hour. I'll take the day, but what do you say to skipping out for a few hours?"

"How can I say no? "I'll text Ashleigh." I reach for my phone, but she covers my hand.

"Maybe wait until six or seven."

It's incredible that the world already feels like it revolves around our plans. "Six. She's used to it."

"She shouldn't be."

"Good point, Miss Bell." Technically, I shouldn't be playing hooky with the possibility of partnership on the line, but Ashleigh will vouch for hours spent working from home. I set my phone back on the coffee table and pick up my 'I'm not feeling worky today' mug. "Something tells me you had this planned all along."

She asks, "What should we do with the next six or seven hours?"

"Movies? Walk in Central Park? Shopping? Baseball Playoffs? Coffee? Go out for lunch? Whatever you want to do, I want, too."

Closing her book, she tosses it to the coffee table and gets to her knees, crawling over to me. I toss the paper behind me, welcoming her onto my lap. "I want to stay in. However long I can have you." She kisses me, and then dips to my ear to whisper, "Tell me something you've never told anyone."

That is not where I saw this headed. Caught by surprise, I tick through a list of contenders. I could tell her I own the building or about how I found out I'm the frontrunner for partnership, but that's bragging stuff. I know that's not what she means or wants. Leaning my head back, I want the honor of seeing her face every night and every day. I don't say that in fear of scaring her off, though. I need to find something in between.

I go with, "The shirt I was wearing the day we met has never been dry-cleaned." Okay, that leans more toward creeper than a neutral admission, but it's out in the open now.

"You tossed it?" I detect a note of disappointment as her eyes fixate on mine.

Shaking my head, I reply, "I still have it in a bag at the top of my closet."

Running the tip of her finger down the bridge of my nose, she says, "I'm intrigued by the fact that you'd tell me that. That would totally creep out some women." *I have no doubt.* She taps the tip of my nose. "I'm not one of them. Why'd you keep it?"

"Because some things are worth holding on to."

"Flattery will get you everywhere, Mr. Wellington." I love that I can see every emotion trailing across her face. "I have a confession. It's going to make you really mad." Despite the fact she knows it will upset me, a smile still wiggles the corners of her mouth.

We're talking about Tealey Bell. *How bad can it be?* "I doubt it, but I'm ready. Confess away."

"Senior year . . ." she starts but pauses, biting her lip. "Don't hate me, okay?"

"I couldn't." If I were wearing a shirt, I might be tugging at my collar, though. She has a knack for amping up the suspense. I have no idea what she's about to tell me, but I might need to brace myself, after all.

"Senior year at NYU, I ran into your date to the bowl game in the bathroom at that bar down from the stadium. We'd gone there to watch since we didn't all get tickets."

"I remember." I nod. "We sold the three we had so we could all watch together."

"Yep." She smiles so sweetly that I'm wondering how this could possibly lead to something bad. "So, we were at that bar, and I needed to use the restroom. She was in there."

"Okay."

Her gaze pivots, and then she takes a deep breath and exhales. "I told her that we had just broken up, and she was a rebound."

Not what I expected. "Kayla."

"Yep." She snaps her fingers. "Kayla. That's right. I'd forgotten her name. She was very nice. Well, before I said that . . ."

Staring at her in disbelief, I try to remember how that worked out with Kayla. *Ah.* "She dumped me during halftime."

Her arms tighten around my neck, and she kisses my face. Probably to hide the guilt. "I know." She giggles. Guess there's no guilt felt. "I'm a terrible person. I'm sorry yet . . . not at all sorry."

Still surprised by how devious that was, I never saw Tealey doing something like that. "You sabotaged my relationship." *And why didn't I think to do this to Steve? Fucker.*

"I did." This time, she doesn't even try to hide her smile. I rub her thigh, finding her devious side a turn-on.

"I'm impressed, Bell. You play dirty."

Tilting my head to face her, she kisses the corners of my mouth. "Only when I want something. How does that make you feel, Counselor?"

Counselor. Hearing that name elicits a possessive growl in my throat. I know Tealey never would have told me about doing that to Kayla if we weren't where we are today. *She was possessive back then. I like that even more.*

Running a hand into the back of her hair, I move her closer, and then whisper, "I wouldn't want it any other way."

Standing, I lift her into my arms and start for the bedroom. "I know what I want to do today."

"And that is?"

I toss her on my bed and plop down next to her. "I want to be inside you."

Running her hands over my comforter, she laughs. "That's all you want to do today?"

"Yep." I roll to the side and tuck her hair behind her ears. "That's all I need."

Our clothes come off as our lips find each other.

My mind spins as I watch her wriggle. She's desperate for my hands on her—my rough touch and my gaze drifting over her body. I want to give her what she wants.

Freckles on her thighs draw me in, and I move to cover her softness with the heat of my hand. Her body moves, her eyes wild with the same desire I feel inside. We made love last night several times over. As great as that felt, seeing her lying in my bed brings out a different craving.

Yearning.

Voracity.

Uncontrollable hunger.

I can't change the power of the hurricane I'm becoming with her, but I'll do my best to control the speed for her enjoyment. Taking the sheet, I push the fabric away from Tealey's body. This amazing woman trusts me not just with her body but also with her mind, her joy, and every inch of skin and emotion like I deserve her.

Covering the hills of her hips, I settle her small frame on top of me. She rolls a condom over my dick before rising, only to sink down again. Seated with me inside her, she rests her palms on my chest, and whispers, "You say you waited years but know that you weren't waiting alone." Leaning down, she kisses me as I devour her words, her kiss, her mouth, and everything she'll give me. I'm greedy when it comes to her.

She takes every thrust, coming back down with her own intensity. As she rocks on top, her breasts summon me. I knead and pinch, watching her react and learning what she likes and needs.

The warmth of her body consuming mine has me falling deeper under her spell.

As she climbs toward her orgasm, I'm spellbound by her beauty. *No other woman has ever done this to me.* Her eyes dip closed, and her head tilts back with her mouth open. She's stunning in her glory, owning every part of me without even trying. If she only knew . . .

She moans, cries out my name, and as she comes, I dive into the deep end of her heavenliness, joining her as I orgasm. *God, this woman.*

Even sated, I can't wait for more of her.

She curls around my side, her breath still uneven. But something makes her giggle, and she says, "I had no clue it could be this good."

I run my thumb over her cheek and lower to her neck to

feel the rapidly thumping beat of her pulse. "Same, baby. Same."

And seeing her gentle smile, I feel content for the first time.

"I want to get married."

So much for the contentedness . . .

Maybe my reaction—eyes bulging like a cartoon character—isn't as controlled as I would have liked. *But what the hell?*

She wants to talk about marriage?

With her hands already thrown up in surrender, she sits up. "One day. I mean one day. Not today. *Oh, God.*" She covers her eyes with her hands. "I totally blew this amazing sex moment—"

"It was more than a moment. I mean, it wasn't that fast." *No need to base skill or prowess on how fast or slow things take.* She turns me on. *That's the bottom line.*

"I shouldn't have said anything." She won't even look at me, yet I can't stop staring at her—probably still bug-eyed. I can't lose my cool. She's not the opposing side. *She's my girlfriend.*

Why did I bristle at the mention of marriage? Is it because I'm not ready—that seems logical. It's also fast. We've only dated a short time. Granted, I've already been with Tealey longer than most women in my past.

Taking a seriously deep breath, I pull her hands from her face and am greeted with mortification. There's nothing I hate more about Tealey Bell than seeing pain or shame in her expression. I swore I'd never be the cause of it, and I stand by that.

Before I have a chance to say anything, she says, "I'm not embarrassed that I just blurted that out, but I am embarrassed at how you're looking at me."

She shifts her weight like she's going to get off me, but I hold her hips with my hands.

I'm not sure what to say—my mind is still reeling from her unexpected admission. I just need a moment to get myself together because I need to choose my words wisely from this point forward.

"I didn't mean to ruin things," she says, swallowing hard. Her gaze falls from me while her fingers torture the sheets by twisting them.

My heart both aches and swells. I hate that she thinks she just ruined things. But at least I can fix that. "Look at me, Tealey." When she finally works her gaze back to me, I add, "We made love last night and just had pretty intense sex. Emotions are running high because we're still undefined. You don't need to question my intentions. I'll tell you where I stand. I'm right here with you. I . . . I'm not quite ready to talk life plans, but . . ." I swallow down any jaded feelings and look at this woman on top of me.

This is like a daydream and a nightmare all rolled into one. Tealey's admission is a game changer—a life changer, actually. It's the one thing I didn't think I'd ever hear her say, nor is it anything I ever thought I'd consider. It doesn't feel wrong, not at all, just quick. And with so many things between us undecided—Marlow, my promotion, Cammie and Cade's wedding shenanigans, and the newness of this whole damn thing—I just feel unprepared. And being unprepared is the worst sin in my book.

Still, losing her isn't an option, even if I'm not sure what the endgame is.

I stroke her hip with my thumb.

"I want to be your boyfriend," I tell her, "for now, until we get our feet under us and figure this out. What do you say to that, Tealey Bell? Will you be my girlfriend?"

The morning sun has wrangled free from the clouds, and the rays through the glass halo her soft, blond hair. Although her face is shadowed, I see embarrassment slipping away from her delicate features. "Do you mean that?"

"I mean it. I have no doubts whatsoever. You make me happy, and I want to do the same for you." I sit up and caress her shoulders before leaning in and kissing her.

She licks her lips when we part, and then says, "I don't question your intentions."

"I didn't mean to imply you didn't trust me. I know you wouldn't be here if you didn't." I can see the questions mounting in her expression, and fuck, if she needs to get things off her chest, I'll let her. "But you're wanting to know how I see things in the long term?"

"Not just with me but in life. How do you see your life? Where do I fit in? How do I fit in your life, in your home? And to throw more honesty your way . . . I stopped returning my real estate agent's calls last week. I've felt guilty for that, but I needed a break from the disappointment of not feeling I could afford something that you'd approve of. I haven't told you because I thought you might get mad."

"There's no expiration date on you staying here. And here's some honesty for you," I say, tapping her nose. "I like you being here, so don't settle for a place because you feel there's an imaginary deadline or you think you're in the way. You're not." The softness of her skin beckons me, and I rub along her leg, resting my hand where it meets her waist. "I want you to find a place that feels like home."

Like my place. I leave that unspoken between us. It may be how I feel, but I need to hold on to logic, not emotions.

"That means more to me than you know. Thank you." She buries herself in my arms.

"As for marriage," I start, but my throat clogs around the

last word, and I have to cough to dislodge it. Understanding her need to know what we are and what we're doing is relatable. It's something I think about and have fallen back on *just friends* as a means to an end. But it's not an answer to the question. It's an opportunity to think beyond today. "We've been friends for a long time now, and even though it does seem premature to have this talk in some respects, I understand why we might need to. We're not new to each other. We're in the dead center of the marrying age. It's all around us and even closer because of Cammie and Cade."

Her eyes are intent on me, not wanting to miss a word. I continue, "My parents' marriage didn't work out. I'm faced with the ugliness of divorce every day." I glance outside before returning to her, wanting to give her what she needs to hear while being honest about my own feelings. That's just it. I can be honest with her, and there's no judgment. "When I think about the future, I'm not spending my life alone. I'm not opposed to marriage. I respect the institution too much to damage it with my baggage, so it's always seemed unattainable for someone like me."

When I see her eyes glass over, I lie down and hold my arm open wide. She snuggles against me, and I wrap my arm around her. I say, "You want to get married one day. You've always been a romantic while I'm a cynic."

She shakes her head, angling it my way. "You want it to last forever. We're alike that way. Deep down, you're a romantic just like me, Rad."

"I don't want to disappoint you." I lose her blues to the far wall as we explore this new territory of sharing our deepest desires and worries. "All I can do is tell you how I feel right now. I've never been happier, and that's because of you. Despite what you think, the idea of being with you doesn't scare me."

"What scares you?"

The idea of being with *anyone* is new. It's been a long time since I dabbled in having a steady girlfriend. The strength of her hold on me hasn't lessened, the way her hands hold mine, and the way my heart holds hers.

"I was never scared to be with you. It's the thought of living without you that scares me."

29

Rad

I'm not sure what happened.

One minute, I'm living life like I always do, and the next, I'm one-half of a couple. I'm coupling. This is going to take some getting used to. Especially when my new girlfriend . . . *Girlfriend . . . Whoa.* I have a girlfriend.

Tealey sits on the bed with crossed legs, watching me choose a tie for court. She says, "Red's nice."

"Too aggressive for this judge."

"Blue is calming."

"Eh. I'm not feeling it." Watching the ties rotate on the holder, uninspired, I release the button, and it comes to a stop. "What does green say to you?"

She stares at me, slowly blinking before she falls back on the bed, kicking her legs in the air. "I don't know. This is exhausting. What does orange say? Purple? Yellow? Polka dot?" Propping herself up on her elbows, she says, "And here I thought facts and principles only mattered. Who knew a tie could make or break a case?"

"So burgundy then?" I grab the tie and loop it around my neck.

As if I've offended her, she stands with her hands on her hips. "I said red first."

"Burgundy isn't red. It's deeper. Richer. It says you can trust me, and my client should win."

Her gaze goes to my tie, and then, in disbelief, she eyes me again. "That's what you think that tie says?"

"Sure, to this judge."

"You pick your clothes based on the presiding judge?"

I'm lost to how she doesn't know this. Doesn't everybody plan their professional clothes around impressions and performance? I glance at her pants with another cat print, suddenly realizing maybe it doesn't matter in all fields. "Nice pants."

"Don't mock me just because you're absorbed by the shade of a tie in hopes it wins you the case. Next, you're going to say the material plays a role."

"Good point. Maybe I should go with the pure silk."

Throwing her arms up in the air, she storms to the door. Just inside the hall, she whips back around. "For your information, these pants are the cat's pajamas," she says, slowly enunciating the last two words.

"I get it. They're pajama pants."

"No." She huffs, shaking her head. "You don't get it. You know, like the bee's knees?" Staring at my blank face, she adds, "Cat's pajamas? *Oh, forget it.* They're awesome. That's all that matters." By seeing how bothered she is when she walks off, I start to wonder if we just had our first argument. *Shit.* I don't even know what it's about.

"Hey, Tealey?" I call, dipping my head into the hall. "So no on the burgundy?"

Her door slams closed. "Okay, I'll go with green. That color always brings me luck."

Before I head out, I stop by her room. Standing there, I begin to wonder how this will work exactly with her room and mine. Will we start shacking up in the same room, or will she want her space, like now? Will I want mine?

I don't think there will be an issue for me. I'll go where she goes, wherever she's most comfortable. I knock. "I'm sorry."

The door cracks open, and she's standing with a cocked eyebrow. "For what?"

Resting against the doorframe, I shrug. "I don't actually know, but I don't want you upset either."

She opens the door and steps into my arms. "Not everyone gets my humor."

"They're idiots."

"You didn't get the joke."

"Sometimes, I'm an idiot as well."

Squeezing me in her arms, she says, "You're not. Not at all." She walks to the kitchen but glances over her shoulder with a smile. "I like your tie. You look very handsome. I'm sure the judge will love it."

"Thanks," I reply coyly. She grins.

"I need to leave in a few minutes, but I wanted to talk about us once more."

"What do you want to talk about?" She hands me a bottle of water and then starts filling a cup with water from the faucet for herself.

"Marlow and her father are scheduled for a meeting today."

"Oh." There's a curtness in the simple response.

"It was supposed to be over lunch or dinner, but I had Ashleigh reschedule to meet at the office."

She perks up a bit. "I see."

Not sure why I'm holding back, but I need to get to my point. "The group gossips."

"They do," she replies and then takes a sip of water. "Is this about keeping us a secret?"

Thank God she said it. Now I don't feel shitty for bringing it up again.

She goes on, "I agree. I still don't have all the details, but what does it hurt to pretend you're together if it's only for her father? And, with the wedding just around the corner, we shouldn't take away the spotlight. Friends aside . . ." She comes closer and straightens my jacket. "I like that we have something that only we share, so I'm good with keeping *us* a secret."

Her nod is full of the same confidence I recognize from the day we met. She may have apologized for ruining my shirt back then, but she wasn't seeking forgiveness for how we did it. *How is it possible she's even more beautiful?*

I say, "We'll keep it until after the wedding. Just to be on the safe side."

Lifting onto her toes, she kisses my chin. "Do you know how sexy being sneaky can be?"

I kiss her because I struggle to keep my lips or hands off her. *She's too gorgeous not to touch.* Especially where I want to touch her repeatedly. *Fuck. Don't go there right now, Wellington.* "I hope I'm about to find out."

"Oh, you will indeed. Now go win those cases, so we can celebrate your victories."

I dip her, holding her low enough for her to give me her trust by relaxing in my arms. I kiss her and then set her back on her feet again.

She slides her hand down my neck and then lower to my chest. Tapping over my heart, she replaces her hand with her lips. "You need to go," she whispers. "The sooner you leave, the sooner you return to me."

"What about you? What will you be doing today?"

Walking toward the elevator, she wiggles her ass. She has no clue how I wish I had a job that I could cancel going in altogether. Court days are not those. "I'll be here waiting for you." There's lightness in her reply, a smile infiltrating her tone.

I punch the button and hold her one last time. In her bare feet, she fits right under my chin. "You have a date, Miss Bell."

The door opens too soon for my liking today. Her arms wrap around me, and she says, "Go be awesome, Counselor."

I kiss her forehead and step into the elevator. Just before the door closes, I give her a wink. "I always am."

STANDING across the street from the courthouse, Ashleigh greets me with a smile. "Nice tie. Green is always good luck."

I chuckle. "Do you know what cat pajamas are?" I raise my hand to run my fingers through my hair but stop because I don't want it a mess for court. I detour to the back of my neck and scratch instead.

"Pajamas for cats?"

"No." I furrow my brow. "Like as in the cat's pajamas," I say it slowly like Tealey did.

Ashleigh starts laughing. "Yeah, it's like great, awesome. The bee's knees."

"Do bees even have knees?"

"That's beside the point."

"Apparently." Why the fuck am I wasting time before court thinking about this? "Anyway, do you have the file?"

"We have thirty minutes before the hearing." Ashleigh digs the file from her burgundy leather briefcase. I'm starting to think this color and dressing for the job is a formality in the legal field. I'm going to owe Tealey another apology.

Ashleigh hands me a file, and I immediately open it to review. She says, "I secured an office for us to go over everything."

We start walking toward the doors of the building. I know this, though. Everything in this file is here because I entered it. I know my client's assets top to bottom, and every offshore account is accounted for. There shouldn't be any surprises unless the *missus* has been hiding something. *I hate surprises.* "Nothing's changed, and I've been going through it all in my mind for weeks now. I'm ready."

She nods. "You're ready."

"Maybe we grab a coffee instead?" We walk half a block in silence before I ask, "Why do you work at the law firm?" I open the door, and we enter the coffee shop. The sound of conversation and orders being called fills the air.

While we wait in line, she replies, "I don't just work there. I'm achieving my goal of being an executive assistant. I also believe in you, and we make a great team."

"We do."

After ordering our drinks, we sit at a table by the window. I shouldn't be exhausted, but I squeeze the bridge of my nose and can't help but ask, "Why do you believe in me? I'm a divorce lawyer, Ashleigh. You could work for any other type of attorney. I'm not changing the world. I'm not helping people in need. I'm breaking families apart and fighting to dismantle a life they built together while destroying their kids' lives in the process." She cocks her head to the side and stares at me like I'm out of my right mind.

"You've got it all wrong, Rad."

I never used to question what I was doing. I've wanted to be a divorce attorney since my family was ripped apart in the middle of a courtroom. I want to make a difference for kids in the same scenario. Ensure they aren't forgotten or used as bargaining chips—*something I refuse to do. Ever.* So why am I seeing my chosen path in life in a new light? "Do I?"

"Bear with me here." She sits forward, resting her hands on the table. "You're wrong about me willingly working for other attorneys. I work for you because you help people out of bad situations, situations that destroy them and the people around them. It's an ugly process that our world dictates, not you. You aren't tearing them apart. You're giving clients hope for a happier future." She stops and looks out the window, seeming to gather her thoughts. "You're more than your job, Rad," she says, her eyes on me. "You're a friend who stands by their side through one of the most difficult times of their lives. And that is why I work for you and not for the firm."

"Like I always say, everyone needs an Ashleigh on their side."

I'm grinning when she says, "Robert Marché canceled again. He's open for a video call next week, but he's stuck in California and can't get back to New York until after the fifteenth."

Personally, that suits me just fine. Professionally, I'm starting to wonder if he even wants this divorce by how much time he's spending back in LA. "He's focusing on business there while reassuring me that his priorities are here. It's not adding up. Can you verify the residency clause? He's walking a fine line, and I can't let him jeopardize my career by not protecting ourselves." Residency is not an issue I've encountered with a client before since they usually live here year-round. It's a given. I do know that if he's trying to get the sweeter deal by lying, that will play into the outcome.

When our names are called, I get up and wait at the counter, not wanting to think about the partner position or get lost in the weeds of the minutiae of my cases. I need a clear head for that.

Thinking about Tealey is much more entertaining, even with the topic of marriage coming at me sooner than expected. Marriage is something that I've let skate by whenever it was even hinted at by a woman. But I'm glad Tealey talked to me, even if it wasn't an easy conversation to have. She's making sure she's on a path that leads to what she wants. She's protecting herself, and I can respect that.

Knowing I'll see her in a few hours helps return my good mood. The way we've flirted for the past month has been fun, and then how we progressed to acting on those flirtations in the Hamptons.

In the last week alone, I've discovered she makes delicious deconstructed eggplant Parmesan and mixes a mean paloma cocktail.

The woman's got mad cooking skills, and though she carries doubts that her bedroom skills are up to par, I tell her the results speak for themselves. And then I apologize for coming so fast.

Retrieving the drinks, I notice how the paper cups are lacking in design. Tealey could fix that.

I set the cups down on the table and sit across from Ashleigh again. I open the file to review that everything is in order and all my paperwork is here as a backup to what I filed online. Ashleigh says, "Can I say something about your personal life? Share an observation?"

Some teens walk in, talking loudly, and cause me to look up. Returning my attention to Ashleigh, I say, "Of course."

"You dedicate so much time to your career that you seem to be searching for answers that can be found outside the office. You've always enjoyed the bachelor awards, but maybe that and your work aren't enough anymore."

We've tiptoed around this topic before. We both know I don't have a life and what I've sacrificed for my career. She only says this stuff because she cares and worries about me, so I'm not upset. But unfortunately, Tealey and I agreed just this morning that we wouldn't share our private lives with others. "Is there a question in there somewhere?"

"No. Just that I see the change. It's slow, but it's happening. Trust me, Rad, you're going to fall so hard you won't know what hit you. And then you'll finally see the light. All the pieces will fall into place after that, and hopefully, you'll find more work-life balance."

"The light? Why is it always about seeing the light?" I sigh, rolling my eyes.

"Did you just roll your eyes?"

"Did I?"

She laughs. "You did. That's new."

"I must have picked it up somewhere over the weekend."

With a knowing grin, she sing-songs, "Must have. Or someone has rubbed off on you."

She sees right through me. *Guilty as charged.* Tealey's definitely been rubbing off on me, and I on her. *Fuck.* Now I can't hide my smile. Ashleigh pounces. "Who has you smiling like that, boss?"

Handing her the file, I stand. I grab my briefcase with one hand and my coffee in the other. "As fun as it has been to analyze my life, let's get to court."

30

Tealey

Rad's magnetism puts women under a spell, and his charisma causes men to envy him. I've seen it firsthand. Rad Wellington is a gifted man when it comes to who he is on the inside, but my goodness, my heart and other parts are enjoying the full package.

Rolled-up shirtsleeves. A black and chrome watch on his wrist. That Adam's apple that dips down to tease me. His jaw that ticks when he's deep in thought . . . or greedily taking me in like he is now. Gah! It's too much!

I'm a lucky woman indeed because he came home to me.

His keys jingle around the hook, and he never breaks his stride on his way to me. A man on a mission. "Are you hungry?" I ask the giant of a man coming toward me. He takes hold of my head and sweeps my hair to the opposite shoulder.

I open myself up, my neck begging to be kissed, and Rad never disappoints. With warm lips against my rapidly heating skin, he breathes, "I don't want to eat food. I don't need anything to drink. I only want you. All I've thought about all day is being buried deep inside you."

"Um . . ." I start, my throat thickening under the intensity. "We should do that. Get right on it. Now's good for me."

His eyes darken in the dim lights of the living room as his pupils widen, devouring me as if I'm dinner instead of the treats I baked him today. The scrape of his tongue along the corner of his mouth mesmerizes me, but when his mouth presses to mine, he breathes life into me again.

Giving and taking, we share our feelings through our caresses without saying a word. The passion in his eyes pierces my skin as he takes in my rising and falling chest with each breath I can't contain. "Looking this good is dangerous for my career. I may never go back to work if you're here waiting."

I point my toe. "They're new leggings. Camo. I'm surprised you could even see me."

Victory is mine. I finally get him to smile.

"The *Friends* shirt gave you away."

"Ah, yes. Ross shouting 'pivot' is always a crowd-pleaser, but I have a feeling it's not my wardrobe you're referring to."

"No."

He dips and takes hold of the back of my legs, carrying me over his shoulder. My ass is squeezed, and then he gives me a good, hard smack. Launching up, I squeal through a fit of giggles. "I take it you won your cases?"

"Damn right, I did." *It all makes sense now.* I promised we'd celebrate his victories.

"Are you claiming your prize?"

Setting me on the bed, he's already tugging my socks off. "I'm claiming you. Hope your schedule is clear for the next few hours."

"Hours? Oh goodness." Starfishing on the mattress, I'm more than ready. "And here I baked cupcakes to celebrate."

Sliding my leggings down, he licks his lips. "Don't worry. We won't let them go to waste." He reaches down and unabashedly drags a fingertip through my lower lips. I suck in a harsh breath, holding it when he raises his finger and slides it into his mouth. "As a matter of fact—"

"I'm not putting a cupcake in my vagina."

He chuckles and then drags me by the legs until I'm wrapped around him. His hands drop to either side of my head, and he hovers over me. "Why eat a cupcake when I can eat you instead?"

Holy hell. I like the way this man thinks.

Standing back up, he kicks off his shoes and strips down until he's naked. He climbs onto the bed and lies down. "C'mere, baby."

I straddle him and then lift my top off. Being naked with him is becoming my favorite part of the day. And I'm pretty sure that's because Rad is incredible in bed.

Taking hold of my breasts, he kisses the tips and then sucks them until they're deep pink, ripe, and ready.

He seems to have a plan, but I'm already rubbing against him, too turned on to wait for direction. But then he says, "I want you on your hands and knees."

I'm scrambling to get into position.

My hair is gathered into one hand, and my hip is held with his other. The anticipation has me squeezing my middle and my eyes closing. The ripping of the packet and the sound of his moan blend. Tilting back, I want him so badly that I don't think I can wait.

Rad still takes his time to leisurely kiss my spine before his tip finds my entrance. I slide back again, this time being rewarded and filled. "Always in a hurry, faster, harder," he says, reminding me of my usual demands.

"I thought you were hungry."

"Oh baby, be careful what you wish for." He slams into me.

By the time I'm lying on the bed again, boneless with no energy and a smirk on my face, I say, "Sometimes wishes do come true."

~ Five Days Later ~

"Tealey?"

I come out of my daydream only to be greeted by an empty room, except for Cammie waiting at the door. Turning around, I discover everyone else has already left the bridal shower.

"How long has it been?" I jump up and grab my purse.

"Long enough for the others to leave."

Her arm wraps with mine, and she asks, "Was it that boring?"

"No." *Yes.* "The party was perfect." I just can't believe I'm living a fairy tale. Every minute away from Rad has me happily reliving every detail. "Do you love the gifts?"

"I do. I never thought I'd be excited over tumblers, but here I am, unwrapping each present, hoping to complete the set."

I'm not usually one for spoilers, but now I need to know. "Did you get them all?"

She holds up two fingers. "Missing two."

"I'll buy them for you."

She smiles. "Don't worry about it. Ten should be enough. When will I ever have ten people at my house anyway?"

"Well," I start, thinking about how to say this. "Marlow and her date. Jackson and his. Me and—"

"Your date," she says, then bites the inside of her cheek so hard I worry she's going to draw blood. "Well, you get what I mean. So? Have you been seeing anyone lately?"

"Oh. Um, you know. . ." I stop just inside the restaurant and toe the floor. I can see Marlow outside, and I don't want her to hear this conversation with Cammie. "I'm sticking close to home these days."

When I turn back, she's smiling like a Cheshire cat. "You called Rad's place home."

"Temporary home. Honest mistake." I try my best to shrug her off.

Her smile faltering, she sighs. "Well, as long as home is fulfilling, then things are all good."

I don't even understand what she's getting at. I wish I could tell her everything from how wonderful Rad is to me, kind and attentive when we're living like any other couple in the evenings, and then sweet to intense in the bedroom. I usually share everything with her, so it's hard to keep this a secret. Rad and I agreed not to tell them, so I need to stick with the plan.

She says, "Then if you have kids—"

"Me and Rad?" I jab my finger into my chest.

"No. Me and Cade. We might need twelve goblets for when we have kids."

My shoulders sag in relief. "I swear you said *you,* as in *me.*"

Laughing as though I'm not in on the joke, she says, "I mean the general you. You ready? That question is aimed at you, though."

"Yeah, definitely ready."

We push out the door and find Marlow standing there.

"There you are, Teals. Want to share a cab?" When I hesitate, she adds, "I'm paying."

"I'm happy to share then." I'm about to hug Cammie when I notice the corners of her mouth turned down. Reactionary crier here. Tears spring to my eyes. "Oh, Cam." I hug her, not sure why I'm feeling emotional all of a sudden. "Why are we crying?"

"I'm scared to enter a new phase in life. Am I losing my best friends?"

Marlow grins at her, sympathy resonating in her eyes. She wraps one arm around Cammie and one around me. "No," she says, "you're gaining a husband and a soul mate. We'll always be there when you need us."

"I've become such a sap," Cammie replies, sniffling along with a smile. Dabbing her eyes with a tissue she pulls from her pocket, she laughs. "Remind me to wear waterproof mascara for the wedding."

Huddling in again, I not only adore my friends but also love my sisters by choice. I say, "We have your back."

I lied. I do know why I'm on the verge of crying. With Cammie getting married, her priorities will shift, as they should, and we might not see each other as much. Then if she starts a family, things will be totally different.

I suspect we've all had similar thoughts. We're smack dab in the middle of major life changes that are personal and unique to each of us.

Although both of them appear to be in a hurry, I ask, "Has anything been decided about the venue?"

Cammie touches my arm. "You know, I'm really thinking about taking Amanda up on her offer."

"You should," I say. "It's so beautiful there, and she's thrown a million parties. She'd have this planned in a week."

Marlow primps her hair. "Prepare for the wind, but nothing a great hairspray can't handle."

Nodding, Cammie says, "So I should do it?"

Excited for my friend, I take her hand. "You should. It's going to be perfect in the Hamptons."

"Yeah, maybe this is meant to be. And since we had to use the hotel for our vendors, we lost everything from the caterer to the florist. They've returned our money, which frees it up to spend again." Her phone rings. "Speaking of, it's Amanda. Gotta run. Thank you for everything and the gifts."

Marlow says, "Enjoy the gravy boat."

I'm not sure if Marlow's being sarcastic, but Cammie laughs as she walks away. Turning back to face us, she says, "I will. Gravy for every occasion."

"I can't wait," I reply, laughing.

Marlow says, "I don't like gravy."

"We've had this discussion before. It's gelatinous to you, but I could eat a vat of cream gravy. So good."

"And so Southern of you."

I shrug unapologetically. Now that I'm thinking about it, I should cook chicken fried steak with cream gravy for dinner. I bet Rad would love it.

When we start for the curb, Marlow checks her phone. From where I stand at her side, I can read the message on the screen: *Wear the red.*

"Wear the red? Sounds sexy," I say, pursing my lips to the side, trying to figure out who she's going to see. "Hot date?"

"It's nothing." The phone is quickly dropped into her purse, and suddenly, everything is way more interesting than me. She's great at avoiding topics that make her uncomfortable, but I still see right through her.

I'd love to give her a hard time and dig for more details,

but even in five-inch heels, she's taking the lead. She hails a cab, and of course, two speed her way. Dressed to kill in a pale pink dress and black heels will do it. She climbs in the back just as I reach the taxi.

She gives the driver directions and then sits back, clutching her purse.

"If you don't want to talk about some guy you're seeing, that's fine, but can we talk about Rad?" I ask.

Rad always says my eyes are beautiful, but Marlow's are striking and piercing when she doesn't want to discuss a certain topic. Like now.

When she doesn't say anything, I say, "I've heard a little about this, but I guess I'm wondering when the charade ends?"

Shrugging, she asks, "What's the hurry? We're not hurting anyone."

Except me, though technically, I don't have a right to that claim. They aren't hurting me at all. *But the thought of them even pretending is starting to bug me more and more.* Among others, this is one of the reasons I can't share my happiness with my friends. *And why isn't she in a hurry to end it?*

Marlow always gets the guy. Now I'm dating the only one I've ever dreamed of, and for him to even pretend to date her feels like a slap in the face of our relationship. Maybe I'm being irrational. They haven't done anything, and they don't plan to, other than put on a little show for her dad. What's the harm in that?

Maybe there is none. . .

"Just curious. It's a little odd to scheme your dad out of an apartment."

Offense tightens her lips. "We're not scheming, Tealey. He *wants* to give me the apartment."

"Under the guise of being with Rad." I hate how angry I sound. It even catches her off guard.

"Why are you so upset, Tealey? Why do you even care?" Something dawns in her eyes before I can think of how to answer that. "Are you jealous?"

And there it is . . . laid out in the simplest form.

I am jealous of their fake relationship. It makes no sense other than I want him all to myself. Leaning forward, I ask the driver, "Do you mind turning up the air-conditioning?"

"Oh, my God," she says, sitting back and angling her knees toward me. "You're jealous. Why? Why would you be . . . Ah. Only you're allowed to have a crush on Rad."

"You have a crush on Rad?"

She stares at me, her expression kicked into neutral. When she sighs, she faces forward again. The silence is killing me, so I start tugging at a loose thread on my shirt's hem. Seconds feel torturously long and turn into minutes. I glance out the window, knowing we'll be approaching Rad's building soon.

Desperate to get answers and then smooth things over before I have to leave, I ask, "Marlow?"

Her sigh is heavier this time, filled with disappointment, like her eyes when she looks at me. "I don't have a crush on Rad. I never did, and I don't now." The car pulls to the curb.

Her tone is steeped in anger, and she looks away from me again.

Having her mad at me hurts, and I'm not sure I can fix this before costing her a fortune in cab fare. "I'm sorry." Lifting her chin minutely, she continues to stare ahead. "I think it's best if I just leave—"

"Yes," she adds.

I open the door and wade through the quicksand of

emotions as I get out of the vehicle. I can't leave it like this. Turning back, I lower my head. "Marlow, I'm—"

"It doesn't bother me that you think I have a crush on Rad. He's the type I usually date—attractive, great body, even better career, and financially well off."

Though I'm tempted to roll my eyes, I don't because it will only add fuel to the fire. This time, I keep my mouth shut. She continues, "So it's not a great leap to assume we'd make a great couple. We're a match on many levels. But what hurts is you think I'd act on it, knowing how you feel about him." She grabs the handle of the door and slams it shut.

The cab pulls away, leaving me standing with my jaw on the sidewalk and a spike through my heart.

Marlow is not my enemy, like Kayla. She's the opposite, my best friend. Of course, she'd never hurt me. I just wish that while they get to go public with their arrangement, I wasn't stuck hiding the real thing.

Just a few more weeks, I remind myself as I head for the apartment. Why'd I let jealousy get in the way of my friendship? I stop and pull out my phone. Texting Marlow, I type: *I'm sorry. I know you'd never hurt me.*

The three dots wave across the screen, not coming soon enough. When they disappear, a message replaces them: *I appreciate that because I wouldn't, but I worry that you're going to be hurt when he starts dating someone seriously. Maybe it's time for you to start dating again. I know this great guy, an art collector, who could take your mind off Rad. I'll shoot him a text.*

Panicking, I start typing: *No.*

Me: *I'm good.*

Me: *I don't need to be set up.*

Me: *I'm good.*

Crap! I already typed that.

Marlow: *Too late. He said yes to being your date to the wedding.*

Beyond a million reasons I can think of why I don't need my friends setting me up, everything from I don't need a man to complete me to dealing with enough life changes at the moment, only one matters most.

Rad.

31

Tealey

A WARM SHOWER clears my head but doesn't wash away my sins.

I'm about to shut off the water when the door opens. I turn to find Rad—shirtless with only his boxer briefs on. "Want some company?"

He makes it hard to say no, but I need to, for me. "Will you hate me if I say no?" I ask, setting the soap down.

"No."

"No," I say with a heavy sigh.

"Rough bridal shower? It's not even five, and you look exhausted."

"I am. Emotionally."

Reaching in, he tips my chin up. "Do you want to talk about what's making you so sad?"

Do I? Do I want to reveal how I got jealous over a relationship that doesn't even exist? *Kind of* . . . just to get it off my chest. "Marlow and I got in a fight."

His eyes jump from my chest to my eyes, losing some of the intimacy we just had. "We should probably wait to talk about that. I have a hard-on looking at my girlfriend naked in the shower. Not something I want to be sporting when we're talking about our friends. That just feels . . .*wrong*."

"Good point," I say, using one of his favorite phrases as I turn the lever. "I'll be out in a minute."

With my hair wrapped in a towel and my most cozy, aka comforting, pj's on, I walk into the living room where Rad is watching a game. Looking over his shoulder, he says, "I take it today didn't go well?"

"I accused her of liking you." I plant myself on the arm of the couch opposite of him.

Staring at me, I don't think he blinks for a solid thirty seconds. "And why would you do that?"

"Honest answer? Jealousy."

Confusion has him shaking his head. "Why would you be jealous of Marlow?"

He makes it sound like such an impossibility to be jealous of a five-foot-seven blond beauty who's prettier than any actress in the movies. She's wealthy, funny, and has great style. What's not to be jealous of? "That you two get to be public when we have to hide what we are."

His brows cinch together. "Marlow and I aren't in public together, not more than friends when the six of us hang out. It's only for her dad, and we haven't even had to perform."

"Yet."

"Yet is correct." He moves closer, leaning forward to rest his hands on my legs. "I know this makes no sense. Believe me when I tell you that it didn't make any sense to me either. But sometimes, we do things as a means to an end. The partners at the firm knew I was having a meeting with Bob Marché, and they expected me to close it to make sure our firm was attached to his case. So I couldn't walk away."

"You couldn't walk away from Bob, but why couldn't you walk away from Marlow on this one thing?"

He rubs his hands down the back of my legs, pausing to hold my calves. When he looks back at me, he says, "It felt like a package deal."

"You work off logic and reasoning, not feelings, Counselor. Why the change in direction this time?"

"My honest answer," he starts, looping to what we should always be—honest. "I don't know. She was trying to talk me into it. I said no at first, but then in some twisted dimension of my brain, she started to make sense. Add in the pressure I feel from the partners to keep her dad as a client, and I can't explain it more than that. But I did make a commitment—to her and the firm."

He runs off logic, but I can't seem to explain his reasoning to my heart. I only know how it makes me feel. "So it doesn't matter what I say? You're going to continue this charade?"

"I made a promise," he says with finality, giving me a peek into his attorney side.

"And you made me your girlfriend."

That's the difference when it all boils down. I could overlook the Marlow thing when Rad and I were just having fun, when I didn't really have a say in anything. But he asked me to be his girlfriend, and for some reason, that makes this thing with Marlow feel different.

Shouldn't it matter what I think? Shouldn't he take my feelings into consideration? I know Rad. He's always so thoughtful. Maybe that's why it feels more like the tip of a betrayal digging into my heart this time.

His jaw hardens, but his eyes remain softer, gazing upon

me—his aura a dichotomy. "Are you making me choose, Tealey?"

Getting to my feet again, I shake my head in frustration and take a deep breath to help stave off the sadness threatening to fill my chest. "No, Rad. I can't make you do the right thing." I start for my bedroom, aware that this conversation is not only coming to an end but also hitting rock bottom. I need to end it before we both say something we'll regret.

He asks, "Is it so wrong?" I stop just shy of the door. "When no one's getting hurt?" *That's what Marlow said.*

I glance back. "You sure about that?"

The first crack in my heart was felt in the cab with Marlow. I didn't expect it to break with Rad altogether.

I shut my door and climb into bed. I can smell his cologne lingering on the pillow, the sheets still rumpled from this morning. We've staked claim to both beds like we always knew we'd have the luxury of using both. Now, lying here with the early evening light sneaking in through the blinds, I start to wonder if we were occupying both so we'd always have the option to return, if needed.

Is it needed?

My heart races, my breathing shallow. I push up on my hands and hate this—all of it. The situation, that it feels like there are sides to choose, and most of all, my jealousy.

These two people are my friends, and I know they aren't out to hurt me. *I know that.* This scenario was in place before I moved in, and I need to give them a bit of grace as they try to navigate it. At least until Rad makes partner.

My emotions swirling, I'm quick to the door. But when I pull it open, he's already standing outside it.

His eyes search mine with a tenderness, a softness that punches me in the heart.

"I'm sorry," I say, embracing him.

Wrapping his arms around me, he kisses my forehead. "You don't have to be."

"But I am."

He takes my hand and leads me to the windowsill, where we sit across from each other. "Look, Tealey, this is an unusual situation. We thought it made sense to hide our relationship for the time being. Things change. We evolve. And though we just made that decision, it's not set in stone." Bridging the gap that divides us, he caresses my cheek. I lean into his comfort as he takes my other hand and kisses my palm. "I don't want us to hide. That's how I feel inside. The man who wins awards for staying single wants to show the rest of the world how I feel."

I kiss his palm and then hold it between us, realizing that though this is hard to talk about, I'm glad I did. "Real sounds very official, Mr. Wellington."

Taking my hands, he brings me in closer and then leans in so we're just a breath apart. "It *is* official. You feel right." Our lips meet in the middle again, and then he adds, "You. This. And us. I'd shout it from the rooftops if that's what you want."

My smile comes quick, my heart turning from ice to a blazing fire because of the lack of shame in his confession. "What do you suggest?"

His eyes are set, a determination tightening his brows. "What you need matters to me."

My heart constricts. "I know, and I appreciate that. But what you want and need matters to me, too. And I know the promotion is important. I shouldn't have put you in that spot . . . I was just jealous."

"I didn't make it easy, but I do want to make it up to you." His expression is bright, as if all the solutions we've been searching for have been found. "We start by telling our friends and family, the people who matter most." These are the words I was craving to hear, but at what cost am I getting what I want?

It's not just the two of us in this relationship. There are six, and I can't pretend what's happening in their lives doesn't matter. "What about Cammie and Cade's wedding?"

Sincere eyes that warm my insides when he looks into mine shine light into the nooks and crannies of my heart, finding a way to fill them. "You know they'll be happy for us." He grins. "I want this with you. No more apartment-only dates or hiding how we feel at dinner with our friends. We walk around holding hands when we want to. We kiss if we feel like kissing. Is that something you want with me?"

My smile is wide and bright at the idea of being together outside of the apartment. "Of course," I reply without hesitation, getting a taste of a future that felt unattainable before. "I don't remember a time when I didn't. I only remember resisting the urge to breathe life into my dreams."

A sense of relief washes through his strong features. "I'll just assure Marlow that I'll play my part with her father." Holding me firmer around my lower back, he says, "But I'm not willing to sacrifice what makes you, Tealey Bell, and me happy."

"I want that. It helps Marlow and you, but it gives me something to hold on to."

I bend back, soaking in the sunshine of this new opportunity before hugging him and kissing his neck. He says, "When we're ready, whenever you're ready, we can go public for the rest of the world to see how happy you've made me." We kiss, and it deepens quickly.

When I catch my breath, I say, "You're such a romantic." The words fall from my tongue. What a change we've become. From attraction to friends to lovers and now all those wonderful things rolled into one—*together*.

I WAKE before my alarm goes off. Reaching over, I don't find my phone on the nightstand. I sit propped up on my elbows and look around.

With his eyes still closed, Rad mumbles, "What are you doing?"

"I thought I was in my room."

His arm slides over my middle, and he pulls me across the sheet to him. I smile, running my nails over his tan shoulder. He says, "You're in mine."

"I know. But I'm starting to think we're living together but still on our own."

His eyes finally open. "Huh?"

I lie back down, facing him. Tucking my hands under my cheek, I ask, "I know it's fast to move in together, but we've already done it. My room feels so far from you sometimes."

Since he's barely awake, I'm probably not catching him at a great time, but what's time when you're in bed with your boyfriend?

Turning to grab his watch from the nightstand, he squints through the low light of early morning to check the time. He sets it back down and then scrubs his hands over his face. "It's 5:45 in the morning. You're going to have to help me out here."

I wave my hand between us and the door. "Our rooms are so far apart in this place that I might as well still live in Brooklyn."

"I've still got nothing, Tealey. You'll have to spoon-feed it to me."

Not sure what he's not understanding, I huff and sit back up. "Why are we still existing in two rooms?"

Now I have his attention—eyes wide open, line between his brows. "You want to move into my room? You're already here."

"I want us to get ready for bed and work together, to have a set space that we go to without asking 'my place or yours' every night. Sure, it's funny, but it's starting to feel like a barrier instead."

Flipping the covers off his body, he gets out of bed and stretches. As he heads for the bathroom, he says, "You can move into my room on one condition."

"Name it."

He returns to me and pulls off the covers, letting his gaze graze down my body. "You take your shower with me in the mornings."

I flop back down on the bed with my hands behind my head and my ankles crossed, soaking in this victory. "I have no problem with that."

"Then you have yourself a deal." His head signals toward the bathroom. "Deal starts now. Get that sexy ass in there."

SITTING at my desk a few hours later, I hear Misty Connor asking for me. I stand. "I'm here. Come on back."

Her eyes meet mine, and she walks down the corridor created by the cubicles, stopping when she reaches mine. I smile, noticing that she's holding her head up and looking me in the eyes. "Hi, you weren't here last week when I came by."

Remembering my day of playing hooky, I try not to let guilt from missing work set in. It's a hard habit to break, though. "Sorry I missed you. I was out that day. Have a seat. I'd like to hear an update."

She sits in the chair, setting the brown purse at her feet. Although it's a gentler smile she's wearing, it's more than any I've seen on her before. She says, "Mr. Wellington has helped my case tremendously. I actually have hope that it's going to work out how it's supposed to. Deacon hasn't violated the restraining order despite threats that he would."

"You need to report those threats. A record of certain types of behavior is critical for a judge to side in your favor."

"Yes. My attorney went over everything that he set up. I can't thank you enough, Tealey. Rad has been a blessing, and he's so nice. You said you were friends, but when I mentioned you, he looked different. I don't mean to pry, but I can tell he thinks very highly of you."

I try not to, but I smile. "I appreciate that, Misty. I don't normally discuss my personal life with clients, so please forgive me."

"No. No." She raises her hands in front of her. "I understand. Just thought it was worth mentioning."

I can feel my heart racing like Rad and I share more than a bedroom now. Our lives have entwined in a way that makes me glad I took a chance involving him. "Do you have time to go over the benefits?"

"Yes, that's why I came. I spoke to a social worker in Philadelphia near where my mom lives."

"If you need me, I can help with the transfer and verifications."

I can't stop looking at how different she appears—healthier, less burdened by life, no bruises or black eyes.

She says, "There's a lot of paperwork. I'm surprised it's not all in the system."

"It's an antiquated system, but we're working on getting it updated." I slide my keyboard closer and type in her name to pull up her file.

"Mr. Wellington suggested I consider serving the divorce papers in the next week. That would give me time to get us moved to Philly and find a job before school starts."

Though she's not asking, I'm not in a position to offer advice. "I can't offer you legal advice, but I would trust Mr. Wellington with my life." And my heart, but that's too personal to mention.

I don't have much time, but I have enough to set her up with a resource director in Philly as well as a contact from one of the social services' offices near her mom's house. As soon as she's gone, Lowell dips his face over the dividing wall. "Come to my office, Tealey."

As soon as I know the clients waiting up front are situated with another social worker, I trek back to Lowell's office. Knocking twice on the door with my knuckle causes him to look up. "Come in and take a seat." I move around the chair to sit, but he stops me. "Close the door first."

That's something he could have told me from the beginning. I do it begrudgingly and then sit down. I don't bother asking questions when I know he's happy to tell me what displeases him.

He says, "From my understanding, you left our protocols at the door to find a lawyer who you approved versus what the state of New York deems appropriate to help a client. I don't like people who step outside the lines. What makes you think you know better than all the people who came before you?" *What the actual hell?* He is such an asshole.

"I don't think I'm smarter. I did what I had to do, which

was find a better lawyer than the advisor she was assigned. That's not going outside of my job description, but actually fulfilling it." I stand, ready to leave this nonsense behind. Let him write me up if he so chooses. I can defend my decision to help my clients. Unlike him.

I open the door and start to leave but stop with the doorknob in my hand when he says, "I'm reassigning you to Poughkeepsie."

My stomach drops as I try to process what he just said. I turn back with my mouth wide open. "Poughkeepsie?"

His chair squeals in protest when he relaxes back in it. Holding a pen in his hands, he says, "I believe it will be a good fit for you."

I have no idea if he's flipping the bird to my career or taking our personal conflicts out on me. "Isn't it great news?" he asks, his tone so flat that I'm still trying to figure out if he's telling the truth.

"Are you for real?" My composure is all but gone, and my emotions are shredded. I'm not sure if I should feel angry or sad.

"I'm for real, all right." He cackles like all evil humans do and clicks the keyboard like he's setting a pack of dogs free to attack me.

"I already approved your transfer. They'll let us know in the next few weeks when you'll be starting." Like an electric shock shooting right through me, I'm astounded by his boldness.

"Why would you do that without consulting me?"

"Because I figured one job in Poughkeepsie was better than no job at all."

Angry works. "You're firing me?"

"No. We have budget cuts. It makes no sense to fire Peggy because she's leaving."

Still struggling to comprehend, I ask, "I don't have a job in this office anymore?"

"That's what budget cuts mean. I have spots for two, and . . .it's easier to let you know so you have time to figure out what you're going to do. I heard you still haven't found a place to live." Lowell leans forward, stabbing his elbows into the worn wood of his desk and folding his fingers together. "This is the sign you've been waiting for. Make the move and start fresh with a new crew."

My temper flares, and my hands fist at my side. *How dare he!* He may see me as meek, but I'm stronger than he can ever imagine. I won't walk away quietly.

"What if I don't want to start fresh? I've earned my position in this office, Lowell. Not even for you. I do a good job. You've never received a complaint. My record is clear. It's glowing, in fact. Tell me the real reason I'm being cut." My heated emotions begin to subside. "Not that I want any of the others to move either. They have family in the area. Kids in the local schools . . ." *And then it all begins to make sense.*

32

Rad

I stared at the two invitations.

Two opposite ends of the relationship spectrum with an obligation that doesn't allow me to turn either of them down. One celebrates two people choosing to spend their lives together. The other celebrates being single.

Both have strings attached . . .

Ashleigh taps the top of the desk. "Yes, to both, I assume?"

"Yes." I pick them up and shove them in a side drawer of my desk. I could take time justifying each, but I'm thinking Tealey won't see it the same way. But if she agrees to be my date, she'll see the Big Apple Most Eligible Bachelor Awards is not a ploy to get laid.

"Thank you," I add when Ashleigh stands to leave, turning my attention to the computer monitor.

She straightens a few files on my desk but continues to linger. I watch her go from the folders to the pens to the legal pads. Her fidgeting is distracting, so I ask, "What's going on?"

Dropping back into the chair, she says, "I need to talk to you about something."

I glance at the time to see how many minutes I can spare. "Now is good." I angle my chair to face her and wait. Eight minutes isn't a lot of time, but I'm confident we can address anything that needs immediate attention.

"I'm pregnant."

I'm pretty sure I blink but can't say one hundred percent. The more selfish thoughts run across my mind: *How will she juggle the demands of the job with a newborn? Or will she leave altogether?*

She holds her hand up, stopping my mind from its thoughtless reeling. *Thank God.* She says, "It's a shock. It was for me as well. I even waited for the lab results before I could process what was happening. Now I'm starting to adjust to the idea of having a baby and how this will change my life." She laughs to herself. "It's a big change, but I've always wanted kids, so I know that will work out how it's supposed to. But I worry how it will affect my career."

I sit back in my chair and watch the emotions play out in her eyes. She's been my right-hand for so many years. She's a good person, a good friend, and she's damn good at her job. She'll also be a damn good mother.

Why should she have to choose between her child or her career?

My mind goes to Tealey, and I know what she would choose. I know what I would want her to choose. And the thought of her being in that situation—and of her being pregnant with my child—creates a lump in my throat that I'm not ready to deal with.

"It won't," I say. "I'll make sure of it." A gentle smile

appears, and she looks apprehensive for the first time since I've known her. "The thing is . . ." She glances back up. "I don't want to hold you back, Rad. You need someone—"

"No." I'm already shaking my head, and that in and of itself is a mindfuck. "We do this together, remember?" She smiles in relief.

"I'm grateful to have you as my boss."

What am I doing? This is Ashleigh, my friend. I finally stand and move around my desk to sit in the chair next to her. "I'm grateful to have you every step of the way. Congratulations on the baby. It's wonderful news."

She scrunches her expression. "I know it's not something we usually do, but I was thinking this one time, we could take off our professional hats and set them aside for a hug?"

I nod once. She moves her stuff from her lap to my desk, and we both stand to hug. It's awkward, not going to lie. She's become a sister to my legal family and someone I care about. She must feel the same because we give each other a good job pat on the back right before stepping back.

The door flies open, and Marlow runs into my office. "It's showtime, Rad. Hurry. Hurry." Marlow mimes zipping her lip, waiting for Ashleigh to leave.

While Ashleigh gathers her things from my desk, I say, "Don't barge into my office, Marlow. I could have been with a client or on a call."

With her hand sliding through the air, like she's presenting evidence, she replies, "But you weren't. Lucky, I caught you, I guess." *I caught you.* I swear I fucking hear it in her tone. She crosses the rest of the distance, but I'm already returning to my side of the desk.

Ashleigh asks, "Do you need anything before your meeting?"

"No, thank you." I'd like to say more, but it's not my place to share her good news. As soon as she leaves, Marlow sits down. "My dad said he has a meeting with you and would like to see the two of us together."

Glaring at her, I say, "We need to discuss his divorce. I don't have his permission—"

"He won't mind." She blows me off. I roll my eyes, and she adds, "You look like Tealey when you do that."

"Or you, from what I remember." She narrows her eyes.

"True, but I picked it up from Tealey. She has no patience for the absurd."

Based on her wardrobe and cup collection, I could argue the opposite, but they've grown on me. I could have never imagined her tchotchkes could live in harmony with my minimal approach to clutter. Even more surprising is how well I've adapted to it. *Got to give me a little credit here.*

My video call comes to life, but I only see Robert Marché's nose. "You're too close, Bob," I say.

"Daddy, back up from the camera." Marlow is behind me, resting her hands on my shoulders as she peers at the screen.

"I'm not that old." He sits back, lounging in a large red leather office chair. "I was getting this from Lorie." Lorie? *His soon-to-be-ex-wife-who-is-challenging-every-claim-we-make Lorie?* He holds up a piece of paper.

Marlow nuzzles the top of my head. Jerking back, I ask, "What are you—?" A knuckle grinding into my back puts that question to bed. *Oh, right.* It's showtime. The back of my neck is pinched because I'm screwing this up somehow. Just wish I knew what she wanted me to do.

I cover her other hand with mine for two reasons: effect and to stop her from trying to hurt me. Since Bob is waggling the paper in front of the camera with a big grin on his face, I ask, "What is that?"

"It's our official declaration to end the war." *Fuck me. Does this mean what I think it does?*

"And by ending the war, what do you mean exactly?" My gut tightens. I can read into his words, but I'm going to need this spelled out for me. Clearly, if my career is going up in flames in front of the partners, I deserve the courtesy of making sure I understand.

Lorie pops into the frame of the camera, rubbing Bob's shoulders. Internally, I roll my eyes because aren't we both just the happy couples...

I've seen her in movies and in interviews. I had to watch to make sure my case was airtight. But seeing her now, sans makeup and dressed in workout clothes, I observe a different side of the famous actress most will never see. Simply looking happy, she says, "This is us agreeing to be together." Her gaze flits back and forth between Marlow and me. "And we want to invite you both to the vow renewal we're having in Maui at the house."

I expect a big reaction from Marlow, something more over-the-top—an outburst or tantrum—per usual. But I don't even hear her swallow.

Over my shoulder, I look up at her but find her expression unreadable. So I spin in the chair, causing her hands to drop away. "Marlow, are you okay?"

She nods, but it's exaggerated. I can only imagine that this announcement has come as a shock. She once said she didn't even bother to get to know her stepmoms anymore, but does she hate the idea of her dad being married so much that she's lost her spirit to fight?

If she can't lead this conversation, I need to step in for both of us. I grasp her hand, which causes her to finally look at me. With my back to the camera, I whisper, "It's going to be okay."

She nods, and as if a switch was flipped, she comes alive for the camera. Throwing her arms in the air, she claps her hands together. "That is such great news. Congratulations. And, yes, of course, we'll be there. We wouldn't miss it." Not going to happen. Not on my watch. I just got out of the doghouse with Tealey because of this arrangement, so no, I won't be flying to Maui with Marlow.

No way. No how.

Bob says, "I'm happy, sweetheart." He kisses Lorie.

"I know," Marlow replies as if she was asked for permission. "I can see it."

Resting his arms forward on his desk, he says, "So about the divorce, Wellington. How do we put this to bed since we're not moving forward?"

I feel sick. There goes making partner. I bet they give it to Rogers, who's been fighting Big Pharma for victims. He has that advantage because it's a more noble legal field.

Do I have a right to feel disappointed that I'm losing an opportunity when he's keeping his marriage together? Sure. I give myself a few seconds to grieve a promotion that was mine to lose. A part of me is angry that I lost it based on Bob dangling a carrot like I'd be a made man if I took his case. I'm also disappointed, but with Ashleigh pregnant and eventually taking leave, maybe now's not my time?

And then there's Tealey. She's making me see things differently. With this hurdle out of my path, I can start being with Tealey and put an end to the strain this charade has caused.

Seeing Bob smiling—and how happy Lorie is—makes me say, "I wish you the best." And I genuinely mean it. "I can send the paperwork that will terminate the proceedings if everything is remaining the same. If you're reevaluating the assets or decide to alter the prenuptial agreement, I can handle that for you."

He says, "We'll talk about it and let you know at the wedding." Yeah, not taking that trip. *Pretending on video call is bad enough.*

I say, "I'm not sure I can get to Maui—"

"No, Cammie and Cade's. I got the invitation today and RSVP'd that Lorie and I will be there since we were already planning a visit to the Hamptons."

Lorie dips back onto the screen. "I hear wedding bells are in the future. Maybe we can look at rings while I'm in New York, Marlow." If only I weren't on camera right now . . . "And we can start planning your wedding. Bond over girl stuff like that. Two brides-to-be."

Gobsmacked, I hold my breath. It's best for all of us.

Marlow's hands return to my shoulder, and she squeezes. "A ring?" I hear the discomfort in her tone, and hope for our sakes, they don't. "You know, I'll leave that to Rad. He has exquisite taste, and I love surprises."

"I'm sure you'll have it back by the wedding." Lorie kisses Bob again and says, "We need to start getting ready. The Mercers give us a hard time when we're late."

He turns back to us, and says, "Thank you for the great work you did, Rad. Send the bill over, and I'll add a little something on top for your efforts."

"It doesn't work like that." I'm quick to correct him. "We don't work on tips."

"No matter then. It will get settled. Some more good news is that I finally got a response from the owner of the apartment. They're open to negotiation. The next step is making an offer, so I'll put that in this week. And I guess I'm seeing you two lovebirds in two weeks. Bye."

The screen of my monitor goes blue, and I spin back to Marlow, who's taken a step back. "Fuck," I say, scrubbing my hands over my face and then taking a deep breath.

She says, "If you'll excuse me. I'm going to need some time to process what just happened."

So do I, but more so, we need to renegotiate our arrangement since I no longer have a stake in the game. I'm about to barrage her with questions, but she says, "I know this just got even more complicated, but . . ." Taking her purse, she slides it to her elbow and walks to the door. "Can we discuss this later?"

Yes, I have a lot of damn questions, but she's acting so out of character that I'm wondering if I should be concerned. "Sure. Call me if you need anything."

"I will." As if something else occurs to her, she glances back at me. "I'm glad you'll be at the wedding. I may need your support."

"You have it, Marlow. Always."

"Thanks." She smiles—it's small but genuine. "Since Cammie and Cade are the guests of honor, they'll be busy. And now that Tealey has a date, I'm glad I have you."

What?

"What do you mean Tealey has a date?"

Her smile is brighter, matching her eyes. "I finally got her to agree to go out with Jean-Luc. He's French and so cute. She's going to eat him alive."

"She better fucking not."

"Why not?"

Fuck, did I say that out loud? "Kidding."

"Oh," she replies, accepting that at face value. *Thank fuck.*

She sighs, not quite shaking off the call with her dad. "Anyway, we'll talk soon."

I wait for the door to close to grab my phone to call Tealey, but then it opens again. "I already said not to barge in—" *Shit. Shit. Shit.*

And there stand Klein and Sable, the senior partners, the names on the letterhead, and my bosses. Irritation is wrangled in the lines of their faces. Mrs. Klein says, "Is everything all right, Mr. Wellington?"

"Yes." I stand, trying to shake off the shrapnel from the bomb Marlow just dropped. "How can I help you?"

Mrs. Klein is more soft-spoken; that's how she takes down her opponent. They misjudge her for weak, but she's always quiet before she attacks her prey. She walks into the room and starts pacing the length of the office.

Mr. Sable, a husky guy who uses his impressively large shoulders to intimidate, gets right to the point. They have a good cop/bad cop relationship that's worked well for them. "We wanted to come by and tell you we appreciate your hard work. I know we've said that before, but you've really notched it up to a new level."

"Thank you," I say, sliding a hand down my tie. "I appreciate you noticing."

"How is the Marché case going?" Mrs. Klein asks.

My mouth goes dry as my brain shuffles back to work. I have to pivot and quickly figure out how to make this situation work for me.

"I have great news," I say, thinking on my feet. "The Marché account is basically closed. Everyone is happy."

Mr. Sable raises a brow. "Really? That seems fast?"

"Yes. It turns out that Mr. Marché was able to save his marriage, thanks, in part, to the approach we took when dealing with Mrs. Marché."

Mrs. Klein looks surprised. "That's nearly unheard of at this level, Mr. Wellington. You do know that, don't you?"

My spirits lift because this may work. "I do. It was a risky strategy, but I felt it was the right one. I'm pleased with how it worked out, as is Mr. Marché."

Mr. Sable nods approvingly. "Well done." He gives his partner a quick look and then switches his gaze back to me. "I think it's safe to say the partnership is yours if you don't fuck it up before the board meeting." Normally, I'd take Ashleigh to lunch and celebrate this news. But it feels like an empty win without sharing it with Tealey, so I just add it to the list of other items we need to discuss.

"I won't," I say with a certainty I don't feel inside. When they leave, I click through my schedule to find the date of the next board meeting. *One month.*

That's a lot of time to screw things up.

It may be too late for my personal life. I grab my phone from the desk because I have too many questions running through my head to even think about work. Like why is she taking a date to Cammie and Cade's wedding?

And who the fuck is Jean-Luc?

33

Tealey

"Who's Jean-Luc?" The elevator door hasn't even closed before the words tumble from his mouth.

"I don't know," I reply. "Who *is* Jean-Luc?" I sit up from the couch, resting my forearms on the back of it, waiting for a kiss. It's the usual drill—closed eyes, pursed lips, and a wish that your prince charming will hurry the heck up.

"You tell me." The kiss is quick, too quick, and it felt more obligatory than coated with sweetness like his regular kisses. I let it slide because I like this guessing game. I'm also two glasses of wine in for the night, thanks to Lowell and my crappy day. S*oooo* . . . I cannot be held responsible for my actions.

"After the day I had, this is fun. Like a mystery. Give me a hint. Nothing major. Just something to send me in the right direction."

"What are you talking about, Tealey?"

My humor is clearly lost on him tonight. That won't

keep me from trying to earn his smile. *A chuckle is a bonus on top.*

I ball up my hands and anchor them on my waist, mimicking him, and then lower my voice. "What are *you* talking about, Rad?" That was nothing like he sounds, but I deserve an A for effort.

He huffs, and I think that's the first time I've ever heard him do that. Something's troubling him, and I hope it's not me. "I'm not playing a game," he says. "Why are you bringing a date to Cade and Cammie's wedding?"

Shifting my gaze from his left eye to his right eye before sinking back on the couch to take him all in, I'm still left wondering what he's talking about. Pointing at my chest, I ask, "Me? I don't have a date. Am I supposed to? And how does that work with our relationship?"

"It doesn't. That's my point. It's you and me," he says, holding a finger up from each hand. I'm assuming these are critical to the point he's trying to make. Pushing them together, he adds, "There is no room for anyone else. I didn't make that clear before, but I'm stating it now."

"For the record?" I'm just messing with him because now this is entertaining, and I still have no clue who Jean-Luc is. Whoever he is, he's wound up Rad something terrible.

"Yes. For the record."

Getting up, I move around the couch, and I tap my fingers against his chest. I flatten my palms and stretch on my tiptoes to kiss underneath his chin. It's stubbly, but I can smell his cologne, which causes my knees to weaken without fail, and tonight is no exception. "By the way, hello. It's good to see you." I bat my eyelashes and stroke the side of his face with my thumb. "Just in case you didn't notice the girl on the couch waiting for you to come home for the past two hours, I missed you. Our greetings are one of my favorite parts of the day, so maybe we can make sure to cover that before diving into the deep end."

While his hands rub my back, I see his shoulders begin to drop as they release the day's tension. Yes, his body knows he's home and safe with me. "I'm sorry," he says, pulling me closer and bending down to kiss me again. This time, he lingers a while before I'm released. "I can't believe I jumped ahead and missed that."

"We got there in the end. Speaking of jumping, it sounds like you might be jumping to conclusions as well." I poke him in the chest, and then ask, "Do you want to fill me in on this Jean-Luc business?"

"Didn't you know? Jean-Luc is your date to the wedding."

I wave him on, narrowing my eyes as if I'll figure this out by homing in on him. "Still lost."

"Marlow—"

"Ah, I see." I nod my head, already knowing it's going to be a mess if she's involved. I love her, but I could use a night off from the excitement. I ask, "Do I even want to know what comes next?"

"Only fair since I had to hear that Jean-Luc is your date to our best friends' wedding." His expression twists. "None of this sounds familiar?"

I walk into the kitchen, stopping in front of the island. I rub the marble counter for luck, hoping we get to make the most of it again sometime soon. It's been a week since I was bent over this very structure, screaming his name in ecstasy. Of course, I can't complain. We make love every day like newlyweds. Newly dating doesn't have the same ring to it. "I think I need a drink for this."

"Make that two."

After the conversation with Lowell left me defeated, and

now I'm accused of dating a Frenchman I've never had the pleasure of meeting, I bend to open the wine fridge and pull out a new bottle since I finished off the last one. Holding it up, he shakes his head, answering without me having to ask the question. I take a bottle of bourbon from the cabinet and then grab two glasses, thinking I might need something stronger for this conversation, too.

Rad hangs up his keys and then slips into our bedroom. When I have the two glasses poured, mine over rocks, his neat, I take a sip.

"Is it that bad?" he asks. Discarding his suit in the room, I don't mind the replacement he's chosen. Who knew sweatpants could be so sexy? I grin, appreciating the way the sleeves of the black T-shirt cling to his biceps. It may be a plain cotton shirt, but he sure does know how to wear it.

"Terrible," I say, trying to keep the fire from consuming my throat. I take another gulp this time to prepare for the unknown direction of this conversation. "I have to hand it to you, Welly. For someone who was told his girlfriend is taking another guy on a date to a wedding, you're fairly calm. Whoever taught you to control your emotions in law school did a stellar job."

He tilts the glass back and empties the liquid, swallowing it down. Okay, maybe he's not so calm. But I appreciate the initial effort.

He says, "They don't teach patience or any other techniques for controlling your temper. I guess you just lucked out with me."

"I sure did." Using my legs, I surround him and encourage him closer with my feet rubbing his great ass until he's in grasp's reach. I tug him closer by the front of the shirt, pulling him between my legs so I can wrap my arms around his neck.

He tilts his head like he's not falling for my antics. Little does he know, he already has. Just like I've fallen for him. I tilt my head to match him, a solid guesstimate at thirty-seven degrees to the right. I smile, and then he mimics me by smiling right back. "What are you doing, Tealey?"

"Lovin' up my man." I slide my hand underneath his T-shirt, and his muscles dance under my fingertips.

"Your hands are cold." He rubs my hips, the heat of his hands felt through my compression leggings.

I'm reminded of the cocktail beside me and pick it up to rattle the ice. "The drink is cold. Hence, cold hands." His eyes never leave mine when I tip it back.

Waiting until I swallow, he licks his lips and then asks, "I take it Jean-Luc is Marlow's idea?"

"Yes, Counselor." My trick doesn't work. Just using the term usually gets me thrown over his shoulder and taken to bed.

His brows pull together instead. "And why, exactly, did you agree to this date?"

"Since we're speaking in exacts, I never did."

I don't think he's in the mood to play my word games. "We could cut to the chase and get to the good part if you stop making me guess."

"We could . . ." I shrug, feeling the whiskey in my veins. "But what's the fun in that?"

"Trust me," he starts, using his bossy voice. Fortunately, there's a playfulness to his eyes, or I'd be worried. "There's more fun once I figure out why my girlfriend is cheating on me."

Throwing my hands up, I jerk my head back. "Whoa. Whoa. Whoa. That escalated quickly."

"Imagine how I felt when she dropped that tidbit on me at work today," he says, exasperated.

"I can imagine it was pretty traumatizing. Why didn't you just call me? This could have been settled hours ago."

"I did but was sent straight to voicemail."

I push him away and hop off the counter to retrieve my phone. "You did? That's odd. What time? My phone died around—"

"Five. Five thirty."

"Oh," I say, the wind knocked from my sails. I return to the kitchen. "That was the same time. I'm sorry."

"If you're not dating Jean-Luc, you have nothing to be sorry for."

"I'm not dating Jean-Luc. I've not even met him." Throwing my arms up, I say, "I didn't even know his name before my boyfriend told me."

But I *am* feeling sorry, sorry for bringing more problems into our little bubble of bliss. Little, if you define a large apartment with a rooftop deck as little.

What happened with Lowell will ruin everything Rad and I have been building together. I'm finally settled, and it feels like home.

Feeling unsteady is an understatement compared to when I left for work this morning. So much has changed, but I'm not sure my transfer to Poughkeepsie needs to be discussed before it's a thing.

With the wedding next week, what I want most is for us to be just how we have been. Once I mention a transfer or moving to Poughkeepsie, I'm not sure we'll be able to get back to where we are now with things left unsettled.

Information. Rad and I both work better and think clearer when we have the full story. I have time to get that this week before presenting the predicament so we can work together to find the solution.

Seeing the trust in Rad's eyes has me lifting on my toes

again and kissing him. The stronger feelings blooming inside have made me more sentimental lately. I'm just unsure when to share them. *When is the right time to say I love you?*

I spin in his arms, keeping him wrapped around me. With my phone still in my hand, I ask, "Would you like me to call Marlow and settle this other man issue?"

"Today was enough for both of us."

His tone—exhausted with a clip to it—has me looking over my shoulder. Then I turn back altogether. "Everything okay?"

"It's quite a story. Want to order dinner first?"

Two hours later, I've heard everything, and we even had time to celebrate what the partners said. I don't like the pretend stuff with Marlow and hearing how it extends to the wedding, but at least he's not hiding any details.

And, truth be told, I feel like an equal. The more time I spend with Rad, the more it's clear how wrong Steve was for me. *Any boyfriend before Rad really.* And I love this part of each day. Sitting down and chatting about our days. I never felt lonely living alone, but this is so much better. "So what does that mean for us telling friends and family?"

He goes into the kitchen with this takeout container and throws it away in the recycling. "It means you tell me."

Thinking long and hard about this, I find there's still so much going on. "Do we tell our friends at the reception?" I want to dance with you and kiss you. Weddings are so romantic, but . . . Bob will be there. How does that work for us?"

Though I feel I should see the debate that always wars in his eyes when we bring up this topic, nothing but calm lies in them tonight. "I'll end it before then."

"I hate that you're in this spot and would never want to

jeopardize your dreams." I move into his strong arms once again and close my eyes. I don't know if what I'm doing is right or wrong, but I guess I'm agreeing to this craziness. "We can play it by ear and aim for the reception. If you and Marlow aren't settled by then, we wait a few more days."

"You're okay with that?" Bending his head down, he looks into my eyes. "Are you sure?"

Smiling, I reply, "What's another two weeks in the scheme of things?"

~ Twelve Days Later ~

Jackson loads my suitcase into the back of the SUV and then comes to stand right next to me . . . *and Rad*, leaving no room or privacy to say or do what we really want. He asks, "Ready to roll? The Hamptons await."

Rad stares at me like he might miss something if his gaze deviates, so I turn to Jackson. "I'll be right there."

Crossing his arms over his chest, Jackson says, "I can wait."

"Wait in the car, St. James," Rad snaps. Rad's tone strikes harshly, surprising both Jackson and me.

Jackson side-eyes him. "Can't say I'm upset you're not riding with us, Wellington. Glad you're staying behind in Manhattan for the night. Wouldn't want to be stuck with you and that mood you're wearing like a chip on your shoulder for the next few hours." He returns to the vehicle, opening the back door before passing Marlow tucked in the passenger's seat.

I look at Rad and reach to touch his chest. "It's okay, Rad. He doesn't know why you're upset, and it's not his fault anyway. So don't take it out on him." I lower my hand, remembering that we're still a secret. *No PDA allowed.*

"It's not normal not to be able to say goodbye to my girlfriend."

I love hearing him call me his girlfriend. We're not in situations that warrant introductions, but when he calls me his girlfriend, even in private, I realize how far he's come. Once a proud eternal bachelor turned loyal boyfriend, I don't take a day with him for granted. "I wish you didn't have court tomorrow."

"Don't worry. I'm packed and will leave as soon as I get home."

We're supposed to be two friends saying a simple good-bye, but like him, I feel the weight of what we really are. Hiding it means that I don't get to hug him or touch his chest when we're talking. It means no kissing, and all that adds up to is missing him before I've even left.

Marlow rolls down her window and pokes her head out. "Kiss goodbye already, and let's get on the road." Her laughter trails across the sidewalk.

I roll my eyes at her teasing, and sigh. "They're quite the pair."

Finally, Rad smiles. I'm glad to see his bad mood lifting. "*They* don't know how spot-on they are when it comes to us. That's what makes it funny." Running his hands through his hair, he says, "I can't wait for this to be over, though, so we can just be ourselves."

"Me too." I force my feet to take a step back because it's so hard to leave him. If I don't start now, I'll never leave.

I reach my hand out once more, knowing full well that it will touch the air. But I'll take that air if it touched him.

Rad glances at the SUV, and then his hand reaches for me, our fingertips catching just before I turn and walk away. I climb into the back seat and shut the door before we say something we can't take back—like three-word phrases—or reveal more to the others than we can share.

Just as the vehicle pulls away from the curb, I take one last look because I won't get to see him again until the wedding, and I want to memorize everything about him. Rolling down my window, I sit forward and shove my arm out to wave. "See you at the altar."

34

Rad

See you at the altar . . .

I scoff. Tealey didn't mean it literally . . . *or did she?*

Focus, Wellington. Get your work done so you can go to the Hamptons and see your girl.

I'm not sure where the past two weeks went, but time is flying when I need it to stand still until I'm caught up.

My phone vibrates across my desk. Mia: *Landing in three hours. Meet at Lobby Bar at The Bowery Hotel. Drinks and my room upstairs. Would love to catch up with you. Up for it?*

Guilt gnaws at my stomach. I didn't even send the text, and I feel I owe Tealey an apology.

There have been a handful of messages from women I've spent time with, wondering if I was free, could meet for a drink, or skip the foreplay and fuck. It's not something I thought needed to be discussed in detail with Tealey because I didn't reciprocate the attention or even bother to respond. I haven't had that desire.

Why would I? I don't need anyone else because I have Tealey.

The guys can pontificate about my sex life, exaggerate the hookups I used to have, and live vicariously all they want, but that's in the past. My future has me dashing up the stairs by two to get home every night even faster.

Except tonight. I'm working late and hoping to cut out after court tomorrow. If I could just focus on the task at hand instead of getting caught up in the last words she said to me. *See you at the altar . . .*

~ Late Friday Night ~

My tires crunch against the gravel driveway as I pull up to my mom's house and park to the side, narrowly avoiding a black party event van parked where the lights don't shine.

My body aches after being stuck in five hours of bumper-to-bumper traffic. The summer season is here.

I was too distracted by my hearing this afternoon to remember to plan accordingly.

But I'm here now, so that's what matters.

At just half past eleven, it's not so late that everyone will be in bed. They could be out by the firepit or having fun down by the beach, but I'm not interested in any of that. My goals are to say hello to my mom and then find Tealey, hoping to disappear with her for the rest of the night.

I carry my bag toward the house and go inside. I'm surprised to find the lights lowered and the great room empty. No stragglers snacking in the kitchen or partiers pouring another drink. The deck looks to be clear of people like everywhere else.

Good. I'm on a mission tonight. Maybe it'll be easier to achieve than expected.

I stand there, now unsure what to do. I set my bag down and cross the great room to see if my mom is awake. No light is shed from under the door, so I take my bag and head upstairs.

Passing the room where Tealey usually sleeps, I'm tempted to knock. I don't, not quite yet. I need to clean up after the long day, probably even take a shower. I enter my room, flip on the light switch, and shut the door.

I leave my bag on the bed and start digging through it.

"I thought you . . ." Tealey's voice causes me to look up. "Could show me your movie collection." There she is, standing in the doorway to my secret media room, dressed in nothing but a smile.

"Aren't you a sight for sore eyes?" I start walking as if my feet have a mind of their own.

Primping her hair playfully, she wiggles her hips. "A girl can dream."

Less than two months ago, she confessed the pain of dealing with insecurities caused by other men. Tonight, I reap the benefits for caring for her heart and watering the seeds of her beauty. I can't take all the credit. I've watched her bloom on her own for years. But the woman before me tonight has me grateful that I was given the chance.

What she doesn't realize is she's done the same for me—watering me with what I needed before I even realized I was in the middle of a drought.

Suddenly, I'm hopeful that my breath isn't bad because I take hold of her, walking her backward into the privacy of the room until the back of her knees hit the arm of the couch. "How long have you been waiting for me?

"Everyone was exhausted after the rehearsal dinner, so we called it an early night. I was reading in the window seat of my room and had only got a chapter in when I saw your car."

"Same rock star hero? What was his name?"

"Johnny Outlaw. And no, though I do love him and will reread again next year. It's sort of a tradition, like Christmas for me to reread my favorite books. Currently though, I'm reading the first book in The Crow Brothers' series, Jet Crow's book. It's called *Spark*." *I only hope I can put that same spark in her eyes that these rock stars do.*

I kiss her because I missed her so fucking much—her rambling about books and life, this body, and her smile, the smile that knocks me on my ass every time she beams it my way.

I may have had a small, *aka HUGE,* crush on Tealey Bell, but now I realize that so much of it was superficial. It was about her beauty and how, out of all the students, we ran into each other that day. Never in a million years did I think I'd get to be the guy on the receiving end of hearing about her daily life, and it's better than I could have ever imagined. Everything is better with her in my life.

She's still talking, not realizing the moment I was having. I see sharing a future with someone for the first time. She continues, "You might enjoy this one. He's a lot like you. He's charming and brooding—"

"Brooding?" I'm not sure if I should be offended. "Charming, sure. But you think I'm brooding?"

Caressing my cheek, she leans closer as a shiver runs through her. "I think you're incredibly sexy when you get that intense look in your eyes, the one that tells me I better brace myself without you having to say a word." She massages my shoulders, and I lean into her touch. "Oh, by the way, I volunteered to fill you in on how to walk down the aisle."

"One step at a time until I reach the front?" I deadpan.

"You got it. I can check that off my list."

"Speaking of lists and checking things off, you do realize you're still naked in front of me, right?"

"I do," she says and then bursts out laughing. "See? I'm in the theme of the weekend."

"You're delirious is what you are."

She shrugs. "It's been a long day. Que será." Running a finger down my chest, she says, "But since I am naked, maybe you'd like to get naked with me."

"And then we could check out my movie collection?"

"I think the kids call it streaming these days." When her hand dips to my dick, it's already ready for her and standing at attention. She rubs twice before taking hold of me. "I bet you know a thing or two about streaming, Counselor."

"I sure do."

As if she had to say anything more, I kiss her, and we "watch movies" for the next few hours . . .

~ The Wedding Day ~

It's a happy occasion, or it's supposed to be.

Not seeing Tealey since she snuck out of my room around five o'clock is getting to me. One of the best nights of my life should allow for the best morning to follow. I don't get that, though, because we're still a secret. The only comfort I found in that empty spot next to me was the fact that we're going public at the reception. And then she's mine all the time to do as I please.

If I want to kiss her? *I can.*

Holding her in my arms for no reason? *Yep, I can do it.*

Tell her I love her? *The floor is mine.*

Wait . . . Do I want to tell her I love her tonight?

That might be taking it too far, even if I do feel that way about her. *Baby steps, Wellington.* Not everything has to be revealed at the same time. I think big gestures can wait until we're back home in New York, and it's just the two of us.

It's Cammie and Cade's special day, after all. Their happiness is what matters. Not mine . . .

Lorie Marché touches my arm, whispering close to my ear. "Emerald cut. Four carats minimum. Marlow's dream is five, though. Platinum band with something special the two of you share engraved on the inside." She thinks she's being sneaky, gathering this information and sharing these little nuggets with me throughout the morning. I'm just glad I had an excuse to miss the rehearsal dinner.

"Like a prison tattoo," I say, unable to stop myself. "Something to mark us, like noting how we're being sentenced to life with the I dos?" She blinks rapidly.

Opening her mouth like a fish out of water, she holds her finger up and then lowers it again. Her eyes shift to Bob, and then she says, "More along the lines of a phrase you say to her regularly—"

"Stop barging in?"

She tightens her lips and then pops them. "A simple I love you should do the trick."

"Got it," I reply.

Unfortunately, Lorie is still clinging to my arm like we're old friends, or lovers by how close she is to my ear. She has no boundaries, something I assume is a luxury you acquire when you hold power in Hollywood. They never hear no.

Bob and Marlow are already at the edge of the lawn where the grass meets the sand when we catch up to them. Standing in a row, we stare ahead at the vast ocean.

Marlow reaches for my hand, and though I like to fuck

with her by shifting, I finally succumb to the inevitable. Our connection elicits the faintest gag sound, causing me to look at Marlow. Leaning over, she says, "It's like holding hands with my brother."

"You don't have a brother."

She shakes her head. "You know what I mean."

"I do," I reply, looking down at our joined hands. "Exactly what you mean."

Lorie steps onto the sand like it's her stage. "Although you don't have the ring yet, you could still propose to our sweet Marlow."

Taken aback, I stare at Lorie with a different intensity than Tealey was talking about last night. *Did she just tell me to propose because she wants me to?*

Coming closer again, and with her hands clasped together, her ten-carat diamond sparkles in the sunshine. She adds, "Just a bauble—"

This needs to stop. It's gone on too long. "I've got it under control, Lorie. You don't need to worry yourself about it."

Bob pulls a set of keys from his pocket and dangles them in front of me, like that damn partnership carrot. "We thought keys to the apartment would be the best way to celebrate the engagement." That's all Marlow wanted, and it's being offered on a silver platter. We did it. I glance at Marlow, who's already looking at me.

I've heard that you should never meet your idols. It's always a disappointment. Same feeling.

Marlow squeals in delight and takes the keys. Guess that phrase only applies to me.

"Do they come with a deed?" Marlow asks, unashamed to dive right in and humor them in the name of owning a piece of Manhattan real estate. Maybe I should be more understanding. I own my building, so I can't judge her for wanting her slice of the pie.

We played by the rules set forth by her father, which is to win at all costs. So why does this victory feel like a dirty win? Like we didn't play fair?

He nods with a jolly grin. "They do indeed."

All eyes are aimed at me, but it's Bob who comes to stand face-to-face. Keeping his voice lowered, he asks, "Would it be so bad to get engaged today, Rad? To make my girl happy?" He holds out his hand. "You've always been the most suitable for my Marlow. Let's make it official so we can be here to celebrate the happy occasion."

Being forced to choose between my career and my personal life makes my blood boil. "Enough."

This has been taken too far.

Holding hands for five minutes, playing a role on a conference call—that's all different than what I'm now being expected to do. And there's no mistaking that it's expected, not being asked. *The partnership is yours if you don't fuck it up,* rings in my ears as if Sable himself is right behind me.

Don't fuck it up.

I got Bob's business, even if he isn't divorcing at this time. *Don't lose his business.*

If Marlow and I "get engaged," how am I supposed to go public with Tealey?

Don't lose Tealey.

We leave in the morning and return to our lives. The breakup with Marlow doesn't even have to be a thing. It can be a call Marlow makes on her own at the end of next week.

Marlow and I have more to gain than to lose with the odds stacked in our corner. Tealey will understand. Making partner means more income and Tealey being able to pursue her own dreams, as well as me setting us up to start our lives together, the real ones, not this pretense bullshit.

Stepping into the sand in front of Marlow, I'm one step closer to making my dreams come true.

35

Rad

After being dragged all over the property by Marlow and the Marchés, I'm happy to be locked away in a room with the boys before the wedding begins.

I only caught a glimpse of Tealey from across the lawn this morning when she was helping my mom with the flower arrangements. Not enough to satisfy the craving twisting my gut. But she was stunning even with her hair in rollers and dressed in a robe over workout pants, maybe more so because of how naturally beautiful she is.

A rap on the door sends Jackson to answer it. My mom pokes her head in. "Does anybody need anything?"

Cade and Jackson are good, so she asks me, "Can you spare a minute?"

Already dressed, I join her in the hallway outside my bedroom, which has been deemed the "groom's room." Her smile is genuine with a glassiness to her eyes. "You always look so handsome in a tuxedo."

Hugging her, I say, "You look beautiful, Mom." She does.

I'm not sure why she doesn't date. She looks younger than her years, but she's not old enough to be sitting on the sidelines for the rest of her life. She also doesn't want to hear a lecture from me, so I let it go for today.

"Thank you." Hooking her arm with mine, she says, "Let's take a quick walk."

I'm not sure what this is about, but something's on her mind. Better to get it off now than let it fester.

We move apart on the deck. I lean on the railing while she stands on the steps, keeping her eyes on the crew as they rush around with the finishing touches. She says, "It really turned out beautiful."

"It did. You and Cammie did an incredible job pulling this off so quickly."

"It was my pleasure." Turning toward me, she says, "Clear something up for me."

"All right." Judging by how her expression contorts, I don't know where this is going. It could be a financial question, a legal dispute, or she might want to talk about my future. I literally have no idea. My mom isn't usually subtle.

"What's going on, Radcliffe?" she starts but then stops when two people carrying more chairs pass between us. As soon as they're out of earshot, she continues, "I could have sworn you were showing interest in Tealey when you were last here, but now you're dating Marlow? And from what it looks like, you're quite chummy with the Marchés." That just about sums up the lies I've been living.

"What do you mean showing interest in Tealey?"

Lowering her chin, she gives me *that* look, the one that stops me from daring to go there. *There*, meaning playing dumb. It's something she hates, but I'm not above it.

"The flirting, the 'trip' into town. Frank, an old friend of mine who works part-time security at Rusco's had lots to talk about. I got more than a lobster roll when I stopped by on Tuesday, let me tell you. I got an earful." *Shit.* I keep my mouth shut. It's best to let her finish than fill in the rest of the story.

She joins me at the railing, keeping her eyes trained on the waves in the distance. "The description based on hair or eye color could have been either Marlow or Tealey. But when he mentioned the yellow dress . . ." Her gaze hits me, but there's no judgment in her eyes or hurt in her tone when she asks, "I didn't realize you were so close." She holds my hand. "Tealey's wonderful. Don't get me wrong, son. Marlow is charming, and there's a je ne sais quoi air about her, but I didn't see her . . . and you . . ." My mom's attention turns to the commotion near the quartet.

She's going to be disappointed in me, but I won't lie to her. "Marlow is a good friend, but there's nothing more between us."

The crinkles around her eyes deepen when she smiles. Resting her hands on the railing again, she says, "I thought as much, but then what's going on?"

"We . . ." I sigh. The situation and the lies are draining me. "I got talked into helping her out with a personal issue, and as strange as it may sound, that involved pretending we're dating."

"That doesn't sound like any good can come of it. Helping a friend is a good thing. Lying, not so much." She tilts her head to the side. "What about Tealey? Does she know the truth?"

"She knows the truth."

"That's good. I'd hate to think there was cheating involved."

I stand in disbelief.

"Mom, you know me. I wouldn't cheat. I'm not that man and never will be."

She rubs my shoulder. Pride and empathy shine a light in her eyes as she dotes on me. "I know. I shouldn't have made you feel I didn't. I wasn't questioning your character. I was making sure things haven't been misconstrued when it comes to how Tealey feels about this fake dating business. Does she know how you feel about her?"

I haven't told her how my heart seems to only beat for her. And as much as I should feel ten pounds lighter for settling Bob's case, I'm worried about Tealey and the toll this scheme with Marlow will take on our relationship. This morning at the beach was the final push I never saw coming. Instead of feeling good about what I've accomplished, I'm left feeling ashamed of what I've done. "Not in so many words."

"In any words?" She grins, already knowing the answer.

"Not exactly."

She pats my arm. "Think about filling her in on your feelings. You might be surprised by her reaction."

"I like her . . . *I love her*, Mom."

The words come staggering out, refusing to be hidden any longer. It feels strange to say them out loud, but not wrong in any way. I don't know how I expected to feel, but it wasn't conflicted. None of my feelings for Tealey are conflicting, but the situation with Marlow I've involved myself in is a direct contradiction.

She walks around me, keeping the tips of her fingers tethered to the wood. "I know, son. Make sure she does too. Honesty in actions and words mean everything."

Turning to go, she stops. She faces me again, shaking her head in pure amusement. "Oh, and I about spit out my water when I heard Cammie say you were showing Tealey your 'movie collection.' Your code words need more origi-nality. Nobody owns DVDs or videotapes anymore. Streaming is the way to go."

I chuckle, thinking about how much she and Tealey are alike and then how the differences bridge the gap between them. I'm a lucky guy. "Yeah, I'll look into that," I joke.

Mulling over Mom's advice, I must agree on one thing. There's no reason to wait.

I shouldn't.

It's settled. Tonight is the night I tell Tealey Bell that I love her. I turn with a grin and head back to the groom's room.

Jean-Luc.

Fucker.

I guess Marlow didn't get the message that my Tealey's not up for grabs. The minute he walked in, kissing cheeks of the women under forty and kissing hands of the women over, he made his presence known. You'd think he'd just landed his private helicopter on the lawn by how much attention he was getting. I peek out the window to check, just to make sure.

Jackson asks Cade, "How does it feel to be getting married?"

"Remember how graduation felt? Nervous for the unknown but excited like the whole world was yours for the taking?" Cade grins. "It feels just like that."

I look over my shoulder at Cade. He just described Tealey's and my relationship.

I think I knew all along that she was going to get the best of me, that I wouldn't be able to lose her once I had her.

Even on the day I met Cade by the water, I chalked my feelings up to having mixed-up emotions so I could try to play it off.

Two months later, I realize—I'm ready to admit—that I'm not mixed up when it comes to Tealey. I want to be what I've never been before—a boyfriend, a partner, a lover, and a friend to this woman who makes my heart beat faster, that allows me to breathe with ease. Tealey Bell gives me a peek into a life I never thought I'd have.

Fuck. I run my fingers through my hair in a sad attempt to wrangle my runaway feelings. *Refocus, Wellington.* Turning to face my friend, I say, "You look happy, man."

Cade maneuvers around us and angles his chin to get a better look in the mirror. "I am. It took eight years to get to this point. I would have married her on day one."

Cade's cousin comes in and holds up the bottle of bourbon that went missing from our room earlier. He asks, "Got another one of these?"

Shooting me a look, I know what he's asking me to do. "The wedding's about to begin. It's an open bar at the reception."

"Cool." Satisfied, the guy closes the door.

Jackson says, "Oh to be twenty-one again."

"All of six years ago?" I ask, teasing.

The wedding planner opens the door and pokes her head in. "Ready to get married?" she asks, a smile reaching the rounds of the apples of her cheeks.

Cade heads for the door with us behind him. He asks, "How's my bride?"

The planner looks as if she's seen an angel. "The most beautiful bride I've ever seen."

They continue talking as she leads us to the great room to wait. Her words have me imagining Tealey dressed in white, taking a walk to be my wife. I rub the bridge of my nose. *Two months*, I remind myself. I can *love* her. I can be *in love* with her. But it's too soon for marriage.

Marriage should be a calculated decision, one that makes sense and is done at the right time. Although Tealey's not afraid to put her dreams into the universe, my dreams are just taking shape.

My mom's bedroom door opens, and Tealey and Marlow walk out in short pale purple gowns—fitted on top and flaring out at the waist. The shoes are simple strappy flats, which my mom will appreciate since heels will mess up her lawn.

But it's Tealey's eyes that shine like the sun hides in them —bright and beautiful, so much like who she is—that render me speechless. She comes to me and adjusts my boutonnière. Looking up, she says, "You look very handsome, Counselor."

I'm not sure what to say. I want to wrap my arms around her, tell her how she's utterly breathtaking, kiss her, claim her, and keep her safe from the rakish Frenchman waiting to pounce on her at the first chance he gets. I'm just not allowed to. Not yet. Not without giving her a say. And there's no room to talk for the time being.

Cade is sent marching down the aisle, and we're told to line up. We pair off as it should be—Marlow and Jackson, Tealey and me. Like a drill sergeant, the wedding planner inspects all of us. She steps back to take us in, and her face sours. "No. This isn't working." Grabbing Jackson, she says, "You and . . ." She doesn't have to say it. There are only two couples.

Tealey's hand tightens around my arm, and I place my hand on hers to hold her right where she is. Then the planner says, "We have to hurry. Tealey," she says with a snap of her fingers. "Come up here."

"I think this works."

"If the two ladies swap partners, it looks better visually. You're going to have to trust me on this. I've been organizing weddings for years, and the photos are what remain long after the vows. Let's make Cammie's look the best they can." *Fuck that.*

Tealey huffs, but then her grip loosens. Looking up at me, she swallows, and then says, "She's probably right. You and Marlow are the better match."

"I disagree," I whisper. She gives me a look to go along with it and turns away. Why is it that every time we think we'll be together, something intervenes?

She's handed her bouquet and then looks back once she's on Jackson's arm. The planner shuffles them out the door before I can tell her that my love for Tealey matters more. *And I fucking oppose the planner's decision.* I prefer Tealey standing next to me over any other woman.

Marlow straightens her shoulders. "This is also better for appearances." Marlow beside me, even for Cammie's benefit, feels wrong.

I look at her in disbelief. "Fuck appearances. I'm done playing games with you. He bought the apartment. You got what you wanted."

She arches a perfectly manicured brow. "You did too. Don't forget that."

The planner gives my shoulder blade a little shove, and we start walking. With each step, my annoyance at Marlow and this entire situation continues to build.

Something about her tone makes it seem as if I owe her father something for making partner—*if I make partner*. And as we pass Bob Marché while we step down the aisle, I realize something: my partnership has nothing to do with him.

I've busted my ass for years. I've worked myself into the ground. I've put my heart and soul into my work, and while Bob's divorce may have helped me get there in the end, I would've gotten there anyway.

And Marlow would've too. I glance at her profile. She's come a long way over the past year. She may be flippant, and she may be shallow, but she works hard. She tries to do the right thing. And she's a good friend and a good person. Her metamorphosis was intentional, and she lost a little bit of that today on the beach with her father and Lorie. She fell back into a persona she's tried so hard to shed.

"You know what?" I ask quietly. "That's bullshit."

"What's bullshit?" she whispers and then flashes a forced smile at someone in the audience.

"I worked for my promotion. I've worked for it longer than the past couple of months. If I get partner, it has nothing to do with you or your dad. Don't get it twisted."

She stutter-steps. Her long blond hair is twisted up in the back, restraining it from swinging through the air as she whips to look at me while we cross the deck. "What the hell is wrong with you?"

"You know what's wrong. That crossed every fucking line in my book." I stop on the grass. "This is not who we are, Marlow. Don't let your dad and stepmom drag you back into a version of yourself that you left behind. On purpose."

A clearing of the throat grabs our attention. The planner grits her teeth. "Go."

Marlow sighs heavily but takes my arm again, and we start walking. Through tight smiles, we continue fighting, though. She says, "Not everyone is handed—"

"Don't go there." I set my eyes on Tealey, standing at the

altar, waiting for me just like she said she would be. She had faith this would all work out in our favor. She believed in me. But I've failed her in so many ways.

A slight sadness lingers in Tealey's eyes at seeing Marlow and me coming down the aisle together, and it feels like a knife through my heart.

This should not be happening. I should not have put her through this.

Any of this.

"I've sacrificed more than you'll ever know to play along with your charade."

"Like what?" I can hear the eye roll through her tone.

"The love of my life."

36

Tealey

"I now pronounce you husband and wife. You may kiss the bride."

The wedding photos took forever, but once they were done, enough time had passed for Rad and Marlow to cool off. Although Jackson and I have made wild guesses, neither of us feels we should broach the situation with either of them just yet.

"They argued all the way down the aisle," I say. "Now they don't appear to be on speaking terms. What should we do?"

"Leave them be," Jackson says. "They'll work it out on their own."

I watch Marlow chat with Cammie's grandmother before she turns, looking a little lost. The most noticeable thing is that she appears to be avoiding us.

And Rad took a call and disappeared when I was helping Cammie touch up her makeup. Fortunately, she seems none the wiser. Although Cade was a witness, he hasn't said a word. I agree with his stance. This is their special day, so I'm kind of surprised that Rad and Marlow would put on such a display.

Both head in separate directions, but I decide to start with Rad to figure out what's going on. One moment, I see him with his mom. The next, he's heading into the house. Both times, he looks upset. I'm thinking he might need some time to cool off, so I head to the bar for a glass of champagne.

Jackson has already found his way and is propped up against the bar when I arrive. "What can I get you, Tealey?"

"A glass of champagne, please." When he hands it to me, I say, "Thank you." I leave the space between us open for conversation. "Soooo . . ."

"Yeah," he replies, tensing his jaw. "Whatever it is, it's bad."

"You think?"

He nods.

"And you don't know what happened?"

This time, he shakes his head. Pushing off the bar, he says, "I think I'll go look for Marlow. She might need a friend."

"Maybe I should go then."

"Marlow and I are friends, Tealey." Offense threads through his tone. "Just like you and Rad."

Nothing like Rad and me, but I'm not going to argue with him. I agreed to this vow of silence on the topic of us, and I'll stick with it.

I set my glass back down, having no interest in alcohol right now. As the newlyweds start ticking through their list of traditional items on the reception agenda, I go in search of Rad again. Cutting across the lawn, I'm just at the edge of the party when I hear, "Bonjour, mademoiselle."

The accent is thick, matching his dark hair. His caramel eyes are set on me like we've met before. We haven't, but I know who he is. "You're even prettier than Marlow described."

"Thank you. You must be Jean-Luc." When he leans in to kiss my cheek, I pull back, his gesture too forward for me. Or maybe I'm just not sophisticated enough to appreciate the greeting. Either way, I say, "It's nice to meet you. I'm Tealey." I know nothing of this man other than he's an art collector. Something tells me he has interests in collecting other things, such as notches on his belt. Just a gut instinct, but one that's served me well.

Of course, I had judged Rad all wrong, so maybe my instincts aren't as reliable as I once believed.

"Yes, Marlow spoke highly of you." He holds his glass forward. "You don't have a drink? Shall we make our way to the bar?"

"No. I'm fine." Antsy to get to Rad, I look toward the house one more time.

"Champagne is for celebrations. Weddings. Engagements. New friends. We have all the makings of a beautiful evening."

"The wedding was so beautiful." I was teary-eyed when Cammie tried on her dress the first time, cried when I saw her today, and bawled like a baby while I listened to her and Cade exchange their vows.

He sips his champagne while I figure out how to ditch him and get back to searching for my boyfriend. "I should apologize for Marlow. I did not agree to—"

"Her engagement, I heard, was quite the surprise today." He sips, his eyes fixed on me.

Marlow? Engaged? He must be mistaken. There's no way. She's not even dating anyone. I try to riddle through what he said, thinking I heard him wrong in the first place. "Marlow's not engaged."

"Oui, she is indeed. The fiancé was ill-prepared, popping the question because her family is here. Americans have lost the art of romance. No honest man would make a mockery of love. Love requires intimacy, not big displays." His flippant comment warrants a comeback, but I'm still stuck on the "popping the question because her family is here" part. The only person with Marlow and her family was Rad.

My hands fist at my side, and I take a deep and staggering breath to control my head from exploding. "Did you see the man, *her fiancé*," I grit, "propose, or is it a rumor?"

"The actress, Lorie Marché, was telling a small group of us at the wedding. Her father is going to give a toast."

"A toast?" Rad is about to have his engagement announced instead of his relationship with me going public. A punch to the gut has me coddling my midsection just as panic sets in.

He must be wrong. Others men are dressed in tuxes. It must be a mix-up. *Please be anyone but Rad.*

"This, uh, man." He looks around and then turns back. "Is the same man as the one coming from the house."

My gaze pivots over his shoulder to see Rad returning to the reception. Just past him, twenty or so feet, Marlow walks out of the house. My heart sinks to the pit of my stomach, and I brace myself by holding it with one arm. It's hard to speak with my throat thickening, but I ask, "Are you sure? Are you sure that's the man?"

"I am. Lorie pointed him out when they walked down the aisle."

I stare at Jean-Luc, watching the shape of his lips when he speaks and the way they creep around the edge of the glass when he drinks. I stare at his mouth because it's a liar just like the man. Only someone cruel like him would spread lies for entertainment.

My Rad wouldn't do this to me.

My Rad wouldn't betray someone he loves.

My Rad wouldn't go against his moral compass, choosing his career over me. I know he wouldn't. Rad has goals, but he's changed for the better. He has a life, with me, for the better. Why would he do something that he knows would destroy me?

He promised never to hurt me, but I stand here unable to walk away from the pain.

Jean-Luc rocks in his loafers and then smiles. "Would you like to dance?"

"Tealey?" The voice cuts past Jean-Luc. When my eyes find the ones that usually bring me comfort, this time, they don't. I'm hit with a glare so piercing that he has me believing I've done something wrong. "I've been looking for you," Rad says, standing behind Jean-Luc.

"I've been looking for you as well," I volley back with caution.

We've had a fight, but it was a rain shower compared to the storm brewing inside him. The tension is so thick that I take another step back from Jean-Luc as if he'll find me guilty from the proximity to another man.

This is not Rad. *Not my Rad.*

He's not like that—unreasonable and threatening. *Who is this man standing before me?* The one who looks so familiar but feels foreign in every other way.

Jean-Luc steps forward and faces Rad. "Is there a problem?"

His accent is much milder now and more in tune with his manners.

Rad's gaze never sways from mine, ignoring Jean-Luc entirely. He holds out his hand, reaching for me.

In. Front. Of. Everyone.

At least anyone who's paying attention to us, but that doesn't seem to be many when I look around at the party happening behind me. It's a violation of the agreement, either way, and I'm all for chucking that damn deal, but it seems he already did way before now.

I take a breath and place my hand in his despite my better judgment, his touch the match igniting the dwindling embers inside me once again. I needed this. I needed him.

But when I glance at Jean-Luc, his words of warning reappear. *No honest man would make a mockery of love.* No honest man.

I pull my hand back, burned by him. *Again.*

Be strong, Tealey.

Confusion rips through Rad's expression, and he comes forward, whispering, "We need to talk."

"Do we?"

"Yes."

One look. That's all it takes for me to see that he's done something that can't be fixed. "I . . ." I start, my breath getting away from me as tears threaten the corners of my eyes. "Why didn't I see it before now?"

"See what, Tealey?" He comes even closer, desperation coating his tongue. "Talk to me."

As soon as Rad grabs my hands, Jean-Luc says, "You should not touch her."

"Fuck off."

"Rad!" I say, shocked by his behavior.

No, this is not the man I've fallen in love with. "I'm glad you showed me your true colors now before you had me fooled completely," I lie, turning around and walking away. I was fooled by him, head over heels in love with him, but I finally see the truth.

I was never going to be the woman by his side. I would always remain the woman he chose to hide.

His priorities would always take precedence. He might ask me for my opinion or offer to listen to how I feel, but it was never going to really matter.

Rad is successful for a reason. Because he does what it takes to win—both inside and outside the courtroom.

And although he might've won my heart, I didn't win his. And that hurts more than I ever even considered it might.

Rushing through the reception, I search for anyone to help me hold my heart together before it shatters across the dance floor.

I'm smacked in the chest by a bundle of flowers, causing my heart to leap from my body as petals fly everywhere. Reactively, I catch the bouquet before I realize what's even happening. Cammie screams in delight. "Tealey! You caught the bouquet." Pointing at me, she's dancing to the song that just got turned up. "You're next, baby!"

Cade steals a glance before he takes her hand and spins her around on the dance floor. That's how it should be— make sure she's happy. This should be the best day of her life. That means I need to leave. I need to get back to Manhattan and find someplace to hide until I can sort the truth from the lies.

Be brave, Tealey.

I can't keep the burden of my pain away much longer. I start running, moving as fast as I can into the darkness of the lawn.

It's not until I reach the side of the house that I fall against it, giving me time to catch my breath.

"Tealey?" Hearing my name has me standing stiff against the siding, praying not to be found. But the tears fall, sending rivulets streaming down my cheeks.

"Tealey, where are you?"

I catch my breath when I realize it's not Rad but Jackson who's calling after me. He comes around the corner and stops. No words. Just one look is exchanged between us, and then he opens his arms and holds me.

He doesn't worry about me soaking his tux or that my makeup might ruin the collar of his shirt. He stands there with me wrapped in his arms and lets me cry until my tears begin stuttering and my eyes dry. I sag against the house again, and when I look into his sympathetic eyes, I say, "I need a favor."

37

Tealey

My phone died near the same convenience store where Rad and I stopped last time. It's the same place that holds fun memories of buying all the snacks to have variety . . . and because, typically, he didn't allow eating in his precious baby. But he allowed me.

Why?

So much doesn't make sense with him.

This time, I used the restroom to wash off the makeup that streaked down my face. I passed the jelly beans and left the Cheetos. I didn't buy a bag of popcorn that made my stomach growl. I got back in the car, and a guy named Rod —*the similarity not lost on me*—drove me straight home.

Home.

That's a luxury that I no longer have in Manhattan.

Leaning forward, I ask the driver, "Do you have a spare charger?"

"No. I need to use the map. That burns my battery, and I have a long night ahead."

You're telling me.

Filing through my memories, from the little moments Rad and I shared—hot dogs at midnight, stolen kisses in the Hamptons, and reading on the couch on Sundays—along with the bigger events from moving day to making love for the first time, I still can't make sense of how I ended up with a guy named Rod driving me home instead of Rad.

Maybe one day, I'll have the hindsight of learning the lesson this relationship was meant to teach me. I just hope my heart won't still be so broken by then.

Leaning my head against the window, I have nothing but miles and time ahead. I stare in the inky night until my eyelids grow as weary as my battered heart. And then close altogether.

"Miss."

I sigh and then yawn. Opening my eyes, I bolt upright. "Where am I?"

"Home," Rod says, pointing out the passenger window.

I look, and for a split second, I could feel my soul come alive again—the warmth and comfort, the excitement of the adventure ahead, falling asleep with Rad, and waking up with him. For a split second, I feel wonderful.

And then the feeling vanishes before I have a chance to cling to the memories.

I get out from the back seat. The driver pulls away before I have a chance to thank him, so when it's me and the build-ing, I take a deep breath and move a few steps closer. I look up, never paying much attention to the other tenants. It always felt like mine and Rad's. I naïvely started to believe that Poughkeepsie wasn't my destiny.

I enter the building and tap the elevator, still holding my dead phone in my hand like I can actually check it. It's painful to be so detached from the world, from *my* world on any given day, but tonight, I'm feeling especially lonely. Yet I know when I charge it, I'll either be mad because of the texts Rad's sent or more shattered by the messages he didn't. It's a no-win situation that has me dreading the elevator door opening and finding out.

When I enter the apartment, it feels unexpectedly the same, as if I didn't have my heart broken by the other occupant and could walk into the bedroom and crawl in bed next to him. Rad would swing his arm wide and wait for me to settle before curling it around me. He'd snore lightly if he drank too much and be spooning me in the morning. My toothbrush would have paste on it when I slipped into the bathroom to get ready for bed. And if I called him about having a hard day, which there have been lots of lately, there'd be a hot bath and a glass of my favorite wine waiting for me.

I don't realize how long I wander through the apartment—remembering all the ways we had started making this our home and how happy he made me—until my stomach growls, bringing me back to reality. I didn't have time to eat at the reception before my world exploded, but I just lost an hour daydreaming about what could have been.

Now, there's nothing left of us.

When I open the cabinet, I don't grab one of my mugs. They don't speak to me the way I need right now. I choose one of his plain white ones and make a cup of hot green tea with chamomile, hoping it will soothe the choppy waters of my feelings.

Taking my tea, I let it steep while I go into my room—the guest room. Guest. I sigh heavily. I'm such a fool. Why'd I ever believe I could be more than a guest in this apartment? More than a visitor passing through at this stage in Rad's life? Or anything more than a "perk" that he meets after dark?

"That's it. I'm just one of the myriads of women coming and going through his revolving elevator door."

My heart hurts even more under that hot dose of reality. I was clearly not as welcome as I thought I was. Are all men jerks? Apparently, it's an impossible feat to find the man I'm meant to meet from the four million who live in this city.

And worse, I believed Rad was my soul mate.

I plug in my phone, sitting on the edge of the bed, and stare at the black screen. When just the low battery symbol shows up, I distract myself from the anxiety causing my hands to shake.

I need to busy myself, to take my mind off what will or won't be on that phone when it recharges.

As I look around, my things feel out of place. I feel out of place. How can I stay here any longer when I know the truth?

Maybe Poughkeepsie was the world looking out for me. The universe knew I'd need an exit plan.

"I need to go," I say, my voice echoing across the room. "Now."

Jackson gave me the keys to his apartment. I don't remember the last time I was there, but I remember it being spacious. I can probably move over to Cade and Cammie's place in Brooklyn tomorrow since they'll be on their honeymoon. That will give me the privacy I need and the time to find a new place in Poughkeepsie.

Is that where I'm going?

I'm still confused as to where I'm meant to be, and I'm not sure working in another office will make the move worth it.

I just wonder how messy this will be if Rad and I are no

longer speaking. Our friends, mutual events, and my heart are jumbled into this mess. Nothing about this breakup will be clean. But will the others even know we broke up since they didn't know we were dating to begin with?

The thought leaves a bitter taste in my mouth.

My screen comes to life just as I change from my bridesmaid's dress. Slipping on yoga pants and a baggy T-shirt, I stop on the other side of the bed. I'm nervous to get too close, to have my heart take another hit tonight, but there's no way I can't look.

When I see the red dot indicating I have messages, I exhale slowly, and whisper, "Don't hurt me, okay?" And then I pick up the phone and press the icon. Messages populate from six different people: Jackson, Cammie, Cade, Marlow, Amanda, and Rad.

I'm not sure where to start, though my heart, a glutton for punishment, sure does. I read Rad's first, scrolling to where they began before the wedding.

Rad: *Where are you? I have something I want to show you in the media room.*

I hate that I smile and that my heart does a somersault.

Rad: *I can't wait to be alone with you tonight.*

Rad: *What's going on? What happened? Where are you, baby?*

He acts like I did a great disappearing act. Nope. I was right there all along.

Rad: *Don't leave, Tealey. We need to talk.*

Yeah, I guess we did need to, after all. I just wonder if he was planning to tell me about the engagement or if the plan was to leave me out of the equation, as usual.

Rad: *Talk to me. Please.*

I'm not even sure what to think anymore. I hate that he has me second-guessing myself. I did nothing wrong but love him. Love? My stomach clenches, and tears well in my eyes again.

Rad: *Why did you leave?*

Rad: *Call me.*

Like a call could cure all our problems. This is too far gone for that.

I can't worry more about him being upset than the pain he caused me. I need to stop putting others first all the time. It's a side effect of my job, but I'm always the one taken advantage of.

Considering how early I woke up to start helping and then to get ready for the wedding, I'm surprised I'm not tired. I guess the nap in the car has given me enough energy to get through a bare minimum of the task at hand. I need to make some quick decisions on what I'm taking with me to last for the next week.

I open my suitcase on the bed and scramble to fill it with everything I'll need, everything that doesn't include the man I thought made my life complete. When it's full, I zip it closed and wheel it to the elevator. I don't know if Rad is coming back to Manhattan tonight or not, but I start moving faster like he just might be. I'm not looking for a confrontation or to work through this. With my emotions in tatters, I'm not clear-headed enough to argue against an attorney who's out to win.

There's no winning for either of us. The moment he got engaged to Marlow, he made his decision, and that had nothing to do with me.

Rad's engaged . . .

I still can't believe there's any truth to the rumor. Or is it that I don't want to believe he'd stoop beneath the morals he claims to have to earn a promotion? Even if it's fake, like so much has been lately, my feelings weren't considered.

This is about his ego and his reputation. I never did feed that part of him. I'm sure the Wellington and Marché nuptials announcement should give both Rad and Marlow what they crave most—attention.

No honest man would make a mockery of love. Jean-Luc saw Rad for who he is.

It's time I do, too.

After getting a minimal charge to my phone, I grab it and the cable and tuck it into my purse that Jackson was kind enough to sneak into the bridal room to retrieve for me. With it anchored around my body, I punch the button to call the elevator and wait anxiously for it to arrive.

When the door slides open, I hold my breath, not breathing again until I see it's empty. Oh, thank God. Nothing good would have come from an argument at this hour when my nerves are frayed.

From the lobby, I call a car. It only takes a minute, but my hands are shaking more now than before, so I busy myself by pulling up Jackson's address and memorizing the code just in case my phone dies again.

The car is close, so I push the suitcase onto the sidewalk and look up.

My eyes meet the ones that I equally love and dread. Standing just twenty feet ahead of me with his hands in his pockets, Rad is waiting for me.

Waiting . . .

His real "baby" is parked at the curb. The jacket and bow tie are gone, but he's still dressed in the tux shirt and pants, the light from above the door shining on his leather shoes. Despite Rad's hair being a mess—he has a habit of tugging it when he's stressed—*why is he here?*

I hate that the bond that tethers us together still exists. The urge to go to him, sweep his hair off his forehead, and embrace him is so strong that I must restrain myself from doing it.

"I'm sorry." His voice is full of the shame it should be, a tone that knows the damage done.

"For what?" I wipe at my eyes, not wanting him to see how vulnerable I am.

He's shaking his head as his gaze briefly looks down. "I don't know. I just don't want to lose you."

"That's not good enough anymore."

He closes his eyes for a long second. "Why'd you leave?"

"I don't owe you an answer. I don't owe you anything." I take a breath and watch a couple holding hands cut between us on the sidewalk.

"Tell me what I did wrong, Tealey, and I'll fix it. I'll do anything to make it better. I thought I was."

My eyes widen. *He can't be serious.* "You thought you were? In what universe were you making things better? Ah. Wait," I say, sarcasm dripping from my lips. "I get it now." Leveling him with a glare, I narrow my eyes at him. "You were making it better for yourself. Job well done." I give him a golf-clap round of applause.

Gripping the handle of my luggage, I start for the curb when I see headlights coming down the street.

"I don't know what you're talking about, Tealey. I know you're upset, but if you give me a chance to explain—"

"I don't have to give you anything, Rad," I snap, the anger preferable to the pain from before. "I don't owe you more than I've already given, and arguing in the middle of a street at one in the morning isn't something I'm willing to do."

The silence stretches between us as I inch closer to the curb. He comes closer but is smart enough to keep some distance between us, and asks, "Tealey, stay. Talk to me.

We'll go upstairs for privacy." I glare at him over my shoulder. "I promise you—"

"Your promises are why we're in this mess, so don't get it twisted. And stop making promises you can't keep."

Don't second-guess yourself, Tealey.

I hate that I feel empathy when I see the sadness in his eyes, the frown that his mouth has probably never felt before as me feeling bad, and defeat is probably something his shoulders have never experienced before. But I can't let him prey on my sympathies anymore either.

I hate that I'm weak to him when I'm the victim.

A blue sedan pulls up behind his car. It's my ride.

Raising his arms out to his sides, he says, "I still don't know what we're fighting about, and you're running away before we have a chance to work it out."

"I'm not running." I stand with my chin raised. "I'm walking right out of your life."

"Leaving without so much as an explanation."

"Which is what you gave me. Nothing."

He flinches from the words.

He was obviously never mine to keep, so I set him free by pushing him away with a bitter goodbye, and say, "Let's just call it what it is, which was fun." I shrug. "For a while."

"*Fun?*" His face contorts under my neutrality. *Good.* "Oh, no. You don't get to demean what we feel—"

"We? You mean *me?* Because from what I recall, you don't feel anything at all. Right, Counselor?"

Despite my obvious intent to leave, he comes closer, lowering his voice, but revealing the ire in his eyes. "Feelings? *Fuck feelings.* They do nothing but shit on logical thinking. Nothing I say is going to change your mind tonight, but I hope that in the morning—"

"In the morning?" I ask, taken aback. "There is no

morning for us." Using his previous demonstration, I hold my fingers together and then pull them apart. "This is us in the morning. You, living your life, and me, living mine. There is no morning for us. This is it."

"Tealey?" Those feelings he tries so hard to ignore wash through him, and for the first time, it's not sadness but pain he feels. "Don't leave."

"I can't stay. The pain's too much for me as well."

This time, he reaches for me, but I move my hand away. He asks, "How did I hurt you?"

"By trying to be something you're not."

"What is that?"

"Honest."

He needs to hear the truth, *mine*, even at the sacrifice of what might have been and now will never be.

This is what I'll always remember, the moment his lies—his selfishness—caught up with him. While searching for the meaning in relation to himself, recognition of my words finally sets in. "I've been honest with you, Tealey."

"No. All you do is lie like the cheaters you represent. You're no better than them. You're just smart enough not to put a ring on it." Turning to the car when the driver comes for my suitcase, I say, "I'll be out of the apartment before you return from work on Monday."

"I don't want you out of the apartment," he says in a plea and takes my hand. I let him this time, wanting to feel the burn of his touch once more to remind me never to trust him again. "I don't want you to leave at all."

Glancing at our hands, I used to wonder what it would be like to have him want to hold me in such a way that the world would know my heart was his and his was mine.

That's not what this is. This is the desperation of a man who thought he could deceive and win.

I pull back once more, putting whatever distance I can between us, and then say, "Let me go, Rad."

His grasp tightens, but I manage to free myself—from him, the entanglements of living together, and our relationship—all at once. "I'm choosing Poughkeepsie."

38

Rad

My soul drove away in a stranger's blue sedan.

And I stood there and let it happen. *Why'd I let her go?*

Why didn't I fight harder to get her to stay?

The answer is simple: I don't know what I was fighting against.

My life has been built around having the better argument to sway a judge, and I couldn't talk my girlfriend into having a five-minute conversation. Five minutes. Would that have been enough time to undo the damage she thinks I've done?

My head throbs from the stress and lack of sleep. Not having Tealey here with me is a loss deeper and more painful than I could've imagined. It's worsened by the fact that I don't know what went wrong.

Does she not understand how I feel about her? How could she not? I did everything to earn her trust by making us the priority. Granted, I fucked up a lot along the way, but I knew she saw me trying.

I was happily changing my life for her. *Only her.* And now she's gone anyway.

Why?

The sun is rising like this is any other ordinary day. It's not. It's the first day that I'm waking up without Tealey. Nothing about that is right. My day starts and ends because she's a part of them. The middle is just a blur of hours I spend trying to get back home to her.

I push the glass across the island, letting it crash into the empty bottle.

Fuck feelings.

I can say it like a mantra, but it doesn't change the fact that I don't believe it. I stood firmly behind that motto until I met Tealey. *Until I fell in love with her.*

With her gone, I feel empty, like the bottle of bourbon.

What happened?

Jean-Luc?

Marlow?

The wedding?

Bob and Lorie?

My work?

There are too many things to list to lead me to what went wrong, except one—the truth.

Staring at the phone in front of me, I've let messages pile up from everyone from Jackson to my mom. Not one of them was from Tealey. I hop off the countertop, needing a shower to help wash away the grime from the past twenty-four hours. I'd like to get a clear head so I can see the situation in a new light.

When the screen on my phone lights up, I'm quick to glance down. I can't lie that I'm disappointed seeing it's not a message from Tealey.

Ashleigh: *Are you available?*

It's Sunday, so her needing to talk is unusual. Business never ends.

Me: *Depends . . .*

My phone rings, and I answer it because she knows I'm always fucking available, which has always been one of Tealey's biggest issues with me. "Hello?"

"Hi, boss, sorry to catch you on the weekend, but I was reviewing the deposition for the Lewis case and found items listed in the file that didn't correlate."

"Why are you working today?" I scrub over my jaw, feeling the need for a shave.

"I like to get a jump start on the week ahead."

I swear I've said those exact words. "I don't want you working today, Ashleigh. Enjoy the Sunday. Spend time with your loved ones. Relax. All of this can be worked out in the office on Monday."

"But—"

"I'm serious. Nothing is more important than spending time with those you care about."

"What's going on?" she asks, her concern traveling the line. "Why are you saying this?"

I swallow my emotions, but it lumps in my throat, refusing to go down. Letting my personal life interfere with work has never been a struggle. Until now. "Sorry. I have a lot on my mind." I walk to crack open a window, thinking fresh air would serve me well, but change my mind at the last second when I realize I'd lose the last of her scent. It may be faint, but it's kept me company all night.

Ashleigh's silence begins to make me uncomfortable. The unflappable attorney is shaken by his own assistant. That'd go over well with the firm. I can't even hold my own with her. "What? Say it. I can tell you want to."

"You're not happy." I could address that accusation a

million different ways, but I let it go because it's not untrue. "And I'm worried about you."

"Don't do this, Ashleigh. I can't get caught up in what's happening in personal dramas. That takes my eye off my job."

"From the sounds of it, you're already caught up in it. As you should be. It's your life. It's what matters most, like finding happiness."

"I'm happiest when my clients are happy."

But as soon as the line that I've spewed a hundred times before passes my lips, I know it's a lie. That's not what makes me happy. *Not anymore.*

"I owe my full attention to my clients."

"No, you don't." Her tone is firm, raised to be heard. "You owe them the hours they paid for. They don't own you outside of the business day. *Day.* Not night."

"Coming from the woman working on Sunday." I sigh, not wanting to argue with her. "My entire fucking career has been built on being available twenty-four seven, Ashleigh."

"Your career is going to be the death of you," she snaps back.

"It already is." I drop my head into my hands, resting my elbows on the island. Squeezing my eyes shut, I say, "She left me, Ashleigh."

There's a pause, and then she whispers, "Who?"

"It was our secret, only for the time being."

Her sigh has me clamping my mouth shut. She knows without me saying the name. "Tealey. Oh Rad, I'm sorry to hear your pain. I can hear how much you care about her."

"I love her." The words came out quieter than how I feel when I say them. Shouting my love for Tealey Bell from the rooftop has always been the goal when it comes to her.

"Aw, boss," she says, her tone not as heavy as before.

"Love is an amazing thing. It can make you feel on top of the world or cut you to the bone. Sometimes the right person makes you experience both."

"The right, or do you mean the wrong person?"

"The wrong person doesn't make you feel anything at all."

Tealey's words from last night come back to haunt me—*you don't feel anything at all. Right, Counselor?*

I do feel, though. Because of her, I feel alive for the first time. "I feel everything for her."

"Talk to her." There's an edge of excitement to her tone, a confidence that I needed to hear. "If you can be as open with your heart and emotions as you have been just now with me, she'll hear you." Seeming satisfied, she adds, "And I'm taking the rest of the day off to enjoy it. I'll see you tomorrow bright and early?"

"Unfortunately, for you, yes."

She laughs lightly. "Good luck, Rad."

"Thanks."

She's right. I must find a way to reach Tealey and beg her to give me a second chance. But first, I need to shower. No way am I facing her smelling like whiskey and looking like shit.

IT TAKES me too long to figure out what to wear. I gravitate toward button-up shirts and dress pants, and although I know Tealey thinks I'm attractive when I'm put together, I need to appeal to her senses. I see the way she stares at my arms and ogles my ass when I'm in a T-shirt and jeans.

The problem is, my wardrobe, like my life, is bland without her. I'm desperate to get to her, so I grab my wallet and keys, needing to make a stop on the way to see her.

I lower my sunglasses when the sunshine hits my face and stop altogether when I hear my name called from behind me.

I turn to see a woman waving her arm in the air as she runs toward me. "Rad, wait." The voice sounds familiar, but nothing about her is . . . holy shit!

Looking like I've never seen her, Marlow is wearing a tank top, leggings, and flip-flops. Not a stitch of makeup graces her face, and her hair is pulled into a mess on top of her head. She looks younger, like she did back in college, and a lot like Tealey has rubbed off on her.

Tealey. I have to get to her. I have to make this right. "I don't have time for this today, Marlow." I start in the opposite direction of her.

She runs, flanking my side. "I need to talk to you."

"No. I need a break from you."

"Please." She tugs my arm, but when I pull free, she stays where I left on the sidewalk. "I'm sorry, Rad. I didn't know about you and Tealey. I would have—"

"You would have what, Marlow?" I ask, turning around. My blood boils. "I'd really like to know what you would've done because this scheme was never about anyone but you. It was about Marlow getting what she wanted at all costs, even if that meant roping me into a fake relationship and then nearly into a fucking engagement." I raise my brows, causing her to flinch. "You screwed me over, and now you've done the same to Tealey. And maybe you didn't know about us, but you might've if you would've paid a little attention to anyone but yourself."

I cross my arms over my chest and glare at her.

She comes close enough for us not to need to yell. Not

making a scene is probably wise, so I try to temper the anger I have toward her. She says, "I would have never asked you to be a part of this if I had known you and Tealey were together." Shading her eyes with her hand, she asks, "Why didn't you guys tell us? I thought we shared everything."

I lower my guard and shove my hands in my pockets. "Because Tealey thought we would ruin your chances of getting the apartment."

She winces. "Of course, she did. She puts everyone else's needs before her own." Her thoughts are heavy, hanging in the tension of her body language. "Do you love her, Rad?"

Nodding would suffice, but I want to say the words. "I do. I love her. I think I always have."

"Two things to note," she starts with a smile creeping into the corners of her mouth. "One, always? I thought you two were enemies. You never talked or hung out with each other."

"I didn't want her to see how weak I was."

"Weak to love, and weak because you feel for a woman isn't the same thing as being a weak man. I think it actually makes you stronger."

I smile, but my body still itches to move, to find my girl. "And two?"

"Why are you still here? She's over at Jackson's apartment." Jealousy envelops me as I think about Tealey staying at Jackson's. But as I calm myself down, I realize it could be worse. At least she had a place to go in her abrupt departure from my life, and I know Jackson will be kind to her.

And hopefully, keep her there until I can figure this out . . . and get her back.

Because I will. I'll get Tealey Bell back. There is no other option.

We start walking again. "We're going to have to walk and

talk, Marlow." I glance at her beside me. "Can you help me with something?"

"Yeah, but can I say something first?" She stops again, and although I get that she wants to chat, I need to keep moving. Every second without Tealey puts distance in a possible reunion. But then I see her vulnerability, a trust exposed in the edges of her eyes that reminds me she's been hurt, disappointed, and has struggled with solid footing for as long as I've known her. The lack of dependability on her father has deepened the insecurity he created in the first place. She says, "I'm sorry for how I treated you and . . ." She looks off, but her eyes return to mine. "I'm really sorry for my dad and Lorie. He's such an asshole, and she's not much better."

I start walking again because my priority is getting to Tealey, but I give Marlow a half-smile. "I'm glad you came to New York to get away from him. And I appreciate the apology."

"Thanks, Rad."

Not a block down, I stop and head to the corner to cross the street. "That's where I need to stop on my way to see Tealey."

39

Rad

I'm more determined than ever. I push the nerves down, ready to fight for my future. Because I've had many regrets in life, but not one was being with Tealey.

The opposite is true, in fact. She made me feel I was invincible. But my pride kept me from seeing what that power was doing to her.

I leave my ego for the courtroom and knock on Jackson's door.

The peephole darkens, but then nothing. *Shit*. I didn't expect her to pretend she wasn't home. "Tealey," I say, pressing my ear to the door. "Can we talk? Please?"

Nothing.

I knock once more, and then the light seeps through the hole again. Just when I think she's going to leave me out here, I hear the door unlock, and the dead bolt turns. The door opens, and although she's only given me a sliver in which to see her, I feel my lungs fill with the air that was lacking from seconds earlier.

"I don't want to talk," she says.

"I know you don't, but can I please say my piece?" I see her gaze lower, and though I hoped for a better reaction upon seeing me—or any, for that matter—it's not why I'm here. "Tealey, I'm begging you."

She tightens the robe at her neck, and replies, "Okay."

When I realize she's not giving me an inch more of her, I'll take what she is offering—her ear.

"I'd crafted this long speech in my head all morning. I had it memorized like I was preparing to read it in court. It was full of points I thought you'd want to hear from me, evidence that made sense for us to be together. But—"

"But?" Her head tilts. It's when she lets the natural light scrape across her skin that I can see how red it is under her eyes, her lids swollen from tears. My heart twists, my chest tightening around it. Anger courses through me for causing her pain.

"I don't want to say things only because I think you want to hear them. I want to speak from my heart and hope I hit the mark. If I don't, then you can walk away. If—"

"What does your heart say, Rad?" I swallow a lump in my throat.

"Having feelings doesn't make me weak. They make me *human*, something I might have forgotten to be in some ways. I had my eyes set on a prize and lost the ability to see what winning was doing to me and, worse, how it was affecting you."

She sighs, but it's not sad or impatient. It's taking a moment to absorb my words. It's everything I hoped would happen. "Okay."

"I don't need awards or accolades. I don't need pats on the back or to make partner, Tealey. Because if I don't have you, none of that matters anymore."

Her eyes are cast down. Not that I blame her, but her blank stare and straight mouth are killing me inside.

"Tealey?"

She looks back up, eyeing me through the crack of the door.

"I wouldn't have hidden us from the world if I thought I'd had a choice. I *did* have a choice, though. I see that now. I was making a choice to play a part of that charade every day."

The tension between us is thick and full of the emotions we both share. I can barely hear Tealey's quick breaths over my own pulse rushing through my veins.

I love her. *God, I love her.* I love her more than I ever thought I could love anyone.

"Tealey . . ."

She pauses, hesitation warring in those sparkling blues. Finally, as I shove my hands in my pockets to stop from reaching out to her, she pulls the door open a bit wider.

Her eyes dart to the floor as if looking at me is too hard. "Jackson went for a run. If you want to come in for a minute, that would be okay."

Relief swamps me as I try not to overreact. "I'd appreciate that."

She moves away from the door as I enter, keeping a wide distance between us. Not having her pressed against me in our usual greeting is another dagger in my heart and a reminder of all I've lost.

All we've lost. Because my actions caused Tealey to lose, too.

She moves to the leather couch, where it looks like she's been camping out. Stuff is littered across the coffee table, from soda cans to snack wrappers, balled-up tissues, and a paperback book.

Closing the door behind me, I take the opening as an opportunity to lay out the rest of my case. Though I'm not sure where to sit or if I should stand. I'm thinking right next to her probably won't go over well, so I sit in a chair on the other side of the coffee table from her.

She settles into the cushions and then twists her hair on top of her head, fastening it with an elastic before she rests back. Gnawing on the inside of her cheek, she toys with the belt of her robe and then takes an audible breath. "Go on."

"Do you have any questions for me? Anything on your mind?"

She glances away with a look of annoyance filtering through her features. "Too many to bother asking at this stage."

"What stage is that?"

"The one that has us going in reverse instead of moving forward with our own lives." *What is my own life without her? Doesn't she see?*

"I don't want that," I say, trying my best to stay calm and not just blurt out that I love her. She needs to be heard, especially after what I put her through. So, I let her lead.

She furrows her brows, seemingly baffled. "You don't want what? The reverse or the forward?"

"Either. Neither option works for me."

She arches a brow. "Well, this isn't only about you anymore."

"It never was *only* about me. I tried to do my best for everyone who wanted a piece of me and failed miserably."

"You failed because you focused on the stuff that was always going to come back at you negatively. Such a tangled web you weaved." She pushes up, her back stiffening. Her hands clasp together in front of her chest. "You had me, Rad. You had me and chose to lose me over what you keep calling a charade. Getting engaged goes beyond a faux romance that was supposedly performed for Marlow's dad."

Taken aback, I stare at her, now knowing why she was so upset. "You heard I was engaged?"

The question makes her bristle. "Every guest heard you were engaged, that you made it official with Marlow down on the beach before the wedding."

What the fuck is going on? "Who'd you hear that from?"

She crosses her arms over her chest again. "Doesn't matter," she says pointedly.

Now everything makes sense. "It sure the fuck does matter. Someone telling you something that they had no right to say is my fucking business."

"Not if it doesn't change things." She summons a deep breath, but it's shaky. "An engagement is a declaration of your love," she says, her voice sounding wistful. "It shows the world you've found your soul mate."

I thought we were on the right track. My heart beats faster, like I might be given the chance that I so desperately want. That I need. To have it lost in an instant based on gossip . . . I'm to blame. I'm the one who hurt her. It's because of me that she would even believe that lie.

Then her eyes pin me to the couch. "Rad, you talk a good talk, but it was about walking the walk as well. You and I were always sitting on the same side of the table. We had nothing to protect from the other. We were on the same team. Team us. But just when I thought we were really coming together, you turned against me. You just didn't give me the courtesy of knowing your feelings had changed."

"We were on the same team. We are. We still are, Tealey."

"I believe you. I really do. I think you're hardwired to work in such a way that you'd rather hide your heart than put it on the line to be hurt. And I think that's why you did this, whether you're conscious of it or not." She stands, leaving me so much to digest.

But the flaw in her argument . . . I rub the bridge of my nose, realizing I do treat us like we're on different sides of a case.

She leans her hip against the kitchen bar with her arms crossed over her chest. Her anger begins to dissipate, but the distrust is still on display in her pursed lips. I slow the questions racing through my head. This isn't a cross-examination. This is the woman I want to be with, the one I want to marry.

I stand, coming around the couch and resting on the back of it. We have enough separating us that I don't want distance to add to it.

"I fucked up," I say. "I'm sorry for that. You're right. I had your devotion and lost your trust. My attention was divided when you gave me all of yours. But I need you to know the truth because somewhere along the grapevine, someone else lied to you."

Her arms tighten their hold around her, making herself smaller. *Fuck.* Have I done that? If given the chance, I'll make sure she always knows how much she means to me and that I value her.

"Who lied?" she asks. "About what?"

"You may think I know nothing about feelings, especially love, but hear me out. I would never, *not ever* sacrifice the chance to ask for your hand in marriage for a ploy to gain financial wealth."

Her blinks have appeared measured until now, when they become erratic. "I'm not following."

"When I ask you to marry me, that will be the only time I ever ask anybody."

She begins to pace in front of me, staring at the floor, but occasionally glancing at me. She stops and stares me directly in the eyes. "Are you saying you didn't ask Marlow to marry you?"

"The only woman I'd ever ask that of is you."

I hear her gulp, and then her bottom lip wobbles. "You want to marry me?" Her hands flail in front of her face. "One day?"

I've never felt more certain about anything than knowing I want her in my life forever. "I'm going to marry you one day, Tealey. If you let me, we can work through the misinformation and get to the truth. But I want you to know that whoever told you that Marlow and I were engaged probably has an ulterior motive. His name probably starts with Jean as well."

Her eyes mist with tears. "He also said Americans have lost the art of romance."

I hold my hand out, palm up for a long couple of seconds. Finally, when she slips her hand in mine, I kiss it. "Give me a second chance to love you, Tealey Bell, and I'll spend the rest of my life proving that fucker wrong."

The tears she's been holding back break the dam and stream down her beautiful face. I close the gap and wrap my arms around my girl instead.

"Tealey?"

"Yeah?"

I lean back just enough to see her. Tilting her chin up to look into her eyes, I say, "I love you. I love you so much."

Tears fall from her eyes again. "I love you," she says. "And I'm sorry for not trusting you." She lifts on her feet to kiss me again. Our lips are together, and our souls are in sync.

When she hugs me, I realize how much I missed not just

her presence and soul that fills mine with life, but her touch, her body against mine, and this connection.

It's been an intense sixteen hours. *I wouldn't want to repeat that again.*

Stepping back, she grins. "I'm glad we got everything out on the table." The belt of her robe loosens, and the ends fall apart. As if I couldn't have planned it better, I strip off the hoodie I had to buy to hide my shirt. Now seems like the right time to reveal it.

I watch as her gaze guides across the design. I see the joy when it rises inside. Looking down, she pulls her shirt away from her chest, and says, "Got Rhubarb?"

I grin. "I got your rhubarb right here, babe."

"Where'd you find that shirt? It's perfect."

"In the *I'm-the-right-guy-for-you* section of the store."

Her lips twist with a smile that warms my heart. "Punny guy."

I wink. "I learn from the best."

I used to think that sex had nothing to do with dating. Dating was about companionship while sex just satisfied physical needs. *I was wrong.* With the right person, you not only find what you want but you also get what you need.

I kiss the top of her head and then lower to her forehead and cheek and then find her lips. When we're left breathless, we part begrudgingly. Tealey's smile lights up my life once again, and she asks, "Is it me or is the best part of fighting the making up?"

"I think it's the only good part of fighting." I smirk. "I think we should get to it. Do you still have those condoms?"

Joy sparks in her eyes. "We've used a lot, but I think I have a good twenty or so left. Except they're at home."

Home.

I wrap my arm around her shoulder and kiss her head

again. "Yes, speaking of, let's go home together. Forever." I kiss her again and then let her go, only temporarily so she can gather her belongings. "I forgot to ask, who's Pough-keepsie and what an unfortunate name."

"What do you mean *who*?"

I narrow my eyes in confusion. "Last night, you said you were choosing Poughkeepsie."

"Oh." She laughs. "The city."

"Still lost." I've learned that eventually, we'll get there, but I'm not in a hurry.

Rolling her suitcase in from the spare room, she says, "I'm being transferred to Poughkeepsie."

"What?" I ask, thinking we just took two steps back. "No way. Not having it. Not on my watch."

With her hand on her hip, she cocks a brow at me over a teasing smile. "You may have a nice watch, Rad, but you have no say."

I grin. "We'll see."

40

Tealey

Lately, Rad's favorite thing to do is to introduce me as his girlfriend . . . to anyone who will listen.

Strangers at the coffee shop.

The poor souls stuck sitting next to us at restaurants.

Don't even get me started on the sweet elderly couple at the movie theater the other night. The memory causes me to blush on command.

I'm not complaining. I always get a compliment or two. He gets a "lucky guy," so I figure we both win. It's just fun to tease him because seeing the former most eligible bachelor brag about how lucky he is for being my boyfriend makes me pretty damn lucky, too.

We walk in, holding hands, and weave through the busy diner until we see our friends in the back. I wave. I know Cammie and Cade were only gone two weeks, but I've missed them. And now they're officially a married couple.

A round of mimosas awaits us, and we hug. "Was it the best?" I ask her about their honeymoon in the Bahamas.

"It's the bluest water I've ever seen. We all need to go sometime." She leans in as the guys shake hands. "And you need to fill me in on everything asap. I've been dying for this to come out."

"You knew?"

She glances to Rad nervously. "Um, someone let it slip in the Hamptons." Just as I give Rad the evil eye, she says, "I was sworn to secrecy and it was nice to see thing evolve naturally. You didn't need all of us in your relationship."

"I appreciate that." Giving Rad a look again, I say, "You owe me a new mug." It's my favorite way to justify my addiction, get him to buy them for me.

He squeezes my hand. "I know other ways to repay you."

"Oh, that sounds interesting."

Kissing the top of my head, he says, "I'll tell you all about it later in bed."

My body heats and I wipe my brow. "Can't wait."

Cade leans in to give me a hug, and then I turn to sit next to Rad right before Jackson and Marlow walk in. Or maybe I should say, arriving at the same time. She looks at him behind her in surprise. "Oh, I didn't see you there." She acts all awkward. "Hey."

He nods . . . *awkwardly*. "Hey."

I notice a few people around our table staring. We never much cared if we made a scene. We're loud. We're a family.

With Rad holding my hand on one side of me, Marlow says, "We should hang out soon."

"We should." We've communicated through text several times and had a call after Rad and I made up, but it's been relatively quiet after that. I ask, "Are you doing okay?"

"I am."

Getting a good look at her, I start to see the subtle changes in her hair—less styled and more natural. Her makeup is lighter, and her clothes are casual. Casual for Marlow anyhow. "You look pretty."

She smiles sheepishly. "Thanks. You always look pretty, Teals, but you look especially happy."

"I am." I hug her. She's my best friend. I know she would never hurt me, not on purpose. I think we've all learned a hard lesson that's made us take inventory of ourselves. "Thanks."

When we pull back, we exchange smiles, and then she hands me a present. I ask, "What is this?"

"I thought it was time for a change. Seems to be the season."

I discard the tissue and pull a T-shirt from the bag. Holding it in front of me, I read, "I'm a Rachel." The *Friends* tee makes me smile and feels a lot like I just got a promotion. "You didn't have to do this. I'm happy to be Phoebe to your Rachel."

She squeezes my hand. "I love you, Teals."

I embrace her again, rubbing her back. "Thank you."

Cammie asks me, "Have the calls stopped?"

The only downside to dating the Big Apple's most eligible bachelor—for three years running, he likes to add—is our relationship became public very fast. The news that Radcliffe Wellington was "taken" hit hard and fast, and then we were old news. I ask, "From the gossip columnists or Rad's lady friends? Yes, to the former. No, to the latter. I guess the news of us dating hasn't landed in Europe yet." I nudge Rad with my elbow and laugh. He rolls his eyes. *Why is it so cute when he does that?*

After we catch up on the past few weeks in each of my friends' lives, we eat, and then Cammie says, "Now for the business at hand."

Cammie, Cade, Rad, and I turn to the guilty parties—

Marlow and Jackson. It helped that we were all in cahoots to figure out exactly what was going on with those two.

Marlow's gaze dashes from one to the next until she's staring at Jackson. He shrugs, so she looks at Cammie, and asks, "What?"

Always direct, Cade asks, "Are you two friends with benefits or the real thing?" He grabs a bagel from the basket in the center of the table and starts smearing cream cheese on it like this is everyday conversation. Gotta love him.

While Marlow sputters the mimosa she just drank, Jackson says, "Huh?"

Rad says, "Playing dumb isn't a defense. For the record, too many things don't add up."

Marlow dabs the corners of her mouth, eyeing the door like she's about to make a break for it. Jackson mutters under his breath, "Let's just tell them."

She does the most minute shake of her head. I say, "Just in case you weren't aware, we can hear *and* see you."

"Fine," she replies, her palms hitting the Formica table and causing the flatware to jump and then clang against our plates. "We had sex."

Jackson sits back with a wry smirk, and adds, "We *have* sex."

Marlow gasps, blinking rapidly. With her mouth hanging open, she scans our faces, but I'm sure we don't look much different. Jackson's arm wings out, nudging her. When she looks at him, he winks. I'm not sure if it was the wink or nudge that sets her off when she blurts, "Fine!" She crosses her arms over her chest. "We *have* sex. Sometimes. When we're lonely. I'm busy with my career, and he's busy, and I guess it's easy. He's easy."

"Geez, thanks, Marlow," he replies sarcastically.

Reaching for her leg, he rests his hand there like any of

this is normal. She glances at it and then calms. "Comforting. I meant comforting with the familiarity." She faces us, and the steadiness of her expression makes me believe her. Her chin rises in the air, and she says, "I'm sure a lot like how you and Rad were."

Rad laughs. "Don't drag us into this. This is all about the two of you."

This is too amusing. I sit back in my chair and watch Marlow squirm. "Do you go on dates?"

Like an old married couple, Jackson takes this one. "We hang out, but we don't go on official dates. It's not like that with us. Though we do order pizza sometimes. She makes me order cauliflower crust, so that doesn't really count as pizza."

"I'm watching my carb intake. You know that. Anyway, there aren't complications with him," she says, joining in. I almost expect him to say tag, you're it. "We already decided that if we meet someone we want to get to know better, then we'll stop doing whatever this is."

Jackson's nodding, and the way they're looking at each other, I guess they're on the same page.

Cade says, "All right. With that out of the way, who's coming over to watch the game?"

Rad stands. "Sorry, Tealey and I already have plans." Tossing money on the table, he says, "Brunch is on me."

Everyone gets up and files out of the restaurant. Just outside the door on the sidewalk, Marlow asks, "So next Sunday?"

"We're in," Cammie replies.

I glance at Rad, but I already know the answer. He takes my hand, and says, "We'll be here." I've never felt so right about my decision to let him back into my life. Hearing the man I can rely on to always be there privately and publicly sound so happy to be one-half of a couple makes my heart melt.

Jackson nudges Marlow. "Since I'll be rolling out of your bed—"

"Ew. You're so crude, Jackson."

"That's why you love me."

"I don't love you," she snaps. "I'm still not sure if I even like you, if I'm telling the truth."

"Well, something keeps you sniffing around my door."

Marlow whacks him on the arm.

Rad chuckles. "Okay, guys. I think it's time to go. Have a good week." Taking my hand, he leads me in the opposite direction as the four of them.

We start down the sidewalk, the warm afternoon air caressing my skin. Birds chirp happily overhead. "What do you plan on doing the rest of the day, Miss Bell?"

"Doing?" I smirk, giving him the grin I usually save for when we're alone. "Nothing but you, Counselor."

His arm flies into the air. "Taxi!"

EPILOGUE

Rad

Eight months later

I WALKED AWAY.

And I couldn't be happier.

It's surreal how much my life has changed. A year ago, I would have been hitting the partners and board members hard with every reason I deserved that promotion.

Today, I stood in the conference room, removing myself from contention. It turns out, Bob Marché is financially bankrupt—morally too, but that's another story.

Apparently, Bob thought that marrying his daughter off to me would give him an in with my family—and our money. Desperate times, desperate measures, I guess, since his last four movies tanked. It does help that Marlow was as unsuspecting as anyone else in the situation.

The mortgage papers he dangled in front of his daughter at the beach? Fake. A desperate attempt to make me close the deal and pop the question. I cut ties early enough to save the firm's reputation. Thankfully.

And my heart had other plans.

Not only do I not want partner anymore but stepping away was the right thing to do. Rogers is coming off a two-billion-dollar settlement deal against a large pharmaceutical company. He wants to work long hours, all weekends, and every holiday. Good for him. He deserves the promotion and will make a great partner.

I didn't elaborate on the new direction my life is taking or the life I'm building with my gorgeous girlfriend. Tealey's shown me that living to work isn't living at all. I think she saved me just in time to fix the errors of my way.

Anyway, my winning streak in court is still intact, so I'm good.

Better than good these days because I got the girl instead.

I arrive home with arms of groceries and a present or two tucked in my bags. I was able to put everything away and get a workout in before Tealey walked in the door.

"You're home early," she says, hanging her keys on the hook and setting her bag on the floor.

She gets more beautiful every day. I come to greet her with a kiss but find myself hanging on to her a little longer. "Light day."

"I didn't know attorneys had light days." She wriggles away after another quick kiss. I'm sweaty but was hoping to take a shower with her.

Returning to the kitchen, I reply, "Normally, no, but the partners thought I might want to leave on time today."

"Why?" Seeing the bowl of cherry tomatoes on the counter, she plucks one and pops it in her mouth. Everything she does is so fucking sexy.

I lean against the counter like I'm not about to drop a

huge bomb in her lap. Grinning, I say, "I'm not going to be a partner."

Her mouth opens to ask the question I see forming in her eyes, but then she looks up at me. "I'm sorry. I know how much that meant to you."

"I'm not upset." I kiss that soft spot behind her ear, sending a thrill of goose bumps over her skin. "I wanted it before I had anything else. That doesn't hold true for me anymore." Rubbing her back, I smile, looking at my bright-eyed girl. "I have you, and I'm pretty damn invested in our future. So tonight, we're celebrating a different kind of victory—a big thing called getting a life. I got one because of my partnership with you, and that is worth more than a promotion at work."

"So I'm the trade-off? A life with me or a successful career?" There's no bitterness in her tone despite the words. She knows what she means to me because I don't just tell her. I show her. But I don't want her to feel guilty like she's taking something away from me.

"There's no competition. You'll win every time." I look into those baby blues, and say, "I took myself out of the running because I've been considering a change of careers for a while now." Her lips twitch.

"The best divorce attorney in the city doesn't want to divorce people?"

It's a struggle not to grin, so I cock my brow. "Do I detect a note of sarcasm?"

She shrugs and then rests her hand on the side of my neck. The caress of her thumb causes my eyelids to dip briefly, savoring her touch and the comfort between us.

Reciprocating, I touch her cheek with the same care. "I've been thinking about your dream."

"Which dream is that?" she asks with her thoughts elsewhere.

Before this conversation moves to the bedroom, I reply, "The dream to help kids. What do you think about setting up a foundation?"

She leans back, her eyes wide. *The dots have connected.* "To help kids find homes and provide meals—"

"And the training and after-school programs. I've been talking to my mom, and it's something she could help us set up. She has experience working with charities. Add in your trained skill set and I think it would work. You could develop it from the ground up, getting the right people in place to help it grow."

Slipping away, Tealey walks through the living room to the window. She rests against the sill, still facing me, her thoughts pinching her brows together. "I don't understand, Rad. You're giving up your career to help me?"

"I still might work, just not as much. I like my career. I just hate the hours. But it became even more apparent when Misty's paperwork came through a couple of days ago that I really liked that. I liked helping her, protecting her. I'd like to do more of that sort of thing with my time."

I come closer, wedging between her legs and rubbing her shoulders. "You could stop commuting to Poughkeepsie three days a week and follow a different dream."

Her expression softens. "Misty's studying to be a social worker in Philly."

"Because you inspire people."

"I appreciate the vote of confidence, but setting up a nonprofit takes money, Rad. A lot of money. If you aren't working—"

"I'll be working, but you've always known that I come from money. I have trust funds."

Cupping her ear, she leans closer. "Did I hear an S, as in plural?"

I chuckle. "Yes, six of them, and only one's been touched." Taking her hand, I turn it over and then lean down to kiss her palm, worried how she'll react to the next part. I suck in a breath. "I lied to you."

Her hand is yanked back, and I'm struck with a glare. "Rad . . ."

She doesn't have to say more. The tone gets her message across loud and clear. White knuckling the windowsill, she asks, "What is it?" I was trying to avoid worrying her.

I start talking faster. "I got notice that the third-floor tenant is moving out."

She tilts her head, worry turning into interest. "I'm not following."

There are reasons I never shared the history of my inheritances or about the building. Simply put, I didn't want to be treated any differently. But she's going to find out one day, so I might as well confess. "It's a small lie by omission. I know that counts but hear me out."

She sighs heavily. "Tell me."

"I own the building."

Unblinking, she stares at me for a disconcerting number of seconds. Maybe it's been minutes. I scratch the back of my neck nervously. Not able to bear the silence, I finally ask, "What are you thinking?"

"I just . . . Um . . ." She directs her gaze out the window, blocking me from reading what's on her mind. When her eyes return to mine, she asks, "Since when?"

"Since college. I bought it with some of the money from one of my trust funds."

"Oh, right, the plural amount of trust funds . . . there's nothing normal about that, just so you know."

"It is in my world." I tuck her hair behind her ears. "*Our* world."

"You say that like I blend in with your world with such ease," she says in disbelief.

"You do. You fit right in. You've become it. You're my whole world."

Another soft sigh escapes her, but a smile graces her face. "I feel the same about you, but I didn't realize how much you were worth."

Nothing I can say will make her feel more comfortable about never having to worry about money. She's lived her entire life doing the opposite. She asks, "How much does that apartment rent for?"

I grin. "Are you in the market?"

"I can't afford your spare bedroom," she deadpans. Her hand covers her mouth, hiding most of her pretty smile from me. "So, I know I can't afford a full-floor apartment in this neighborhood or any apartment in the city." I breathe easier when all signs of concern disappear from her features. "But I am curious."

"Ten thousand."

Her mouth falls open. "A month?" Stumbling back, she catches herself on the frame of the window. "Good lord, Rad. You're rich rich. Richie Rich rich. Rockefeller rich."

"Not Rockefeller rich."

Fanning herself, she jokes, "I'm going to need a second to process this new information. Do Jackson and Cade know?"

"I've never given them my financials, but Jackson *St. James* isn't far off. His last name's a staple in this city. I'm only sharing this information with you."

"You're telling me because you have the money to start the nonprofit? Just lying around?"

"I've never rolled in a pile of money exactly, but I could, so yes. I have my trust funds, but I've also made a lot of money in the stock market." Now everything's just pouring out, financial vomiting is probably not something I should make a habit of, but for her—anything. "My career. Basically, everything I touch turns to gold." *I smirk because I'm not called the golden boy for nothing.*

Pursing her lips, she then laughs. "Your humility is something I've always admired about you."

That's my opening. I move in and take hold of her hips. "My girl's got jokes." I kiss her neck, nuzzling against her soft skin until I score a mewl from her.

"Boy, do I." She cracks up. "I started as an opening act and recently moved into headlining."

"You'll always be my shining star."

I try to kiss her, but her hands are on my chest, and she says, "Before we get sidetracked, because we often do, you want to use your money to not only make my dream come true but also to change countless lives for the better?"

"Yes. Now can we kiss?"

"No, *and for the record . . .*" Tealey loves using my words against me. She has the courtesy of kissing me, at least. "You think it's your hands, but I know it's your heart that's pure gold. That's why I love you, Rad."

Who's charming whom? She might just be winning. "I love you, too."

I'm still fairly new to this coupling thing, but I feel like I caught on quickly. It's never been about time for us. If that were the case, I would have given up eight years ago. But with the mileage of our friendship and the journey of dating, I don't want to waste any more time.

Lowering her head to her shoulder, she cradles my head, and whispers, "Did you always know we were meant to be?"

Inhaling her scent that's become like air to me, I savor these times when I can just be me. With her, that's who I am. The better man. "I always knew you were the one. I just hoped that one day you'd see me as more than *just friends*."

"I always saw you as more, my love. I just thought we were an impossibility. You proved me wrong." A sweet kiss lands on my cheek.

"But now?" I ask timidly.

"I don't bet the odds anymore, gambling man. When it comes to you, I'm not leaving anything to chance. Why would I? You're more than I could have ever asked for."

That's all I ever need to be—hers. "If you want me naked, all you have to do is ask."

"I want you naked, Counselor."

Lifting her into my arms, I walk toward the door. "Your wish is my command."

CALL me a genie because I made all her wishes come true last night. Sexually speaking. I'm hoping she grants my wish this morning.

I have her coffee down to a science. One-third half and half, two sugar-in-the-raw cubes, and a heavy splash of coffee.

"What are you doing up so early on a Saturday?" Tealey's arms wrap around me from behind. I like when she hugs me like I'm her lifeline.

Spinning in her arms, I embrace her. "I had some stuff on my mind, so I went for a run to clear my head."

Stroking my hair back from my forehead, she kisses my lips, closing her eyes and lingering. "Did it help?"

"No, only you can help me."

"At your service." Her eyes flick to the mug, her expression lighter. "Is that a new mug?"

"It is."

"You bought me a gift?" Picking it up with care, she reads the front. "I love you a latte. *Awww.* That is so sweet, Rad. Thank you. I absolutely love it." She kisses me again and then takes a sip. "Sorry, I was distracted by the cuteness of this mug." Waving her arm, she says, "Okay, back to you. What's going on that you needed to clear your head?"

"It's actually related to the mugs." For effect and added drama to this buildup, I open the cabinet door.

"How so?" She glances at the collection and then gives me puppy eyes.

"I used to be content with plain white mugs." Pointing to the mostly barren left side of the cabinet, I say, "How did I live a life so—"

"Boring."

I laugh. "I was going to say orderly."

"Orderly. *Boring.*" She shrugs and then takes another sip. "Same thing. I mean, look at the adorable drawing of the face on this illustration on the front of my mug."

"Yeah, it's very meta."

"I don't know what you mean."

"Like Fight Club . . . Okay, never mind. It's not important. What *is* important is that I love you a latte. I mean, a lot. I like your mugs in my cabinet, and I'm not even bothered by the way you squeeze the toothpaste in the middle of the tube like a serial killer."

Slow blinking, she twists her mouth. "Serial killer might be taking it a little too far, don't you think?"

I shrug. "Is it?"

"A wee bit, but I get the intention behind it. Carry on."

We've gotten off track, so to steer this baby back into the right lane, I tap the mug. "Bottoms up."

"That's what he said. Last night, in fact." Her giggle-snort causes her body to vibrate with laughter. "I'll be here all week, folks." She's my regular comedian, but she's not making this easy.

"So yeah, um. What I'm trying to say—"

"I've never known you to struggle with words."

I've never done this before.

Is it hot in here?

I casually bump the mug closer to her mouth. "Drink the coffee!" I shout, and then whisper, "please."

"Good gracious, Rad." Her brow creases, and her tone is cross. "Why? Did you poison me?"

"No," I reply an octave too loud. *Shit. I'm fucking this up.*

Her eyebrow cocks. Now we're off the rails entirely.

"For Pete's sake," I say, "I didn't poison you."

"Who's Pete?"

This is not how it was supposed to go. "I don't know who Pete is. I don't care who Pete is. It's just an expression."

"I know. I was only teasing." She giggles. "What's wrong?"

I grab the mug and dump the remaining coffee down the drain. With her hands on her hips, she scowls. "Why'd you do that?"

I practically shove the mug back at her and then sink to one knee. "Look at the mug."

"It's adorable. Thank you," she says, irritation coating her tone. "I already said I love it, but you didn't have to waste perfectly good coffee."

I take a deep breath. I love this woman with my whole heart. Apparently, I'm not making it easy on her either. This was a terrible plan. Rubbing my forehead, I say, "*Look inside the mug, Tealey.*"

She does . . . and then it happens. She finally sees what I've been anxious for her to read. Her lips part, and her chest rises and falls with a heavy breath. "Will you marry me, Tealey?" Each word sounded out as tears sprang to her eyes. When her attention pivots to me, she sets the mug on the counter and caresses my cheek. "Did you have that made for me?"

"No," I say casually, like it's not hard to find the name Tealey on anything. The confusion written on her face was not exactly what I was aiming for with this proposal. "Yes, I had it made. Trust me, there are no other Tealeys in the Tri-state area."

Since I've already screwed it up, I flip open the velvet box to reveal the ring I had designed for her, with the help of Marlow and Cammie, who insisted on input. My stomach does a flip, and my heart is beating out of my chest.

I clear my throat, trying to be serious and sincere. "I love you, baby, your punny mugs, cat pjs, and rock star romance reading ways. There's no one else I want to wake up to each morning or go to bed with each night other than with you. Destiny introduced us, but we made it happen. Now, I can't imagine my life without you. I may not be an odds man, but I'd bet on us every time, baby." I look at her and lick my lips. "Will you marry me, Tealey Bell?"

Not the best argument I've ever laid out, but it's us—a little orderly and a dash of chaos.

She sits on my bent knee, wrapping her arms around my neck, and says, "Yes, because underneath those tailored suits and behind those crystal awards, you were always a man who knew what he wanted. You just momentarily lost your way, but you got here in the end. So, yes, I'll marry you, Counselor."

"How's tomorrow?"

She giggles again and then kisses me.

At one time, divorce just about destroyed my belief in love, but then along came Tealey to prove me wrong. The chance to love her for a lifetime is a gift that I'll never take for granted. Not in this life, or in the next. And every time I get to kiss her sweet lips, it's like the entire universe is rooting for us.

Ashleigh once told me I'd fall so hard that I wouldn't know what hit me. I know exactly what hit me—a pretty, blue-eyed beauty not watching where she was going with a bag full of strawberries. And that's how I fell head over feels for the woman of my dreams.

When Tealey tells the story, she says she was on her way to psychology. When I tell it, I say she was on her way to me. Either version makes for a good story, but mine makes for a happy ending.

If I do say so myself.

And I do.

Bam, and here we are.

TEALEY'S BOOK RECOMMENDATIONS

Tealey is an avid reader and the following are not only her recommendations but also the books she was reading. Hope you enjoy them as much as she does.

In addition to Tealey and Rad's story in Head Over Feels, which is part of the *New York Love Stories* series, I think you'll enjoy reading the following books. They are all standalones that will grab your heart and carry it on the journey along some familiar names. All are FREE to read in Kindle Unlimited.

New York Love Stories series includes:
  Never Got Over You
  The One I Want
  Crazy in Love
  Head Over Feels

Never Got Over You - You must meet Natalie and Nick. The universe shifts and their stars realign. Third time's a charm . . . or is it? *Now Available.*

The One I Want - Juni and Andrew are a breath of fresh air that will have your heart swooning and have you smiling. *Now Available.*

Crazy in Love - You've never met a more determined and devoted hero as Harrison. The girl of his dreams slipped away, their lives taking them in different directions. When destiny brings them back together, they find the chemistry still remains. *Now Available.*

Tealey's Reads in Head Over Feels:

New York Times and *USA Today Bestseller: The Resistance* - Torn between what Holliday Hughes knew about Jack Dalton and a mysterious side he tried to hide, could she walk away or was he simply too hard to resist? *Now Available.*

Spark - Meet these up-and-coming rock star brothers and the fierce women they fall for. Spark is all the heart and passion, depth of characters, and originality of We Were Once. *Now Available.*

We Were Once - Read the Bestselling Book that's been called **"The Most Romantic Book Ever"** by readers and have them raving. Turn the page for a sneak peek. *Now Available.*

NEVER GOT OVER YOU

NEVER GOT OVER YOU CHAPTER 1

Natalie St. James

I'm the first to admit I have no business taking another shot.

Especially after the past two.

But what's a girl to do when a room full of strangers is chanting my name and a particularly wild best friend places the shot hat on my head along with a small glass of liquor in my hand?

I drink.

In a little hole-in-the-wall hidden from the main street in Avalon on Catalina Island, I down the liquid like a champ, then promptly proceed to fall from grace, also known as the barstool.

My eyes close, bracing for impact, except . . . someone catches me just before landing. With my breath caught in my throat, I hang in the balance of arms made of steel and open my eyes.

Laughter fades away with any drunken shame that threatened as I stare into the soulful eyes of a stranger.

"Hi," whispers the future hero of my dirty dreams . . . *oh, wait.*

Maybe I'm unconscious? Maybe I was knocked out cold, and I'm dreaming. I blink. Why are my eyes open? Letting my lids fall, I keep them closed long enough to pray, "Please let him be real. If he's not, I'm begging you to leave me in this dream a little longer." My lids drift back open to find him still staring at me.

"Are you okay?"

"Perfect," I reply. *I think.* I'm not sure if I actually voice the response or not. I feel pretty damn perfect in his arms, though, the response still fitting in any circumstance that involves me, him, and those arms wrapped around my body.

Naked would be nice, but I'll save that for our second date.

His brow furrows, but a smile curls the corners of his lips.

The fog of alcohol clouds my mind, creating a heavy blanket on my brain. Regardless, I try to calculate the odds of a ridiculously sexy stranger—the exact man I'd craft if Create-a-Hottie was an actual thing—being in the right place at the right time to catch me if I fell.

It's impossible, so the only logical answer to this conundrum is that either he is the best college graduation gift ever or I'm dreaming. "How are you so hot?" I ask, worried he'll disappear in a puff of smoke and mirrors. Clamping my eyes closed again, I whisper, "Dear Lord, please don't let him be a mirage."

"I'm real." *Yes!*

Does that mean my friend set up this encounter for me? She's always been a great gift giver. It is our job, after all. I squint one eye open, biting my bottom lip. "*Mm*, so real," I purr. *Too perfect to be real, though. I must be dreaming.*

His grin creates dimples that could compete with the Grand Canyon. *How did I know I liked dimples enough to add them into this delirium?* I don't know, but score one for me.

"I think you're going to be okay," my dream man says, his voice as delectable as his face.

Wait, what? No. "As for me being okay, not so fast, buddy. No need to rush toward the waking hours. Anyway . . ." I drape my hand across my forehead. "Dream or real, I'm going to need mouth-to-mouth resuscitation."

His dimples dig deeper. "Is that so?"

"*So* right," I pant.

"Do you think I should call a paramedic?"

"That's a little kinky for me, but if you're into it . . ." I press my lips into a pretty little pout to seriously consider this twist. "Nah. Changed my mind. I only want you. Just the two of us resuscitating each other."

"You want me?" he asks, surprise tingeing his tone as he cocks an eyebrow. He readjusts me in his strong, manly arms. "Circling back to the real part, you do realize you're not dreaming, right?"

I reach up and wrap my arms around his neck, wanting to melt in his arms again. Totally obsessed with how I fit so perfectly, I pull him closer and hold tight. "You do realize you're stupidly attractive, right?"

He chuckles, his grin lifting higher on one side.

That smirk would totally get me into bed, given what it's doing to me while dreaming. I close my eyes again. "I'm ready."

"For what?" His deep, dulcet tones vibrate through my body.

"Resuscitation. I'm ready. Resuscitate away."

When nothing happens, I peek one eye open. He's still

staring at me with the smirk I'm ready to kiss off his sexy face, and whispers, "I don't think you need me—"

"Trust me." Opening both eyes, I also run my fingers through his shiny, chestnut-hued hair, taking in the feel of the soft strands. "I really, *really* need you."

When he leans down, I prepare my lips with a quick lick before meeting his . . . or at least, that's the direction I hope this dream is going.

"I was thinking—"

"Yes?" My gaze floats from his mouth to his eyes again.

"We've been at this a while. Maybe we should get you off the floor?" His head tilts to the side, and the industrial lights above him shine bright in my eyes, almost like a place of business, a restaurant, or a bar would hang. My senses begin to return, starting with the stench of old beer scenting the air.

"Yuck." Next comes a wave of cedar-y cologne and salty air. That's a scent I approve of, but that's when something else hits me. *What if I'm not dreaming?*

"Up you go," he says, shadowing me again as he tries to lift me to my feet.

I don't budge. "Dream or not, I quite enjoy being horizontal with you."

"Are you always this, *should we say*, flirtatious?" he asks, laughter punctuating his question.

"Not when I'm awake, no."

As if he couldn't be more gorgeous, little lines whisker from the outer corners of his eyes, enticing me to drag my fingertip along each one. I don't, but I want to. "Are your eyes hazel or brown? It's hard to tell in this light."

"Brown."

"Brown does them a disservice. A kaleidoscope of colors

is trapped inside them. I'm going to need a closer look in the sunshine."

"The sun will be setting soon."

"Then we should hurry."

A restrained chuckle wriggles his lips. "You can stare into my eyes, but I have to warn you, once you do, you'll fall madly in love with me. And I'm leaving tomorrow, so if we're falling in love, you better get to the loving part since you've already fallen."

"Good point."

"Get up, Natalie," my best friend says, rudely barging into my fantasy and peering at me from beside his shoulder. "The floor is filthy! Now you're going to have to wash your hair."

My eyes shift her way. "Please go away and let me have this one little dream, Tatum."

Snapping her fingers twice in front of my face has me jerking my head back. "You're wide awake and making a fool of yourself."

Noise from the crowded bar filters into my consciousness. Instead of looking around to confirm, I stare into Dreamy's eyes a moment longer and then exhale as embarrassment becomes reality, returning me to the present. "You're real, aren't you?"

A slow nod accompanies a smug expression.

The heat of my cheeks has me pressing my hands to them in hopes of cooling my skin down. "Do you mind helping me up?"

"I need to know something first."

"What?" I ask, knowing I should leave before I'm sober enough to realize how absurd I've been behaving.

Still holding me in his arms as if I'm light as a feather, he leans closer with his eyes on my mouth. When his gaze rises to meet mine, he asks, "Did you fall in love?"

My heart rate spikes, and the sound of it beating whooshes in my ears. Maybe I did hit my head because I swear at that moment, the one with my dream man so close I can kiss him or even lick him if I want, I can answer honestly.

Despite all the physical signs of me feeling otherwise, I reply, "You know. I think it's time for me to go." *Before the last few minutes really sink in.*

My feet are set on solid flooring while his hands remain on the underside of my forearms to steady me. Like the perfect gentleman. "I wish—"

"Nat," Tatum says under her breath. She moves in and grabs my hand.

"What?"

Her hair catches the light when she flips it over her shoulder, an exhausted sigh following right after. Every blonde needs a brunette bestie, and Tatum Devreux was destined to be mine since our mothers exchanged silver spoons from Tiffany's as baby shower gifts. I'm not exactly the calm to her wild ways, but she can out party me any day.

"A party on a yacht down in the harbor. We have to go now, though."

Panic rises in my chest. I know I should want to hightail it out of here to save myself from further mortification, but I don't want to go. I'm perfectly content right here.

I'm not shy about it. I look straight at him, but I'm smacked with a dose of candor I wasn't ready for, my ego crushed under his expression that mirrors pity. Now I regret not making a quick getaway when I had the chance.

My stomach plummets to the floor I was just hovering

above. "Yeah, it's time to go," I tell Tatum, my hand pressing to my belly in an attempt to keep myself together. My hand is grabbed, and I'm tugged after her as she calls, "Ciao, darlings."

I turn back to catch Mr . . . *Dreamy, Smug, Sexy, Pity-er of Drunk Girls* watching me. I'm left with two options to make an escape without further incident. I *could* blame the craziness on a head injury, or I *could* just leave. "So . . . thanks," I say awkwardly as I back toward the door. *Yes. Choosing the latter.*

"Are you sure you're okay?" His voice carries over the lively crowd.

I dust the dirt off my ass. "I'm fine. Guess I'm not a tequila girl."

"You drank rum," he replies with a lopsided smile that could sweep me off my feet again if I'm not careful.

"Rum. Tequila. Same difference." I wave off the idea because it doesn't really matter. "I'm not good with liquor." That should settle it, but I make the mistake of daring to look into his eyes again. The five feet between us virtually disappears, and mentally, I'm back in his arms again, reading the prose that makes up his features. It would take me days to interpret, capturing not only his thoughts but a history that's worn in the light lines. He makes it hard to look away.

Stepping forward, he raises his hand and then lowers it to his side again as conflict invades his expression. "You sure you're okay? You might have a concussion."

I can't say I'm not touched by his concern. Grinning, I ask, "Does a concussion involve my heart?"

"What's happening with your heart?"

"It's beating like crazy."

Smiles are exchanged. "I think you're experiencing something else, but if you'd like me to call an ambulance—"

"Nope," Tatum cuts in, yanking me toward the door again, and laughs. "He's cute, but we don't want to miss the yacht." She whips the straw hat off me and tosses it to him.

I twist to look back. "Thanks for the lift. *Literally*."

"Anytime," he says with his eyes set on mine. When he shoves his hands in his pockets, he looks like he's posing for a Ralph Lauren ad. Tan. Rugged good looks. Tall. Those dreamy eyes and a grin that call me back to him. But life isn't a dream. It's time to return to reality.

Goodbye, dream man. It was nice hanging with . . . onto you.

———

CONTINUE READING NEVER GOT **Over You on Amazon.**

To keep up to date with her writing and more, visit S.L. Scott's website: **www.slscottauthor.com**

To receive the newsletter about all of her publishing adventures, free books, giveaways, steals and more:

https://geni.us/intheknow

Follow me on TikTok: https://geni.us/SLTikTok
Follow on IG: https://geni.us/IGSLS
Follow on Bookbub: https://geni.us/SLScottBB

THANK YOU

Thank you from the bottom of my heart. I have the ability to do what I love because of you. Thank you for reading my books, for the love, and the kindness always.

I wanted to give a shoutout to my awesome team. This book took me three years to write but came together in the last few months. They were there walking this journey with me and giving me, Tealey, and Rad all their attention.

Thank you, Adriana Locke. You came in when I was struggling and picked me, dusted off my confidence, and set me on me feet again . . . technically, made me sit and finish this book. You read every word and page and gave so much of yourself that I'll always be eternally grateful.

Thank you to Andrea Johnston for listening to my crazy ideas for years regarding this book and not treating me like was nuts. Ha! Also, thank you for reading 38 billion versions of this book over the years.

Jenny Sims, thank you for working tirelessly into the night on impossible deadlines and then doing it again to make sure we catch as much as humanly possible. You are a gem! And I'll try my best to stop using last for past, like "last few months . . . " Some habits are hard to break but I'm working on it.

Dear Kristen Johnson, you are always there for me whether it's in the group or ready with your eagle eyes. Thank you. You are so amazing.

Thank you, Marion (Making Manuscripts), for trying your best to work with my insane deadlines and for the chats as I muddle through a million ideas and we try to reign them in.

Thank you!